1

The Bronze Bell

by Louis Joseph Vance

Copyright © 8/13/2015
Jefferson Publication

ISBN-13: 978-1516892372

Printed in the United States of America

Contents

CHAPTER I

DESTINY AND THE BABU

Breaking suddenly upon the steady drumming of the trucks, the prolonged and husky roar of a locomotive whistle saluted an immediate grade-crossing.

Roused by this sound from his solitary musings in the parlour-car of which he happened temporarily to be the sole occupant, Mr. David Amber put aside the magazine over which he had been dreaming, and looked out of the window, catching a glimpse of woodland road shining white between sombre walls of stunted pine. Lazily he consulted his watch.

"It's not for nothing," he observed pensively, "that this railroad wears its reputation: we are consistently late."

His gaze, again diverted to the flying countryside, noted that it had changed character, pine yielding to scrub-oak and second-growth—the ragged vestments of an area some years since denuded by fire. This, too, presently swung away, giving place to cleared land—arable acres golden with the stubble of garnered harvests or sentinelled with unkempt shocks of corn.

In the south a shimmer of laughing gold and blue edged the faded horizon.

Eagerly the young man leaned forward, dark eyes the functions of waiting-room and ticket and telegraph offices. From its eaves depended a weather-worn board bearing the legend: "Nokomis."

The train, pausing only long enough to disgorge from the baggage-car a trunk or two and from the day-coaches a thin trickle of passengers, flung on into the wilderness, cracked bell clanking somewhat disdainfully.

By degrees the platform cleared, the erstwhile patrons of the road and the station loafers—for the most part hall-marked natives of the region—straggling off upon their several ways, some afoot, a majority in dilapidated surreys and buckboards. Amber watched them go with unassumed indifference; their type interested him little. But in their company he presently discovered one, a figure so thoroughly foreign and aloof in attitude, that it caught his eye, and, having caught, held it clouded with perplexity.

Abruptly he abandoned his belongings and gave chase, overtaking the object of his attention at the far end of the station.

"Doggott!" he cried. "I say, Doggott!"

His hand, falling lightly upon the man's shoulder, brought him squarely about, his expression transiently startled, if not a shade truculent.

Short and broad yet compact of body, he was something round-shouldered, with the stoop of those who serve. In a mask of immobility, full-colored and closely shaven, his lips were thin and tight, his eyes steady, grey and shallow: a countenance neither dishonest nor repellent, but one inscrutable. Standing solidly, once halted, there remained a suggestion of alertness in the fellow's pose.

"Doggott, what the deuce brings you here? And Mr. Rutton?"

Amber's cordiality educed no response. The grey eyes, meeting eyes dark, kindly, and penetrating, flickered and fell; so much emotion they betrayed, no more, and that as disingenuous as you could wish.

"Doggott!" insisted Amber, disconcerted. "Surely you haven't forgotten me—Mr. Amber?"

The man shook his head. "Beg pardon, sir," he said; "you've got my nyme 'andy enough, but I don't know *you*, and—"

"But Mr. Rutton?"

"Is a party I've never 'eard of, if you'll excuse my sayin' so, no more'n I 'ave of yourself, sir."

"Well!" began Amber; but paused, his face hardening as he looked the man up and down, nodding slowly.

"Per'aps," continued Mr. Doggott, unabashed, "you mistyke me for my brother, 'Enery Doggott. 'E was 'ome, in England, larst I 'eard of 'im. We look a deal alike, I've been told."

"You would be," admitted Amber drily; and, shutting his teeth upon his inherent contempt for a liar, he swung away, acknowledging with a curt nod the civil "Good-arfternoon, sir," that followed him.

4

The man had disappeared by the time Amber regained his kit-bag and gun-case; standing over which he surveyed his surroundings with some annoyance, discovering that he now shared the station with none but the ticket-agent. A shambling and disconsolate youth, clad in a three-days' growth of beard, a checked jumper and khaki trousers, this person lounged negligently in the doorway of the waiting-room and, caressing his rusty chin with nicotine-dyed fingers, regarded the stranger in Nokomis with an air of subtle yet vaguely melancholy superiority.

"If ye're lookin' for th' hotel," he volunteered unexpectedly, "there aint none;" and effected a masterly retreat into the ticket-booth.

Amused, the despised outlander picked up his luggage and followed amiably. "I'm not looking for the hotel that aint," he said, planting himself in front of the grating; "but I expected to be met by someone from Tanglewood—"

"Thet's the Quain place, daown by th' ba-ay," interpolated the youth from unplumbed depths of mournful abstraction.

"It is. I wired yesterday—"

"Yeour name's Amber, aint it?"

"Yes, I—"

"Well, Quain didn't get yeour message till this mornin'. I sent a kid daown with it 'baout ten o'clock."

"But why the—but I wired yesterday afternoon!"

"I knaow ye did," assented the youth wearily. "It come through raound closin' time and they wa'n't nobody baound that way, so I held it over."

"This craze for being characteristic," observed Mr. Amber obscurely, "is the only thing that really stands in the way of Nokomis becoming a thriving metropolis. Do you agree with me? No matter." He smiled engagingly: a seasoned traveller this, who could recognise the futility of bickering over the irreparable. Moreover, he had to remind himself in all fairness, the blame was, in part at least, his own; for he had thoughtlessly worded his telegram, "Will be with you to-morrow afternoon"; and it was wholly like Quain that he should have accepted the statement at its face value, regardless of the date line.

"I *can* leave my things here for a little while, I presume?" Amber suggested after a pause.

The ticket-agent stared stubbornly into the infinite, making no sign till a coin rang on the window-ledge; when he started, eyed the offering with fugitive mistrust, and gloomily possessed himself of it. "I'll look after them," he said. "Be ye thinkin' of walkin'?"

"Yes," said Amber over his shoulder. He was already moving toward the door.

"Knaow yeour wa-ay?"

"I've been here before, thank you."

"Fer another quarter," drawled the agent with elaborate apathy, "I'd leave the office long enough to find somebody who'd fetch ye daown in a rig for fifty cents."

But Amber was already out of ear-shot.

Crossing the tracks, he addressed himself to the southward-stretching highway. Walking briskly at first, he soon left behind the railway-station with its few parasitic cottages; a dip in the land hid them, and he had hereafter for all company his thoughts, the desultory road, a vast and looming sky, and bare fields hedged with impoverished forest.

A deep languor brooded over the land: the still, warm enchantment of an Indian Summer which, protracted though it were unseasonably into the Ides of November, had

5

yet lost nothing of its witchery. There was no wind, but now and again the air stirred softly, and when it stirred was cool; as if the earth sighed in sheer lassitude. Out of a cloudless sky, translucent sapphire at its zenith fading into hazy topaz-yellow at the horizon, golden sunlight slanted, casting shadows heavy and colourful; on the edge of the woodlands they clung like thin purple smoke, but motionless, and against them, here and there, a clump of sumach blazed like a bed of embers, or some tree loath to shed its autumnal livery flamed scarlet, russet, and mauve. The peace of the hour was intense, and only emphasised by a dull, throbbing undertone—the muted murmur of the distant sea.

Amber had professed acquaintance with his way; it seemed rather to be intimacy, for when he chose to forsake the main-travelled road he did so boldly, striking off upon a wagon-track which, leading across the fields, delved presently into the heart of the forest. Here it ran snakily and, carved by broad-tired wheels and beaten out by slowly plodding hoofs in a soil more than half sand, glimmered white as rock-salt where the drifting leaves had left it naked.

Once in this semi-dusk made luminous by sunlight which touched and quivered upon dead leaf and withered bush and bare brown bough like splashes of molten gold, the young man moved more sedately. The hush of the forest world bore heavily upon his senses; the slight and stealthy rustlings in the brush, the clear dense ringing of some remote axe, an attenuated clamour of cawing from some far crows' congress, but served to accentuate its influence. On that windless day the vital breath of the sea might not moderate the bitter-sweet aroma of decay that swam beneath the unmoving branches; and this mournful fragrance of dying Autumn wrought upon Amber's mood as might a whiff of some exquisite rare perfume revive a poignant memory in the bosom of a bereaved lover. His glance grew aimless, his temper as purposeless, lively anticipation giving way to a retrospection tinged with indefinable sadness.

Then into the silence crept a sound to rouse him from his formless reverie: at first a mere pulsing in the stillness, barely to be distinguished from the song of the surf; but presently a pounding, ever louder and more insistent. He paused, attentive; and while he waited the drumming, minute by minute gaining in volume, swept swiftly toward him— the rhythmic hoofbeats of a single horse madly ridden. When it was close upon him he stepped back into the tangled undergrowth, making room; for the track was anything but wide.

Simultaneously there burst into view, at the end of a brief aisle of trees, the horse—a vigorous black brute with white socks and muzzle—running freely, apparently under constraint neither of whip nor of spur. In the saddle a girl leaned low over the horn—a girl with eyes rapturous, face brilliant, lips parted in the least of smiles. A fold of her black habit-skirt, whipping out, almost snapped in Amber's face, so close to him she rode; yet she seemed not to see him, and very likely did not. A splendid sketch in black-and-white, of youthful spirit and joy of motion: so she passed and was gone....

Hardly, however, had the forest closed upon the picture, ere a cry, a heavy crashing as of a horse threshing about in the underbrush, and a woman's scream of terror, sent Amber, in one movement, out into the road again and running at a pace which, had he been conscious of it, would have surprised him.

A short fifty yards separated him from the bend in the way round which the horse and its rider had vanished. He had no more than gained this point than he was obliged to pull up sharply to avoid running into the girl herself.

Although dismounted, she was on her feet, and apparently uninjured. She stood with one hand against the trunk of a tree, on the edge of a small clearing wherein the axes of the local lumbermen had but lately been busy. Her horse had disappeared; the rumble of his hoofs, diminuendo, told the way he had gone.

So much Amber comprehended in a single glance; with a second he sought the cause of the accident, and identified it with a figure so *outré* and bizarre that he momentarily and excusably questioned the testimony of his senses.

At a little distance from the girl, in the act of addressing her, stood a man, obese, gross, abnormally distended with luxurious and sluggish living, as little common to the scene as a statue of Phoebus Apollo had been: a babu of Bengal, every inch of him, from his dirty red-and-white turban to his well-worn and cracked patent-leather shoes. His body was enveloped in a complete suit of emerald silk, much soiled and faded, and girt with a sash of many colours, crimson predominating. His hands, fat, brown, and not overclean, alternately fluttered apologetically and rubbed one another with a suggestion of extreme urbanity; his lips, thick, sensual, and cruel, mouthed a broken stream of babu-English; while his eyes, nearly as small and quite as black as shoe-buttons —eyes furtive, crafty, and cold—suddenly distended and became fixed, as with amazement, at the instant of Amber's appearance.

Instinctively, as soon as he had mastered his initial stupefaction, Amber stepped forward and past the girl, placing himself between her and this preposterous apparition, as if to shield her. He was neither overly imaginative nor of a romantic turn of mind; but, the circumstances reviewed, it's nothing to his discredit that he entertained a passing suspicion of some curious conspiracy against the girl, thought of an ambuscade, and with quick eyes raked the surroundings for signs of a confederate of the Bengali.

He found, however, nothing alarming, no indication that the man were not alone; nor, for that matter, could he reasonably detect in the fellow's bearing anything but a spirit of conciliation almost servile. None the less he held himself wary and alert, and was instant to halt the babu when he, with the air of a dog cringing to his master's feet for punishment, would have drawn nearer.

"Stop right there!" Amber told him crisply; and got for response obedience, a low salaam, and the Hindu salutation accorded only to persons of high rank: "Hazoor!" But before the babu could say more the American addressed the girl. "What did he do?" he inquired, without looking at her. "Frighten your horse?"

"Just that." The girl's tone was edged with temper. "He jumped out from behind that woodpile; the horse shied and threw me."

"You're not hurt, I trust?"

"No—thank you; but"—with a nervous laugh—"I'm furiously angry."

"That's reasonable enough." Amber returned undivided attention to the Bengali. "Now then," he demanded sternly, "what've you got to say for yourself? What do you mean by frightening this lady's horse? What are you doing here, anyway?"

Almost grovelling, the babu answered him in Urdu: "Hazoor, I am your slave—"

Without thinking Amber couched his retort in the same tongue: "Count yourself lucky you are not, dog!"

"Nay, hazoor, but I meant no harm. I was resting, being fatigued, in the shelter of the wood, when the noise of hoofs disturbed me and I stepped out to see. When the woman was thrown I sought to assist her, but she threatened me with her whip."

"That is quite true," the girl cut in over Amber's shoulder. "I don't think he intended to harm me, but it's purely an accident that he didn't."

Inasmuch as the babu's explanation had been made in fluent, vernacular Urdu, Amber's surprise at the girl's evident familiarity with that tongue was hardly to be concealed. "You understand Urdu?" he stammered.

"Aye," she told him in that tongue, "and speak it, too."

"You know this man, then?"

7

"No. Do you?"

"Not in the least. How should I?"

"You yourself speak Urdu."

"Well but—" The situation hardly lent itself to such a discussion; he had the babu first to dispose of. Amber resumed his cross-examination. "Who are you?" he demanded. "And what is your business in this place?"

The fat yellowish-brown face was distorted by a fugitive grimace of deprecation. "Hazoor, I am Behari Lal Chatterji, solicitor, of the Inner Temple."

"Well? And your business here?"

"Hazoor, that is for your secret ear." The babu drew himself up, assuming a certain dignity. "It is not meet that the message of the Bell should be uttered in the hearing of an Englishwoman, hazoor."

"What are you drivelling about?" In his blank wonder, Amber returned to English as to a tongue more suited to his urgent need of forcible expression. "And, look here, you stop calling me 'Hazoor.' I'm no more a hazoor than you are—idiot!"

"Nay," contended the babu reproachfully; "is it right that you should seek to hoodwink me? Have I not eyes with which to see you, ears that can hear you speak our tongue, hazoor? I am no child, to be played with—I, the appointed Mouthpiece of the Voice!"

"I know naught of your 'Voice' or its mouthpiece; but certainly you are no child. You are either mad, or insolent—or a fool to be kicked." And in exasperation Amber took a step toward the man as if to carry into effect his implied threat.

Alarmed, the babu cringed and retreated a pace; then, suddenly, raising an arm, indicated the girl. "Hazoor!" he cried. "Be quick—the woman faints!" And as Amber hastily turned, with astonishing agility the babu sprang toward him.

Warned by his moving shadow as much as by the girl's cry, Amber leapt aside and lifted a hand to strike; but before it could deliver a blow it was caught and a small metallic object thrust into it. Upon this his fingers closed instinctively, and the babu sprang back, panting and quaking.

"The Token, hazoor, the Token!" he quavered. "It is naught but that—the Token!"

"Token, you fool!" cried Amber, staring stupidly at the man. "What in thunder——!"

"Nay, hazoor; how should I tell you now, when another sees and hears? At another time, hazoor, in a week, or a day, or an hour, mayhap, I come again—for your answer. Till then and forever I am your slave, hazoor: the dust beneath your feet. Now, I go."

And with a haste that robbed the courtesy of its grace, the Bengali salaamed, then wheeled square about and, hitching his clothing round him, made off with a celerity surprising in one of his tremendous bulk, striking directly into the heart of the woods.

For as much as a minute he was easily to be followed, his head and shoulders rising above the brush through which he forged purposefully, with something of the heedless haste of a man bent on keeping a pressing engagement—or a sinner fleeing the wrath to come. Not once did he look back while Amber watched—himself divided between amusement, annoyance, and astonishment. Presently the trees blotted out the red-and-white turban; the noise of the babu's elephantine retreat diminished; and Amber was left to knit his brows over the object which had been forced upon him so unexpectedly.

It proved to be a small, cubical box, something more than an inch square, fashioned of bronze and elaborately decorated with minute relief work in the best manner of ancient Indian craftsmanship.

"May I see, please?" The voice of the girl at his side recalled to Amber her existence. "May I see, too, please, Mr. Amber?" she repeated.

8

CHAPTER II

THE GIRL AND THE TOKEN

In his astonishment he looked round quickly to meet the gaze of mischievous eyes that strove vainly to seem simple and sincere. His own, in which amusement was blended with wonder, noted that they were very handsome eyes and rather curiously colourful, the delicate sepia shade of the pupils being lightened by a faint sheen of gold in the irides; they were, furthermore, large and set well apart. On the whole he decided that they were even beautiful, for all the dancing glimmer of perverse humour in their depths; he could fancy that they might well seem very sweet and womanly when their owner chose to be serious.

Aware that he faced an uncommonly pretty woman, who chose to study him with a straightforward interest he was nothing loath to imitate, he took time to see that she was very fair of skin, with that creamy, silken whiteness that goes with hair of the shade commonly and unjustly termed red. This girl's hair was really brown, a rich sepia interwoven with strands of raw, ruddy gold, admirably harmonious with her eyes. Her nose he thought a trace too severely perfect in its modelling, but redeemed by a broad and thoughtful brow, a strong yet absolutely feminine chin, and a mouth.... Well, as to her mouth, the young man selected a rosebud to liken it to; which was really quite a poor simile, for her lips were nothing at all like rose-leaves save in colour; but they were well-shapen and wide enough to suggest generosity, without being in the least too wide.

Having catalogued these several features, together with the piquant oval of her face, and remarked that her poise was good and gracious in the uncompromising lines of her riding-habit, he had a mental portrait of her he was not likely soon to forget. For it's not every day that one encounters so pretty a girl in the woods of Long Island's southern shore—or anywhere else, for that matter. He felt sure of this.

But he was equally certain that he was as much a stranger to her as she to him.

She, on her part, had been busy satisfying herself that he was a very presentable young man, in spite of the somewhat formidable reputation he wore as a person of learned attainments. There could be no better way to show him to you than through her eyes, so you must know that she saw a man of less than thirty years, with a figure slight and not over-tall but well-proportioned, and with a complexion as dark as hers was light. His eyes, indeed, were a very dark grey, and his hair was black, and his face and hands had been coloured by the sun and wind until the tan had become indelible, almost, so that his prolonged periods of studious indoor seclusion worked little toward lightening it. If his looks attracted, it was not because he was handsome, for that he wasn't, but because of certain signs of strength to be discerned in his face, as well as an engaging manner which he owned by right of ancestry, his ascendants for several generations having been notable representatives of one of the First Families of Virginia. Amber was not inordinately proud of this fact, at least not more so than nine out of any ten Virginians; but his friends—who were many but mostly male—claimed that he wrote "F.F.V." before the "F.R.S." which he was entitled to inscribe after his name.

The pause which fell upon the girl's use of his name, and during which they looked one another over, was sufficiently prolonged to excuse the reference to it which Amber chose to make.

"I'm sure," he said with his slow smile, "that we're satisfied we've never met before. Aren't we?"

"Quite," assented the girl.

"That only makes it the more mysterious, of course."

"Yes," said she provokingly; "doesn't it?"

"You know, you're hardly fair to me," he asserted. "I'm rapidly beginning to entertain doubts of my senses. When I left the train at Nokomis station I met a man I know as well as I know myself—pretty nearly; and he denied me to my face. Then, a little later, I encounter a strange, mad Bengali, who apparently takes me for somebody he has business with. And finally, you call me by name."

"It isn't so very remarkable, when you come to consider it," she returned soberly. "Mr. David Amber is rather well known, even in his own country. I might very well have seen your photograph published in connection with some review of—let me see.... Your latest book was entitled 'The Peoples of the Hindu Kush,' wasn't it? You see, I haven't read it."

"That's sensible of you, I'm sure. Why should you?... But your theory doesn't hold water, because I won't permit my publishers to print my picture, and, besides, reviews of such stupid books generally appear in profound monthlies which abhor illustrations."

"Oh!" She received this with a note of disappointment. "Then my explanation won't do?"

"I'm sorry," he laughed, "but you'll have to be more ingenious—and practical."

"And you won't show me the present the babu made you?"

He closed his fingers jealously over the bronze box. "Not until...."

"You insist on reciprocity?"

"Absolutely."

"That's very unkind of you."

"How?" he demanded blankly.

"You will have it that I must surrender my only advantage—my incognito. If I tell you how I happen to know who you are, I must tell you who I am. Immediately you will lose interest in me, because I'm really not at all advanced; I doubt if I should understand your book if I had to read it."

"Which Heaven forfend! But why," he insisted mercilessly, "do you wish me to be interested in you?"

She flushed becomingly at this and acknowledged the touch with a rueful, smiling glance. But, "Because I'm interested in you," she admitted openly.

"And ... why?"

"Are you hardened to such adventures?" She nodded in the direction the babu had taken. "Are you accustomed to being treated with extraordinary respect by stray Bengalis and accepting tokens from them? Is romance commonplace to you?"

"Oh," he said, disappointed, "if it's only the adventure—! Of course, that's easily enough explained. This half-witted mammoth—don't ask me how he came to be here—thought he recognised in me some one he had known in India. Let's have a look at this token-thing."

He disclosed the bronze box and let her take it in her pretty fingers.

"It must have a secret spring," she concluded, after a careful inspection.

"I think so, but...."

She shook it, holding it by her ear. "There's something inside—it rattles ever so slightly. I wonder!"

"No more than I."

"And what are you going to do with it?" She returned it reluctantly.

"Why, there's nothing to do but keep it till the owner turns up, that I can see."

"You won't break it open?"

"Not until curiosity overpowers me and I've exhausted every artifice, trying to find the catch."

"Are you a patient person, Mr. Amber?"

"Not extraordinarily so, Miss Farrell."

"Oh, how did you guess?"

"By remembering not to be stupid. You are Miss Sophia Farrell, daughter of Colonel Farrell of the British Diplomatic Service in India." He chuckled cheerfully over this triumph of deductive reasoning. "You are visiting the Quains for a few days, while *en route* for India with some friends whose name I've forgotten—"

"The Rolands," she prompted involuntarily.

"Thank you.... The Rolands, who are stopping in New York. You've lived several years with your father in India, went back to London to 'come out' and are returning, having been presented at the Court of St. James. Your mother was an American girl, a schoolmate of Mrs. Quain's. I'm afraid that's the whole sum of my knowledge of you."

"You've turned the tables fairly, Mr. Amber," she admitted. "And Mr. Quain wrote you all that?"

"I'm afraid he told me almost as much about you as he told you about me; we're old friends, you know. And now I come to think of it, Quain has one of the few photographs of me extant. So my chain of reasoning's complete. And I think we'd better hurry on to Tanglewood."

"Indeed, yes. Mrs. Quain will be wild with worry if that animal finds his way back to the stable without me; I've been very thoughtless." She caught up her riding-skirt and started down the path with Amber trudging contently beside her. "However," she considered demurely, "I'm not at all sorry, really; it's quite an experience to have a notability at a disadvantage, even if only for a few minutes."

"I wish you wouldn't," he begged in boyish embarrassment. "I'm not a notability, really; Quain's been talking too much. I'll get even with him, though."

"That sounds so modest that I almost believe I've made a mistake about your identity. But I've no doubt you're right; Mr. Quain does exaggerate in praise of his friends. Very likely it is as you insist, and you're only an ordinary person, after all. At least, you would be if stray babus didn't make you mysterious presents."

"So long as there is that to hold your interest in me, I'm content," he told her, diverted. "How much longer shall you stay at Tanglewood, Miss Farrell?"

"Unhappily," she sighed, "I must leave on the early train to-morrow, to join the Rolands in New York."

"You don't want to go?"

"I'm half an American, Mr. Amber. I've learned to love the country already. Besides, we start immediately for San Francisco, and it'll be such a little while before I'll be in India."

"You don't care for India?"

"I've known it for less than six years, but already I've come to hate it as thoroughly as any exiled Englishwoman there. It sits there like a great, insatiable monster, devouring English lives. Indirectly it was responsible for my mother's death; she never recovered from the illness she contracted when my father was stationed in the Deccan. In the course of time it will kill my father, just as it did his father and his elder brother. It's a cruel, hateful, ungrateful land—not worth the price we pay for it."

11

"I know how you feel," he said with sympathy. "It's been a good many years since I visited India, and of course I then saw and heard little of the darker side. Your people are brave enough, out there."

"They are. I don't know about Government; but its servants are loyal and devoted and unselfish and cheerful. And I don't at all understand," she added in confusion, "why I should have decided to inflict upon you my emotional hatred of the country. Your question gave me the opening, and I forgot myself."

"I assure you I was thoroughly shocked, Miss Farrell."

"You should have been—surprised, at least. Why should I pour out my woes to you—a man I've known not fifteen minutes?"

"Why not, if you felt like it? After all, you know, we're both of us merely making talk to—ah—to cover our interest in one another."

She paused momentarily to laugh at his candour. "You are outspoken, Mr. Amber! It's very pretty of you to assert an interest in me; but why should you assume that I—"

"You said so, didn't you?"

"Wel-l ... yes, so I did."

"You can change your mind, of course."

"I shan't, honestly, until you turn stupid. And you can't do that until you stop having strange adventures. Will you tell me something?"

"If I can."

"About the man who wouldn't acknowledge knowing you? You remember saying three people had been mistaken about your identity this afternoon."

"No, only one—the babu. You're not mistaken—"

"I knew you must be David Amber the moment I heard you speaking Urdu."

"And the man at the station wasn't mistaken—unless I am. He knew me perfectly, I believe, but for reasons of his own refused to recognise me."

"Yes—?"

"He was an English servant named Doggott, who is—or once was—a valet in the service of an old friend, a man named Rutton."

She repeated the name: "Rutton? It seems to me I've heard of him."

"You have?"

"I don't remember," she confessed, knitting her level brows. "The name has a familiar ring, somehow. But about the valet?"

"Well, I was very intimate with his employer for a long time, though we haven't met for several years. Rutton was a strange creature, a man of extraordinary genius, who lived a friendless, solitary life—at least, so far as I knew; I once lived with him in a little place he had in Paris, for three months, and in all that time he never received a letter or a caller. He was reticent about himself, and I never asked any questions, of course, but in spite of the fact that he spoke English like an Englishman and was a public school man, apparently, I always believed he had a strain of Hungarian blood in him—or else Italian or Spanish. I know that sounds pretty broad, but he was enigmatic—a riddle I never managed to make much of. Aside from that he was wonderful: a linguist, speaking a dozen European languages and more Eastern tongues and dialects, I believe, than any other living man. We met by accident in Berlin and were drawn together by our common interest in Orientalism. Later, hearing I was in Paris, he hunted me up and insisted that I stay with him there while finishing my big book—the one whose title you know. His assistance to me then was invaluable. After that I lost track of him."

"And the valet?"

"Oh, I'd forgotten Doggott. He was a Cockney, as silent and self-contained as Rutton.... To get back to Nokomis: I met Doggott at the station, called him by name, and he refused to admit knowing me—said I must have mistaken him for his twin brother. I could tell by his eyes that he lied, and it made me wonder. It's quite impossible that Rutton should be in this neck of the woods; he was a man who preferred to live a hermit in centres of civilisation.... Curious!"

"I don't wonder you think so. Perhaps the man had been up to some mischief.... But," said the girl with a note of regret, "we're almost home!"

They had come to the seaward verge of the woodland, where the trees and scrub rose like a wild hedgerow on one side of a broad, well-metalled highway. Before them stretched the eighth of a mile of neglected land knee-deep with crisp, dry, brown stalks of weedy growths, beyond which the bay smiled, a still lake of colour mirroring the intense lapis-lazuli of the calm eastern skies of evening. Over across its waters the sand dunes of a long island glowed like a bar of new red gold, tinted by the transient scarlet and yellow glory of the smouldering Autumnal sunset. Through the woods the level, brilliant, warmthless rays ran like wild-fire, turning each dead, brilliant leaf to a wisp of incandescent flame, and tingeing the air with an evanescent ruby radiance against which the slim young boles stood black and stark.

To the right, on the other side of the road, a rustic fence enclosed the trim, well-groomed plantations of Tanglewood Lodge; through the dead limbs a window of the house winked in the sunset glow like an eye of garnet. And as the two appeared a man came running up the road, shouting.

"That's Quain!" cried Amber; and sent a long cry of greeting toward him.

"Wait!" said the girl impulsively, putting out a detaining hand. "Let's keep our secret," she begged, her eyes dancing—"just for the fun of it!"

"Our secret!"

"About the babu and the Token; it's a bit of mystery and romance to me—and we don't often find that in our lives, do we? Let us keep it personal for a while—between ourselves; and you will promise to let me know if anything unusual ever comes of it, after I've gone. We can say that I was riding carelessly, which is quite true, and that the horse shied and threw me, which again is true; but the rest for ourselves only.... Please.... What do you say?"

He was infected by her spirit of irresponsible mischief. "Why, yes—I say yes," he replied; and then, more gravely: "I think it'll be very pleasant to share a secret with you, Miss Farrell. I shant say a word to any one, until I have to."

* * * * *

As events turned he had no need to mention the incident until the morning of the seventh day following the girl's departure. In the interim nothing happened, and he was able to enjoy some excellent shooting with Quain, his thoughts undisturbed by any further appearance of the babu.

But on that seventh morning it became evident that a burglary had been visited upon the home of his hosts. A window had been forced in the rear of the house and a trail of burnt matches and candle-grease between that entrance and the door of Amber's room, together with the somewhat curious circumstance that nothing whatever was missing from the personal effects of the Quains, forced him to make an explanation. For his own belongings had been rifled and the bronze box alone abstracted—still preserving its secret.

In its place Amber found a soiled slip of note-paper inscribed with the round, unformed handwriting of the babu: "Pardon, sahib. A mistake has been made. I seek but to regain that which is not yours to possess. There will be naught else taken. A thousand excuses from your hmbl. obt. svt., Behari Lal Chatterji."

CHAPTER III

MAROONED

A cry in the windy dusk; a sudden, hollow booming overhead; a vision of countless wings in panic, sketched in black upon a background of dulled silver; two heavy detonations and, with the least of intervals, a third; three vivid flashes of crimson and gold stabbing the purple twilight; and then the acrid reek of smokeless drifting into Amber's face, while from the sky, where the V-shaped flock had been, two stricken bundles of blood-stained feathers fell slowly, fluttering....

Honking madly, the unscathed brethren of the slain wheeled abruptly and, lashed by the easterly gale, fled out over the open sea, triangular formation dwindling rapidly in the clouded distances.

Shot-gun poised abreast, his keen eyes marking down the fall of his prey, Amber stood without moving, exultation battling with a vague remorse in his bosom—as always when he killed. Quain, who had dropped back a pace after firing but one shot and scoring an unqualified miss at close range, now stood plucking clumsily, with half frozen fingers, at an obstinate breech-lock. This latter resisting his every wile, his temper presently slipped its leash; as violently as briefly he swore: "Damn!"

"Gladly," agreed Amber, without turning. "But what?"

"This gun!"

"Your gun?"

"Of course." There were elaborations which would not lend themselves to decorative effect upon a printed page.

"Then damn it yourself, Quain; I'm sure you can do it ever so much more thoroughly than I. But what's the matter?"

"Rim-jammed cartridge," explained Quain between his teeth. The lock just then yielding to his awkward manipulation, stock and barrel came apart in his hands. "Just my beastly luck!" he added gratuitously. "It wouldn't've been me if—! How many'd you pot, Davy?"

"Only two," said Amber, lowering his weapon, extracting the spent shells, and reloading.

"Only *two!*" The information roused in Quain a demon of sarcasm. Fumbling in his various pockets for a shell-extractor, he grunted his disgust. "Here, lend us your thingumbob; I've lost mine. Thanky.... Only two! How many'd you expect to drop, on a snapshot like that?"

"Two," returned Amber so patiently that Quain requested him, explosively, to go to the devil. "If you don't mind," he said, "I'll go after my ducks instead. You'll follow? They're over there, on our way." And accepting Quain's snort for an affirmative he strolled off in the direction indicated, hugging his gun in the crook of his arm.

Fifty yards or so away he found the ducks, side by side in a little hollow. "Fine fat birds," he adjudged sagely, weighing each in his hand ere dropping it into his lean game-bag. "This makes up for a lot of cold and waiting."

Satisfaction glimmering in his grave dark eyes, he lingered in the hollow, while the frosty air, whipping madly through the sand-hills, stung his face till it glowed beneath the brown. But presently, like the ghost of a forgotten kiss, something moist and chill touched gently his cheek, and was gone. Startled, he glanced skywards, then extended an arm, watching it curiously while the rough fabric of his sleeve was salted generously with fine white flakes. Though to some extent apprehended (they had been blind indeed to have ignored the menace of the dour day just then dying) snow had figured in their calculations as little as the scarcity of game. Amber wondered dimly if it would work a change in their plans, prove an obstacle to their safe return across the bay.

The flurry thickening in the air, a shade of anxiety colored his mood. "This'll never do!" he declared, and set himself to ascend a nearby dune. For a moment he slipped and slid vainly, the dry sand treacherous to his feet, the brittle grasses he clutched snapping off or coming away altogether with their roots; but in time he found himself upon the rounded summit, and stood erect, straining the bitter air into panting lungs as he cast about for bearings.

Behind him a meagre strip of sand held back a grim and angry sea; before him lay an eighth of a mile of sand-locked desolation, and then the weltering bay—a wide two miles of leaping, shouting waves, slate-coloured but white of crests. Beyond, seen dimly as a wall through driving sheets of snow, were the darkly wooded rises of the mainland. In the west, to his left, the blank, impersonal eye of the light-house, its pillar invisible, winked red, went out, and flashed up white. Over all, beneath a low and lustreless sky as flat as a plate, violet evening shadows were closing in like spectral skirts of the imminent night. But, in the gloom, their little cat-boat lay occult to his searching gaze.

Quain's voice recalling him, he turned to discover his host stumbling through a neighbouring vale, and obeying a peremptory wave of the elder man's hand, descended, accompanied by an avalanche in miniature.

"Better hurry," shouted Amber, as soon as he could make himself heard above the screaming of the gale. "Wind's freshening; it looks like mean weather."

"Really?" Quain fell into step at his side. "You 'stonish me. But the good Lord knows I'm willin'. Whereabout's the boat?"

"Blessed if I know: over yonder somewhere," Amber told him, waving toward the bay-shore an arm as vaguely helpful as his information.

"Thank you so much. Guess I can find her all right. Hump yo'self, Davy."

They plodded on heavily, making fair progress in spite of the hindering sand. Nevertheless it had grown sensibly darker ere they debouched upon the frozen flats that bordered the bay; and now the wind bore down upon them in full-winged fury, shrieking in their ears, searing their eyes, tearing greedily at the very breath of their nostrils, and searching out with impish ingenuity the more penetrable portions of their clothing.

For a moment Quain paused, irresolute, peering right and left, then began to trudge eastwards, heavy boots crunching the thin sedge-ice. A little later they came to the water's edge and proceeded steadily along it, Quain leading confidently. Eventually he tripped over some obstacle, stumbled and lurched forward and recovered his balance with an effort, then remained with bowed head, staring down at his feet.

"Hurt yourself, old man?"

"No!" snapped Quain rudely.

"Then what in—"

"Eh?" Quain roused, but an instant longer looked him blankly in the eye. "Oh," he added brightly—"oh, she's gone."

"The boat——?"

15

"The boat," affirmed Quain, too discouraged for the obvious retort ungracious. He stooped and caught up a frayed end of rope, exhibiting it in witness to his statement. "Ain't it hell?" he inquired plaintively.

Amber's gaze followed the rope, the further end of which was rove through the ring of a small grapnel anchor half buried in the spongy earth. "Gone!" he echoed dismally.

"Gone away from here," said Quain deliberately, nodding at the rope's end. "The tide floated her off, of course; but how this happened is beyond me. I could kill Antone." He named the Portuguese labourer charged with the care of the boats at Tanglewood. "It's his job to see that these cables are replaced when they show signs of wear." He cast the rope from him in disdain and wheeled to stare baywards. "There!" he cried, levelling an arm to indicate a dark and fleeting shadow upon the storm-whipped waters. "There she goes— not three hundred feet off. It can't be five minutes since she worked loose. I don't see why…! If it hadn't been for that damned cartridge…! It's the devil's own luck!"

A blur of snow swept between boat and shore; when it had passed the former was all but indistinguishable. From a full heart Quain blasphemed fluently…. "But if she holds as she stands," he amended quickly, his indomitable spirit fostering the forlorn hope, "she'll go aground in another five minutes—and I know just where. I'll go after her."

"The deuce you will! How?"

"There's an old skimmy up the shore a ways." Already Quain was moving off in search of it. "Noticed her this morning. Daresay she leaks like a sieve, but at worst the water's pretty shoal inshore, hereabouts."

"Cold comfort in that."

"Better than none, you amiable—"

"Can you swim?" Amber demanded pointedly.

"Like a fish. And you?"

"Not like a fish."

"Damn!" Quain brought up short with a shin barked against a thwart of the rowboat he had been seeking, and in recognition of the mishap liberally insulted his luck.

Amber, knowing that his hurt was as inconsiderable as his ill-temper, which was more than half-feigned to mask his anxiety, laughed quietly, meanwhile inspecting their find with a critical eye.

"You don't seriously mean to put off in this crazy hen-coop, do you?" he asked.

"Just precisely that. It's the only way."

"It simple madness. I won't—"

"You don't want to stay here all night, do you?"

"No, but—"

"Well, then, lend us a hand and don't stand there grumbling. Be thankful for what you've got, which is me and my enterprise."

"Oh, all right."

Together they put their shoulders to the bows of the old, flat-bottomed rowboat, with incredible exertions uprooting it from its ancient bed, and at length had it afloat.

Panting, Quain mopped his forehead with a handkerchief much the worse for a day's association with gun-grease, and peered beneath his hand into the murk that veiled the bay.

"There she is," he declared confidently: "aground." He pointed. "I'll fetch up with her in no time."

But Amber could see nothing in the least resembling the catboat, and said so with decision.

"She's there, all right," insisted Quain. "'Tain't my fault if you're blind. Here, hold this, will you, while I find me a pole of some sort." He thrust into Amber's hand an end of rotten painter at which the rowboat strained, and wandered off into the night, in the course of time returning with an old eel-pot stake, flotsam of some summer storm. "Pure, bull-headed luck!" he crowed, jubilant, brandishing his trophy; and jumped into the boat. "Now sit tight till I come back?... Huh—what?"

"I'm coming, too," Amber repeated quietly.

"The hell you are! D'you want to sink us? What do you think this is, anyway—an excursion steamer? You stay where you are and—I say—take care of this till I come back, like a good fellow."

He thrust the butt of his shot-gun into Amber's face, and the latter, seizing it, was rewarded by a vigorous push that sent him back half a dozen feet. At the same time the painter slipped from his grasp and Quain, lodging an end of the eel-pot stake on the hard sand bottom, put his weight upon it. Before Amber could recover, the boat had slid off and was melting swiftly into the shadows.

After a bit Quain's voice came back: "Don't fret, Davy. I'm all right."

Amber cupped hands to mouth and sent a cheerful hail ringing in response. Simultaneously the last, least, indefinite blur that stood for the boat in the darkness, vanished in a swirl of snow; and he was alone with the storm and his misgivings. Upon these he put a check—would not dwell upon them; but their influence none the less proved strong enough to breed in him a resistless restlessness and keep him tramping up and down a five-yard stretch of comparatively solid earth: to and fro, stamping his feet to keep his blood circulating, lugging both guns, one beneath either arm, hunching his shoulders up about his ears in thankless attempt to prevent wet flakes from sifting in between his neck and collar—thus, interminably it seemed, to and fro, to and fro....

In the course of time this occupation defeated its purpose; the very monotony of it sent his thoughts winging back to Quain; he worried more than ever for his friend, reproaching himself unmercifully for that he had suffered him to go alone—or at all. Quain had a wife and children; that thought proved insupportable.... Had he missed the catboat altogether? Or had he gained it only to find the motor disabled or the propeller fouled with the wiry eel-grass that choked the shoals? In either instance he would be at the mercy of the wind, for even with the sail close-reefed he would have no choice other than to fly before the fury. Or had the boat possibly gone aground so hard and fast that Quain had found himself unable to push her off and doomed to lie in her, helpless, against the fulling of the tide? Or (last and most grudged guess of all) had the "skimmy" proved as unseaworthy as its dilapidated appearance had proclaimed it?

Twenty minutes wore wearily away. Falling ever more densely, the snow drew an impenetrable wan curtain between Amber and the world of life and light and warmth; while with each discordant blast the strength of the gale seemed to wax, its high hysteric clamour at times drowning even the incessant deep bellow of the ocean surf. Once Amber paused in his patrol, having heard, or fancying he had heard, the staccato *plut-plut-plut* of a marine motor. On impulse, with a swelling heart, he swung his gun skywards and pulled both triggers. The double report rang in his ears loud as a thunderclap.

In the moments that followed, while he stood listening, with every fibre of his being keyed to attention, the sense of his utter isolation chilled his heart as with cold steel.

A little frantically he loaded and fired again; but what at first might have been thought the faint far echo of a hail he in the end set down reluctantly to a trick of the hag-ridden wind; to whose savage voice he durst not listen long; in such a storm, on such a night, a man had but to hearken with a credulous ear to hear strange and terrible voices whispering, shrieking, gibbering, howling untold horrors....

An hour passed, punctuated at frequent intervals by gunshots. Though they evoked no answer of any sort, hope for Quain died hard in Amber's heart. With all his might he laboured to convince himself that his friend must have overtaken the drifting boat, and, forced to relinquish his efforts to regain the beach, have scudded across the bay to the mainland and safety; but this seemed a surmise at best so far-fetched, and one as well not overlong to be dwelt upon, lest by that very insistence its tenuity be emphasised, that Amber resolutely turned from it to a consideration of his own plight and problematic way of escape.

His understanding of his situation was painfully accurate: he was marooned upon what a flood tide made a desert island but which at the ebb was a peninsula—a long and narrow strip of sand, bounded on the west by the broad, shallow channel to the ocean, on the east connected with the mainland by a sandbar which half the day lay submerged.

He had, then, these alternatives: he might either compose himself to hug the leeward side of a dune till daybreak (or till relief should come) or else undertake a five-mile tramp on the desperate hope of finding at the end of it the tide out and the sandbar a safe footway from shore to shore. Between the two he vacillated not at all; anything were preferable to a night in the dunes, beaten by the implacable storm, haunted by the thought of Quain; and even though he were to find the eastern causeway under water, at least the exercise would have served to keep him from freezing.

Ten minutes after his last cartridge had been fruitlessly discharged, he set out for the ocean beach, pausing at the first dune he came upon to scrape a shallow trench in the sand and cache therein both guns and his game-bag. Marking the spot with a bit of driftwood stuck upright, he pressed on, eventually pausing on the overhanging lip of a twenty-foot bluff. To its foot the beach below was aswirl knee-deep with the wash of breakers, broad patches of water black and glossy as polished ebony alternating with vast expanses of foam and clotted spume, all aglow with pale winter phosporescence. Momentarily, as he watched, at once fascinated and appalled, mountainous ridges of blackness heaved up out of the storm's grey heart, offshore, and, curling crests edged with luminous white, swung in to crash and shatter thunderously upon the sands.

Awed and disappointed, Amber drew back. The beach was impassable; here was no wide and easy road to the east, such as he had thought to find; to gain the sandbar he had now to thread a tortuous and uncertain way through the bewildering dunes. And the prospect was not a little disconcerting; afraid neither of wind nor of cold, he was wretchedly afraid of going astray in that uncertain, shifting labyrinth. To lose oneself in that trackless wilderness…!

A demon of anxiety prodded him on: he must learn Quain's fate, or go mad. Once on the mainland it were a matter of facility to find his way to the village of Shampton, telephone Tanglewood and charter a "team" to convey him thither. He shut his teeth on his determination and set his face to the east.

Beset and roughly buffeted by the gale; the snow settling in rippling drifts in the folds of his clothing and upon his shoulders clinging like a cloth; his face cut by clouds of sand flung horizontally with well-nigh the force of birdshot from a gun: he bowed to the blast and plodded steadily on.

Imperceptibly fatigue benumbed his senses, blunted the keen edge of his emotions; even the care for Quain became a mere dull ache in the back of his perceptions; of physical suffering he was unconscious. He fell a prey to freakish fancies—could stand aside and watch himself, an atom whirling in the mad dance of the tempest, as the snow-flakes whirled, as little potent. He saw himself pitting his puny strength of mind and body against the infinite force of the elements: saw himself fall and rise and battle on, gaining nothing: an atom, sport of high gods! To the flight of time he grew quite oblivious, his thoughts wandering in the past, oddly afar to half-remembered scenes, to experiences more than half-forgotten, both wholly irrelevant; picturesque and painful memories cast up from the deeps of the subconsciousness by some inexplicable convulsion of the imagination. For a long time he moved on in stupid, wondering contemplation of a shining crescent of sand backed by a green, steaming wall of jungle; there was a dense blue sky above, and below, on the beach, dense blue waters curled lazily up the feet of a little, naked, brown child that played contentedly with a shell of rainbow hues. Again he saw a throng upon a pier-head, and in its forefront an unknown woman, plainly dressed, with deep brown eyes wherein Despair dwelt, tearless but white to the lips as she watched a steamer draw away. And yet again, he seemed to stand with others upon the threshold of the cardroom of a Hong-Kong club: in a glare of garish light a man in evening dress lay prone across a table on whose absorbent, green cloth a dark and ugly stain was widening slowly.... But for the most part he fancied himself walking through scented, autumnal woods, beside a woman whose eyes were kind and dear, whose lips were sweet and tempting: a girl he had known not an hour but whom already he loved, though he himself did not dream it nor discover it till too late.... And with these many other visions formed and dissolved in dream-like phantasmagoria; but of them all the strongest and most recurrent was that of the girl in the black riding-habit, walking by his side down the aisle of trees. So that presently the tired and overwrought man believed himself talking with her, reasoning, arguing, pleading desperately for his heart's desire;... and wakened with a start, to hear the echo of her voice as though she had spoken but the instant gone, to find his own lips framing the syllables of her name—"Sophia!"

Thus strangely he came to know that beyond question he loved. And he stopped short and stood blinking blindly at nothing, a little frightened by the depth and strength of this passion which had come to him with such scant presage, realising for the first time that his need for her was an insatiable hunger of the soul.... And she was lost to him; half a world lay between them—or soon would. All his days he had awaited, a little curiously, a little sceptical, the coming of the thing men call Love; and when it had come to him he had not known it nor guessed it until its cause had slipped away from him.... Beyond recall?

Abruptly he regained consciousness of his plight, and with an effort shook his senses back into his head. It was not precisely a time when he could afford to let his wits go wool-gathering. And he realised that he had been, in a way, more than half-asleep as he walked; even now he was drowsy, his eyes were heavy, his feet leaden—and numb with cold besides. He had no least notion of what distance he might have travelled or whether he had walked in a straight line or a circle; but when he thought to glance over his shoulder—there was at the moment perhaps more wind with less snow than there had been for some time—he found the lighthouse watching him as it had from the first: as if he had not won a step away from it for all his struggle and his pains. The white, staring eye winked sardonically through a mist of flakes, was blotted out and turned up a baleful red. It seemed to mock him, but Amber nodded at it with no unfriendly feeling. It still might serve his purpose very well, if his strength held, since he had merely to keep his back to the light and the ocean beach upon his right to win to the Shampton sandbar, whether soon or late.

Inflexible of purpose in the face of all his weariness and discouragement, he was on the point of resuming his march when he was struck by the circumstance that the whitened shoulder of a dune, quite near at hand, should seem as if frosted with light—coldly luminous.

Staring, speculative, he hung in the wind—inquisitive as a cat but loath to waste time in footless inquiry. The snow-fall, setting in with augmented violence, decided him. Where light was, there should be man, and where man, shelter.

His third eager stride opened up a wide basin in the dunes, filled with eddying veils of snow, and set, at some distance, with two brilliant squares of light—windows in an invisible dwelling. In the space between them, doubtless, there would be a door. But a second time he paused, remembering that the island was said to be uninhabited. Only yesterday he had asked and been so informed.... Odd!

So passing strange he held it, indeed, that he was conscious of a singular reluctance to question the phenomenon. That superstitious dread of the unknown which lies dormant in us all, in Amber stirred and awoke and held him back like a strong hand. Or, if there be such a thing as a premonition of misfortune, he may be said to have experienced it in that hour; certainly a presentiment of evil crawled in his brain, and he hesitated at a time when he desired naught in the world so much as that which the windows promised— light, heat and human companionship. He had positively to force himself on to seek the door, and even when he had stumbled against its step he twice lifted his hand and let it fall without knocking.

There was not a sound within that he could hear above the clamour of the goblin night.

In the end, however, he knocked stoutly enough.

CHAPTER IV

THE MAN PERDU

A shadow swept swiftly across one of the windows, and the stranger at the door was aware of a slight jarring as though some more than ordinarily brutal gust of wind had shaken the house upon its foundation, or an inner door had been slammed violently. But otherwise he had so little evidence that his summons had fallen on aught but empty walls or deaf ears that he had begun to debate his right to enter without permission, when a chain rattled, a bolt grated, and the door swung wide. A flood of radiance together with a gust of heated air struck him in the face. Dazzled, he reeled across the threshold.

The door banged, and again the house in the dunes shuddered as the storm fell upon it with momentarily trebled ferocity; as if, cheated of its foreordained prey, it would rend apart his frail refuge to regain him.

Three paces within the room Amber paused, waiting for his eyes to adjust themselves to the light. Vaguely conscious of a presence behind him, he faced another—the slight, spare silhouette of a man's figure between him and the lamp; and at the same time felt that he was being subjected to a close scrutiny—both searching and, at its outset, the reverse of hospitable. But he had no more than become sensitive to this than the man before him stepped quickly forward and with two strong hands clasped his shoulders.

"David Amber!" he heard his name pronounced in a voice singularly resonant and pleasant. "So you've run me to earth at last!"

Amber's face was blank with incredulity as he recognised the speaker.
"Rutton!" he stammered. "Rutton—why—by all that's strange!"

"Guilty," said the other with a quiet laugh. "But sit down." He swung Amber about, gently guiding him to a chair. "You look pretty well done up. How long have you been out in this infernal night? But never mind answering; I can wait. Doggott!"

"Yes, sir."

"Take Mr. Amber's coat and boots and bring him my dressing-gown and slippers."

"Yes, sir."

"And a hot toddy and something to eat—and be quick about it."

"Very good, sir."

Rutton's body-servant moved noiselessly to Amber's side, deftly helping him remove his shooting-jacket, whereon snow had caked in thin and brittle sheets. His eyes, grey and shallow, flickered recognition and softened, but he did not speak in anticipation of Amber's kindly "Good-evening, Doggott." To which he responded quietly: "Good-evening, Mr. Amber. It's a pleasure to see you again. I trust you are well."

"Quite, thank you. And you?"

"I'm very fit, thank you sir."

"And"—Amber sat down again, Doggott kneeling at his feet to unlace and remove his heavy pigskin hunting-boots—"and your brother?"

For a moment the man did not answer. His head was lowered so that his features were invisible, but a dull, warm flush overspread his cheeks.

"And your brother, Doggott?"

"I'm sorry, sir, about that; but it was Mr. Rutton's order," muttered the man.

"You're talking of the day you met Doggott at Nokomis station?" interposed his employer from the stand he had taken at one side of the fireplace, his back to the broad hearth whereon blazed a grateful driftwood fire.

Amber looked up inquiringly, nodding an unspoken affirmative.

"It was my fault that he—er—prevaricated, I'm afraid; as he says, it was by my order."

Rutton's expression was masked by the shadows; Amber could make nothing of his curious reticence, and remained silent, waiting a further explanation. It came, presently, with an effect of embarrassment.

"I had—have peculiar reasons for not wishing my refuge here to be discovered. I told Doggott to be careful, should he meet any one we knew. Although, of course, neither of us anticipated…."

"I don't think Doggott was any more dumfounded than I," said Amber. "I couldn't believe he'd left you, yet it seemed impossible that you should be here—of all places—in the neighbourhood of Nokomis, I mean. As for that—" Amber shook his head expressively, glancing round the mean room in which he had found this man of such extraordinary qualities. "It's altogether inconceivable," he summed up his bewilderment.

"It does seem so—even to me, at times."

"Then why—in Heaven's name—"

By now Doggott had invested Amber in his master's dressing-gown and slippers; rising he left them, passing out through an inner door which led, evidently, to the only other room in the cottage. Rutton delayed his reply until the man had shut the door behind him, then suddenly, with the manner of one yielding to the inevitable, drew a chair up to face Amber's and dropped into it.

"I see I must tell you something—a little; as little as I can help—of the truth."

"I'm afraid you must; though I'm damned if I can detect a glimmer of either rhyme or reason in this preposterous situation."

Rutton laughed quietly, lounging in his armchair and lacing before him the fingers of hands singularly small and delicate in view of their very considerable strength—to which Amber's shoulder still bore aching testimony.

"In three words," he said deliberately: "I am hiding."

21

"Hiding!"

"Obviously."

Amber bent forward, studying the elder man's face intently. Thin and dark—not tanned like Amber's, but with a native darkness of skin like that of the Spanish—it was strongly marked, its features at once prominent and finely modelled. The hair intensely black, the eyes as dark and of peculiar fire, the lips broad, full, and sympathetic, the cheekbones high, the forehead high and something narrow: these combined to form a strangely striking ensemble, and none the less striking for its weird resemblance to Amber's own cast of countenance.

Indeed, their likeness one to the other was nothing less than weird in that it could be so superficially strong, yet so elusive. No two men were ever more unalike than these save in this superficial accident of facial contours and complexion. No one knowing Amber (let us say) could ever have mistaken him for Rutton; and yet any one, strange to both, armed with a description of Rutton, might pardonably have believed Amber to be his man. Yet manifestly they were products of alien races, even of different climes—their individualities as dissimilar as the poles. Where in Rutton's bearing burned an inextinguishable, almost an insolent pride, beneath an ice-like surface of self-constraint, in Amber's one detected merely quiet consciousness of strength and breeding—his inalienable heritage from many generations of Anglo-Saxon forebears; and while Rutton continually betrayed, by look or tone or gesture, a birthright of fierce passions savagely tamed, from Amber one seldom obtained a hint of aught but the broad and humourous tolerance of an American gentleman.

But to-night the Virginian had undergone enough to have lost much of his habitual poise. "Hiding!" he reiterated in a tone scarcely louder than a whisper.

"And you have found me out, my friend."

"But—but I don't—"

Rutton lifted a hand in deprecation; and as he did so the door in the rear of the room opened and Doggott entered. Cat-like, passing behind Amber, he placed upon the table a small tray, and from a steaming pitcher poured him a glass of hot spiced wine. At a look from his employer he filled a second.

"There's sandwiches, sir," he said; "the best I could manage at short notice, Mr. Amber. If you'll wait a bit I can fix you up something 'ot."

"Thank you, Doggott, that won't be necessary; the sandwiches look mighty good to me."

"Thank you, sir. Will there be anything else, Mr. Rutton?"

"If there is, I'll call you."

"Yes, sir. Good-night, sir. Good-night, Mr. Amber."

As Doggott shut himself out of the room, Amber lifted his fragrant glass. "You're joining me, Rutton?"

"With all my heart!" The man came forward to his glass. "For old sake's sake, David. Shall we drink a toast?" He hesitated, with a marked air of embarrassment, then impulsively swung his glass aloft. "Drink standing!" he cried, he voice oddly vibrant. And Amber rose. "To the King—the King, God bless him!"

"To the King!" It was more an exclamation of surprise than an echo to the toast; nevertheless Amber drained his drink to the final drop. As he resumed his seat, the room rang with the crash of splintering glass; Rutton had dashed his tumbler to atoms on the hearthstone.

"Well!" commented Amber, lifting his brows questioningly. "You *are* sincere, Rutton. But who in blazes would ever have suspected you of being a British subject?"

"Why not?"

"But it seems to me I should have known——"

"What have you ever really known about me, David, save that I am myself?"

"Well—when you put it that way—little enough—nothing." Amber laughed nervously, disconcerted.

"And I? Who and what am I?" No answer was expected—so much was plain from Rutton's tone; he was talking to himself more than addressing his guest. His long brown fingers strayed to the box and conveyed a cigarette to his lips; staring dreamily into the fire, he smoked a little ere continuing. "What does it mean, this eternal 'I' round which the world revolves?" His voice trailed off into silence.

Amber snapped the tension with a chuckle. "You can search me," he said irreverently. And his host returned his smile. "Now, will you please pay attention to me, my friend? Or do you wish me to turn and rend myself with curiosity—after I've attended to these excellent sandwiches?… Seriously, I want to know several things. What have you been doing with yourself these past three years?"

Rutton shook his head gravely. "I can't say."

"You mean you won't?"

"If you will have it that way."

"Well … I give you up."

"That's the most profitable thing you could do, David."

"But, seriously now, this foolish talk about hiding is all a joke, isn't it?"

"No," said Rutton soberly; "no, it's no joke." He sighed profoundly. "As for my recent whereabouts, I have been—ah—travelling considerably; moving about from pillar to post." To this the man added a single word, the more significant in that it embodied the nearest approach to a confidence that Amber had ever known him to make: "Hunted."

"Hunted by whom?"

"I beg your pardon." Rutton bent forward and pushed the cigarettes to Amber's elbow. "I am—ah—so preoccupied with my own mean troubles, David, that I had forgotten that you had nothing to smoke. Forgive me."

"That's no matter, I——"

Amber cut short his impatient catechism in deference to the other's mute plea. And Rutton thanked him with a glance—one of those looks which, between friends, are more eloquent than words. Sighing, he shook his head, his eyes once more seeking the flames. And silently studying his face—the play of light from lamp and hearth throwing its features into salient relief—for the first time Amber, his wits warmed back to activity from the stupor the bitter cold had put upon them, noticed how time and care had worn upon the man since they had last parted. He had never suspected Rutton to be his senior by more years than ten, at the most; to-night, however, he might well be taken for fifty were his age to be reckoned by its accepted signs—the hollowing of cheek and temple, the sinking of eyes into their sockets, the deepening of the maze of lines about the mouth and on the forehead.

Impulsively the younger man sat up and put a hand upon the arm of Rutton's chair. "What can I do?" he asked simply.

Rutton roused, returning his regard with a smile slow, charming, infinitely sad. "Nothing," he replied; "absolutely nothing."

"But surely——!"

"No man can do for me what I cannot do for myself. When the time comes"—he lifted his shoulders lightly—"I will do what I can. Till then…." He diverged at a tangent. "After all, the world is quite as tiny as the worn-out aphorism has it. To think that you should find me here! It's less than a week since Doggott and I hit upon this place and settled down, quite convinced we had, at last, lost ourselves … and might have peace, for a little space at least!"

Amber glanced curiously round the room; sparely furnished, bare, unlovely, it seemed a most cheerless sort of spot to be considered a haven of peace.

"And now," concluded Rutton, "we have to move on."

"Because I've found you here?"

"Because you have found me."

"I don't understand."

"My dear boy, I never meant you should."

"But if you're in any danger—"

"I am not."

"You're not! But you just said—"

"I'm in no danger whatever; humanity is, if I'm found."

"I don't follow you at all."

Again Rutton smiled wearily. "I didn't expect you to, David. But this misadventure makes it necessary that I should tell you something; you must be made to believe in me. I beg you to; I'm neither mad nor making game of you." There was no questioning the sane sincerity of the man. He continued slowly. "It's a simple fact, incredible but absolute, that, were my whereabouts to be made public, a great, a staggering blow would be struck against the peace and security of the world…. Don't laugh, David; I mean it."

"I'm not laughing, Rutton; but you must know that's a pretty large order. Most men would—"

"Call me mad. Yes, I know," Rutton took up his words as Amber paused, confused. "I can't expect you to understand me: you couldn't unless I were to tell you what I may not. But you know me—better, perhaps, than any living man save Doggott … and one other. You know whether or not I would seek to delude you, David. And, knowing that I could not, you know why it seems to me imperative that, this hole being discovered, Doggott and I must betake ourselves elsewhere. Surely there must be solitudes——!" He rose with a gesture of impatience and began restlessly to move to and fro.

Amber started suddenly, flushing. "If you mean—"

Rutton's kindly hand forced him back into his chair. "Sit down, David. I never meant that—never for an instant dreamed you'd intentionally betray my secret. It's enough that you should know it, should occasionally think of me as being here, to bring misfortune down upon me, to work an incalculable disaster to the progress of this civilisation of ours."

"You mean," Amber asked uncertainly, "thought transference?"

"Something of the sort—yes." The man came to a pause beside Amber, looking down almost pitifully into his face. "I daresay all this sounds hopelessly melodramatic and neurotic and tommyrotic, David, but … I can tell you nothing more. I'm sorry."

"But only let me help you—any way in my power, Rutton. There's nothing I'd not do…."

"I know, David, I know it. But my case is beyond human aid, since I am powerless to apply a remedy myself."

"And you *are* powerless?"

24

Rutton was silent a long moment. Then, "Time will tell," he said quietly. "There is one way...." He resumed his monotonous round of the room.

Mechanically Amber began to smoke, trying hard to think, to penetrate by reasoning or intuition the wall of mystery which, it seemed, Rutton chose to set between himself and the world. The intense earnestness of the man's hopeless confession had carried conviction. Amber believed him, believed in the reality of his trouble; and, divining it dimly, a monstrous, menacing shape in the vagueness of the unknown, was himself dismayed and a little fearful. He owed much to this man, was bound to him by ties not only of gratitude but of affection, yet, finding him distressed, found himself simultaneously powerless to render aid. Inwardly mutinous, he had to school himself to quiescence; lacking the confidence which Rutton so steadfastly refused him, he was impotent.

Presently he grew conscious that Rutton was standing as if listening, his eyes averted to the windows. But when Amber looked they showed, beneath their half-drawn muslin shades, naught save the grey horizontal rush of snow beyond the panes. And he heard nothing save the endless raving of the maniac wind.

"What is it?" he inquired at length, unable longer to endure the tensity of the pause.

"Nothing. I beg your pardon, David." Rutton returned to his chair, making a visible effort to shake off his preoccupation. "It's an ugly night, out there. Lucky you blundered on this place. Tell me how it happened. What became of the other man—your friend?"

The thought of Quain stabbed Amber's consciousness with a mental pang as keen as acute physical anguish. He jumped up in torment. "God!" he cried chokingly. "I'd forgotten! He's out there on the bay, poor devil!—freezing to death if not drowned. Our boat went adrift somehow; Quain would insist on going after her in a leaky old skiff we found on the shore ... and didn't come back. I waited till it was hopeless, then concluded I'd make a try to cross to Shampton by way of the tidal bar. And I must!"

"It's impossible," Rutton told him with grave sympathy.

"But I must; think of his wife and children, Rutton! There's a chance yet—a bare chance; he may have reached the boat. If he did, every minute I waste here is killing him by inches; he'll die of exposure! But from Shampton we could send a boat—"

"The tide fulls about midnight to-night," interrupted Rutton, consulting his watch. "It's after nine,—and there's a heavy surf breaking over the bar now. By ten it'll be impassable, and you couldn't reach it before eleven. Be content, David; you're powerless."

"You're right—I know that," groaned Amber, his head in his hands. "I was afraid it was hopeless, but—but—"

"I know, dear boy, I know!"

With a gesture of despair Amber resumed his seat. For some time he remained deep sunk in dejection. At length, mastering his emotion, he looked up. "How did you know about Quain—that we were together?" he asked.

"Doggott saw you land this morning, and I've been watching you all day with my field-glasses, prepared to take cover the minute you turned my way. Don't be angry with me, David; it wasn't that I didn't yearn to see you face to face again, but that ... I didn't dare."

"Oh, that!" exclaimed Amber with an exasperated fling of his hand. "Between the two of you—you and Quain—you'll drive me mad with worry."

"I'm sorry, David. I only wish I might say more. It hurts a bit to have you doubt me."

"I don't doubt," Amber declared in desperation; "at least, I mean I won't if you'll be sensible and let me stand by and see you through this trouble—whatever it is."

25

Rutton turned to the fire, his head drooping despondently. "That may not be," he said heavily. "The greatest service you can do me is to forget my existence, now and henceforth, erase our friendship from the tablets of your memory, pass me as a stranger should our ways ever cross again." He flicked the stub of a cigarette into the flames. "Kismet!… I mean that, David, from my heart. Won't you do this for me—one last favour, old friend?"

"I'll try; I'll even promise, on condition that you send me word if ever you have need of me."

"That will be never."

"But if—"

"I'll send for you if ever I may, David; I promise faithfully. And in return I have your word?"

Amber nodded.

"Then…." Rutton attempted to divert the subject. "I think you said Quain? Any relation to Quain's 'Aryan Invasion of India?'"

"The same man. He asked me down for the shooting—owns a country place across the bay: Tanglewood."

"A very able man; I wish I might have met him…. What of yourself? What have you been doing these three years? Have you married?"

"I've been too busy to think of that…. I mean, till lately."

"Ah?"

Amber flushed boyishly. "There was a girl at Quain's—a guest…. But she left before I dared speak. Perhaps it was as well."

"Why?"

"Because she was too fine and sweet and good for me, Rutton."

"Like every man's first love."

The elder man's glance was keen—too keen for Amber to dissimulate successfully under it. "You're right," he admitted ruefully. "It's the first sure-enough trouble of the sort I ever experienced. And, of course, it had to be hopeless."

"Why?" persisted Rutton.

"Because—I've half a notion there's a chap waiting for her at home."

"At home?"

"In England." The need for a confidant was suddenly imperative upon the younger man. "She's an English girl—half English, that is; her mother was an American, a schoolmate of Quain's wife; her father, an Englishman in the Indian service."

"Her name?"

"Sophia Farrell." A peculiar quality, a certain tensity, in Rutton's manner, forced itself upon Amber's attention. "Why?" he asked. "Do you know the Farrells? What's the matter?"

Rutton's eyes met his stonily; out of the ashen mask of his face, that suddenly had whitened beneath the brown, they glared, afire but unseeing. His hands writhed, the fingers twisting together with cruel force, the knuckles grey. Abruptly, as if abandoning the attempt to reassert his self-control, he jumped up and went quickly to a window, there to stand, his back to Amber, staring fixedly out into the storm-racked night. "I knew her father," he said at length, his tone constrained and odd, "long ago, in India."

"He's out there now—a Political, I believe they call him, or something of the sort."

"Yes."

26

"She's going out to rejoin him."

"What!" Rutton came swiftly back to Amber, his voice shaking. "What did you say?"

"Why, yes. She travels with friends by the western route to join Colonel Farrell at Darjeeling, where he's stationed just now. Shortly after I came down she left; Mrs. Quain had a wire a day or so ago, saying she was on the point of sailing from San Francisco…. Good Lord, Rutton! are you ill?"

Something in the man's face had brought Amber to his feet, a prey to inexpressible concern; it was as if a mask had dropped and he were looking upon the soul of a man in mortal torture.

"No," gasped Rutton, "I'm all right. Besides," he added beneath his breath, so that Amber barely caught the syllables, "it's too late."

As rapidly as he had lost he seemed to regain mastery of his inexplicable emotion. His face became again composed, almost immobile, and stepping to the table he selected a cigarette and rolled it gently between his slim brown fingers. "I'm sorry to have alarmed you," he said, his tone a bit too even not to breed a doubt in the mind of his hearer. "It's nothing serious—a little trouble of the heart, of long standing, incurable—I hope."

Perplexed, yet hesitating to press him further, Amber watched him furtively, instinctively assured that between this man and the Farrells there existed some extraordinary bond; wondering how that could be, convinced in his soul that somehow the entanglement involved the woman he loved, he still feared to put his suspicions to the question, lest he should learn that which he had no right to know … and while he watched was startled by the change that came over Rutton. At ease, one moment, outwardly composed if absorbed in thought, the next he was rigid, every muscle taut, every nerve tense as a steel spring, his keen, thoughtful face hardening with a look of brutal hatred, his eyes narrowing until no more than a glint of fire was visible between the lashes, lips straining apart until they showed thin and bloodless, with a gleam of white, set teeth between. His head jerked back suddenly, his gaze fixing itself first upon the window, then shifting to the door. And his fingers, contracting, tore the cigarette in half.

"Rutton, what the deuce is the matter?"

Rutton seemed not to hear; Amber got his answer from the door, which was swung wide and slammed shut. A blast of frosty air and a flurry of snow swept across the room. And against the door there leaned a man puffing for breath and coughing spasmodically—a gross and monstrous bulk of flesh, unclean and unwholesome to the eye, attired in an extravagant array of coloured garments, tawdry silks and satins clinging, sodden, to his ponderous and unwieldy limbs.

"The babu!" cried Amber unconsciously; and was rewarded by a flash of recognition from the coal-black, beady, evil eyes of the man.

But for that involuntary exclamation the tableau held unbroken for a space; Rutton standing transfixed, the torn halves of the cigarette between his fingers, his head well up and back, his stare level, direct, uncompromising, a steady challenge to the intruder; the babu resting with one shoulder against the door, panting stertorously and trembling with the cold and exposure he had undergone, yet with his attention unflinchingly concentrated upon Rutton; and, finally, Amber, a little out of the picture and quite unconsidered of the others, not without a certain effect as of a supernumerary standing in the wings and watching the development of the drama.

Then, demanding Amber's silence with an imperative movement of his hand, Rutton spoke. "Well, babu?" he said quietly, the shadow of a bitter and weary smile curving his thin, hard lips.

The Bengali moved a pace or two from the door, and plucked nervously at the throat of his surtout, finally managing to insert one hand in the folds of silk across his bosom.

"I seek," he said distinctly in Urdu, and not without a definite note of menace in his manner, "the man calling himself Rutton Sahib?"

Very deliberately Rutton inclined his head. "I am he."

"Hazoor!" The babu laboriously doubled up his enormous body in profound obeisance. Having recovered, he nodded to Amber with the easy familiarity of an old acquaintance. "To you, likewise, greeting, Amber Sahib."

"What!" Rutton swung sharply to Amber with an exclamation of amazement. "You know this fellow, David?"

The babu cut in hastily, stimulated by a pressing anxiety to clear himself. "Hazoor, I did but err, being misled by his knowledge of our tongue as well as by that pale look of you he wears. And, indeed, is it strange that I should take him for you, who was told to seek you in this wild land?"

"Be silent!" Rutton told him angrily.

"My lord's will is his slave's." Resignedly the babu folded his fat arms.

"Tell me about this," Rutton demanded of Amber.

"The ass ran across me in the woods south of the station, the day I came down," explained Amber, summarising the episode as succinctly as he could. "He didn't call me by your name, but I've no doubt he's telling the truth about mistaking me for you. At all events he hazoor-ed me a number of times, talked a lot of rot about some silly 'Voice,' and finally made me a free gift of a nice little bronze box that wouldn't open. After which he took to his heels, saying he'd call later for my answer—whatever he meant by that. He did call by night and stole the box. That's about all I know of him, thus far. But I'd watch out for him, if I were you; if he isn't a raving lunatic, I miss my guess."

"Indeed, my lord, it is all quite as the sahib says," the babu admitted graciously, his eyes gleaming with sardonic amusement. "Circumstances conspired to mislead me; but that I was swift to discover. Nor did I lose time in remedying the error, as you have heard. Moreover—"

He shut up suddenly at a sign from Rutton, with a ludicrous shrug of his huge shoulders disclaiming any ill-intent or wrong-doing; and while Rutton remained deep in thought by the table, the babu held silence, his gaze flickering suspiciously round the room, searching the shadows, questioning the closed door behind which Doggott lay asleep (evidence of which fact was not wanting in his snores), resting fleetingly on Amber's face, returning to Rutton. His features were composed; his face, indeed, might have been taken as a model for some weird mask of unctuous depravity, but for his eyes, which betrayed a score of differing phases of emotion. He was by turns apparently possessed by fear, malice, distrust, a subtle sense of triumph, contempt for Amber, deference to Rutton, and a feeling that he was master not alone of the situation but of the man whom he professed to honor so extravagantly.

At length Rutton looked up, suppressing a sigh. "Your errand, babu?"

"Is it, then, your will that I should speak before this man?" The Bengali nodded impudently at Amber.

"It is my will."

"Shabash! I bear a message, hazoor, from the Bell."

"You are the Mouthpiece of the Voice?"

"That honor is mine, hazoor. For the rest I am—"

28

"Behari Lal Chatterji," interrupted Rutton impatiently; "solicitor of the Inner Temple—disbarred; anointed thief, liar, jackal, lickspittle, and perjurer—I know you."

"My lord," said the man insolently, "omits from his catalogue of my accomplishments my chiefest honour; he forgets that, with him, I am an accepted Member of the Body."

"The Body wears strange members that employs you, babu," commented Rutton bitterly. "It has fallen upon evil days when such as you are charged with a message of the Bell."

"My lord is harsh to one who would be his slave in all things. Fortunate indeed am I to own the protection of the Token." A slow leer widened greasily upon his moon-like face.

"Ah, the Token!" Rutton repeated tensely, beneath his breath. "It is true that you have the Token?" "Aye; it is even here, my lord." The heavy brown hand returned to the spot it had sought soon after the babu's entrance, within the folds of silk across his bosom, and groped therein for an instant. "Even here," he iterated with a maddening manner of supreme self-complacency, producing the bronze box and waddling over to drop it into Rutton's hand. "My lord is satisfied?" he gurgled maliciously.

Without answering Rutton turned the box over in his palm, his slender fingers playing about the bosses of the relief work; there followed a click and one side of it swung open. The Bengali fell back a pace with a whisper of awe—real or affected: "The Token, hazoor!" Amber himself gasped slightly.

Unheeded, the box dropped to the floor. Between Rutton's thumb and forefinger there blazed a great emerald set in a ring of red old gold. He turned it this way and that, inspecting it critically; and the lamplight, catching on the facets, struck from it blinding shafts of intensely green radiance. Rutton nodded as if in recognition of the stone and, turning, with an effect of carelessness, tossed it to Amber.

"Keep that for me, David, please," he said. And Amber, catching it, dropped the ring into his pocket.

"My lord is satisfied with my credentials, then?" the babu persisted.

"It is the Token," Rutton assented wearily. "Now, your message. Be brief."

"The utterances of the Voice be infrequent, hazoor, its words few—but charged with meaning: as you know of old." The Bengali drew himself up, holding up his head and rolling forth his phrases in a voice of great resonance and depth. "These be the words of the Voice, hazoor:

"'_To all my peoples:

"'Even now the Gateway of Swords yawns wide, that he who is without fear may pass within; to the end that the Body be purged of the Scarlet Evil.

"'The Elect are bidden to the Ordeal with no exception._'"

The sonorous accents subsided, and a tense wait ensued, none speaking. Rutton stood in stony apathy, his eyes lifted to a dim corner of the ceiling, his gaze—like his thoughts—perhaps ranging far beyond the dreary confines of the cabin in the dunes. Minute after minute passed, he making no sign, the babu poised before him in inscrutable triumph, watching him keenly with his black and evil eyes of a beast. Amber hung breathless upon the issue, sensing a conflict of terrible forces in Rutton's mind, but comprehending nothing of their natures. In the hush within-doors he became acutely conscious of the war of elements without: the mad elfin yammering of the gale tearing at the cabin as though trying to seize it up bodily and whirl it off into the witches' dance of the storm; the deep and awful booming of the breakers, whose incessant impact upon the beach seemed to rock the very island on its base. Somehow he divined a similitude between the struggle within and the struggle without, seemed to see the contending elements personified before his eyes—the spirit of evil incarnate in the Bengali, vast,

29

loathsome, terrible in his inflexibility of malign purpose; the force of right symbolized in Rutton, frail of stature, fine of mould, strong in his unbending loyalty to his conception of honour and duty. The Virginian could have predicted the outcome confidently, believing as he did in his friend. It came eventually on the heels of a movement of the babu's; unable longer to hold his pose, he shifted slightly. And Rutton awoke as from a sleep.

"The Voice has spoken, babu," he said, not ungently, "and I have heard."

"And your answer, lord?"

"There is no answer."

"Hazoor!"

"I have said," Rutton confirmed evenly, "there is no answer."

"You will obey?"

"That is between me and my God. Go back to the Hall of the Bell, Behari Lal Chatterji, and deliver your report; say that you have seen me, that I have listened to the words of the Voice, and that I sent no answer."

"Hazoor, I may not. I am charged to return only with you."

"Make your peace with the Bell in what manner you will, babu; it is no concern of mine. Go, now, while yet time is granted you to avoid a longer journey this night."

"Hazoor!"

"Go." Rutton pointed to the door, his voice imperative.

Upon this the babu abandoned argument, realising that further resistance were futile. And in a twinkling his dignity, his Urdu and his cloak of mystery, were discarded, and he was merely an over-educated and over-fed Bengali, jabbering babu-English.

"Oah, as for thatt," he affirmed easily, with an oleaginous smirk, "I daresay I shall be able to make adequate explanation. It shall be as you say, sar. I confess to fright, however, because of storm." He included Amber affably in his confidences. "By Gad, sar, thees climate iss most trying to person of my habits. The journey hither *via* causeway from mainland was veree fearful. Thee sea is most agitated. You observe my wetness from association with spray. I am of opinion if I am not damn-careful I jolly well catch-my-death on return. But *thatt* is all in day's work."

He rolled sluggishly toward the door, dragging his inadequate overcoat across his barrel-like chest; and paused to cough affectingly, with one hand on the knob. Rutton eyed him contemptuously.

"If you care to run the risk," he said suddenly, "you may have a chair by the fire till the storm breaks, babu."

"Beg pardon?" The babu's eyes widened. "Oah, yess; I see. 'If I care to run risk.' Veree considerate of you, I'm sure. But as we say in Bengal, 'thee favour of kings iss ass a sword of two edges.' Noah, thanks; the servants of thee Bell do not linger by wayside, soa to speak. Besides, I am in great hurree. Mister Amber, good night. Rutton Sahib"—with a flash of his sinister humour—"*au revoir*; I mean to say, till we meet in thee Hall of thee Bell. Good night."

He nodded insolently to the man whom a little time since he had hailed as "my lord," shrugged his coat collar up round his fat, dirty neck, shivered in anticipation, jerked the door open and plunged ponderously out.

A second later Amber saw the confused mass of his turban glide past the window.

CHAPTER V

THE GOBLIN NIGHT

Amber whistled low. "Impossible!" he said thoughtfully.

Rutton had crossed to and was bending over a small leather trunk that stood in one corner of the room. In the act of opening it, he glanced over his shoulder. "What?" he demanded sharply.

"I was only thinking; there's something I can't see through in that babu's willingness to go."

"He was afraid to stay."

"Why?"

Rutton, rummaging in the trunk, made no reply. After a moment Amber resumed.

"You know what Bengalis are; that fellow'd do anything, brave any ordinary danger, rather than try to cross that sandbar again—if he really came that way; which I am inclined to doubt. On the other hand, he's intelligent enough to know that a night like this in the dunes would kill him. Well, what then?"

Rutton was not listening. As Amber concluded he seemed to find what he had been seeking, thrust it hurriedly into the breast-pocket of his coat, and with a muttered word, unintelligible, dashed to the door and flung it open and himself out.

With a shriek of demoniac glee the wind entered into and took possession of the room. A cloud of snow swept across the floor like a veil. The door battered against the wall as if trying to break it down. A pile of newspapers was swept from the table and scattered to the four corners of the room. The rug lifted beneath the table and flapped against it like a broken wing. The cheap tin kerosene lamp jumped as though caught up by a hand; its flame leapt high and blue above the chimney—and was not. In darkness but for the fitful flare of the fire that had been dying in embers on the hearth, Amber, seeking the doorway, fell over a chair, blundered flat into the wall, and stumbled unexpectedly out of the house.

His concern was all for Rutton; he had no other thought. He ran a little way down the hollow, heartsick with horror and cold with dread. Then he paused, bewildered. Other than the wan glimmer of the snow-clad earth he had no light to guide him; with this poor aid he could see no more than that the vale was deserted. Whither in that white whirling world Rutton might have wandered, it was impossible to surmise. In despair the Virginian turned back.

When he had found his way to the door of the cabin, it was closed; as he entered and shut it behind him, a match flared and expired in the middle of the room, and a man cursed brokenly.

"Rutton?" cried Amber in a flush of hope.

"Is that you, Mr. Amber? Thank Gawd! Wyte a minute."

A second match spluttered, its flame waxing in the pink cup of Doggott's hands. The servant's head and shoulders stood out in dim relief against the darkness.

"I've burnt me 'and somethin' 'orrid on this damn' 'ot chimney," he complained nervously.

He succeeded in setting fire to the wick. The light showed him barefoot and shivering in shirt and trousers. He lifted a bemused red face to Amber, blinking and nursing his scorched hand. "For pity's syke, sir, w'at's 'appened?"

"It's hard to say," replied Amber vaguely, preoccupied. He went immediately to a window and stood there, looking out.

"But w'ere's Mr. Rutton, sir?"

"Gone—out there—I don't know just where." Amber moved back to the table. "You see, he had a caller."

"A caller, sir—on a night like this?"

"The man he came here to hide from," said Amber.

"I knew 'e was tryin' to dodge somethin', sir; but 'e never told me aught about it. What kind of a person was 'e, sir, and what made Mr. Rutton go aw'y with 'im?"

"He didn't; he went after him to...." Amber caught his tongue on the verge of an indiscretion; no matter what his fears, they were not yet become a suitable subject for discussion with Rutton's servant. "I think," he amended lamely, "he had forgotten something."

"And 'e's out there now! My Gawd, what a night!" He hung in hesitation for a little. "Did 'e wear 'is topcoat and 'at, sir?"

"No; he went suddenly. I don't think he intended to be gone long."

"I'd better go after 'im, then. 'E'll 'ave pneumonia ... I'll just jump into me clothes and—" He slipped into the back room, to reappear with surprisingly little delay, fully dressed and buttoning a long ulster round his throat. "You didn't 'appen to notice which w'y 'e went, sir?"

"As well as I could judge, to the east."

Doggott took down a second ulster and a cap from pegs in the wall. "I'll do my best to find 'im; 'e might lose 'imself, you know, with no light nor nothin'."

"And you?"

"I'll be all right; I'll follow 'is footprints in the snow. I've a 'andy little electric bull's-eye to 'elp me, in my pocket."

"Are you armed, Doggott?"

"By Mr. Rutton's orders, sir, I've carried a revolver for years. You aren't thinkin' it's come to that, sir?"

"I don't know.... If I was sure I wouldn't let you go alone," said Amber, frowning. "It's only that Mr. Rutton may not want me about ... I wish I knew!"

"It'll be better, sir, for you to stay and keep the fire up—if you don't mind my makin' so free as to advise—in case 'e's 'arf-froze when 'e gets back, as is likely. But I'd better 'urry, 'specially if...." Doggott's color faded a little and his mouth tightened. "But I 'ope you're mistyken, sir. Good-night."

The door slammed behind him.

Alone, and a prey to misgivings he scarce dared name to himself, Amber from the window watched the blot of light from Doggott's handlamp fade and vanish in the storm; then, becoming sensible to the cold, went to the fireplace, kicked the embers together until they blazed, and piled on more fuel.

A cosy, crackling sound began to be audible in the room; sibilant jets of flame, scarlet, yellow, violet, and green, spurted up from the driftwood. Under the hypnotic influence of the comforting warmth, weariness descended upon Amber like a burden; he was afraid to close his eyes or to sit down, lest sleep should overcome him for all his intense excitement and anxiety. He forced himself to move steadily round the room, struggling against a feeling that all that he had witnessed must have been untrue, an evil dream, akin to the waking visions that had beset him between the loss of Quain and the finding of

Rutton. The very mediocrity of the surroundings seemed to discredit the testimony of his wits.

Unmistakably a camp erected for its owners' convenience during the hunting season, alike in design and furnishing the cabin was almost painfully crude and homely. The walls were of rough-hewn logs from which the bark had not been removed; the interstices were stopped only with coarse plaster; the partition dividing it into two rooms was of pine, unpainted. In one corner near Rutton's trunk, a bed-hammock swung from a beam. The few chairs were plain and rude. There were two deal tables, a plate-rack nailed to the partition, and a wall-seat in the chimney-corner. On the centre table, aside from the lamp, were a couple of books, some out-of-date magazines, and a common tin alarm-clock ticking stolidly.

In a setting so hopelessly commonplace and everyday, one act of a drama of blood and fire had been played; into these mean premises the breath of the storm, as the babu entered, had blown Romance.... Incredible!

And yet Amber's hand, dropping idly in his coat-pocket, encountered a priceless witness to the reality of what had passed. Frowning, troubled, he drew forth the ring and slipped it upon his finger; rays of blinding emerald light coruscated from it, dazzling him. With a low cry of wonder he took it to the lamplight. Never had he looked upon so fine a stone, so strangely cut.

It was set in ruddy soft gold, worked and graven with exquisite art in the semblance of a two-headed cobra; inside the band was an inscription so worn and faint that Amber experienced some difficulty in deciphering the word RAO (king) in Devanagari, flanked by swastikas. Aside from the stone entirely, he speculated, the value of the ring as an antique would have proven inestimable. As for the emerald itself, in its original state, before cutting, it must have been worth the ransom of an emperor; much had certainly been sacrificed to fashion it in its present form. The cunning of a jewel-cutter whose art was lost before Tyre and Nineveh upreared their heads must have been taxed by the task. Its innumerable facets reproduced with wonderful fidelity a human eyeball, unwinking, sleepless. In the enigmatic heart of its impenetrable iris cold fire lived, cold passionless flames leaped and died and leaped again like the sorcerous fire of a pythoness.

To gaze into its depths was like questioning the inscrutable green heart of the sea. Fascinated, Amber felt his consciousness slip from him as a mantle might slip from his shoulders; awake, staring wide-eyed into the emerald eye, he forgot self, forgot the world, and dreamed, dreamed curiously....

The crash of the door closing behind him brought him to the right-about in a panic flutter. He glared stupidly for a time before comprehending that Rutton and Doggott had returned. How long they had been absent he had no means of reckoning; the interval might have been five minutes or an hour in duration. The time since he had stooped to examine the ring was as indefinite; but his back was aching and his thoughts were drowsy and confused. He had a sensation as of being violently recalled to a dull and colourless world from some far realm of barbaric enchantment. His brain reeled and his vision was blurred as if by the flash and glamour of many vivid colours.

With an effort he managed to force himself to understand that Rutton was back. After that he felt more normal. His thoughts slid back into their accustomed grooves.

If there were anything peculiar in his manner, Rutton did not remark it. Indeed, he seemed unconscious, for a time, of the presence either of Amber or of Doggott. The servant relieved him of his overcoat and hat, and he strode directly to the fire, bending over to chafe and warm his frost-nipped hands. Unquestionably he laboured under the influence of an extraordinary agitation. His limbs twitched and jerked nervously; his eyebrows were tensely elevated, his eyes blazing, his nostrils dilated; his face was ashen grey.

From across the room Doggott signalled silence to Amber, with a forefinger to his lips; and with a discretion bred of long knowledge of his master's temper, tiptoed through into the back room and shut the door.

Amber respected the admonition throughout a wait that seemed endless.

The tin clock hammered off five minutes or more. Suddenly Rutton started and wheeled round, every trace of excitement smoothed away. Meeting Amber's gaze he nodded as if casually, and said, "Oh, Amber," quietly, with an effect of faint surprise. Then he dropped heavily into a chair by the table.

"Well," he said slowly, "that is over."

Amber, without speaking, went to his side and touched his shoulder with that pitifully inadequate gesture of sympathy which men so frequently employ.

"I killed him," said Rutton dully.

"Yes," replied Amber. He was not surprised; he had apprehended the tragedy from the moment that Rutton had fled him, speechless; the feeling of horror that he had at first experienced had ebbed, merged into a sort of apathetic acknowledgment of the inevitable.

After a bit Rutton turned to the table and drew an automatic pistol from his pocket, opening the magazine. Five cartridges remained in the clip, showing that two had been exploded. "I was not sure," he said thoughtfully, "how many times I had fired." His curiosity satisfied, he reloaded the weapon and returned it to his pocket. "He died like a dog," he said, "whimpering and blaspheming in the face of eternity ... out there in the cold and the night.... It was sickening—the sound of the bullets tearing through his flesh...."

He shuddered.

"Didn't he resist?" Amber asked involuntarily.

"He tried to. I let him pop away with his revolver until it was empty. Then...."

"What made you wait?"

"I didn't care; it didn't matter. One of us had to die to-night; he should have known that when I refused to accompany him back to ... I was hungry for his bullet more than for his life; I gave him every chance. But it had to be as it was. That was Fate. Now...." He paused and after a little went on in a more controlled voice. "Quaintly enough, if there's anything in the theory of heredity, David, my hands have been stained with no man's blood before to-night. Yet my forebears were a murderous lot.... Until this hour I never realised how swift and uncontrollable could be the impulse to slay...."

His voice trailed off into silence and he sat staring into the flickering flames that played about the driftwood. Now and again his lips moved noiselessly.

With a wrench Amber pulled himself together. He had been mentally a witness to the murder—had seen the Bengali, obese, monstrous, flabby, his unclean carcass a gross casing for a dark spirit of iniquity and treachery, writhing and whining in the throes of death.... "Rutton," he demanded suddenly, without premeditation, "what are you going to do?"

"Do?" Rutton looked up, his eyes perplexed.

"Why, what is there to do? Get away as best I can, I presume—seek another hole to hide in."

"But how about the law?"

"The law? Why need it ever be known—what has happened to-night? I can count on your silence—I have no need to ask. Doggott would die rather than betray me. He and I can dispose of—it. No one comes here at this time of the year save hunting parties; and their eyes are not upon the ground. You will go your way in the morning. We'll clear out immediately after."

"You'd better take no chances."

Suddenly Rutton smote the table with his fist. "By Indur!" he swore strangely, his voice quavering with joy; "I had not thought of that!" He jumped up and began to move excitedly to and fro. "I am free! None but you and I know of the passing of the Token and the delivery of the message—none can possibly know for days, perhaps weeks. For so much time at least I am in no danger of—"

He shut his mouth like a trap on words that might have enlightened Amber.

"Of what?"

"Let me see: there are still waste places in the world where a man may lose himself. There's Canada—the Hudson Bay region, Labrador...."

A discreet knock sounded on the door in the partition, and it was opened gently. Doggott appeared on the threshold, pale and careworn. Rutton paused, facing him.

"Well?"

"Any orders, sir?"

"Yes; begin packing up. We leave to-morrow."

"Very good, sir."

"That is all to-night."

"Yes, sir. Good-night. Good-night, Mr. Amber." The man retired and at intervals thereafter Amber could hear him moving about, apparently obeying orders.

Rutton replenished the fire and stood with his back to it, smiling almost happily. All evidence of remorse had disappeared. He seemed momentarily almost light-hearted, certainly in better spirits than he had been at any time that night. "Free!" he cried softly. "And by the simplest of solutions. Strange that I should never have thought before to-night of—" He glanced carelessly toward the window; and it was as if his lips had been wiped clean of speech.

Amber turned, thrilling, his flesh creeping with the horror that he had divined in Rutton's transfixed gaze.

Outside the glass, that was lightly silvered with frost, something moved—the spectral shadow of a turbaned head—moved and was stationary for the space of twenty heartbeats. Beneath the turban Amber seemed to see two eyes, wide staring and terribly alight.

"God!" cried Rutton thickly, jerking forth his pistol.

The shadow vanished.

With a single thought Amber sprang upon Rutton, snatched the weapon from his nerveless fingers, and, leaping to the door, let himself out.

The snow had ceased; only the wind raved with untempered force. Overhead it was blowing clear; through rifts and rents in the fast-moving cloud-rack pale turquoise patches of moonlit sky showed, here and there inlaid with a far shining star. The dunes were coldly a-glimmer with the meagre light that penetrated to the earth and was cast back by its white and spotless shroud.

But Amber, at pause a few paces beyond the doorstep, his forefinger ready upon the trigger of the automatic pistol, was alone in the hollow.

Cautiously, and, to be frank, a bit dismayed, he made a reconnaissance, circling the building, but discovered nothing to reward his pains. The snow lay unbroken except in front of the cabin, where the traces of feet existed in profuse confusion; Amber himself, Rutton, Doggott, the babu, and perhaps another, had passed and repassed there; the trail they had beaten streamed out of the vale, to the eastwards. Only, before the window, through which he had seen the peering turbaned head, he found the impressions of two feet, rather deep and definite, toes pointing toward the house, as though some one had lingered there, looking in. The sight of them reassured him ridiculously.

"At least," he reflected, "disembodied spirits leave no footprints!"

He found Rutton precisely as he had left him, his very attitude an unuttered question.

"No," Amber told him, "he'd made a quick getaway. The marks of his feet were plain enough, outside the window, but he was gone, and … somehow I wasn't over-keen to follow him up."

"Right," said the elder man dejectedly. "I might have known Chatterji would not have come alone. So my crime was futile." He spoke without spirit, as if completely fagged, and moved slowly to the door. "I don't want another interruption to-night," he continued, shooting the bolts. He turned to the windows, "Nor peeping Toms," he added, drawing the shade of one down to the sill.

Amber started for him in a panic. "Get away from that window, Rutton! For the love of heaven don't be foolhardy!"

Rutton drew the second shade deliberately. "Dear boy!" he said with his slow, tired smile, "I'm in no danger personally. Not a hair of my head will be touched until…." Again he left his thought half-expressed.

"But if that fellow out there was Chatterji's companion——!"

"He undoubtedly was. But you don't understand; my life is not threatened—yet."

"Chatterji fired at you," Amber argued stubbornly.

"Only when he found it was his life or mine. I tell you, David, if our enemy in the outer darkness were the babu's brother, he would not touch a hair of my head unless in self-defense."

"I don't understand. It's all so impossible!" Amber threw out his hands helplessly, "Unbelievable! For God's sake wake me up and tell me I've had a nightmare!"

"I would that were so, David. But the end is not yet."

"What do you mean by that?" demanded Amber, startled.

"Simply, that we have more to endure, you and I. Consider the limitations of the human understanding, David; a little while ago I promised to ask your aid if ever the time should come when I might be free to do so; I said, 'That hour will never strike.' Yet already it is here; I need you. Will you help me?"

"You know that."

"I know…. One moment's patience, David." Rutton glanced at the clock. "Time for my medicine," he said; "that heart trouble I mentioned…."

He drew from a waistcoat pocket a small silver tube, or phial, and uncorking this, measured out a certain number of drops into a silver spoon. As he swallowed the dose the phial slipped from his fingers and rang upon the hearthstone, spilling its contents in the ashes. A pungent and heady odour flavoured the air.

"No matter," said Rutton indifferently. "I shan't need it again for some time." He picked up and restored the phial to his pocket. "Now let me think a bit." He took a quick turn up the room and down again. Amber remarked that the medicine was having its effect; though the brilliance of Rutton's eyes seemed somewhat dimmed a dull flush had crept into his dark cheeks, and when he spoke it was in stronger accents—with a manner more assured, composed.

"A mad dance," he observed thoughtfully: "this thing we call life. We meet and whirl asunder—motes in a sunbeam. To-night Destiny chose to throw us together for a little space; to-morrow we shall be irrevocably parted, for all time."

"Don't say that, Rutton."

"It is so written, David." The man's smile was strangely placid. "After this night, we'll never meet. In the morning Doggott will ferry you over—"

"Shan't we go together?"

"No," said Rutton serenely; "I must leave before you."

"Without Doggott?"

"Without Doggott; I wish him to go with you."

"Where?"

"On the errand I am going to ask you to do for me. You are free to leave this country for several months?"

"Quite. I corrected the final galleys of my 'Analysis of Sanskrit Literature' just before I came down. Now I've nothing on my mind—or hands. Go on."

"Wait." Rutton went a second time to the leather trunk, lifted the lid, and came back with two small parcels. The one, which appeared to contain documents of some sort, he cast negligently on the fire, with the air of one who destroys that which is no longer of value to him. It caught immediately and began to flame and smoke and smoulder. The other was several inches square and flat, wrapped in plain paper, without a superscription, and sealed with several heavy blobs of red wax.

Rutton drew a chair close to Amber and sat down, breaking the seals methodically.

"You shall go a long journey, David," he said slowly—"a long journey, to a far land, where you shall brave perils that I may not warn you against. It will put your friendship to the test."

"I'm ready."

The elder man ripped the cover from the packet, exposing the back of what seemed to be a photograph. Holding this to the light, its face invisible to Amber, he studied it for several minutes, in silence, a tender light kindling in his eyes to soften the almost ascetic austerity of his expression. "In the end, if you live, you shall win a rich reward," he said at length. He placed the photograph face down upon the table.

"How—a reward?"

"The love of a woman worthy of you, David."

"But——!" In consternation Amber rose, almost knocking over his chair. "But—Great Scott, man!"

"Bear with me, David, for yet a little while," Rutton begged. "Sit down."

"All right, but——!" Amber resumed his seat, staring.

"You and Doggott are to seek her out, wherever she may be, and rescue her from what may be worse than death. And it shall come to pass that you shall love one another and marry and live happily ever after—just as though you were a prince and she an enchanted princess in a fairy tale, David."

"I must say you seem pretty damn' sure about it!"

"It must be so, David; it shall be so! I am an old man—older than you think, perhaps—and with age there sometimes comes something strangely akin to the gift of second-sight. So I know it will be so, though you think me a madman."

"I don't, indeed, but you.... Well! I give it up." Amber laughed uneasily. "Go on. Where's this maiden in distress?"

"In India—I'm not sure just where. You'll find her, however."

"And then——?"

"Then you are to bring her home with you, without delay."

"But suppose—"

"You must win her first; then she will come gladly."

"But I've just told you I loved another woman, Rutton, and besides—"

"You mean the Miss Farrell you mentioned?"

"Yes. I—"

"That will be no obstacle."

"What! How in thunder d'you know it won't?" Amber expostulated. A faint suspicion of the truth quickened his wits. "Who is this woman you want me to marry?"

"My daughter."

"Your daughter!"

"My only child, David."

"Then why won't my—my love for Sophia Farrell interfere?"

"Because," said Rutton slowly, "my daughter and Sophia Farrell are the same.... No; listen to me; I'm not raving. Here is my proof—her latest photograph." He put it into Amber's hands.

Dazed, the younger man stared blankly at the likeness of the woman he loved; it was unquestionably she. Fair, sweet, and imperious, her face looked up to his from the bit of cardboard in his hands; the direct and fearless eyes met his—eyes frank, virginal, and serene, beautiful with the beauty of a soul as unsullied and untroubled as the soul of a child.

He gasped, trembling, astounded. "Sophia...!" he said thickly, colouring hotly. He was conscious of a tightening of his throat muscles, making speech a matter of difficulty. "But—but—" he stammered.

"Her mother," said Rutton softly, looking away, "was a Russian noblewoman. Sophia is Farrell's daughter by adoption only. Farrell was once my closest friend. When my wife died...." He covered his eyes with his hand and remained silent for a few seconds. "When Sophia was left motherless, an infant in arms, Farrell offered to adopt her. Because I became, about that time, aware of this horror that has poisoned my life—this thing of which you have seen something to-night—I accepted on condition that the truth be never revealed to her. It cost me the friendship of Farrell; he was then but lately married and—and I thought it dangerous to be seen with him too much. I left England, having settled upon my daughter the best part of my fortune, retaining only enough for my needs. From that day I never saw her or heard from Farrell. Yet I knew I could trust him. Last summer, when my daughter was presented at Court, I was in London; I discovered the name of her photographer and bribed him to sell me this." He indicated the photograph.

"And she doesn't know!"

"She must never know." Rutton leaned forward and caught Amber's hand in a compelling grasp. "Remember that. Whatever you do, my name must never pass your lips—with reference to herself, at least. No one must even suspect that you know me— Farrell least of all."

"Sophia knows that now," said Amber. "Quain and I spoke of you one night, but the name made no impression on her. I'm sure of that."

38

"That is good; Farrell has been true. Now ... you will go to India?"

"I will go," Amber promised.

"You will be kind to her, and true, David? You'll love her faithfully and make her love you?"

"I'll do my best," said the young man humbly.

"It must be so—she must be taught to love you. It is essential, imperative, that she marry you and leave India with you without a day's delay."

Amber sat back in his chair, breathing quickly, his mouth tense. "I'll do my best. But, Rutton, why? Won't you tell me? Shouldn't I know—I, who am to be her husband, her protector?"

"Not from me. I am bound by an oath, David. Some day it may be that you will know. Perhaps not. You may guess what you will—you have much to go on. But from me, nothing. Now, let us settle the details. I've very little time." He glanced again at the shoddy tin clock, with a slight but noticeable shiver.

"How's that? It's hours till morning."

"I shall never see the dawn, David," said Rutton quietly.

"What—"

"I have but ten minutes more of life.... If you must know—in a word: poison.... That I be saved a blacker sin, David!"

"You mean that medicine—the silver phial?" Amber stammered, sick with horror.

"Yes. Don't be alarmed; it's slow but sure and painless, dear boy. It works infallibly within half an hour. There'll be no agony—merely the drawing of the curtain. Best of all, it leaves no traces; a diagnostician would call it heart-failure.... And thus I escape that." He nodded coolly toward the door.

"But this must not be, Rutton!" Amber rose suddenly, pushing back his chair. "Something must be done. Doggott—"

"Not so loud, please—you might alarm him. After it's all over, call him. But now—it's useless; the thing is done; there's no known antidote. Be kind to me, David, in this hour of mine extremity. There's much still to be said between us ... and in seven minutes more...."

Rutton retained his clutch upon Amber's hand; and his eyes, their lustre dimmed, held Amber's, pitiful, passionate, inexorable in their entreaty. Amber sat down, his soul shaken with the pity of it.

"Ah-h!" sighed Rutton. Relieved, the tension relaxed; he released Amber's hand; his body sank a little in the chair. Becoming conscious of this, he pulled himself together.... "Enter India by way of Calcutta," he said in a dull and heavy voice. "There, in the Machua Bazaar, you will find a goldsmith and money-lender called Dhola Baksh. Go to him secretly, show him the ring—the Token. He will understand and do all in his power to aid you, should there be any trouble about your leaving with Sophia. To no one else in India are you to mention my name. Deny me, if taxed with knowing me. Do you understand?"

"No. Why?"

"Never mind—but remember these two things: you do not know me and you must under no circumstances have anything to do with the police. They could do nothing to help you; on the other hand, to be seen with them, to have it known that you communicate with them, would be the equivalent of a seal upon your death warrant. You remember the money-lender's name?"

"Dhola Baksh of the Machua Bazaar."

"Trust him—and trust Doggott.... Four minutes more!"

"Rutton!" cried Amber in a broken voice. Cold sweat broke out upon his forehead.

The man smiled fearlessly. "Believe me, this is the better way—the only way.... Some day you may meet a little chap named Labertouche—a queer fish I once knew in Calcutta. But I daresay he's dead by now. But if you should meet him, tell him that you've seen his B-Formula work flawlessly in one instance at least. You see, he dabbled in chemistry and entomology and a lot of uncommon pursuits—a solicitor by profession, he never seemed to have any practice to speak of—and he invented this stuff and named it the B-Formula." Rutton tapped the silver phial in his waistcoat pocket, smiling faintly. "He was a good little man.... Two minutes. Strange how little one cares, when it's inevitable...."

He ceased to speak and closed his eyes. A great stillness made itself felt within the room. In the other, Doggott was silent—probably asleep. Amber noted the fact subconsciously, even as he was aware that the high fury of the wind was moderating. But consciously he was bowed down with sorrow, inexpressibly racked.

In the hush the metallic hammering of the mean tin clock rang loud and harsh; Amber's heart seemed to beat in funeral time to its steady, unhurried, immutable ticking.

It was close upon two in the morning.

"Amber," said Rutton suddenly and very clearly, "you'll find a will in my despatch box. Doggott is to have all I possess. The emerald ring—the Token—I give to you."

"Yes, I—I—"

"Your hand.... Mine is cold? No? I fancied it was," said the man drowsily. And later: "Sophia. You will be kind to her, David?"

"On my faith!"

Rutton's fingers tightened cruelly upon his, then relaxed suddenly. He began to nod, his chin drooping toward his breast.

"The Gateway ... the Bell...."

The words were no more than whispers dying on lips that stilled as they spoke. For a long time Amber sat unmoving, his fingers imprisoned in that quiet, cooling grasp, his thoughts astray in a black mist of mourning and bewilderment.

Through the hush of death the tin clock ticked on, placidly, monotonously, complacently. In the fireplace a charred log broke with a crash and a shower of live cinders.

Out of doors something made a circuit of the cabin, like a beast of the night, stealthy footsteps muffled by the snow: *pad—pad—pad....*

In the emerald ring on Amber's finger the deathless fire leaped and pulsed.

CHAPTER VI

RED DAWN

Presently Amber rose and quietly exchanged dressing-gown and slippers for his own shooting-jacket and boots—which by now were dry, thanks to Doggott's thoughtfulness in placing them near the fire.

The shabby tin clock had droned through thirty minutes since Rutton had spoken his last word. In that interval, sitting face to face, and for a little time hand in hand, with the man to whom he had pledged his honour, Amber had thought deeply, carefully weighing ways and means; nor did he move until he believed his plans mature and definite.

But before he could take one step toward redeeming his word to Rutton, he had many cares to dispose of. In the hut, Rutton lay dead of poison; somewhere amongst the dunes the babu lay in his blood, shot to death—foully murdered, the world would say. Should these things become known, he would be detained indefinitely in Nokomis as a witness—if, indeed, he escaped a graver charge.

It was, then, with a mind burdened with black anxiety that he went to arouse Doggott.

The rear room proved to be as cheerless as the other. Of approximately the same dimensions, it too had been furnished with little regard for anything but the barest conveniences of camp-life. It contained a small sheet-iron stove for cooking, a table, a rack of shelves, two chairs, and a rickety cot-bed in addition to another trunk. On the table a tin kerosene-lamp had burned low, poisoning the air with its bitter reek. On the cot Doggott sprawled in his clothing, his strained position—half reclining, feet upon the floor—suggesting an uncontemplated surrender to fatigue. His face was flushed and he was breathing heavily.

The Virginian stood over him for several minutes before he could bring himself to the point of awakening the man to the news of Rutton's death. Aware of that steadfast loyalty which Doggott had borne his master through many years of service, he shrank with conceivable reluctance from the duty. But necessity drove him with a taut rein; and finally he bent over and shook the sleeper by the shoulder.

With a jerk the man sat up and recognised Amber.

"Beg pardon, sir," he muttered, lifting himself sluggishly; "I didn't mean to fall asleep—I'd only sat down for a moment's rest. Has—has anything gone bad, sir?" he added hastily, remarking with troubled eyes the sympathy and concern in Amber's expression.

Amber looked away. "Mr. Rutton is dead, Doggott," he managed to say with some difficulty.

Doggott exclaimed beneath his breath. "Dead!" he cried in a tone of daze. In two strides he had left Amber and was kneeling by Rutton's side. The most cursory examination, however, sufficed to resolve his every doubt: the hanging head and arms, the livid face with its staring yet sightless eyes, the shrunken figure seeming so pitifully slight and unsubstantial in comparison with its accustomed strong and virile poise, hopelessly confirmed Amber's statement.

"Dead!" whispered the servant. He rose and stood swaying, his lips a-tremble, his eyes blinking through a mist, his head bowed. "'E always was uncommon' good to me, Mr. Amber," he said brokenly. "It's a bit 'ard, comin' this w'y. 'Ow—'ow did it—" He broke down completely for a time, and staggered away to the wall, there to stand with his head pillowed on his crossed forearms.

When he had himself in more control Amber told him as briefly as possible of the head at the window and of its sequel—Rutton's despairing suicide.

Doggott listened in silence, nodding his comprehension. "I've always looked for it, sir," he commented. "'E'd warned me never to touch that silver tube; 'e never said poison, but I suspected it, 'e being blue and melancholy-like, by fits and turns—'e never told me why."

Then, reverently, they took up the body and laid it out upon the hammock-bed, Doggott arranging the limbs and closing the eyes before spreading a sheet over the rigid form.

"And now, what, Mr. Amber?" he asked.

Amber had returned to the table. He pondered his problems for some time before answering; a distasteful duty devolved upon him of questioning the servant about his master's secrets, of delving into the mystery which Rutton had chosen always to preserve about himself—which, indeed, he had chosen to die without disclosing to the man whom he had termed his sole intimate. Yet this task, too, must be gone through with.

"Mr. Rutton spoke of a despatch-box, Doggott. You know where to find it?"

"Yes, sir."

The servant brought from Rutton's leather trunk a battered black-japanned tin box, which, upon exploration, proved to contain little that might not have been anticipated. A bankbook issued by the house of Rothschild Frères, Paris, showed a balance to the credit of H.D. Rutton of something slightly under a million francs. There was American money, chiefly in gold certificates of large denominations, to the value of, roundly, twenty thousand dollars, together with a handful of French, German and English bank-notes which might have brought in exchange about two hundred and fifty dollars. In addition to these there was merely a single envelope, superscribed: "To be opened in event of my death only. H.D.R."

Amber broke the seal and read the enclosures once to himself and a second time aloud to Doggott. The date was barely a year old.

"For reasons personal to myself and sufficient," Rutton had written, "I choose not to make a formal will. I shall die, probably in the near future, by my own hand, of poison. I wish to emphasise this statement in event the circumstances surrounding my demise should appear to attach suspicion of murder upon any person or persons whatever. I am a widower and childless. What relations may survive me are distant and will never appear to claim what estate I may leave—this I know. I therefore desire that my body-servant, Henry Doggott, an English citizen, shall inherit and appropriate to his own use all my property and effects, providing he be in my service at the time of my death. To facilitate his entering into possession of my means, whatever they may be, without the necessity of legal procedure of any kind, I enclose a cheque to his order upon my bankers, signed by myself and bearing the date of this memorandum. He is to fill it in with the amount remaining to my credit upon my bank-book. Should he have died or left me, however, the disposition of my effects is a matter about which I am wholly careless."

The signature was unmistakably genuine—the formal "H.D. Rutton" with which Amber was familiar. It was unwitnessed.

The Virginian put aside the paper and offered Doggott the blank cheque on Rothschilds'. "This," he said, "makes you pretty nearly independently rich, Doggott."

"Yes, sir." Doggott took the slip of paper in a hand that trembled even as his voice, and eyed it incredulously. "I've never 'ad anything like this before, sir; I 'ardly know what it means."

"It means," explained Amber, "that, when you've filled in that blank and had the money collected from the Rothschilds, you'll be worth—with what cash is here—in the neighbourhood of forty five thousand pounds sterling."

Doggott gasped, temporarily inarticulate. "Forty-five thousand pounds!... Mr. Amber," he declared earnestly, "I never looked for nothin' like this I—I never—I—" Quite without warning he was quiet and composed again. "Might I ask it of you as a favour, sir, to look after this"—he offered to return the cheque—"for a while, till I can myke up my mind what to do with it."

"Certainly." Amber took the paper, folded it and placed it in his card-case. "I'd suggest that you deposit it as soon as possible in a New York bank for collection. In the meantime, these bills are yours; you'd better take care of them yourself until you open the banking account. I'll keep Mr. Rutton's bank-book with the cheque." He placed the book in his pocket with the singular document Rutton had called his "will," and motioned Doggott to possess himself of the money in the despatch-box.

"It'll keep as well in 'ere as anywheres," Doggott considered, relocking the box. "I 'aven't 'ardly any use for money, except, of course, to tide me over till I find another position."

"What!" exclaimed Amber in amaze.

"Yes, sir," affirmed Doggott respectfully. "I'm a bit too old to chynge my w'ys; a valet I've been all my life and a valet I'll die, sir. It's too lyte to think of anything else."

"But with this money, Doggott—"

"Beg pardon, sir, but I know; I could live easy like a gentleman if I liked—but I wouldn't be a gentleman, so what's the use of that? I could go 'ome and buy me a public-'ouse; but that wouldn't do neither. I'd not be 'appy; if you'll pardon my s'ying so, I've associated too long with gentlemen and gentlemen's gentlemen to feel at ease, so to speak, with the kind that 'angs round publics. So the w'y I look at it, there's naught for me but go on valeting until I'm too old; after that the money'll be a comfort, I dares'y.... Don't you think so, sir?" "I believe you're right, Doggott; only, your common-sense surprises me. But it makes it easier in a way...." Amber fell thoughtful again.

"'Ow's that, sir—if I m'y ask?"

"This way," said Amber: "Before he died, Mr. Rutton asked me to do him a service. I agreed. He suggested that I take you with me."

"I'm ready, sir," interrupted Doggott eagerly. "There's no gentleman I'd like to valet for better than yourself."

"But there will be dangers, Doggott—I don't know precisely what. That's the rub: we'll have to travel half-way round the world and face unknown perils. If Mr. Rutton were right about it, we'll be lucky to get away with our lives."

"I'll go, sir; it was 'is wish. I'll go with you to India, Mr. Amber."

"Very well...." Amber spoke abstractedly, reviewing his plans. "But," he enquired suddenly, "I didn't mention India. How did you know——?"

"Why—I suppose I must 'ave guessed it, sir. It seemed so likely, knowing what I do about Mr. Rutton."

Amber sat silent, unable to bring himself to put a single question in regard to the dead man's antecedents. But after a pause the servant continued voluntarily.

"He always 'ad a deal to do with persons who came from India—niggers—I mean, natives. It didn't much matter where we'd be—London or Paris or Berlin or Rome— they'd 'unt 'im up; some 'e'd give money to and they'd go aw'y; others 'e'd be locked up with in 'is study for hours, talking, talking. They'd 'ardly ever come the same one twice. 'E 'ated 'em all, Mr. Rutton did. And yet, sir, I always 'ad a suspicion—"

Doggott hesitated, lowering his voice, his gaze shifting uneasily to the still, shrouded figure in the corner.

"What?" demanded Amber tensely.

"I alw'ys thought per'aps 'e was what we call in England a man of colour, 'imself, sir."

"Doggott!"

"I don't mean no 'arm, sir; it was just their 'ounding him, like, and 'is being a dark-complected man the syme as them, and speakin' their language so ready, that made me think it. At least 'e might 'ave 'ad a little of their blood in 'im, sir. Things 'd seem unaccountable otherwise," concluded Doggott vaguely.

"It's impossible!" cried Amber.

"Yes, sir; at least, I mean I 'ope so, sir. Not that it'd myke any difference to me, the w'y I felt towards 'im. 'E was a gentleman, white or black. I'd've died for 'im any d'y."

"Doggott!" The Virginian had risen and was pacing excitedly to and fro. "Doggott! don't ever repeat one word of this to man or woman—while you're faithful to the memory of Mr. Rutton."

The servant stared, visibly impressed. "Very good, Mr. Amber. I'll remember, sir. I don't ordinarily gossip, sir; but you and him being so thick, and everything 'appening to-night so 'orrible, I forgot myself. I 'ope you'll excuse me, sir."

"God in Heaven!" cried the young man hoarsely. "It can't be true!" He flung himself into his chair, burying his face in his hands. "It can't!"

Yet irresistibly the conviction was being forced upon him that Doggott had surmised aright. Circumstance backed up circumstance within his knowledge of or his experience with the man, all seeming to prove incontestably the truth of what at the first blush had seemed so incredible. What did he, Amber, know of Rutton's parentage or history that would refute the calm belief of the body-servant of the dead man? Rutton himself had consistently kept sealed lips upon the subject of his antecedents; in Amber's intercourse with him the understanding that what had passed was a closed book had been implicit. But it had never occurred to Amber to question the man's title to the blood of the Caucasian peoples. Not that the mystery with which Rutton had ever shrouded his identity had not inevitably of itself been a provocation to Amber's imagination; he had hazarded many an idle, secret guess at the riddle that was Rutton. Who or what the man was or might have been was ever a field of fascinating speculation to the American, but his wildest conjecture had never travelled east of Italy or Hungary. He had always fancied that one, at least, of Rutton's parents had been a native of the European Continent. He had even, at a certain time when his imagination had been stimulated by the witchery of "Lavengro" and "The Romany Rye," gone so far as to wonder if, perchance, Rutton were not descended from Gipsy stock—a fancy which he was quick to dismiss as absurd. Yet now it seemed as if he had not been far wrong; if Doggott were right—and Amber had come to believe that the valet was right—it was no far cry from the Hindu to the Romany, both offshoots of the Aryan root.

And then Amber's intelligence was smitten by a thought as by a club; and he began to tremble violently, uncontrollably, being weakened by fatigue and the strain of that endless, terrible night. A strangled cry escaped him without his knowledge: "Sophia!"

Sophia Farrell, the woman he had promised to wed, nay even the woman he loved with all his being—a half-breed, a mulatto! His mind sickened with the horror of that thought. All the inbred contempt of the Southerner for the servile races surged up to overwhelm his passion, to make it seem more than impossible, revolting, that the mistress of his dreams should be a creature tainted by the blood of a brown-skinned people. Though her mother had been of noble Russian family, as her father had declared; though her secret were contained in his knowledge and Farrell's alone, and though it were to be preserved by them ever inviolate—could he, David Amber, ever forget it? Could he make her his bride and take her home to his mother and his sisters in Virginia—offer them as daughter and sister a woman who, though she were fairer than the dawn, was in part a product of intermarriage between white and black?

His very soul seemed to shudder and his reason cried out that the thing could never be.... Yet in his heart of hearts still he loved her, still desired her with all his strength and will; in his heart there was no wavering. Whatever Rutton had been, whatever his daughter might be, he loved her. And more, the honour of the Ambers was in pledge, holding him steadfast to his purpose to seek her out in India or wherever she might be and to bear her away from the unnamed danger that threatened her—even to marry her, if she would have him. He had promised; his word had passed; there could now be no withdrawal....

An hour elapsed, its passing raucously emphasised by the tin clock. Amber remained at the table, his head upon it, his face hidden by his arms, so still that Doggott would have thought him sleeping but for his uneven breathing.

On tiptoe the man-servant moved in and out of the room, making ready for the day, mechanically carrying out his dead master's last instructions, to pack up against an early departing. His face was grave and sorrowful and now and again he paused in the midst of his preparations to watch for an instant the sheeted form upon the hammock-bed, his head bowed, his eyes filling; or to cast a sympathetic glance at the back and shoulders of the living, his new employer. In his day Doggott had known trouble; he was ignorant of the cause, but now intuitively he divined that Amber was suffering mental torment indescribable and beyond his power to assuage.

At length the young man called him and Doggott found him sitting up, with a haggard and careworn face but with the sane light of a mind composed in his eyes.

"Doggott," he asked in an even, toneless voice, "have you ever mentioned to anybody your suspicion about Mr. Rutton's race?"

"Only to you, sir."

"That's good. And you won't?"

"No, sir."

"Have you," continued Amber, looking away and speaking slowly, "ever heard him mention his marriage?"

"Never, sir. 'E says in that paper 'e was a widower; I fancy the lady must have died before I entered 'is service. 'E was always a lonely man, all the fifteen year I've been with 'im, keepin' very much to 'imself, sir."

"He never spoke of a—daughter?"

"No, sir. Didn't 'e say 'e was childless?"

"Yes. I merely wondered.... Tell me, now, do you know of any letters or papers of his that we should destroy? If there are any, he would wish us to."

"'E never 'ad many, sir. What letters 'e got 'e answered right away and destroyed 'em. There was a little packet in 'is trunk, but I see that's gone."

"He burned it himself this evening. There's nothing else?"

"Nothing whatever, sir."

"That's all right, then. We have nothing to do but ... see that he's decently buried and get away as soon as we can. There's no time to lose. It's after four, now, and as soon as it's daylight——You must have a boat somewhere about?"

"Yes, sir. Mr. Rutton 'ad me 'ire a little power launch before 'e came down. It's down by the bayside, 'alf a mile aw'y."

"Very well. The wind is dying down and by sunrise the bay will be safe to cross—if it isn't now. These shallow waters smoothe out very quickly. We'll—"

He cut his words short and got up abruptly with a sharp exclamation: "What's that?"

Doggott, too, had heard and been startled. "It sounded like a gun-shot, sir, and a man shouting," he said, moving toward the door.

But Amber anticipated him there.

As he stepped out into the bitter-cold air of early morning, he received an impression that a shadow in the hollow had been alarmed by his sudden appearance and had flitted silently and swiftly out upon the beaten eastward path. But of this he could not be sure.

He stood shivering and staring, waiting with attentive senses for a repetition of the sound. The wind had indeed fallen, and the world was very still—a hush that overspread and lay unbroken upon the deep, ceaseless growling of the sea, like oil on water. The moon had set and the darkness was but faintly tempered by the starlight on the snow—or was it the first wan promise of the dawn that seemed to quiver in the formless void between earth and sky?

In the doorway Doggott grew impatient. "You don't 'ear anything, sir?"

"Not a sound."

"It's cruel cold, Mr. Amber. 'Adn't you better come inside, sir?"

"I suppose so." He abandoned hope disconsolately and returned to the hut, his teeth inclined to chatter and his stomach assailed by qualms—premonitions of exhaustion in a body insufficiently nourished.

Doggott, himself similarly affected, perhaps, was quick to recognise the symptoms. "I'll get a bite of breakfast, sir," he suggested; "you 'aven't 'ad enough to eat, and 'unger's tyking 'old of you. If you'll pardon my saying so, you look a bit sickly; but a cup of hot coffee'll set that right in a jiffy."

"Thank you, Doggott; I believe you're right. Though disappointment has a good deal to do with the way I look. I'd hoped it might be Mr. Quain come to look for me."

Doggott disappeared to prepare the meal, but within five minutes a second gun-shot sounded startlingly near at hand. The Virginian's appearance at the door was coincident with a clear hail of "Aho-oy, Amber!"—unmistakably Quain's voice, raised at a distance of not over two hundred yards.

Amber's answering cry quavered with joy. And with a bear-like rush Quain topped the nearest dune, dropped down into the hollow, and was upon him.

"By the Lord Harry!" he cried, almost embracing Amber in his excitement and relief; "I'd almost given you up for good and all!"

"And I you," said Amber, watching curiously and somewhat distrustfully a second man follow Quain into the vale. "Who's that?" he demanded.

"Only Antone. We've him to thank. He remembered this old camp here—I'd completely forgotten it—and was sure you'd taken refuge in it. Come inside." He dragged Amber in, the Portuguese following. "Let's have a look at you by the light. Lord! you seem to be pretty comfortable—and I've been worrying myself sick for fear you—" He swept the room with an approving glance which passed over Doggott and became transfixed as it rested upon the hammock-bed with its burden; and his jaw fell. "What's this? What's this?" He swung upon Amber, appraising with relentless eyes the havoc his night's experience had wrought upon the man. "You look like hell!" he exploded. "What's up here? Eh?"

Amber turned to Doggott. "Take Antone out there with you and keep him until I call, please. This is Mr. Quain; I want to talk with him undisturbed.... But you can bring us coffee when it's ready."

Quain motioned to Antone; the Portuguese disappeared into the back room with Doggott, who closed the communicating door.

"You first," said Amber. "If you've fretted about me, I've been crazy about you—what time I've had to think."

Quain deferred to his insistence. "It was simple enough—and damned hard," he explained. "I caught the *Echo* by the skin of my teeth, the skimmy almost sinking under me. She was hard and fast aground, but I managed to get the motor going and backed her off. As soon as that was all right we got a wave aboard that soused the motor—like a fool I'd left the hatch off—and short-circuited the coil. After that there was hell to pay. I worked for half an hour reefing, and meanwhile we went aground again. The oar broke and I had to go overboard and get wet to my waist before I got her off. By that time it was blowing great guns and dead from the beach. I had to stand off and make for the mainland—nothing else to do. We beached about a mile below the lighthouse and I had the four-mile tramp home. Then after I'd thawed out and had a drink and a change of clothes, we had to wait two hours for the sea to go down enough to make a crossing in the launch practicable. That's all for mine. Now you? What's that there?"

"A suicide; a friend of mine—the man Rutton whom we were discussing the night I came down. And that's not half. There's a man out there somewhere, shot to death by Rutton—a Bengali babu.... Quain, I've lived in Purgatory ever since we parted and now … I'm about done."

He was; the coming of Quain with the ease of mind it brought had snapped the high nervous tension which had sustained Amber. He was now on the edge of collapse and showed it plainly. But two circumstances aided him to recover his grip upon himself: Quain's compassionate consideration in forbearing to press his story from him, and Doggott's opportune appearance with a pot of coffee, steaming and black. Two cups of this restored Amber to a condition somewhat approaching the normal. He lit a cigarette and began to talk.

For all his affection for and confidence in his friend, there were things he might not tell Quain; wherefore he couched his narrative in the fewest possible words and was miserly of detail. Of the coming of the babu and his going Amber was fairly free to speak; he suppressed little if any of that episode. Moreover he had forgotten to remove the Token from his finger, and Quain instantly remarked it and demanded an explanation. But of the nature of the errand on which he was to go, Amber said nothing; it was, he averred, Rutton's private business. Nor did he touch upon the question of Rutton's nationality. Sophia Farrell he never mentioned.

Nevertheless, he said enough to render Quain thoughtful.... "You're set on this thing, I suppose?" he asked some time after Amber had concluded.

"Set upon it, dear man? I've no choice. I must go—I promised."

"Of course. That's you, all over. Personally, I think it'll turn out a fool's errand. But there's something you haven't told me—I'm not ass enough to have missed that and no doubt that influences you."

"I've told you everything that, in honor, I could."

"Hmm—yes; I dare say...." Quain scowled over the problem for some time. "It's plain enough," he asserted forcibly: "that man was involved in some infernal secret society. Just how and why's the question. Think I'll have a look at him."

Amber would have protested, but thought better of it and held his peace while Quain went to the hammock-bed, turned back the sheet, and for several minutes lingered there, scrutinising the stony, upturned face.

"So!" he said, coming back. "Here's news that'll help you some. You were blind not to see it yourself. That man's—was, I should say—a Rajput." He waited for the comment which did not come. "You knew it?"

"I … suspected, to-night."

"It's as plain as print; the mark of his caste is all over him. But perhaps he was able to disguise it a little with his manner—alive; undoubtedly, I'd say. He was a genius of his kind—a prodigy; a mental giant. That translation of the 'Tantras'——! Wonderful!... Well, he's gone his own way: God be with him.... When do you want to start?"

"As soon as possible—sooner. I've not a day to lose—not an hour."

"Urgent as that, eh?" Quain peered keenly into his face. "I wish I knew what you know. I wish to Heaven I might go with you. But I'm married now—and respectable. If I "ear the East a-callin" and daren't answer, it's my own fault for ever being fool enough to have heard it. Well...." He proceeded to take charge of the situation with his masterful habit. "The morning train leaves Nokomis at seven-thirty. You can make that, if you must. But you need sleep—rest."

"I'll get that on the train."

"'Knew you'd say that. Very well. This is Tuesday. The *Mauretania*—or the *Lusitania*, I don't know which—sails to-morrow. You can catch that, too. It's the quickest route, eastwards—"

"But I've decided to go west."

"That means a week more, and you said you were in a hurry."

"I am; but by going westwards it's barely possible I may be able to transact or wind up the business on the way."

As a matter of fact Amber was hoping the Rolands, with Sophia Farrell, might linger somewhere *en route*, remembering that the girl had discussed a tentative project to stop over between steamers at Yokohama.

"Very well," Quain gave in; "you're the doctor. Now as for things here, make your mind easy. I'll take charge and keep the affair quiet. There's no reason I can see for its ever getting out. I can answer for myself and Antone; and the two of us can wind things up. That man Rutton is at peace now—'chances are he'd prefer a quiet grave here on the island. Then that devilish babu—he doesn't count; Antone and I'll get him under the ground in a jiffy. No one ever gets over here but me, now; come summer and there'll be a few wanderers, but by that time.... The dunes'll hold their secrets fast: be sure of that. Finally, if any one round here knows about this place being occupied, your departure'll be public enough to make them think it's being abandoned again. Keep your hat-brim down and your coat-collar up at the station; and they'll never know you aren't Rutton himself; and you'll have Doggott to back up the deception. So there'll be no questions asked.... Get ready now to trot along, and I'll take care of everything."

"There's no way of thanking you."

"That's a comfort. Call Doggott now and tell him to get ready. You haven't much time to lose. I'd land at the lighthouse dock, if I were you, and take the short-cut up to the station by the wood road. If you land at Tanglewood, Madge'll hold you up for a hot breakfast and make you miss your train. I'll cook up some yarn to account for your defection; and when you get back with your blooming bride you can tell her the whole story, by way of amends."

Amber wheeled upon him, colouring to the brows. "My bride! What do you mean by that? I said nothing—"

Quain rubbed his big hands, chuckling. "Of course you didn't. But I'm wise enough to know there's bound to be a woman in this case. Besides, it's Romance—and what's a romance without a woman?"

"Oh, go to thunder," said Amber good-naturedly, and went to give Doggott his orders.

While they waited for the servant to pack his handbag—it being obvious that to take the trunks with them was not feasible; while Quain was to care for Amber's things at Tanglewood until his return from India—Quain was possessed by an idea which he was pleased to christen an inspiration.

"It's this," he explained: "what do you know about Calcutta?"

"Little or nothing. I've been there—that's about all."

"Precisely. Now *I* know the place, and I know you'll never find this goldsmith in the Machua Bazaar without a guide. The ordinary, common-or-garden guide is out of the question, of course. But I happen to know an Englishman there who knows more about the dark side of India than any other ten men in the world. He'll be invaluable to you, and you can trust him as you would Doggott. Go to him in my name—you'll need no other introduction—and tell him what you've told me."

"That's impossible. Rutton expressly prohibited my mentioning his name to any one in India."

"Oh, very well. You haven't, have you? And you won't have to. I'll take care of that, when I write and tell Labertouche you're coming."

"What name?"

"Labertouche. Why? You don't know him."

"No; but Rutton did. Rutton got that poison from him."

Quain whistled, his eyes round. "Did, eh? So much the better; he'll probably know all about Rutton and'll take a keener interest."

"But you forget—"

"Hang your promise. I'm not bound by it and this is business—blacker business than you seem to realise, Davy. You're bent on jumping blindfold and with your hands tied into the seething pool of infamy and intrigue that is India. And I won't stand for it. Don't think for an instant that I'm going to let you go without doing everything I can to make things as pleasant as possible for you.... No; Labertouche is your man."

And to this Quain held inflexibly; so that, in the end, Amber, unable to move him, was obliged to leave the matter in his hands.

A sullen and portentous dawn hung in the sky when the little party left the cabin. In the east the entire firmament was ensanguined with sinister crimson and barred with long reefs of purple-black clouds in motionless suspense. Upon the earth the red glare fell ominously; the eastern faces of the snow-clad dunes shone like rubies; westward the shadows streamed long and dense and violet. The stillness was intense.

A little awed, it may be, and certainly more than a little depressed, they left the hollow by the beaten way, the Portuguese Antone leading with a pick and spade, Amber and Quain following side by side, Doggott with his valise bringing up the rear. Beyond the hollow the tracks diverged toward the bay shore; and presently they came to the scene of the tragedy.

Between two sandhills the Bengali lay supine, a huddled heap of garish colour—scarlet, yellow, tan—against the cold bluish-grey of snow. A veil of unmelted flakes blurred his heavy, contorted features and his small, black eyes—eyes as evil now, staring glassily up to the zenith, as when quickened by his malign intelligence. About him were many footprints, some recently made—presumably by his companion. The latter, however, kept himself discreetly invisible.

At a word from Quain the Portuguese paused and began to dig. Quain, Amber, and Doggott went on a little distance, then, by mutual consent, halted within sight of Antone.

"I wouldn't leave him if I were you," Amber told Quain, nodding back at the Portuguese. "It mightn't be safe, with that other devil skulking round—Heaven knows where."

"Right-O!" agreed Quain. His hand sought Amber's. "Good-bye, and God be with you," he said huskily.

Amber tightened his clasp upon the man's fingers. "I can't improve on that, Tony," said he with a feeble smile. "Good-bye, and God be with you." He dropped his hand and turned away. "Come along, Doggott."

The servant led the way baywards. Behind them the angry morning blazed brighter in the sky.

In the sedge of the shore they found a rowboat and, launching it, embarked for the power-boat, which swung at her mooring in deeper water. When they were aboard the latter, Doggott took charge of the motor, leaving to Amber the wheel, and with little delay they were in motion.

As their distance from the shore increased Amber glanced back. The island rested low against the flaming sky, a shape of empurpled shadows, scarcely more substantial to the vision than the rack of cloud above. In the dark sedges the pools, here and there, caught the light from above and shone blood-red. And suddenly the attention of the Virginian was arrested by the discovery of a human figure—a man standing upon a dune-top some distance inland, and staring steadfastly after the boat. He seemed of extraordinary height and very thin; upon his head there was a turban; his arms were folded. While Amber watched he held his pose, a living menace—like some fantastic statue bulking black against the grim red dawn.

CHAPTER VII

MASKS AND FACES

Like many a wiser and a better man, Amber was able upon occasion to change his mind without entertaining serious misgivings as to his stability of purpose. Therefore, on second thought, he elected to journey India-wards *via* the Suez Canal rather than by the western route. As he understood the situation, he had no time to waste; the quicker way to his destination was the eastern way; and, viewed soberly, the chance upon which he had speculated, that of overtaking the girl's party somewhere *en route*, appeared a long one—a gambler's risk, and far too risky if he did not exaggerate the urgency of his errand. Rutton's instructions had, moreover, been explicit upon one point: Amber was to enter India only by the port of Calcutta. In deferring to this the Virginian lost several days waiting in London for the fortnightly P. & O. boat for Calcutta: a delay which might have been obviated by taking the overland route to Brindisi, connecting there with the weekly P. & O. boat for Bombay, from which latter point Calcutta could have been quickly reached by rail across the Indian Peninsula.

Now Quain's letter to Labertouche went by this quicker route and so anticipated Amber's arrival at the capital of India by about a week; during all of which time it languished unread.

A nice young English boy in Mr. Labertouche's employ received and stamped it with the date of delivery and put it away with the rest of the incoming correspondence in a substantial-looking safe. After which he returned to his desk in the ante-room and resumed his study of the law; which he pursued comfortably enough with a cigarette in his mouth, his chair tilted back, and his feet gently but firmly implanted upon the fair printed pages of an open volume of Blackstone. His official duties, otherwise, seemed to consist solely in imparting to all and sundry the information that Mr. Labertouche was "somewhere up in the Mofussil, hunting bugs—I don't know exactly where."

This was, broadly speaking, perfectly true, within the limitations of the youth's personal knowledge. He was a pleasant-mannered boy of twenty or thereabouts, with an engaging air of candour which successfully masked a close-mouthed reticence, even as his ostensibly heedless, happy-go-lucky ways disguised a habit of extreme caution and keen and particular observation: qualities which caused him to be considered an invaluable office-assistant to a solicitor without any clientele worth mentioning, and who chose to spend most of his time somewhere up in the Mofussil hunting bugs.

The Mofussil, by the way, is an extremely elastic term, standing as it does in the vocabulary of the resident Calcutta-man, for the Empire of India outside the seat of its Government.

Precisely why Mr. Labertouche maintained his office was a matter for casual conjecture to his wide circle of acquaintances; although it's not unlikely that, were he the subject of discussion, the bulk of the wonder expressed would be inspired by his unreasonable preference for Calcutta as a place of residence. The Anglo-Indian imagination is incapable of comprehending the frame of mind which holds existence in Calcutta tolerable when one has the rest of India—including Simla—open to one. And Labertouche was unmarried, unconnected with the Government, and independent of his profession; certainly it would seem that the slender stream of clients which trickled in and out of the little offices on Dhurrumtollah Street, near the Maidan, could hardly have provided him with a practice lucrative enough to be a consideration. On the other hand it had to be admitted that the man kept up his establishment in Calcutta rather than lived there; for he was given to unexpected and extended absences from home, and was frequently reported as having been seen poking sedulously over this plain or through that jungle, with a butterfly net, a bottle of chloroform, and an air of abstraction. In view of all of which he was set down as an original and wholly irresponsible. The first of which he was and the second of which he emphatically was not.

Henry Charles Beresford Labertouche was, in person, a quiet and unassuming body, with nothing particularly remarkable about him save his preference for boot-heels nearly three inches high and a habit of dying his hair—naturally greyish—a jet-black. Inasmuch as he was quite brazen about these matters and would cheerfully discuss with comparative strangers the contrasted merits of this hair-dye and that and the obvious advantages of being five feet nine and one-half inches in height instead of five feet seven, his idiosyncrasies were not held against him. Otherwise he was a man strikingly inconspicuous; his eyes were a very dark brown, which is nothing remarkable, and his features were almost exasperatingly indefinite. You would have found him hard to recall to memory, visually, aside from the boot-heels, which might easily have been overlooked, and the black hair, which was, when all's said, rather becoming than otherwise. Living with two native servants in a modest bungalow somewhere between Chitpur and Barrackpur, he went to and from his office, or didn't, at his whim, with entire lack of ostentation. Soft-spoken and gifted with a distinct sense of the humorous, he would converse agreeably and intelligently upon any impersonal topic for hours at a time, when the spirit so moved him. As an entomologist his attainments were said to be remarkable; he was admittedly an interested student of ethnology; and he filled in his spare time compounding unholy smells in a little laboratory connected with his suburban home. This latter proceeding earned him the wholesome fear and respect of the native population, who firmly believed him an intimate of many devils.

Such, at least, was the superficial man.

Now upon the morning of the day that found the steamship *Poonah* nuzzling up the Hooghly's dirty yellow flood, Mr. Labertouche's clerk arrived at the Dhurrumtollah Street office at the usual hour; which, in the absence of his employer, was generally between eleven o'clock and noon. Having assorted and disposed of the morning's mail, he donned his office-coat, sat down, thumbed through Blackstone until he found two perfectly clean pages, opened the volume at that place, tipped back his chair, and with every indication of an untroubled conscience imposed his feet upon the book and began the day's labours with a cigarette.

51

The window at his right was open, affording an excellent view, from an elevation of one storey, of the tide of traffic ebbing and flowing in Dhurrumtollah Street. The clerk watched it sleepily, between half-closed eyelids. Presently he became aware that an especially dirty and travel-worn Attit mendicant had squatted down across the way, in the full glare of sunlight, and was composing himself for one of those apparently purposeless and interminable vigils peculiar to his vocation. Beneath their drooping lashes the eyes of the clerk brightened. But he did not move. Neither did the Attit mendicant.

In the course of the next half-hour the clerk consumed two cigarettes and entertained a visitor in the person of a dapper little Greek curio-dealer from the Lal Bazaar, who left behind him an invitation to Mr. Labertouche to call and inspect some scarabs in which he had professed an interest. It was quite a fresh importation, averred the Greek; the clerk was to be careful to remember that.

When he had gone the clerk made a note of it. Then, glancing out the window, he became aware that the Attit mendicant, for some reason dissatisfied, was preparing to move on. Yawning, the clerk resumed his street coat, and went out to lunch, carelessly leaving the door unlocked, and the memorandum of the Greek's invitation exposed upon his blotter. When he returned at three o'clock, the door of Mr. Labertouche's private office was ajar and that gentleman was at his desk. The memorandum was, however, gone.

Mr. Labertouche was in the process of opening and reading a ten-days' accumulation of correspondence, an occupation which he suspended temporarily to call his clerk in and receive his report. This proved to be a tolerably lengthy session, for the clerk, whose name appeared to be Frank, demonstrated his command of a surprising memory. Without notes he enumerated the callers at the office day by day from the time when Labertouche had left for the Mofussil with his specimen-box and the rest of his bug-hunting paraphernalia; naming those known to his employer, minutely describing all others, even repeating their words with almost phonographic fidelity.

Labertouche listened intently, without interrupting, abstractedly tapping his desk with a paper-cutter. At the end he said "Thank you," with a dry, preoccupied air; and resumed consideration of his letters. These seemed to interest him little; one after the other he gave to his clerk, saying "File that," or "Answer that so-and-thusly." Two he set aside for his personal disposition, and these he took up again after the clerk had been dismissed. The first he read and reconsidered for a long time; then crumpled it up and, drawing to him a small tray of hammered brass, dropped the wadded paper upon it and touched a match to it, thoughtfully poking the blazing sheets with his paper-cutter until they were altogether reduced to ashes.

Quain's was the second letter. Having merely glanced at the heading and signature, Labertouche had reserved the rather formidable document—for Quain had written fully— as probably of scant importance, to be dealt with at his absolute leisure. But as he read his expression grew more and more serious and perturbed. Finishing the last page he turned back to the first and went over it a second time with much deliberation and frequent pauses, apparently memorising portions of its contents. Finally he said, "Hum-m!" inscrutably and rang for Frank.

"He left New York by the *Lusitania*, eh?" said Mr. Labertouche aloud. The clerk entering interrupted his soliloquy. "Bring me, please," he said, "Bradshaw, the *News*— and the latest P. & O. schedule." And when Frank had returned with these articles, he desired him to go at once and enquire at Government House the whereabouts of Colonel Dominick James Farrell, and further to search the hotels of Calcutta for a Miss Farrell, or for information concerning her. "Have this for me to-night—come to the bungalow at seven," he said. "And ... I shall probably not be at the office again for several days."

52

"Insects?" enquired the clerk.

"Insects," affirmed Mr. Labertouche gravely.

"In the Mofussil?"

"There or thereabouts, Frank."

"Yes, sir. I presume you don't feel the need of a capable assistant yet?"

"Not yet, Frank," said Labertouche kindly. "Be patient. Your time will come; you're doing famously now."

"Thank you."

"Good-afternoon. Lock the door as you leave."

Immediately that he found himself alone, Labertouche made of Quain's letter a second burnt offering to prejudice upon the tray of hammered brass. He was possessed of an incurable aversion to waste-paper baskets and other receptacles from which the curious might fish out torn bits of paper and, with patience, piece together and reconstruct documents of whose import he preferred the world at large to remain unadvised. Hence the tray of brass—a fixture among the furnishings of his desk.

This matter attended to, he lost himself in Bradshaw and the Peninsular & Oriental Steamship Company's list of sailings; from which he derived enlightenment. "He was to come direct," mused Labertouche. "In that case he'll have waited over in London for the *Poonah*." He turned to the copy of the *Indian Daily News* which lay at his elbow, somewhat anxiously consulting its shipping news. Under the heading of "Due this Day" he discovered the words: "*Poonah*, London—Calcutta—Straits Settlements." And his face lengthened with concern.

"That's short notice," he said. "Lucky I got back to-day—uncommon lucky!... Still I may be mistaken." But the surmise failed to comfort him.

He drew a sheet of paper on which there was no letter-head to him and began to write, composing deliberately and with great care.

The building in which his offices were located stood upon a corner; at either end of the long corridor on the upper floor, upon which the various offices opened, were stairways, one descending to Dhurrumtollah Street, the other to a side street little better than an alley. It may be considered significant that, whereas Labertouche himself was not seen either to enter or to leave the building at any time that day, an Attit mendicant did enter from Dhurrumtollah Street shortly after Frank had gone to lunch—and disappeared forthwith; while, in the dusk of evening, a slim Eurasian boy with a clerkly air left by the stairs to the alley. I say a boy, but he may have been thirty; he was carefully attired in clothing of the mode affected by the Anglo-Indian, but wore shoes that were almost heelless. His height may have been five-feet seven inches, but he carried himself with a slight, studious rounding of the shoulders that assorted well with the effect of his large gold-rimmed spectacles.

He stumbled out of the alley into Free School Street and set his face to the Maidan, shuffling along slowly with a peering air, his spectacles catching the light from the shop-windows and glaring glassily through the shadows.

CHAPTER VIII

FIRST STEPS

Forward on the promenade deck of the *Poonah*, in the shadow of the bridge, Amber stood with both elbows on the rail, dividing his somewhat perturbed attention between a noisy lot of lascar stewards, deckhands, and native third-class passengers in the bows below, and the long lines of Saugor Island, just then slipping past on the starboard beam.

On either hand, ahead, the low, livid green banks of the Hooghly were closing in, imperceptibly constricting the narrow channel through which the tawny tide swirled down to the sea at the full force of its ebb. Struggling under this handicap, the *Poonah* trembled from stem to stern with the heavy labouring of the screw, straining forward like a thoroughbred, its strength almost spent, with the end of the race in sight. Across the white gleaming decks, as the bows swung from port to starboard and back again, following the channel, purple-black shadows slipped like oil. A languid land-wind blew fitfully down the estuary, in warm puffs dense with sickly-sweet jungle reek. The day was hot and sticky with humidity; a haze like a wall of dust coloured the skies almost to the zenith.

It was ten o'clock in the morning; Calcutta lay a hundred miles up the river, approximately. By evenfall Amber expected to be in the city, whether he stuck by the steamer until she docked in the port, or left her at Diamond Harbour, sixty miles upstream, and finished his journey by rail. At the present moment he hardly knew which to do; in the ordinary course of events he would have gone ashore at Diamond Harbour, thereby gaining an hour or two in the city. But within the last eighteen hours events had been diverted from their normal course; and Amber was deeply troubled with misgivings.

Up to the day that the Poonah had sailed from Tilbury Dock, London, from the time he had left Quain among the sand-dunes of Long Island, he had not been conscious of any sort of espionage upon his movements. That gaunt and threatening figure which he had seen silhouetted against the angry dawn had not again appeared to disturb or trouble him. His journey across the Atlantic had been uneventful; he had personally investigated the saloon passenger lists, the second and third cabins and the steerage of the *Lusitania,* not forgetting the crew, only to be reassured by the absence of anybody aboard who even remotely suggested an Indian spy. But from the hour that the *Poonah* with its miscellaneous ship's company, white, yellow, brown, and black, had warped out into the Thames, he had felt he was being watched—had realised it instinctively, having nothing definite whereon to base his feeling. He was neither timorous nor given to conjuring up shapes of terror from the depths of a nervous imagination; the sensation of being under the surveillance of unseen, prying eyes is unmistakable. Yet he had tried to reason himself out of the belief—after taking all sensible precautions, such as never letting the photograph of Sophia Farrell out of his possession and keeping the Token next his skin, in a chamois bag that nestled beneath his arm, swinging from a leather cord round his neck. And as day blended into eventless day, he had lulled himself into an uneasy indifference. What if he were watched? What could it profit any one to know what he did or how he did it, day by day? And with increasing infrequency he had come to question himself as to the reason for the spying on his movements.

Possibly the fruitlessness of any such speculation had much to do with his gradual cessation of interest in the enigma. He was not credulous of the power of divination popularly ascribed to the Oriental; he was little inclined to believe that the nature of his errand to India had been guessed, or that any native intelligence in India knew or suspected the secret of Sophia Farrell's parentage—Rutton's solicitude to the contrary notwithstanding. The theory that he most favoured in explanation of the interest in him was that it had somehow become known that he bore with him the emerald. It was quite conceivable that that jewel, intrinsically invaluable, was badly wanted by its former possessors, whether for the simple worth of it or because it played an important part in the intrigue, or whatever it was, that had resulted in Rutton's suicide. For his own part, Amber cared nothing for it; he had christened it, mentally, the Evil Eye—with a smile to himself; nonetheless he half-seriously suspected it of malign properties. He was imaginative enough for that—or superstitious, if you prefer.

He would, however, gladly have surrendered the jewel to those who coveted it, in exchange for a promise of immunity from assassination, had he known whom to approach with the offer and been free to make it. But he must first show it to Dhola Baksh of the Machua Bazaar. After that, when its usefulness had been discharged, he would be glad of the chance to strike such a bargain....

Such, in short, had been his frame of mind up to eight o'clock of the previous evening. At that hour he had made a discovery which had diverted the entire trend of his thoughts.

Doggott, ever a poor sailor, had been feeling ill and Amber had excused him early in the afternoon. About six o'clock he had gone to his stateroom and dressed for dinner, unattended. Absorbed in anticipations of the morrow, when first he should set foot in Calcutta and take the first step in pursuit of Sophia Farrell, he had absent-mindedly neglected to empty the pockets of his discarded clothing. At seven he had gone to dinner, leaving his stateroom door open, as was his habit—a not unusual one with first-cabin passengers on long voyages—and his flannels swinging from hooks in the wall. About eight, discovering his oversight through the absence of his cigarette-case, he had hurried back to the stateroom to discover that he had been curiously robbed.

His watch, his keys, his small change and his sovereign purse, his silver cigarette-case—all the articles, in fact, that he was accustomed to stuff into his pockets—with one exception, were where he had left them. But the leather envelope containing the portrait of Sophia Farrell was missing from the breast-pocket of his coat.

From the hour in which he had obtained it he had never but this once let it out of his personal possession. The envelope he had caused to be constructed for its safe-keeping during his enforced inaction in London. He had never once looked at it save in strict privacy, secure even from the eyes of Doggott; and the latter did not know what the leather case contained.

Thus his preconceived and self-constructed theory as to the extent of The Enemy's knowledge, was in an instant overthrown. "They" had seized the very first relaxation of his vigilance to rob him of that which he valued most. And in his heart he feared and believed that the incident indicated "their" intimacy not alone with his secret but with that which he shared with Colonel Farrell.

Since then his every move toward regaining the photograph had been fruitless. His stateroom steward, a sleek, soft Bengali boy who had attended him all through the voyage with every indication of eagerness to oblige him, professed entire ignorance of the theft. That was only to be expected. But when Amber went to the purser and the latter cross-examined the steward in his presence, the Bengali stuck to his protestations of innocence without the tremor of an eyelash. In fact, he established an alibi by the testimony of his fellow-stewards. Further, when Amber publicly offered a reward of five guineas "and no questions asked" and in private tempted the Bengali with much larger amounts, he accomplished nothing.

In the end, and in despair, Amber posted a notice on the ship's bulletin-board, offering fifty guineas reward for the return of the photograph to him either before landing or at the Great Eastern Hotel, Calcutta, and having thereby established his reputation as a mild lunatic, sat down to twirl his thumbs and await the outcome, confidently anticipating there would be none. "They" had outwitted him and not five hundred guineas would tempt "them," he believed. It remained only to contrive a triumph in despite of this setback.

But how to set about it? How might he plan against forces of whose very nature he was ignorant—save that he guessed them to be evil? How could he look ahead and scheme to circumvent the unguessable machinations of the unknown?... His wits, like wild things in a cage, battered themselves to exhaustion against the implacable bars of his understanding.

For the thousand-and-first time he reviewed the maddeningly scanty store of facts at his command, turning them over and over in his mind, vainly hopeful of inferring a clue. But, as always, he found his thoughts circling a beaten track of conjecture.... What dread power had hounded Rutton, forth from the haunts of his kind, from pillar to post of the world (as he had said) to his death among the desolate dunes of Long Island? What "staggering blow against the peace and security of the world" could that or any power possibly strike, with Rutton for its tool, once it had caught and bent him to its will? What fear had set upon his lips a seal so awful that even in the shadow of death he had not dared speak, though to speak were to save the one being to whom his heart turned in the end? To save his daughter from what, had he voluntarily renounced her, giving her into another's care, forswearing his paternal title to her love, refusing himself even the cold comfort of seeing her attain to the flower of her womanly beauty as another's child? What—finally—was the ordeal of the Gateway of Swords, and what could it be that made the Gateway of Death seem preferable to it?

For the thousand-and-first time Amber abandoned his efforts to divine the inscrutable, to overcome the insurmountable, to attain to the inaccessible, but abandoned them grudgingly, grimly denying the possibility of ultimate failure. Though he were never to know the dark heart of the mystery, yet would he snatch from its pythonic coils the woman he had sworn to save, the woman he loved!

And while the black steamer with the buff super-structure toiled on, cleaving its arduous way through the turbulent yellow flood between the contracting shores of the Sunderbunds, while the offshore wind buffeted Amber's cheeks with the hot panting breath of Bengal, his eyes, dimmed with dreaming, saw only Her face.

So often of late had he in solitude pondered her photograph, striving to solve the puzzle of her heart that was to him a mystery as unfathomable as that which threatened her, that he had merely to think of her to bring her picture vividly before him. He could close his eyes (he closed them now, shutting out the moving panorama of the river) and see the girl that he had known in those few dear hours: the girl with eyes as brown as sepia but illumined by traces of gold in the irides—eyes that could smile and frown and be sweetly grave, all in the time that a man needs to catch his breath; the girl with the immaculate, silken skin, milk-white, with the rose-blush of young blood beneath; with lips softly crimson as satin petals of a flower, that could smile a man into slavery; the girl to contemplate whose adorably modelled chin and firm, round, young neck would soften the austerity of an anchorite; in whose hair was blended every deep shade of bronze and gold....

Something clutched at his heart as with a hand of ice. He could never forget, dared not remember what he could not believe yet dared not deny. To him, reared as he had been, the barrier of mixed blood rose between them, a thing surmountable only at the cost of caste; the shadow of that horror lay upon his soul like ink—as black as the silhouetted rails and masts and rigging of the *Poonah* on her dead white decks. He could win her heart only to lose his world. And still he loved, still pursued his steadfast way toward her, knowing that, were he to find her and his passion to be returned, death alone could avert their union in marriage. He might not forget but ... he loved. With him the high wind of Romance was a living gale, levelling every obstacle between him and the desire of his heart.

This is to be borne in mind: it was the man's first love. Theretofore the habits of a thinker had set his feet in paths apart from those of other men. Pretty women he had always admired—from a discreet distance; that distance abridged, he had always found himself a little afraid of and dismayed by them. They were the world's disturbing element; they took men's lives in the rosy hollows of their palms and moulded them as they would. While Amber had desired to mould his own life. The theme of love that runs a golden thread through the drab fabric of existence had to him been an illusion—a hallucination to which others were subject, from which he was happily, if unaccountably, exempt. But that had been yesterday; to-day....

In the afternoon the *Poonah* touched at Diamond Harbour, landing the majority of her passengers. Amber was among those few who remained aboard.

When the steamer swung off from the jetty and, now aided by a favourable tide, resumed her progress up the river, he replaced his notice on the bulletin-board with one offering a hundred guineas for the return of the photograph before they docked in the port of Calcutta; the offer of fifty guineas for its return to the Great Eastern Hotel remained unaltered.

His anticipations were not disappointed; positively nothing came of it. All afternoon the *Poonah* plodded steadily on toward the pall of smoke that hemmed the northern horizon. The reedy river banks narrowed and receded, gorgeous with colour, unvaryingly monotonous, revealing nothing. Behind walls of rank foliage, dense green curtains almost impenetrable even to light, the flat and spongy delta of the Ganges lay decorously screened. If now and again the hangings parted they disclosed nothing more than a brief vista of half-stagnant water or a little clearing, half-overgrown, with the crumbling red brick walls of some roofless and abandoned dwelling.

In the lavender and gold and scarlet of a windless sunset, Calcutta lifted suddenly up before them, a fairy city, mystic and unreal with its spires and domes and minarets a-glare with hot colour behind a hedge of etched black masts and funnels—all dimmed and made indefinite by a heavy dun haze of smoke: lifted up in glory against the evening sky and was blotted out as if by magic by the swooping night; then lived again in a myriad lights pin-pricked upon the dense bluish-blackness.

The *Poonah* slipped in to her dock under cover of darkness. Amber, disembarking with Doggott, climbed into an open ghari on the landing stage and was driven swiftly to his hotel.

As he alighted and, leaving Doggott to settle with the ghariwallah, crossed the sidewalk to the hotel entrance, a beggar slipped through the throng of wayfarers, whining at his elbow:

"Give, O give, Protector of the Poor!"

Preoccupied, Amber hardly heard, and passed on; but the native stuck leech-like to his side.

"Give, hazoor—and the mercy of God shall be upon the Heaven-born for ten-thousand years!"

Now "Heaven-born" is flattery properly reserved for those who sit in high places. Amber turned and eyed the man curiously, at the same time dropping into the filthy, importunate palm a few annas.

"May the shadow of the Heaven-born be long upon the land, when he shall have passed through the Gateway of Swords!"

And like a flash the man was gone—dodging nimbly round the ghari and across Old Court House Street, losing himself almost instantly in the press of early evening traffic.

"The devil!" said Amber thoughtfully. "Why should it be assumed that I have any shadow of an intention of entering that damnable Gateway of Swords?"

An incident at the desk, while he was arranging for his room, further mystified him. He had given his name to the clerk, who looked up, smiling.

"Mr. David Amber?" he said.

"Why, yes—"

"We were expecting you, sir. You came by the *Poonah*?"

"Yes, but—"

"There's a note for you." The man turned to a rack, sorting out a small square envelope from others pigeon-holed under "A."

Could it be possible that Sophia Farrell had been advised of his coming? Amber's hand trembled slightly with eagerness and excitement as he took the missive.

"An Eurasian boy left it for you half an hour ago," said the clerk.

"Thank you," returned Amber, controlling himself sufficiently to wait until he should be conducted to his room before opening the note.

It was not, he observed later, superscribed in a feminine hand. Could it be from Quain's friend Labertouche? Who else?... Amber lifted his shoulders resignedly. "I wish Quain had minded his own business," he said ungratefully; "I can take care of myself. This Labertouche'll probably make life a misery for me."

There was a quality in the note, however, to make him forget his resentment of Quain's well-meant interference.

"My dear Sir," it began formally: "Quain's letter did not reach me until this afternoon; a circumstance which I regret. Otherwise I should be better prepared to assist you. I have, on the other hand, set afoot enquiries which may shortly result in some interesting information bearing upon the matters which engage you. I expect to have news of the Fs. to-night, and shall be glad to communicate it to you at once. I am presuming that you purpose losing no time in attending to the affair of the goldsmith, but I take the liberty of advising you that to attempt to find him without proper guidance or preparation would be an undertaking hazardous in the extreme. May I offer you my services? If you decide to accept them, be good enough to come before ten to-night to the sailors' lodging house known as 'Honest George's,' back of the Lal Bazaar, and ask for Honest George himself, refraining from mentioning my name. Dress yourself in your oldest and shabbiest clothing; you cannot overdo this, since the neighbourhood is questionable and a well-dressed man would immediately become an object of suspicion. Do not wear the ring; keep it about you, out of sight. Should this fail to reach you in time, try to-morrow night between eight and ten. You would serve us both well by *burning* this immediately. Pray believe me yours to command in all respects."

There was no signature.

Amber frowned and whistled over this. "Undoubtedly from Labertouche," he considered. "But why this flavour of intrigue? Does he know anything more than I do? I presume he must. It'd be a great comfort if.... Hold on. 'News of the Fs.' That spells the Farrells. How in blazes does he know anything about the Farrells? I told Quain nothing.... Can it be a trap? Is it possible that the chap who took that photograph recognised...?"

The problem held him in perplexity throughout the evening meal. He turned it over this way and that without being able to arrive at any comforting solution. Impulse in the end decided him—impulse and a glance at his watch which told him that the time grew short. "I'll go," he declared, "no matter what. It's nearly nine, but the Lal Bazaar's not far."

In the face of Doggott's unbending disapproval he left the hotel some twenty minutes later, having levied on Doggott's wardrobe for suitable clothing. Dressed in an old suit of soft grey serge, somewhat too large for him, and wearing a grey felt hat with the brim pulled down over his eyes, he felt that he was not easily to be identified with his everyday self—the David Amber whose exacting yet conservative "correctness" had become a by-word with his friends.

Once away from the Great Eastern he quietly insinuated himself into the tide of the city's night life that tirelessly ebbs and flows north of Dalhousie Square—the restless currents of native life that move ceaselessly in obedience to impulses so meaningless and strange to the Occidental understanding. Before he realised it he had left civilisation behind him and was breathing the atmosphere, heady and weird, of the Thousand-and-One Nights. The Lal Bazaar seethed round him noisily, with a roaring not unlike that of a surf in the hearing of him who had so long lived separate from such scenes. But gradually the strangeness of it passed away and he began to feel at home. And ere long he passed in a single stride from the glare of many lights and the tumult of a hundred tongues to the dark and the quiet hush of an alley that wormed a sinuous way through the hinterland of the bazaar. Here the air hung close and still and gravid with the odour of the East, half stench, half perfume, wholly individual and indescribable; here black shadows clung jealously to black and slimy walls, while lighter ones but vaguely suggestive of robed figures glided silently hither and yon; and odd noises, whispers, sobs, sounds of laughter and of rage, assailed the ear and excited the imagination....

At a corner where there was more light he came upon a policeman whose tunic, helmet, and truncheon were so closely patterned after those of the London Bobby that the simple sight of them was calculated to revive confidence in the security of one's person. He inspected Amber shrewdly while the latter was asking his way to Honest George's, and in response jerked a white-gloved thumb down the wide thoroughfare.

"You carn't miss it, sir—s'ylors' boardin'-'ouse, all lit up and likely with a row on at the bar. Mind your eye, guv'nor. It ayn't a plyce you'd ought to visit on your lone."

"Thanks; I've business there. I reckon to take care of myself."

Nevertheless it was with a mind preyed upon by forebodings that Amber stumbled down the cobbled way, reeking with filth, toward the establishment of Honest George. Why on earth should Labertouche make an appointment in so unholy a spot? Amber's doubts revived and he became more than half persuaded that this must be a snare devised by those acute intelligences which had instigated both the theft of the photograph and that snarled mock-benediction of the mendicant.

"I don't like it," he admitted ruefully; "it's so canny."

He stopped in front of a building whose squat brick facade was lettered with the reassuring sobriquet of its proprietor. A bench, running the width of the structure, was thick with sprawling loafers, who smoked and spat and spoke a jargon of the seas, the chief part of which was blasphemy. Within, visible through windows never closed, was a crowded barroom ablaze with flaring gas-jets, uproarious with voices thick with drink.

One needed courage of no common order to run the gauntlet of that rowdy room and brave the more secret dangers of the infamous den. "You've got to have your nerve with you," Amber put it. "But I suppose it's all in the game. Let's chance it." And he entered.

Compared with the atmosphere of that public-room a blast from Hell were sweet and cooling, thought Amber; the first whiff he had of it all but staggered him; and he found himself gasping, perspiration starting from every pore. Faint with disgust he elbowed his way through the mob to the bar, thankful that those about him, absorbed in the engrossing occupation of getting drunk, paid him not the least heed. Flattening himself against the rail he cast about for the proprietor. A blowsy, sweating barmaid caught his eye and without a word slapped down upon the sloppy counter before him a glass four fingers deep with unspeakable whiskey. And he realised that he would have to drink it; to refuse would be to attract attention, perhaps with unpleasant consequences. "It's more than I bargained for," he grumbled, making a pretence of swallowing the dose, and to his huge relief managing to spill two-thirds of it down the front of his coat. What he swallowed bit like an acid. Tears came to his eyes, but he choked down the cough, and as soon as he could speak paid the girl. "Where's the boss?" he asked.

"Who?" Her glance was penetrating. "Oh, he's wytin' for you." She nodded, lifting a shrill voice. "Garge, O Garge! 'Ere's that Yankee." With a bare red elbow she indicated the further end of the room. "You'll find 'im down there," she said, her look not unkindly.

Amber thanked her quietly and, extricating himself from the press round the bar, made his way in the direction indicated. A couple of billiard tables with a small mob of onlookers hindered him, but by main strength and diplomacy he wormed his way past and reached the rear of the room. There were fewer loafers here and he had little hesitation about selecting from an attendant circle of sycophants the genius of the dive— Honest George himself, a fat and burly ruffian who filled to overflowing the inadequate accommodation of an armchair. Sitting thus enthroned in his shirt-sleeves, his greasy and unshaven red face irradiating a sort of low good-humour that was belied by the cold cunning of his little eyes, he fulfilled admirably the requirements of the role he played self-cast.

"'Ere, you!" he hailed Amber brusquely. "You're a 'ell of a job-'unter, ain't you? Mister Abercrombie's been wytin' for you this hour gone. 'Know the w'y upstairs?"

His tone was boisterous enough to fix upon Amber the attention of the knot of loafers round the arm-chair. Amber felt himself under the particular regard of a dozen pair of eyes, felt that his measure was taken and his identification complete. Displeased, he answered curtly: "No."

"This w'y, then." Honest George hoisted himself ponderously out of his arm-chair and lumbered heavily across the room, shouldering the crowd aside with a high-handed contempt for the pack of them. Jerking open a small door in the side wall, he beckoned Amber on with a backward nod of his heavy head. "Be a bit lively, carn't you?" he growled; and Amber, in despite of qualms of distrust, followed the fellow into a small and noisome hallway lighted by a single gas-jet. On the one hand a flight of rickety steps ran up into repellent obscurity; on the other a low door stood open to the night.

The crimp lowered his voice. "Your friend's this w'y." He waved his fat red hand toward the door. "Them fools back there 'll think you're tryin' for a berth with Abercrombie, the ship-master. I 'opes you'll not tyke offense at the w'y I 'ad to rag you back there, sir."

"No," said Amber, and Honest George led the way out into a small, flagged well between towering black walls and left him at the threshold of a second doorway. "Two flights up, the door at the top," he said; "knock twice and then twice." And without waiting for an answer he lurched heavily back to his own establishment.

Amber watched his broad back fill the dimly-lighted doorway opposite and disappear, of two minds whether or not to turn tail and run. Suspicious enough in the beginning, the affair had now an exceeding evil smell—as repulsive figuratively as was the actual effluvium of the premises. He hung hesitant in doubt, with a heart oppressed by those grim and silent walls of blackness that loomed above him. With feet slipping on slimy flags he might be pardoned for harbouring suspicions of some fouler treachery. The yawning mouth of the narrow doorway, with the blackness of Erebus within, was deterring at its best; in such a hole a man might be snared and slain and his screams, though they rang to high Heaven, would fall meaningless on mundane ears. Honest George's with its flare of lights and its crowd had been questionable enough....

With a shrug, at length, he took his courage in his hands—and his life, too, for all he knew to the contrary—and moved on into the blackness, groping his way cautiously down a short corridor, his fingers on either side brushing walls of rotten plaster. He had absolutely nothing to guide him beyond the crimp's terse instructions. Underfoot the flooring seemed to sag ominously; it creaked hideously. Abruptly he stumbled against an obstruction, halted, and lighted a match.

The insignificant flame showed him a flight of stairs, leading up to darkness. With a drumming heart he began to ascend, counting twenty-one steps ere his feet failed to find another. Then groping again, one hand encountered a baluster-rail; with this for guide he turned and followed it until it began to slant upwards. This time he counted sixteen steps before his eyes, rising above the level of the upper floor, discovered to him a thin line of light, bright along the threshold of a door. He began to breathe more freely, yet apprehension kept him strung up to a high tension of nerves.

He knuckled the door loudly—one double knock followed by another.

From within a voice called cheerfully, in English: "Come in."

He fumbled for the knob, found and turned it, and entered a small, low-ceiled chamber, very cosy with lamplight, and simply furnished with a single chair, a charpoy, a water-jug, a large mirror, and beneath the latter a dressing-table littered with a collection of toilet gear, cosmetics and bottles, which would have done credit to an actress.

There was but a single person in the room and he occupied the chair before the dressing-table. As Amber came in, he rose; a middle-aged babu in a suit of pink satin, very dirty. In one hand something caught the light, glittering.

"Oah, Mister Amber, I believe?" he gurgled, oily and affable. "Believe me most charmed to make acquaintance." And he laughed agreeably.

But Amber's face had darkened. With an oath he sprang back, threw his weight against the door, and with his left hand shot the bolt, while his right whipped from his pocket Rutton's automatic pistol.

"Drop that gun, you monkey!" he cried sharply. "I was afraid of this, but I think you and I'll have an accounting before any one else gets in here."

CHAPTER IX

PINK SATIN

Shaking with rage, Amber stood for a long moment with pistol poised and eyes wary; then, bewildered, he slowly lowered the weapon. "Well," he observed reflectively, "I'm damned." For the glittering thing he had mistaken for a revolver lay at his feet; and it was nothing more nor less than a shoehorn. While as for the babu, he had dropped back into the chair and given way to a rude but reassuring paroxysm of gusty, silent laughter.

"I'm a fool," said Amber; "and if I'm not mistaken you're Labertouche."

With a struggle the babu overcame his emotion. "I am, my dear fellow, I am," he gasped. "And I owe you an apology. Upon my word, I'd forgotten; one grows so accustomed to living the parts in these masquerades, after a time, that one forgets. Forgive me." He offered a hand which Amber grasped warmly in his unutterable relief. "I'm really delighted to meet you," continued Labertouche seriously. "Any man who knows India can't help being glad to meet the author of 'The Peoples of the Hindu Kush.'"

"You did frighten me," Amber confessed, smiling. "I didn't know what to expect—or suspect. Certainly,"—with a glance round the incongruously furnished room—"I never looked forward to anything like this—or you, in that get-up."

"You wouldn't, you know," Labertouche admitted gravely. "I might have warned you in my note; but that was a risky thing, at best. I feared to go into detail—it might have fallen into the wrong hands."

"Whose?" demanded Amber.

"That, my dear man, is what we're here to find out—if we can. But sit down; we shall have to have quite a bit of talk." He scraped a heap of gaily-coloured native garments off one end of the charpoy and motioned Amber to the chair. At the same time he fished a cigar-case out of some recess in his clothing. "These are good," he remarked, opening the case and offering it to Amber; "I daren't smoke anything half so good when at work. The native tobacco is abominable, you know—*quite* three-fourths filth."

"At work?" questioned Amber, clipping the end of his cigar and lighting it. "You don't mean to say you travel round in those clothes?"

"But I do. It's business with me—though few people know it. Quain didn't; only I had a chance, one day, to tell him some rather startling facts about native life. This sort of thing, done properly, gives a man insight into a lot of unusual things."

Labertouche puffed his cigar into a glow and leaned back, clasping one knee with two brown hands and squinting up at the low, discoloured ceiling. And Amber, looking him over, was amazed by the absolute fidelity of his make-up; the brownish stain on face and hands, the high-cut patent-leather boots, the open-work socks through which his tinted calves showed grossly, his shapeless, baggy, soiled garments—all were hopelessly babu-ish.

"And if it isn't done properly?"

"Oh, then——!" Labertouche laughed, lifting his shoulders expressively. "No Englishman incapable of living up to a disguise has ever tried it more than once in India; few, very few, have lived to tell of the experiment."

"You're connected with the police?" Amber's brows contracted as he remembered Rutton's emphatic prohibition.

But Quain had not failed to mention that. "Officially, no," said Labertouche readily. "Now and again, of course, I run across a bit of valuable information; and then, somehow, indirectly, the police get wind of it. But this going *fantee* in an amateur way is simply my hobby; I've been at it for years—and very successfully, too. Of course, it'll have its end. One's bound to slip up eventually. You can train yourself to live the life of the native, but you can't train your mind to think as he thinks. That's how the missteps happen. Some day...." He sighed, not in the least unhappily.... "Some day I'll dodge into this hole, or another that I know of, put on somebody else's rags—say, these I'm wearing—and inconspicuously become a mysterious disappearance. That's how it is with all of us who go in for this sort of thing. But it's like opium, you know; you try it the first time for the lark of it; the end is tragedy."

Amber drew a long breath, his eyes glistening with wonder and admiration of the man. "You don't mean to tell me you run such risks for the pure love of it?"

"Well ... perhaps not altogether. But we needn't go into details, need we?" Labertouche's smile robbed the rebuke of its sting. "The opium simile is a very good one, though I say it who shouldn't. One acquires a taste for the forbidden, and one hires a little room like this from an unprincipled blackguard like Honest George, and insensibly one goes deeper and deeper until one gets beyond one's depth. That is all. It explains me sufficiently. And," he chuckled, "you'd never have known it if your case hadn't been exceptional."

"It is, I think." Amber's expression became anxious. "I want to know what you think of it—now Quain's told you. And, I say, what did you mean by 'news of the Fs.'?"

"News of the Farrells—father and daughter, of course." Labertouche's eyes twinkled.

"But how in the name of all that's strange—!"

"Did I connect the affair Rutton with the Farrells? At first by simple inference. You were charged with a secret errand, demanding the utmost haste, by Rutton; your first thought was to travel by the longer route—which, as it happens, Miss Farrell had started upon a little while before. You had recently met her, and I've heard she's rather a striking young woman. You see?"

"Yes," admitted Amber sheepishly. "But—"

"And then I remembered something," interrupted Labertouche. "I recalled Rutton. I knew him years ago, when he was a young man.... You know the yarn about him?"

"A little—mighty little. I know now that he was a Rajput—though he never told me that; I know that he married a Russian noblewoman"—Amber hesitated imperceptibly—"that she died soon after, that he chose to live out of India and to die rather than return to it."

"He was," said Labertouche, "a singular man, an exotic result of the unnatural conditions we English have brought about in India. The word renegade describes him aptly, I think: he was born and bred a Brahmin, a Rajput, of the hottest and bluest blood in Rajputana; he died to all intents and purposes a European—with an English heart. He is—was—by rights Maharana of Khandawar. As the young Maharaj he was sent to England to be educated. I'm told his record at Oxford was a brilliant one. He became a convert to Christianity—that was predestined—was admitted to the Church of England, a communicant. When his father died and he was summoned to take his place, Rutton at first refused. Pressure was brought to bear upon him by the English Government and he returned, was enthroned, and for a little time ruled Khandawar. It was then that I knew him. He was continually dissatisfied, however, and after a year or two disappeared. It was rumoured that he'd struck a bargain with his prime-minister, one Salig Singh. At all events Salig Singh contrived to usurp the throne, Government offering no objection. Rutton turned up eventually in Russia and married a woman there who died in childbirth—twenty years ago, perhaps. The child did not survive its mother...." Labertouche paused deliberately, his glance searching Amber's face. "So the report ran, at least," he concluded quietly.

"How do you know all this?" Amber countered evasively.

"Government watches its wards very tenderly," said Labertouche with a grin. "Besides, India's a great place for gossip.... And then," he pursued tenaciously, "I remembered something else. I recalled that Rutton had one very close friend, an Englishman named Farrell—"

"Oh, what's the use?" Amber cut in nervously. "You understand the situation too well. It's no good my trying to keep anything from you."

"Such as the fact that Colonel Farrell adopted Rutton's daughter, who, as it happens, did survive her mother? Yes; I knew that—or, rather, part I knew and part I guessed. But don't worry, Mr. Amber; I'll keep the secret."

"For the girl's sake," said Amber, twisting his hands together.

"For her sake. I pledge you my word."

"Thank you."

"And now ... for what purpose did Rutton ask you to come to India? Wasn't it to get Miss Farrell out of the country?"

"I think you're the devil himself," said Amber.

"I'm not," confessed Labertouche; "but I am a member of the Indian Secret Service—not officially connected with the police, observe!—and I know a deal that you don't. I think, in short, I can place my finger on the reason why Rutton was so concerned to get his daughter out of the country."

Amber looked his question.

"You read the papers, don't you, in America?"

"Rather." Amber smiled.

"You've surely not been so blind as to miss the occasional reports that leak out about native unrest in India?"

"Surely you don't mean——"

"I assuredly do mean that the Second Mutiny impends," declared Labertouche solemnly. "Such, at least, is my belief, and such is the belief of every thinking man in India who is at all informed. The entire country is undermined with conspiracy and sedition; day after day a vast, silent, underground movement goes on, fomenting rebellion against the English rule. The worst of it is, there's no stopping it, no way of scotching the serpent; its heads are myriad, seemingly. And yet—I don't know—since yesterday I have hoped that through you we might eventually strike to the heart of the movement."

"Through me!" cried Amber, startled.

Labertouche nodded. "Just so. The information you have already brought us is invaluable. Have you thought of the significance of Chatterji's 'Message of the Bell'?"

"'*Even now,*'" Amber quoted mechanically, "'*The Gateway of Swords yawns wide, that he who is without fear may pass within; to the end that the Body be purged of the Scarlet Evil.*'" He shook his head mystified. "No; I don't understand."

"It's so simple," urged Labertouche; "all but the Gateway of Swords. I don't place that—yet…. But the 'Body'—plainly that is India; the 'Scarlet Evil'—could anything more fittingly describe English rule from the native point of view?"

Amber felt of his head solicitously. "And yet," he averred plaintively, "it doesn't *feel* like wood."

Labertouche laughed gently. "Now to-night you will learn something from this Dhola Baksh—something important, undoubtedly. May I see this ring—this Token?"

Unbuttoning his shirt, Amber produced the Eye from the chamois bag. Labertouche studied it for a long time in silence, returning it with an air of deep perturbation.

"The thing is strange to me," he said. "For the present we may dismiss it as simply what it pretends to be—a token, a sign by which one man shall know another…. Wear it but turn the stone in; and keep your hands in your pockets when we're outside."

Amber obeyed. "We'll be going, now?"

"Yes." Labertouche rose, throwing away his cigar and stamping out its fire.

"But the Farrells?"

"Forgive me; I had forgotten. The Farrells are at Darjeeling, where the Colonel is stationed just now—happily for him."

"Then," said Amber, with decision, "I leave for Darjeeling to-morrow morning."

"I know no reason why you shouldn't," agreed Labertouche. "If anything turns up I'll contrive to let you know." He looked Amber up and down with a glance that took in every detail. "I'm sorry," he observed, "you couldn't have managed to look a trace shabbier. Still, with a touch here and there, you'll do excellently well as a sailor on a spree."

"As bad as that?"

"Oah, my dear fallow!"—it was now the babu speaking, while he hopped around Amber with his head critically to one side, like an inquisitive jackdaw, now and again darting forward to peck at him with hands that nervously but deftly arranged details of his attire to please a taste fastidious and exacting in such matters—"Oah, my dear fellow, surely you appreciate danger of venturing into nateeve quarters in European dress? As regular-out-and-out sahib, I am meaning, of course. It is permeesible for riff-raff, sailors and Tommies from the Fort, and soa on, to indulge in debauchery among nateeves, but first-class sahib—Oah, noah! You would be mobbed in no-time-at-all, where we are going."

"All right; I guess I can play the part, babu. At least, I've plenty of atmosphere," Amber laughed, mentioning the incident of the peg he had not consumed over Honest George's bar.

"I had noticed that; a happy accident, indeed. I think"—Labertouche stepped back to look Amber over again—"I think you will almost do. One moment."

He seized Amber's hat and, dashing it violently to the floor, deliberately stamped it out of shape; when restored to its owner it had aged five years in less than half as many minutes. Amber laughed, putting it on. "Surely you couldn't ask me to look more disreputable," he said with a dubious survey of himself in the mirror.

His collar had been confiscated with his tie; his coat collar was partially turned up in the back; what was visible of his shirt was indecently dirty. His polished shoes had been deprived of their pristine lustre by means of a damp rag, vigorously applied, and then rubbed with dust. An artistic stain had been added to one of his sleeves by the simple device of smudging it with the blacking from his shoes. As for his hat, with the brim pulled down in front, it was nothing more nor less than shocking.

"You'll do," chuckled Labertouche approvingly. "Just ram your hands into your trouser pockets without unbuttoning your coat, and shuffle along as if nocturnal rambles in the slums of Calcutta were an everyday thing to you. If you're spoken to, don't betray too much familiarity with the vernacular. You know about the limit of the average Tommy's vocabulary; don't go beyond it." He unbolted and locked the door by which Amber had entered, putting the key in his pocket, and turned to a second door across the room. "We'll leave this way; I chose this place because it's a regular rabbit warren, with half a dozen entrances and exits. I'll leave you in a passage leading to the bazaar. Wait in the doorway until you see me stroll past; give me thirty yards lead and follow. Keep in the middle of the way, avoid a crowd as the plague, and don't lose sight of me. I'll stop in front of Dohla Baksh's shop long enough to light a cheroot and go on without looking back. When you come out I'll be waiting for you. If we lose one another, get back to your hotel as quickly as possible. I may send you word. If I don't, I shall understand you've taken the first morning train to Darjeeling. I think that's all."

As Amber left the room Labertouche extinguished the lamp, shut and locked the door, and followed, catching Amber by the arm and guiding him through pitch darkness to the head of the stairs. "Don't talk," he whispered; "trust me." They descended an interminable flight of steps, passed down a long, echoing corridor, and again descended. From the foot of the second flight Labertouche shunted Amber round through what seemed a veritable maze of passages—in which, however, he was evidently quite at home. At length, "*Now go ahead!*" was breathed at Amber's ear and at the same time his arm was released.

He obeyed blindly, stumbling down a reeking corridor, and in a minute more, to his unutterable relief, was in the open air of the bazaar.

Blinking with the abrupt transition from absolute night to garish light, he skulked in the shadow of the doorway, waiting. Beneath his gaze Calcutta paraded its congress of peoples—a comprehensive collection of specimens of every tribe in Hindustan and of nearly every other race in the world besides: red-bearded Delhi Pathans, towering Sikhs, lean sinewy Rajputs with bound jaws, swart agile Bhils, Tommies in their scarlet tunics,

Japanese and Chinese in their distinctive dress, short and sturdy Gurkhas, yellow Saddhus, Jats stalking proudly, brawling knots of sailormen from the Port, sleek Mahrattas, polluted Sansis, Punjabis, Bengalis, priests, beggars, dancing girls; a blaze of colour ever shifting, a Babel of tongues never stilled, a seething scum on a witch's brew of humanity....

Like a fat, tawdry moth in his garments of soiled pink, a babu loitered past, with never a sidelong glance for the loaferish figure in the shadowed doorway; and the latter seemed himself absorbed in the family of Eurasians who were shrilly squabbling with the keeper of a vegetable-stall adjacent. But presently he wearied of their noise, yawned, thrust both hands deep in his pockets, and stumbled away. The bazaar accepted him as a brother, unquestioning, and he picked his way through it with an ease that argued nothing but absolute familiarity with his surroundings. But always you may be sure, he had the gleam of pink satin in the corner of his eye.

Before long Pink Satin diverged into the Chitpur Road, with Amber a discreet shadow. So far the latter had been treading known ground, but a little later, when Pink Satin dived abruptly into a darksome alleyway to the right, drawing Amber after him as a child drags a toy on a string, the Virginian lost his bearings utterly and was thereafter helplessly dependent upon the flutter of Pink Satin, and unworried only so long as he could see him, in a fidget of anxiety whenever the labyrinth shut Labertouche from his sight for a moment or two.

It was quiet enough away from the main thoroughfare, but with a sinister quiet. Tall dwellings marched shoulder to shoulder along the ways, shuttered, dark, grim, with an effect of conspirators, their heads together in lawless conference. The streets were intolerably narrow, the paving a farce; pools of stagnant water stood in the depressions, piles of refuse banked the walls. The fetid air hung motionless but sibilant with stealthy footsteps and whisperings.... Preferable to this seemed even the infinitely more dangerous and odorous Coolootollah purlieus into which they presently passed—nesting place though it were for the city's most evil and desperate classes.

In time broad Machua Bazaar Street received them—Pink Satin and the sailorman out for a night of it. And now Pink Satin began to stroll more sedately, manifesting a livelier interest in the sights of the wayside. Amber's impatience—for he guessed that they neared the goldsmith's stall—increased prodigiously; the shops, the stalls, the thatched dance-halls in which arose the hideous music of the nautch, had no lure for him, though they illustrated all that was most evil and most depraved in the second city of the Empire. He was only eager to have done with this unsavoury adventure, to know again the clean walls of his room in the Great Eastern, to taste again the purer air of the Maidan.

Without warning Pink Satin pulled up, extracted from the recesses of his costume a long, black and vindictive-looking native cigar, and lighted it, thoughtfully exhaling the smoke through his nose while he stared covetously at the display of a slipper-merchant whose stand was over across from the stall of a goldsmith.

With true Oriental deliberation Pink Satin finally made up his mind to move on; and Amber lurched heavily into the premises occupied by one Dhola Baksh, a goldsmith.

A customer, a slim, handsome Malayan youth, for the moment held the attention of the proprietor. The two were haggling with characteristic enjoyment over a transaction which seemed to involve less than twenty rupees. Amber waited, knowing that patience must be his portion until the bargain should be struck. Dhola Baksh himself, a lean, sharp-featured Mahratta grey with age, appraised with a single look the new customer, and returned his interest to the Malay. But Amber garnered from that glance a sensation of recognition. He wondered dimly, why; could the goldsmith have been warned of his coming?

Two or three more putative customers idled into the shop. Beyond its threshold the stream of native life rolled on, ceaselessly fluent; a pageant of the Middle Ages had been no more fantastic and unreal to Western eyes. Now and again a wayfarer paused, his interest attracted by the goldsmith's rush of business.

Unexpectedly the proprietor made a substantial concession. Money passed upon the instant, sealing the bargain. The Malay rose to go. Dhola Baksh lifted a stony stare to Amber.

"Your, pleasure, sahib?" he enquired with a thinly-veiled sneer. What need to show deference to a down-at-the-heel sailor from the Port?

"I want money—I want to borrow," said Amber promptly.

"On your word, sahib?"

"On security."

"What manner of security can you offer?"

"A ring—an emerald ring."

Dhola Baksh shrugged. His eyes shifted from Amber to the encircling faces of the bystanders. "I am a poor man," he whined. "How should I have money to lend? Come to me on the morrow; then mayhap I may have a few rupees. To-night I have neither cash nor time."

The hint was lost upon Amber. "A stone of price——" he persisted.

With a disturbed and apprehensive look, the money-lender rose. "Come, then," he grumbled, "if you must——"

A voice cried out behind Amber—"*Heh!*"——more a squeal than a cry. Intuitively, as at a signal of danger, he leaped aside. Simultaneously something like a beam of light sped past his head. The goldsmith uttered one dreadful, choking scream, and went to his knees. For as many as three seconds he swayed back and forth, his features terribly contorted, his thin old hands plucking feebly at the handle of a broadbladed dagger which had transfixed his throat. Then he tumbled forward on his face, kicking.

There followed a single instant of suspense and horror, then a mad rush of feet as the street stampeded into the shop. Voices clamoured to the skies. Somehow the lights went out.

Amber started to fight his way out. As he struggled on, making little headway through the press, a hand grasped his arm and drew him another way.

"Make haste, hazoor!" cried the owner of the hand, in Hindustani. "Make haste, lest they seek to fasten this crime upon your head."

CHAPTER X

MAHARANA OF KHANDAWAR

Both hand and voice might well have been Labertouche's; Amber believed they were. And the darkness rendered visual identification impossible. No shadow of doubt troubled him as he yielded to the urgent hand, and permitted himself to be dragged, more than led, through the reeking, milling mob, whose numbers seemed each instant augmented. He had thought, dully, to find it a difficult matter to worm through and escape, but somehow his guide seemed to have little trouble. Others, likewise, evidently wished to get out of sight before the arrival of the police, and in the wake of a little knot of these Amber felt himself drawn along until, within less than two minutes, they were on the outskirts of the crowd.

He drew a long breath of relief. Ever since that knife had flown whining past his cheek, his instinct of self-preservation had been dominated by a serene confidence that Pink Satin was at hand to steer him in safety away from the brawl. For his own part he was troubled by a feeling of helplessness and dependence unusual with him, who was of a self-reliant habit, accustomed to shift for himself whatever the emergency. But this was something vastly different from the run of experiences that had theretofore fallen to his lot. In the foulest stews of a vast city, with no least notion of how to win his way back to the security of the Chowringhee quarter; in the heart of a howling native rabble stimulated to a pitch of frenzy by the only things that ever seem really to rouse the Oriental from his apathy—the scent and sight of human blood; and with a sense of terror chilling him as he realised the truth at which his guide had hinted—that the actual assassin would not hesitate an instant to cry the murder upon the head of one of the Sahib-logue: Amber felt as little confidence in his ability to work out his salvation as though he had been a child. He thanked his stars for Labertouche—for the hand that clasped his arm and the voice that spoke guardedly in his ear.

And then, by the light of the street, he discovered that his gratitude had been premature and misplaced. His guide had fallen a pace behind and was shouldering him along with almost frantic energy; but a glance aside showed Amber, in Labertouche's stead, a chunky little Gurkha in the fatigue uniform of his regiment of the British Army in India. Pink Satin was nowhere in sight and it was immediately apparent that an attempt to find him among the teeming hundreds before the goldsmith's stall would be as futile as foolish—if not fatal. Yet Amber's impulse was to wait, and he faltered—something which seemed to exasperate the Gurkha, who fairly danced with excitement and impatience.

"Hasten, hazoor!" he cried. "Is this a time to loiter? Hasten ere they charge you with this spilling of blood. The gods lend wings to our feet this night!"

"But who are you?" demanded Amber.

"What matter is that? Is it not enough that I am here and well disposed toward you, that I risk my skin to save yours?" He cannoned suddenly against Amber, shunting him unceremoniously out of the bazaar road and into a narrow black alley.

Simultaneously Amber heard a cry go up, shrill above the clamour of the mob, screaming that a white sailor had knifed the goldsmith. And he turned pale beneath his tan.

"You hear, hazoor? They are naming you to the police-wallahs. Come!"

"You're right." Amber fell into a long, free stride that threatened quickly to distance the Gurka's short, sturdy legs. "Yet why do you take this trouble for me?"

"Why ask?" panted the Gurkha. "Did I not stand behind you and see that you did not throw the knife? Am I a dog to stand by and see an innocent man yoked to a crime?" He laughed shortly. "Am I a fool to forget how great is the generosity of Kings? This way, hazoor!"

"Why call me King?" Amber hurdled a heap of offal and picked up his pace again. "Yet you will find me generous, though but a sahib."

"The sahibs are very generous." Again the Gurkha laughed briefly and unpleasantly. "But this is no time for words. Save your breath, for now we must run."

He broke into a springy lope, with his chin up, elbows in and chest distended, his quick small feet slopping regardlessly through the viscous mud of the unpaved byway. "Hear that!" he cried, as a series of short, sharp yells rose in the bazaar behind them. "The dogs have found the scent!" And for a time terror winged their flight. Eastern mobs are hard to handle; if overtaken the chances were anything-you-please to one that the fugitives would be torn to pieces as by wild animals ere the police could interfere.

They struck through stranger and more awful quarters than Amber had believed could be tolerated, even in India. For if there were a better way of escape they had no time to pause and choose it. From the racket in their rear the pursuit was hot upon their trail, and with every stride, well-nigh, they were passing those who would mark them down and, when the rabble came up, cry it on with explicit directions.

And so Amber found himself pounding along at the heels of his Gurkha, threading acres of flimsy huts huddled together in meaningless confusion—frail boxes of bamboo, mud, and wattles thrown roughly together upon corrupt, naked earth that reeked of the drainage of uncounted generations. Whence they passed through long, brilliant, silent streets lined with open hovels wherein Vice and Crime bred cheek-by-jowl, the haunts of Shame, painted and unabashed, sickening in the very crudity of its nakedness.... There is no bottom to the Pit wherein the native sinks.... And on, panting, with labouring chests and aching limbs, into the abandoned desolation of the Chinese quarter, and back through the still, deadly ways which Amber had threaded in the footsteps of Pink Satin—where the houses towered high and were ornamented with dingy, crumbling stucco and rusty, empty, treacherous balconies of iron, and the air hung in stagnation as if the very winds here halted to eavesdrop upon the iniquities that were housed behind the jealous, rotting blinds of wood and iron.

By now the voice of the chase had subsided to a dull and distant muttering far behind them, and the way was clear. Beyond its age-old, ineradicable atmosphere of secret infamy there was nothing threatening in the aspect of the neighbourhood. And the Gurkha pulled up, breathing like a wind-broken horse.

"Easily, hazoor!" he gasped. "There is time for rest."

Willingly Amber dropped into a wavering stride, so nearly exhausted that his legs shook under him and he reeled drunkenly; and, fighting for breath, they stumbled on, side by side, in the shadow of the overhanging walls, until as they neared a corner the Gurkha stopped and halted Amber with an imperative gesture.

"The police, sahib, the police!" he breathed, with an expressive sweep of his hand toward the cross street. "Let us wait here till they pass." And in evident panic he crowded Amber into the deep and gloomy recess afforded by a door overhung by a balcony.

Taken off his guard, but with growing doubt, Amber was on the point of remonstrating. Why should the police concern themselves with peaceful wayfarers? They could not yet have heard of the crime in the Bazaar, miles distant. But as he opened his lips he heard the latch click behind him, and before he could lift a finger, the Gurkha had flung himself bodily upon him, fairly lifting the American across the threshold.

They went down together, the Gurkha on top. And the door crashed to with a rattle of bolts, leaving Amber on his back, in total darkness, betrayed, lost, and alone with his enemies....

Now take a man—a white man—an American by preference—such an one as David Amber—who has led an active if thoughtful life and lived much out of doors, roughing it cheerfully in out-of-the-way corners of the world, and who has been careful to maintain his physical condition at something above par; bedevil him with a series of mysterious circumstances for a couple of months, send him on a long journey, entangle him in a passably hopeless love affair, work his expectations up to a high pitch of impatience, exasperate him with disappointment, and finally cause him to be tripped up by treachery and thrust into a pitch-black room in an unknown house in one of the vilest quarters of Calcutta: treat him in such a manner and what may you expect of him? Not discretion, at least.

Amber went temporarily mad with rage. He was no stranger to fear—no man with an imagination is; but for the time being he was utterly foolhardy. He forgot his exhaustion, forgot the hopelessness of his plight, forgot everything save his insatiable thirst for vengeance. He was, in our homely idiom, fighting-mad.

One instant overpowered by and supine beneath the Gurkha, the next he had flung the man off and bounded to his feet. There was the automatic pistol in his coat-pocket, but he, conscious that many hands were reaching out in the darkness to drag him down again, found no time to draw it. He seemed to feel the presence of the nearest antagonist, whom he could by no means see; for he struck out with both bare, clenched fists, one after the other, with his weight behind each, and both blows landed. The sounds of their impact rang like pistol-shots, and beneath his knuckles he felt naked flesh crack and give. Something fell away from him with a grunt like a poled ox. And then, in an instant, before he could recover his poise, even before he knew that the turned-in stone of the emerald ring had bitten deep into his palm, he was the axis of a vortex of humanity. And he fought like a devil unchained. Those who had thrown themselves upon him, clutching desperately at his arms and legs and hanging upon his body, seemed to be thrown off like chips from a lathe—for a time. In two short minutes he performed prodigies of valour; his arms wrought like piston-rods, his fists flew like flails; and such was the press round him that he struck no blow that failed to find a mark. The room rang with the sounds of the struggle, the shuffle, thud, and scrape of feet both booted and bare, the hoarse, harsh breathing of the combatants, their groans, their whispers, their low tense cries....

And abruptly it was over. He was borne down by sheer weight of numbers. Though he fought with the insanity of despair they were too many for him. He went a second time to the floor, beneath a dozen half-nude bodies. Below him lay another, with an arm encircling his throat, the elbow beneath his chin compressing his windpipe. Powerless to move hand or foot, he gave up ... and wondered dully why it was that a knife had not yet slipped between his ribs—between the fifth and sixth—or in his back, beneath the left shoulder-blade, and why his gullet remained unslit.

Gradually it was forced upon him that his captors meant him no bodily harm, for the present at least. His wrath subsided and gave place to curiosity while he rested, regaining his wind, and the natives squirmed away from him, leaving one man kneeling upon his chest and four others each pinioning a limb.

There followed a wait, while some several persons indulged in a whispered confabulation at a distance from him too great for their words to be articulate. Then came a croaking laugh out of the darkness and words intended for his ear.

"By Malang Shah! but my lord doth fight like a Rajput!"

Amber caught his breath and exploded. "Half a chance, you damned thugs, and I'd show you how an American can fight!"

But he had spoken in English, and his hearers gathered the import of his words only from his tone, apparently. He who had addressed him laughed applausively.

"It was a gallant fight," he commented, "but like all good things hath had its end. My lord is overcome. Is my lord still minded for battle or for peace? Dare I, his servant, give orders for his release, or——"

Here Amber interrupted; stung by the bitter irony, he told the speaker in fluent idiomatic Hindustani precisely what he might expect if his "lord" ever got the shadow of a chance to lay hands upon him.

The grim cackling laugh followed his words, a mocking echo, and was his only answer. But for all his defiance, he presently heard orders issued to take him up and bear him to another chamber. Promptly the man on his chest moved away, and his fellows lifted and carried Amber, gently and with puzzling consideration, some considerable distance through what he surmised to be an underground corridor. He suffered this passively, realising his impotence, and somewhat comforted if perplexed by the tenderness accorded him in return for his savage fight for freedom.

Unexpectedly he was let down upon the floor and released. Bare feet scurried away in the darkness and a door closed with a resounding bang. He was alone, for all he could say to the contrary—alone and unharmed. He was more: he was astonished; he had not been disarmed. He got up and felt of himself, marvelling that his pocket still sagged with the weight of the pistol as much as at the circumstance that, aside from the inevitable damage to his clothing—a coat-sleeve ripped from the arm-hole, several buttons missing, suspenders broken—he had come out of the melee unhurt, not even bruised, save for the hand that had been cut by the emerald. He wrapped a handkerchief about this wound, and took the pistol out, deriving a great deal of comfort from the way it balanced, its roughened grip nestling snugly in his palm.

He fairly itched to use the thing, but lacking an excuse, had time to take more rational counsel of himself. It were certainly unwise to presume upon the patience of his captors; though he had battered some of them pretty brutally and himself escaped reprisals, the part of wisdom would seem to be to save his ammunition.

With this running through his mind, the room was suddenly revealed to his eyes, that had so long strained fruitlessly to see. A flood of lamplight leaped through some opening behind him and showed him his shadow, long and gigantic upon a floor of earth and a wall of stone. He wheeled about, alert as a cat; and the sight of his pistol hung steady between the eyes of one who stood at ease, with folded arms, in an open doorway. Over his shoulder was visible the bare brown poll of an attendant whose lank brown arm held aloft the lamp.

One does not shoot down in cold blood a man who makes no aggressive move, and he who stood in the doorway endured impassively the mute threat of the pistol. Above its sight his eyes met Amber's with a level and unwavering glance, shining out of a dark, set face cast in a mould of insolence and pride. A bushy black beard was parted at his chin and brushed stiffly back. Between his thin hard lips, parted in a shadowy smile, his teeth gleamed white. Standing a head taller than Amber and very gracefully erect in clothing of a semi-military cut and of regal magnificence, every inch of his pose bespoke power, position, and the habit of authority. His head was bound with a turban of spotless white from whose clasp, a single splendid emerald, a jewelled aigret nodded; the bosom of his dark-green tunic blazed with orders and decorations; at his side swung a sabre with richly jewelled hilt. Heavy white gauntlets hid his hands, top-boots of patent leather his legs and feet.

At once impressed and irritated by his attitude, Amber lowered his weapon. "Well?" he demanded querulously. "What do you want? What's your part in this infamous outrage?"

On the other's face the faint smile became more definite. He nodded nonchalantly at Amber's pistol. "My lord intends to shoot?" he enquired in English, his tone courteous and suave.

"That's as may be," retorted Amber defiantly. "I'm going to have satisfaction for this outrage if I die getting it. You may count on that, first and last."

The man lifted his eyebrows and his shoulders in deprecation; then turned to his attendant. "Put down the light and leave us," he said curtly in Hindustani.

Bowing obsequiously, the servant entered and departed, leaving the lamp upon a wooden shelf braced against one side of the four-square, stone-walled dungeon. As he went out he closed the door, and Amber noted that it was a heavy sheet of iron or steel, very substantial. His face darkened.

"I presume you know what that means," he said, with a significant jerk of his head toward the door. "It'll never be shut on me alone. We'll leave together, you and I, if we both go out feet first." He lifted the pistol and took the measure of the man, not in any spirit of bravado but with absolute sincerity. "I trust I make my meaning plain?"

"Most clear, hazoor." The other showed his teeth in an appreciative smile. "And yet"—with an expressive outward movement of both hands—"what is the need of all this?"

"What!" Amber choked with resentment. "What was the need of setting your thugs upon me—of kidnapping me?"

"That, my lord, was an error of judgment on the part of one who shall pay for it full measure. I trust you were not rudely treated."

"I'd like to know what in blazes you call it," snapped Amber. "I'm dogged by your spies—Heaven knows why!—lured to this place, butted bodily into the arms of a gang of ruffians to be manhandled, and finally locked up in a dark cell. I don't suppose you've got the nerve to call that courteous treatment."

He had an advantage, and knowing it, was pushing it to the limit; for all his nonchalance the black man was not unconscious of the pistol; his eye never forgot it. And Amber's eyes left his not an instant. Despite that the fellow's next move was a distinct surprise.

Suddenly and with superb grace, he stepped forward and dropped to one knee at Amber's feet, bowing his head and offering the hilt of his sword to the American.

"My lord," he said swiftly in Hindustani, "if I have misjudged thee, if I have earned thy displeasure, upon my head be it. See, I give my life into thy hands; but a little quiver of thy forefinger and I am as dust.... An ill report of thee was brought to me, and I did err in crediting it. It is true that I set this trap for thee; but see, my lord! though I did so, it was with no evil intent. I thought but to make sure of thee and bid thee welcome, as a faithful steward should, to thy motherland.... Maha Rao Rana, Har Dyal Rutton Bahadur, Heaven-born, King of Kings, Chosen of the Voice, Cherished of the Eye, Beloved of the Heart, bone of the bone and flesh of the flesh of the Body, Guardian of the Gateway of Swords!... I, thy servant, Salig Singh, bid thee welcome to Bharuta!"

Sonorous and not unpleasing, his voice trembled with intense and unquestionable earnestness; and when it ceased he remained motionless in his attitude of humility. Amber, hardly able to credit his hearing, stared down at the man stupidly, his head awhirl with curiously commingled sensations of amazement and enlightenment. Presently he laughed shortly.

"Get up," he said; "get up and stand over there by the wall and don't be a silly ass."

"Hazoor!" There was reproach in Salig Singh's accents; but he obeyed, rising and retreating to the further wall, there to hold himself at attention.

"Now see here," began Amber, designedly continuing his half of the conversation in English—far too much misunderstanding had already been brought about by his too-ready familiarity with Urdu. He paused a little to collect his thoughts, then resumed: "Now see here, you're Salig Singh, Maharana of Khandawar?" This much he recalled from his conversation with Labertouche a couple of hours gone.

"Hazoor, why dost thou need ask? Thou dost know." The Rajput, on his part, steadfastly refused to return to English.

"But you are, aren't you?"

"By thy favour, it is even so."

"And you think I'm Rutton—Har Dyal Rutton, as you call him, the former Maharana who abdicated in your favour?"

The Rajput shrugged expressively, an angry light in his dark, bold eyes. "It pleases my lord to jest," he complained; "but am I a child, to be played with?"

72

"I'm not joking, Salig Singh, and this business is no joke at all. What I'm trying to drive into your head is the fact that you've made the mistake of your life. I'm not Rutton and I'm nothing like Rutton; I am an American citizen and———"

"Pardon, hazoor, but is this worth thy while? I am no child; what I know I know. If thou art indeed not Har Dyal Rutton, how is it that thou dost wear upon thy finger the signet of thy house"—Salig Singh indicated the emerald which Amber had forgotten— "the Token sent thee by the Bell? If thou are not my lord the rightful Maharana of Khandawar, how is it that thou hast answered the summons of the Bell? Are the servants of the Body fools who have followed the hither, losing trace of thee no single instant since thou didst slay the Bengali who bore the Token to thee? Am I blind—I, Salig Singh, thy childhood's playmate, the Grand Vizier of thy too-brief rule, to whom thou didst surrender the reins of government of Khandawar? I know thee; thou canst not deceive me. True it is that thou art changed—sadly changed, my lord; and the years have not worn upon thee as they might—I had thought to find thee an older man and, by thy grace, a wiser. But even as I am Salig Singh, thou art none other than my lord, Har Dyal Rutton."

Salig Singh put his shoulders against the wall and, leaning so with arms folded, regarded Amber with a triumph not unmixed with contempt. It was plain that he considered his argument final, his case complete, the verdict his. While Amber found no words with which to combat his false impression, and could only stare, open-mouthed and fascinated. But at length he recollected himself and called his wits together.

"That's all very pretty," he admitted fairly, "but it won't hold water. I don't suppose these faithful servants of the Bell you mentioned happened to tell you that Chatterji himself mistook me for Rutton, to begin with, and just found out his mistake in time to recover the Token. Did they?"

The man shook his head wearily. "Nothing to that import hath come to mine ears," he said.

"All right. And of course they didn't tell you that Rutton committed suicide down there on Long Island, just after he had killed the babu?"

Again Salig Singh replied by a negative movement of his head.

"Well, all I've got to say is that your infernal 'Body' employs a giddy lot of incompetents to run its errands."

Salig Singh said nothing, and Amber pondered the situation briefly. He understood now how the babu's companion had fallen into error: how Chatterji, possessing sufficient intelligence to recognise his initial mistake, had, having rectified it, saved his face by saying nothing to his companion of the incident; and how the latter had remained in ignorance of Rutton's death after the slaying of Chatterji, and had pardonably mistaken Amber for the man he had been sent to spy upon. The prologue was plain enough, but how to deal with this its sequel was a problem that taxed his ingenuity. A single solution seemed practicable, of the many he debated: to get in touch with Labertouche and leave the rest to him.

He stood for so long in meditation that the Rajput began to show traces of impatience. He moved restlessly, yawned, and at length spoke.

"Is not my lord content? Can he not see, the dice are cast? What profit can he think to win through furtherance of this farce?"

"Well," curiosity prompted Amber to ask, "what do you want of me, then?"

"Is there need to ask? Through the Mouthpiece, the Bengali, Behari Lai Chatterji, whom thou didst slay, the message of the Bell was brought to thee. Thou hast been called; it is for thee to answer."

"Called——?"

"To the Gateway of Swords, hazoor."

"Oh, yes; to be sure. But where in thunderation is it?"

"That my lord doth know."

"You think so? Well, have it your own way. But suppose I decline the invitation?"

Salig Singh looked bored. "Since thou hast come so far," he said, "thou wilt go farther, hazoor."

"Meaning—by force?"

"Of thine own will. Those whom the Voice calleth are not led to the Gateway by their noses."

"But," Amber persisted, "suppose they won't go?"

"Then, hazoor, doth the Council of the Hand sit in judgment upon them."

The significance was savagely obvious, but Amber merely laughed. "And the Hand strikes, I presume?" Salig Singh nodded. "Bless your heart, I'm not afraid of your 'Hand'! But am I to understand that compulsion is not to be used in order to get me to the Gateway—wherever that is? I mean, I'm free to exercise my judgment, whether or not I shall go—free to leave this place and return to my hotel?"

Gravely the Rajput inclined his head. "Even so," he assented. "I caused thee to be brought hither solely to make certain what thou hast out of thine own mouth confirmed— the report that thou hadst become altogether traitor to the Bell. So be it. There remains but the warning that for four days more, and four days only, the Gateway remains open to those summoned. On the fifth it closes."

"And to those who remain in the outer darkness on that fifth day, Salig Singh——?"

"God is merciful," said the Rajput piously.

"Very well. If that is all, I think I will now leave you, Salig Singh," said Amber, fondling his pistol meaningly.

"One word more," Salig Singh interposed, very much alive to Amber's attitude: "I were unfaithful to the trust thou didst once repose in me were I not to warn thee that whither thou goest, the Mind will know; what thou dost, the Eye will see; the words thou shalt utter, the Ear will hear. To all things there is an end, also—even to the patience of the Body. Shabash!"

"Thank you 'most to death, Salig Singh. Now will you be good enough to order a ghari to take me back to the Great Eastern?"

"My lord's will is his servant's." Salig Singh started for the door the least trace too eagerly.

"One moment," said Amber sharply. "Not so fast, my friend." He tapped his palm with the barrel of the pistol to add weight to his peremptory manner. "I think if you will lift your voice and call, some one will answer. I've taken a great fancy to you, if you don't know it, and I don't purpose letting you out of my sight until I'm safely out of this house."

With a sullen air the Rajput yielded. From his expression Amber would have wagered much that there was a bad quarter of an hour in store for those who had neglected to disarm him when the opportunity was theirs.

"As you will," conceded Salig Singh; and he clapped his hands smartly, crying: "Ohe, Moto!"

Almost instantly the iron door swung open and the lamp-bearer appeared, salaaming.

"Tell him," ordered Amber, "to bring me a cloak of some sort—not too conspicuous. I've no fancy to kick up a scandal at the hotel by returning with these duds visible. You can charge it up to profit and loss; if it hadn't been for the tender treatment your assassins gave me, I'd be less disreputable."

A faint smile flickered in Salig Singh's eyes—a look that was not wholly devoid of admiration for the man who had turned the tables on him with such ease. "Indeed," he said, "I were lacking in courtesy did I refuse thee that." And turning to the servant he issued instructions in accordance with Amber's demands, adding gratuitously an order that the way of exit should be kept clear.

As the man bowed and withdrew Amber grinned cheerfully. "It wasn't a bad afterthought, Salig Singh," he observed; "precautions like that relieve the mind wonderfully sometimes."

But the humour of the situation seemed to be lost upon the Rajput.

In the brief wait that followed Amber shifted his position to one wherefrom he could command both the doorway and Salig Singh; his solicitude, however, was without apparent warrant; nothing happened to justify him of his vigilance. Without undue delay the servant returned with a light cloak and the announcement that the ghari was in waiting.

His offer to help the American don the garment was graciously declined. "I've a fancy to have my arms free for the present," Amber explained; "I can get it on by myself in the ghari." He took the cloak over his left arm. "I'm ready; lead on!" he said, and with a graceful wave of the pistol bowed Salig Singh out of the cellar.

Moto leading with the light, they proceeded in silence down a musty but deserted passage, Amber bringing up the rear with his heart in his mouth and his finger nervous upon the trigger. After a little the passage turned and discovered a door open to the street. Beyond this a ghari could be seen.

Amber civilly insisted that both the servant and his master leave the house before him, but, once outside, he made a wary detour and got between them and the waiting conveyance. Then, "It's kind of you, Salig Singh," he said; "I'm properly grateful. I'll say this for you: you play the game fairly when anybody calls your attention to the rules. Good-night to you—and, I say, be kind enough to shut the door as you go in. I'll just wait until you do."

The Rajput found no answer; conceivably, his chagrin was intense. With a curt nod he turned and reentered the house, Moto following. The door closed and Amber jumped briskly into the ghari.

"Home, James," he told the ghariwallah, in great conceit with himself.
"I mean, the Great Eastern Hotel—and *juldee jao*!"

The driver wrapped a whiplash round the corrugated flanks of his horse and the ghari turned the corner with gratifying speed. In half a minute they were in the Chitpur Road. In fifteen they drew up before the hotel.

It was after midnight and the city had begun to quiet down, but Old Court House Street was still populous with carriages and pedestrians, black and tan and white. There was a Viceregal function of some sort towards in the Government House, and broughams and victorias, coaches, hansoms, and coupes, with lamps alight and liveried coachmen—turn-outs groomed to the last degree of smartness—crowded the thoroughfare to the peril and discomfort of the casual ghari. The scene was unbelievably brilliant. Amber felt like rubbing his eyes. Here were sidewalks, pavements, throbbing electric arcs, Englishmen in evening dress, fair Englishwomen in dainty gowns and pretty wraps, the hum of English voices, the very smell of civilisation. And back there, just across the border he had so recently crossed, still reigned the midnight of the Orient, glamorous with the glamour of the Arabian Nights, dreadful with its dumb menace, its atmosphere of plot and counterplot, mutiny, treason, intrigue, and death. Here, a little island of life and light and gay, heedless laughter; there, all round it, pressing close, silence and impenetrable darkness, like some dark sea of death lapping its shores....

In a cold sweat of horror Amber got out of the vehicle and paid his fare. As he turned he discovered an uniformed policeman stalking to and fro before the hotel, symbol of the sane power that ruled the land. Amber was torn by an impulse to throw himself upon the man and shriek aloud his tale of terror—to turn and scream warning in the ears of those who lived so lightly on the lip of Hell....

A Bengali drifted listlessly past, a bored and blasé babu in a suit of pink satin, wandering home and interested in nothing save his own bland self and the native cigarette that drooped languidly from his lips. He passed within a foot of Amber, and from somewhere a voice spoke—the Virginian could have taken an oath that the babu's lips did not move—in a clear yet discreet whisper.

"To-morrow," it said; "Darjeeling."

Amber hitched his cloak round him and entered the hotel.

CHAPTER XI

THE TONGA

"Badshah Junction, Mr. Amber ... Badshah Junction ... We'll be there in 'alf an hour ..."

Inexorably the voice droned on, repeating the admonition over and over.

Mutinous, Amber stirred and grumbled in his sleep; stirred and, grumbling, wakened to another day. Doggott stood over him, doggedly insistent.

"Not much time to dress, sir; we're due in less than 'alf an hour."

"Oh, *all* right." Drowsy, stiff and sore in bone and muscle, Amber sat up on the edge of the leather-padded bunk and stared out of the window, wondering. With thundering flanges the train fled from east to west across a landscape that still slept wrapped in purple shadows. Far in the north the higher peaks of a long, low range of treeless hills were burning with a pale, cold light. A few stars glimmered in the cloudless vault—glimmered wan, doomed to sudden, swift extinction. Beside the railroad a procession of telegraph poles marched with dipping loops of wire between. There was nothing else to see. None the less the young man, now fully alive to the business of the day, said "Thank God!" in all sincerity.

"Even a tonga will be a relief after three days of this, Doggott," he observed, surrendering himself to the ministrations of the servant.

It was the third morning succeeding that on which he had risen from his bed in the Great Eastern Hotel in Calcutta, possessed by a wild anxiety to find his way with the least possible delay to Darjeeling and Sophia Farrell—a journey which he was destined never to make. For while he breakfasted a telegram had been brought to him.

"*Your train for Benares*," he read, "*leaves Howrah at nine-thirty. Imperative.*" It was signed: "*Pink Satin.*"

He acted upon it without thought of disobedience; he was in the hands of Labertouche, and Labertouche knew best. Between the lines he read that the Englishman considered it unwise to attempt further communication in Calcutta. Something had happened to eliminate the trip to Darjeeling. Labertouche would undoubtedly contrive to meet and enlighten him, either on the way or in Benares itself.

In the long, tiresome, eventless journey that followed his faith was sorely tried; nor was it justified until the train paused some time after midnight at Mogul Serai. There, before Amber and Doggott could alight to change for Benares, their compartment was invaded by an unmistakable loafer, very drunk. Tall and burly; with red-rimmed eyes in a pasty pockmarked face, dirty and rusty with a week-old growth of beard; clothed with sublime contempt for the mode and exalted beyond reason with liquor—a typical loafer of the Indian railways—he flung the door open and himself into Amber's arms, almost knocking the latter down; and resented the accident at the top of his lungs.

"You miserable, misbegotten blighter of a wall-eyed American——" At this point he became unprintably profane, and Doggott fell upon him with the laudable intention of throwing him out. In the struggle Amber caught his eye, and it was bright with meaning. "Pink Satin!" he hissed. "He's gone ahead.... You're to keep on to Agra.... Change for Badshah Junction, Rajputana Route.... Then tonga to Kuttarpur.... Farrell's there and his daughter.... That's right, my man, throw me out!..."

His downfall was spectacular. In his enthusiasm for the part he played, he had erred to the extent of delivering a blow in Doggott's face more forcible, probably, than he had intended it to be. Promptly he landed sprawling on the station platform and, in the sight of a multitude of natives, but the moment gone by his shrieks roused from their sleep in orderly ranks upon the floor, was gathered into the arms of the stationmaster and had the seriousness of his mistake pointed out to him forthwith and without regard to the sensitiveness of human anatomy.

And the train continued on its appointed way, bearing both Amber and the injured Doggott.

Thus they had come to the heart of Rajputana.

In the chill of dawn they were deposited at Badshah Junction. A scanty length of rude platform received them and their two small travelling bags.

On their left the Haiderabad express roared away, following the night, its course upon the parallel ribbons of shining steel marked by a towering pillar of dust. On their right, beyond the sharp-cut edge of the world, the sun had kindled a mighty conflagration in the skies. On every hand, behind and before them, the desert lay in ebbing shadows, a rolling waste seared by arid nullahs—the bone-dry beds of long-forgotten streams. Off in the north the hills cropped up and stole purposelessly away over the horizon.

They stood, then, forlorn in a howling desolation. For signs of life they had the station, a flimsy shelter roofed with corrugated iron, a beaten track that wandered off northwards and disappeared over a grassless swell, a handful of mud huts at a distance, and the ticket-agent. The latter a sleepy, surly Eurasian in pyjamas, surveyed them listlessly from the threshold of the station, and without a sign either of interest or contempt turned and locked himself in.

Amber sat down on his upturned suit-case and laughed and lit a cigarette. Doggott growled. The noise of the train died to silence in the distance, and a hyena came out of nowhere, exhibited himself upon the ridge of a dry desert swell, and mocked them sardonically. Then he, like the ticket-agent, went away, leaving an oppressive silence.

Presently the sun rose in glory and sent its burning level rays to cast a shadow several rods long of an enraged American beating frantically with clenched fists upon the door of an unresponsive railway station.

He hammered until he was a-weary, then deputised his task to Doggott, who resourcefully found him a stone of size and proceeded to make dents in the door. This method elicited the Eurasian. He came out, listened attentively to abuse and languidly to their demands for a tonga to bear them to Kuttarpur, and observed that the mail tonga left once a day—at three in the afternoon. Doggott caught him as he was on the point of returning to his interrupted repose and called his attention to the unwisdom of his ways.

Apparently convinced, this ticket-agent announced his intention of endeavouring to find a tonga for the sahib. Besides, he was not unwilling to acquire rupees. He scowled thoughtfully at Amber, ferociously at Doggott, went back into the station, gossiped casually with the telegraph sounder for a quarter of an hour, and finally reappearing, without a word or a nod left the platform for the road and walked and walked and walked and walked. Within thirty yards his figure was blurred by the dance of new-born heat devils. Within a hundred he disappeared; the desert swallowed him up.

An hour passed as three. The heat became terrific; not a breath of wind stirred. The face of the world lost its contours in wavering mirage. The travellers found lukewarm water in the station and breakfasted sparingly from their own stores of biscuit and tinned things. Then, in the shadow of the station, they settled down to wait, bored to extinction. Lulled by the hushed chatter of the telegraph sounder, Doggott nodded and slept audibly; Amber nodded, felt himself going, roused with a struggle, and lapsed into a dreary mid-world of semi-stupor.

In the simple fulness of Asiatic time a tonga came from Heaven knew where and roused him by rattling up beside the platform. He got up and looked it over with a just eye and a temper none the sweeter for his experience. It was a brute of a tonga, a patched and ramshackle wreck of what had once been a real tonga, with no top to protect the travellers from the sun, and accommodation only for three, including the driver.

The Eurasian ticket-agent alighted and solicited rupees. He got them and with them Amber's unvarnished opinion of the tonga; something which was not received with civility by the driver.

He remained in his seat—a short, swart native with an evil countenance and, across his knees, a sheathed tulwar—arguing with Amber in broken English and, abusing him scandalously in impurest Hindi, flinging at him in silken tones untranslatable scraps of bazaar Billingsgate. For, as he explained in an audible aside to the ticket-agent, this sahib was an outlander and, being as ignorant as most sahibs, could not understand Hindi. At this the Eurasian turned away to hide a grin of delight and the driver winked deliberately at Amber the while he broadly sketched for him his ancestry and the manner of his life at home and abroad.

Thunderstruck, Amber caught himself just as he was on the point of attempting to drag the driver from his seat and beat him into a more endurable frame of mind. He swallowed the hint and gave up the contest.

"Oh, very well," he conceded. "I presume you're trying to say there isn't another tonga to be had and it can't be helped; but I don't like your tone. However, there doesn't seem to be anything to do but take you. How much for the two of us?"

"Your servant, sahib? He cannot ride in this tonga," asserted the driver impassively.

"He can't! Why not?"

"You can see there is room for but two, and I have yet another passenger."

"Where?"

"At the first dak-bungalow, Sahib, where the mail-tonga broke down last night. This tonga, which I say is an excellent tonga, an *aram* tonga, a tonga for ease, is sent to take its place. More than this, I am bidden to go in haste; therefore there is little time for you to decide whether or not you will go with me alone. As for your servant, he can follow by this afternoon's mail tonga."

Upon this ultimatum he stood, immovable; neither threats nor bribery availed. It was an order, he said: he had no choice other than to obey. Shabash! Would the sahib be pleased to make up his mind quickly?

Perforce, the sahib yielded. "It'll be Labertouche; he's arranged this," he told himself. "That loafer said he'd gone on ahead of us." And comforted he issued his orders to Doggott, who received and acceded to them with all the ill-grace imaginable. He was to remain and follow to Kuttarpur by the afternoon's tonga. He forthwith sulked—and Amber, looking round upon the little Tephet that was Badshah Junction, had not the heart to reprove the man.

"It's all very well, sir," said Doggott. "I carn't s'y anything, I know. But, mark my words, sir—beggin' your pardon—there'll be trouble come of this. That driver's as ill-favoured a scoundrel as ever I see. And as for this 'ere ape, if 'e smiles at me just once more, I'll give 'im what-for." And he scowled so blackly upon the Eurasian that that individual hastily sought the seclusion which the station granted.

Amber left him, then, with a travelling-bag and a revolver for company, and the ticket-agent and his bad temper to occupy his mind.

Climbing aboard, the Virginian settled himself against the endless discomforts of the ride which he foresaw; the tonga was anything but "an *aram* tonga—a tonga for ease," there was no shade and no breeze, and the face of the land crawled with heat-bred haze.

To a crisp crackling of the whip-lash over the backs of the two sturdy, shaggy, flea-bitten ponies, the tonga swept away from the station, swift as a hunted fox with a dusty plume. The station dropped out of sight and the desert took them to its sterile heart.

On every hand the long swales rolled away, sunbaked, rocky, innocent of any sign of life other than the trooping telegraph poles in the south, destitute of any sort of vegetation other than the inevitable ak and gos. Wherever the eye wandered the prospect was the same—limitless expanses of raw blistering ochres, salmon-pinks, and dry faded reds, under a sky of brass and fire.

Amber leaned forward, watching the driver's face. "Your name, tonga-wallah?" he enquired.

"Ram Nath, sahib." The man spoke without moving his head, attending diligently to the management of his ponies.

"And this other passenger, who awaits us at the dak-bungalow, Ram Nath—is he, perchance, one known both to you and to me?"

Ram Nath flicked the flagging ponies. "How should I know?" he returned brusquely.

"One," persisted Amber, "who might be known by such a name as, say, Pink Satin?"

"What manner of talk is this?" demanded Ram Nath. "I am no child to be amused by a riddle. I know naught of your 'Pink Satin.'" He bent forward, shortening his grasp upon the reins, as if to signify that the interview was at an end.

Amber sat back, annoyed by the fellow's impudence yet sensitive to a suspicion that Ram Nath was playing his part better than his passenger, that the rebuke was merited by one who had ventured to speak of secret things in a land whose very stones have ears. For all that he could say their every move was watched by invisible spies, of whom the rock-strewn waste through which they sped might well harbour a hidden legion.... But perhaps, after all, Ram Nath had nothing whatever to do with Labertouche. Undeniable as had been his wink, it might well have been nothing more than an impertinence. At the thought Amber's eyes darkened and hardened and he swore bitterly beneath his breath. If that were so, he vowed, the tonga-wallah would pay dearly for the indiscretion. He set his wits to contrive a way to satisfy his doubts.

Meanwhile the tonga rocked and bounded fiendishly over an infamous parody of a road, turning and twisting between huge boulders and in and out of pebbly nullahs, Ram Nath tooling it along with the hand of a master. But all his attention was of necessity centred upon the ponies, and presently his tulwar slipped from his knees and clattered upon the floor of the tonga. Amber saw his chance and put his foot upon it.

"Ram Nath," he asked gently, "have you no other arms?"

"I were a fool had I not." The man did not deign to glance round. "He hath need of weapons who doth traffick with the Chosen of the Voice, sahib."

"Ah, that Voice!" cried Amber in exasperation. "I grow weary of the word, am Nath."

"That may well be," returned the man, imperturbable. "None the less it were well for you to have a care how you fondle the revolver in your pocket, sahib. Should it by any chance go off and the bullet find lodgment in your tonga-wallah, you are like to hear more of that Voice, and from less friendly lips."

"I think you have eyes in the back of your head, Ram Nath." Amber withdrew his hand from his coat pocket and laughed shortly as he spoke.

"There is a saying in this country, sahib, that even the stones in the desert have ears to hear and eyes to see and tongues withal to tell what they have seen and heard."

"Ah-h!... That is a wise saying, Ram Nath."

"There be those I could name who would do well to lay that saying to heart, sahib."

"You are right, indeed.... Now if there be aught of truth in that saying, and if one were unwisely to speak a certain name, even here——"

"The echo of that name might be heard beyond the threshold of a certain Gateway, sahib."

Amber grunted and said no more, contented now with the assurance that he was in truth in touch with Labertouche, that this Ram Nath was an employee of the I.S.S. The wink was now explained away with all the rest of the tonga-wallah's churlishness. Since there was a purpose behind it all, the Virginian was satisfied to contain his curiosity. Nevertheless he could not help thinking that there must be some fantastic exaggeration in the excessive degree of caution that was thus tacitly imposed upon him.

He looked round him, narrowing his eyes against the sun-glare; and the desert showed itself to his eyes a desert waste and nothing more. The day lay stark upon its lifeless face and it seemed as if, within the wide rim of the horizon, no thing moved save the tonga. They were then passing rapidly over higher ground and seemed to have drawn a shade nearer to the raw red northern hills. Amber would have said that they could never have found a solitude more absolute.

The thought was still in his mind when the tonga dipped unexpectedly over another ridge, began to descend another long grade of dead, parched earth, and discovered some distance ahead of them on the wagontrack a cloud of dust like a tinted veil, so dense, opaque, and wide and high that its cause was altogether concealed in its reddish, glittering convolutions. But the Virginian knew the land well enough to recognise the phenomenon and surmise its cause, even before his ears began to be assailed by the hideous rasping screech of wheels of solid wood revolving reluctantly on rough-hewn axles guiltless of grease. And as the tonga swiftly lessened the distance, his gaze, penetrating the thinning folds, discerned the contours of a cotton-wain drawn by twin stunted bullocks, patient noses to the ground, tails a-switch. Beside his cattle the driver plodded, goad in hand, a naked sword upon his hip. Within his reach, between the rude bales of the loaded cart, the butt of a brass-bound musket protruded significantly.... All men went armed in that wild land: to do as much is one of the boons attendant upon citizenship in an unprogressive, independent native State.

Deliberately enough the carter swerved his beasts aside to make way for the tonga, lest by undue haste he should make himself seem other than what he was—a free man and a Rajput. But when his fierce, hawk-like eyes encountered those of the dak traveller, his attitude changed curiously and completely. Recognition and reverence fought with surprise in his expression, and as Ram Nath swung the tonga past the man salaamed profoundly. His voice, as he rose, came after them, resonant and clear:

"Hail, thou Chosen of the Gateway! Hail!"

Amber neither turned to look nor replied. But his frown deepened. The incident passed into his history, marked only by the terse comment it educed from Ram Nath—words which were flung curtly over the tonga-wallah's shoulder: "Eyes to see and ears to hear and a tongue withal ... sahib!"

The Virginian said nothing. But it was in his mind that he had indeed thrust his head into the lion's mouth by thus adventuring into the territory which every instinct of caution and common-sense proclaimed taboo to him—the erstwhile kingdom of the Maharana Har Dyal Rutton. It was, in a word, foolhardy—nothing less. But for his pledged word it had been so easy to order Ram Nath to convey him back to Badshah Junction to order and to enforce obedience at the pistol's point, if needs be! Honour held him helpless, bound upon the Wheel of his Destiny: he must and would go on....

He sat in silent gloom while sixty minutes were drummed out by the flying hoofs. The hills folded in about the way, diverting it hither and yon with raw, seamed spurs, whose flanks flung back harsh and heavy echoes of the tonga's flight through riven gulch and scrub-grown valley. And then it was that Ram Nath proved his mettle. Hardened himself, he showed no mercy to his passenger, and never once drew rein, though the tonga danced from rock to ridge and ridge to rut and back again, like a tin can on the tail of an astonished dog. As for Amber, he wedged his feet and held on with both hands, grimly, groaning in spirit when he did not in the flesh, foreseeing as he did nine hours more of this heroic torture punctuated only by brief respites at the end of each stage.

CHAPTER XII

THE LONG DAY

One travels dak by relays casually disposed along the route at the whim of the native contractor. Between Badshah Junction and Kuttarpur there were ten stages, of which the conclusion of the first was at hand—Amber having all but abandoned belief in its existence.

Slamming recklessly down the bed of an ancient watercourse, the tonga spun suddenly upon one wheel round a shoulder of the banks and dashed out upon a rolling plain, across which the trail snaked to other farther hills that lay dim and low, a wavy line of blue, upon the horizon—the hills in whose heart Kuttarpur itself lay occult. And, by the roadside, in a compound fenced with camel-thorn, sat an aged and indigent dak-bungalow, marking the end of the first stage, the beginning of the second.

It wore a look of Heaven to the traveller. In the shade of its veranda he read an urgent invitation to rest and surcease of sunlight. He approved it thoroughly; the ramshackle rest-house itself, the sheds in the rear for the accommodation of relays, the syce squatting asleep in the sunshine, the few scrawny chickens squabbling and scratching over their precarious sustenance in the deep hot dust of the compound, even the broken tonga reposing with its shafts uplifted at a piteous angle of decrepitude—all these Amber surveyed with a kindly eye.

Ram Nath reined in with a flourish and lifted a raucous voice, hailing the syce, while Amber, painfully disengaging his cramped limbs, climbed down and stumbled toward the veranda. The abrupt transition from violent and erratic motion to a solid and substantial footing affected him unpleasantly, with an undeniable qualm; the earth seemed to rock and flow beneath him as if under the influence of an antic earthquake. He was for some seconds occupied with the problem of regaining his poise, and it was not until he heard an Englishwoman's voice uplifted in accents of anger, that he remembered the other wayfarer with whom he was to share his tonga, or associated the white-clad figure in the dark doorway of the bungalow with anything but the khansamah, coming to greet and cheat the chance-brought guest.

"Where is that tonga-wallah who deserted me here last night?" the woman was demanding of Ram Nath, too preoccupied with her resentment to have eyes for the other traveller, who at sight of her had stopped and removed his pith helmet and now stood staring as if he had come from a land in which there were no women. "Where," she continued, with an imperative stamp of a daintily-shod foot, "is that wretched tonga-wallah?"

"Sahiba," protested Ram Nath, with a great show of deference, "how should I know? Belike he is in Badshah Junction, whither he returned very late last night, being travel-worn and weary, and where I left him, being sent with this excellent tonga to take his place."

"You were? And why have I been detained here, alone and unprotected, this long night? Simply because that other tonga-wallah was a fool, am I to be imposed upon in this fashion?"

"What am I," whimpered Ram Nath, "to endure the wrath of the sahiba for a fault that is none of mine?"

"I beg your pardon, sir," said the girl, turning to Amber, "but it is very annoying." She looked him over, first with abstraction, then with a puzzled gathering of her brows, for he was far from her thoughts—the last person she would have expected to meet in that place, and very effectually disguised in dust and dirt besides, "The tire came off the wheel just as we got here, late yesterday evening, and in trying, or pretending to try, to fit it on again, that block-head of a tonga-wallah hammered the rim with a rock as big as his head and naturally smashed it to kindling-wood. Then, before I could stop him, he flung himself on the back of a pony and went away, saying that it was the will of God that he should return to Badshah for a better tonga. Since when I have had for company one stable-syce, one deaf-and-dumb patriarch of a khansamah and ... the usual dak-bungalow discomforts—insects, bad food, and a terrible fear of dacoits."

"I am so sorry, Miss Farrell," Amber put in. "If I had only been here...."

The girl gave a little gasp and sat down abruptly in one of the veranda chairs, thereby threatening it with instant demolition and herself with a bad spill; for the chair was feeble with the burden of its many years, and she was a quite substantial young person. Indeed, so loudly did it croak a protest and a warning that she immediately arose in alarm.

"Mr. Amber!" she said; and, "Well ...!"

"You'll forgive me the surprise?" he begged, going up on the veranda to her. "I myself had no hope of finding you here."

"But," she protested, with a pretty flush of colour—"but I left you in the States such a little while ago!"

"Yes?" he said gravely. "It seems so long to me.... And when you had gone, Long Island was a very lonely place indeed," he added, with calculated impudence.

Her colour deepened and she sought another chair, seating herself with gingerly decision. "I'm sure you don't mean me to assume that you've followed me half round the world?"

"Why not?" He brought another chair to face her. "Besides, I haven't seen anything of … India for a good many years."

"Mr. Amber!"

"Ma'am?" he countered with affected humility.

"You're spoiling it all. I was so glad to see you—I'd have been glad to see any white man, of course——"

"Much obliged, I'm sure."

"And now you're actually flirting with me—or pretending to."

"I'm not," he declared soberly. "As a matter of solemn fact, I had to come to India."

"You *had* to?"

"On a matter of serious business. Please don't ask me what, just yet; but it's very serious, to my way of thinking. This happy accident—I count myself a very happy man to have been so fortunate—only makes my errand the more pleasant."

She regarded him intently, chin in hand, her brown eyes sedate with speculation, for some time. "I believe you've been speaking in parables," she asserted, at length. "If I'm unjust, bear with me; appearances are against you. There isn't any reason I know of why you should tell me what brought you here——"

"There's every reason, in point of fact, Miss Farrell; only … I can't explain just now."

"Very well," she agreed briskly; "let's be content with that. I am glad to see you again, truly; and—we're to travel on to Kuttarpur in the same tonga?"

"If you'll permit——"

"After what I've endured, this awful night, I wouldn't willingly let you out of my sight."

"Or any other white man?"

She laughed, pleased. "I presume you're wondering what I'm doing here?"

"You were to join your father in Darjeeling, I believe?" he countered, cautious.

"But I found he'd been transferred unexpectedly to Kuttarpur. So, of course, I had to follow. I telegraphed him day before yesterday when I was to arrive at Badshah Junction, and naturally expected he'd come in person or have some one meet me, but I presume the message must have gone astray. At all events there was no one there for me and I had to come on alone. It's hardly been a pleasant experience; that incompetent tonga-wallah behaved precisely as though he had deliberately made up his mind to delay me…. And the tonga's nearly ready; I must lock my kit-bag."

She went into the bungalow, leaving him thoughtful, for perhaps…. But the back of Ram Nath, as that worthy busied himself superintending the harnessing in of fresh ponies, conveyed to him no support for his half-credited hypothesis that this "accident" had been carefully planned by Labertouche for Amber's especial benefit.

He vexed himself with vain speculations, for it was perfectly certain that he would get nothing in the way of either denial or confirmation out of Ram Nath; and, presently, acknowledging this, he called the khansamah and ordered a peg for the sake of the dust in his throat.

The girl joined him on the veranda in due course, very demure and sweet to look upon in her travelling-dress of light pongee and her pith helmet, whose green under-brim and puggaree served very handsomely to set off her fair colouring. If she overlooked the adoration of his eyes, she was rather less than woman; for it was in them, plain to be seen for the looking. The khansamah followed her from the bungalow, staggering under the weight of her box and kit-bag, and with Ram Nath's surly assistance made them fast to the front seat. While Amber gave the girl his hand to help her to her place, and lifted himself to her side in a mute glow of ecstasy. Fate, he thought with reason, was most kind to him.

They rattled headlong from the compound, making for the distant hills of blue. The girl drew down her puggaree, with its soft, thin folds sheltering the pure contours of her face from the dust and burning sun-glare. He watched her hungrily, holding his breath as the thought came to him that he was seated elbow to elbow with the woman who was to be his wife, his hand still a-tingle with the reminiscence of her gloved fingers that had touched it so transiently. She caught his intent look and smiled, her eyes lustrous through the veiling.

She was very tired after her night-long vigil, and after a few words of commonplace as they drew away from the station, he forebore to weary her with talk, and a silence as sweet as communion lengthened between them as the stage lengthened. He was very intent upon her presence; the consciousness of her there beside him seemed, at times, almost suffocating. He could by no means forget that she had in a curious way been assigned to him—set aside to be his wife, the partner of all his days; and she tolerated him kindly, all unsuspicious of the significance of his advent into her life…. If she were made to suspect, to understand, what effect would it have upon their relations, slight and but lately established as they were? Would she shrink from or encourage him?

His wife! He wagged his head in solemn stupefaction, trying to appreciate the intangible, the chimerical dream of yesterday resolved into the actuality of to-day; realising that, even when most intrigued by the adventure of which she was at once the cause and the prize, even though he had met and been charmed by her before becoming enmeshed in its web of incident, he had thought of her with a faint trace of incredulity, as though she had been a thing of fable, trapped with all the fanciful charms of beleaguered fairy princesses, rather than a living woman of flesh and fire and blood—such as she proved to be who rode with him, her thoughts drowsily astray in the vastnesses of her inscrutable, virginal moods.

To think that she was foreordained to be his wife was not more unbelievable than the consciousness that he, her undeclared lover, her predestined mate and protector, was listlessly permitting her to delve further into the black heart of a land out of which he had promised to convey her with all possible speed, for the salvation of her body and soul…. Yet what could he do, save be passive for the time, and wait upon the turn of events? He could not, dared not seize her in his arms and insist that she love him, marry him, fly with him—all within the compass of an hour or even of a day. For words of love came haltingly to his unskilled tongue, though they came from a surcharged heart, and to him the strategy of love was as a sealed book, at whose contents he could but guess, and that with a diffidence and distrust sadly handicapping to one who had urgent need of expedition in his courting.

With a rueful smile and a perturbed heart he pondered his problem. The second stage wore away without a dozen words passing between them; so also the third. The pauses were brief enough, the ponies being exchanged with gratifying despatch. The tonga would pull up, Ram Nath would jump down … and in a brace of minutes or little more the vehicle would be *en route* again, Amber engaged with the infinite ramifications of this labyrinthal riddle of his, and the girl insensibly yielding to the need of sleep. She passed, at length, into sound unconsciousness.

Thus the morning stages flowed beneath the tonga, personified in a winding ribbon of roadway, narrow, deep-rutted, inexpressibly dusty, lined uncertainly over a scrubby, sun-scorched waste. Sophia napped uneasily by fits and starts, waking now and again with a sleepy smile and a fragmentary, murmured apology. She roused finally very much refreshed for the midday halt for rest and tiffin, which they passed at one of the conventional bungalows, in nothing particularly unlike its fellows unless it were that they enjoyed, before tiffin, the gorgeous luxury of plenty of clean water, cooled in porous earthen jars. Amber, overwhelmed by the discovery of this abundance, promptly went to the extreme of calling in the khansamah to sluice him down with jar after jar, and felt like himself for the first time in five days when, shaved and dressed, he returned to the common living-room of the resthouse.

The girl kept him waiting but a little while. Lacking the attentions of an ayah she had probably been unable to bathe so extensively as he, but eventually she appeared in an immeasurably more happy state of body and mind, calling up to him the simile, stronger than any other, of a tall, fair lily after a morning shower. And she was in a bewitching humour, one that ingenuously enough succeeded in entangling him more thoroughly than ever before in the web of her fascinations. Over an execrable curry of stringy fowl and questionable rice, eked out with tea and tinned delicacies of their own, their chatter, at the beginning sufficiently gay and inconsequent, drifted by imperceptible and unsuspected gradations perilously close to the shoals of intimacy. And subsequently, when they had packed themselves back into the narrow tonga-seat and again were being bounced and juggled breathlessly over shocking roads, the exchange of confidences continued with unabated interest. Amber on his part was led to talk of his life and work, of his adventures in the name of Science, of his ambitions and achievements. In return he received a vivid impression of the lives of those women who share with their men the burden of official life in British India: of serene days in the brisk, invigorating, clear atmosphere of hill stations; of sunsmitten days and steaming nights in the Deccan; of the uncertain, anchorless existences of those who know not from one day to another when they may be whisked half across an Empire at the whim of that awful force simply nominated Government....

For all the taint upon her pedigree, she proved herself to Amber at heart a simple, lonely Englishwoman—a stranger in a sullen and suspicious land, desiring nothing better than to return to the England she had seen and learned to love, the England of ample lawns, of box-hedges, and lanes, of travelled highways, pavements and gaslights, of shops and theatres, of home and family ties....

But India she knew. "I sometimes fancy," she told him with the conscious laugh that deprecates a confessed superstition, "that I must have lived here in some past incarnation." She paused, but he did not speak. "Do you believe in reincarnation?" Again he had no answer for her, though temporarily he saw the daylight as darkness. "It's hard to live here for long and resist belief in it.... But as a matter of fact I seem to understand these people better than they're understood by most of *my* people. Don't you think it curious? Perhaps it's merely intuition——"

"That's the birthright of your sex," he said, rousing. "On the other hand, you have to remember that your father is one of a family that for generations has served the Empire. And your mother?"

"She, too, came of an Anglo-Indian family. Indeed, they met and courted here, though they were married in England.... So you think my insight into native character a sort of birthright—a sense inherited?"

"Perhaps—something of the sort."

"You may be right. We'll never know. At all events, I seem to have a more—more painful comprehension of the native than most of the English in this country have; I seem to feel, to sense their motives, their desires, aspirations, even sometimes their untranslatable thoughts. I believe I understand perfectly their feeling toward us, the governing race."

"Then," said Amber, "you know something his Highness the Viceroy himself would give his ears to be sure of."

"I know that; but I do."

"And that feeling is——?"

"Not love, Mr. Amber."

"Much to the contrary——?"

"Very much," she affirmed with deep conviction.

"This 'Indian unrest' one reads of in the papers is not mere gossip, then?"

"Anything but that; it's the hidden fire stirring within the volcano we told ourselves was dead. The quiet of the last fifty years has been not content but slumber; deep down there has always been the fire, slow, deadly, smouldering beneath the ashes. The Mutiny still lives in spirit; some day it will break out afresh. You must believe me—I *know*. The more we English give our lives to educate the natives, the further we spread the propaganda of discontent; day by day we're teaching them to understand that we are no better than they, no more fit to rule; they are beginning to look up and to see over the rim of the world— and we have opened their eyes. They have learned that Japanese can defeat Caucasians, that China turns in its sleep, that England is no more omnipotent than omniscient. They've heard of anarchy and socialism and have learned to throw bombs. Only the other day a justice in Bengal was killed by a bomb.... I fancy I talk," the girl broke off with her clear laugh, "precisely like my father, who talks precisely as a political pamphleteer writes. You'll see when you meet him."

"Do you take much interest in politics?"

"No more than the every-day Englishwoman; it's one of our staples of conversation, when we've exhausted the weather, you know. But I'm not in the least advanced, if that's what you mean; I hunger after fashion-papers and spend more time than I ought, devouring home-made trash imported in paper-covers. I only feel what I feel by instinct—as I said awhile ago."

Perhaps if he had known less about the girl, he would have attached less importance to her statements. As it was, she impressed him profoundly. He pondered her words deeply, storing them in his memory, remembering that another had spoken in the same manner— one for whose insight into the ways of the native he had intense respect.

As the slow afternoon dragged out its blazing hours, their spirits languished, and they fell silent, full weary and listless. Towards the last quarter of the journey their road forsook the spacious, haggard plain and again entered a hilly country, but this time one wherein there was no lack either of water or of life: a green and fertile land parcelled into farms and dotted with villages.

Night overtook the tonga when it was close upon Kuttarpur, swooping down upon the world like a blanket of darkness, at the moment that the final relay of ponies was being hitched in. The sun dipped behind the encircling hills; the west blazed with the lambent flame of fire-opal; the wonderful translucent blue of the sky shaded suddenly to deep purple lanced by great shafts of mauve and amethyst light, and in the east stars popped out; the hills shone like huge, crude gems—sapphire, jade, jasper, malachite, chalcedony—their valleys swimming with mists of mother-of-pearl.... And it was night, the hills dark and still, the sky a deeper purple and opaque, the ruddy fires of wayfarers on the roadside leaping clear and bright.

With fresh ponies the tonga took the road with a wild initial rush soon to be moderated, when it began to climb the last steep grade to the pass that gives access to Kuttarpur from the south. For an hour the road toiled up and ever upward; steep cliffs of rock crowded it, threatening to push it over into black abysses, or to choke it off between towering, formidable walls. It swerved suddenly into a broad, clear space. The tonga paused. Voluntarily Ram Nath spoke for almost the first time since morning.

"Kuttarpur," he said, with a wave of his whip.

Aloof, austere and haughty, the City of Swords sits in the mouth of a ravine so narrow that a wall no more than a hundred yards in length is sufficient to seal its southerly approach. Beneath this wall, to one side of the city gate, a river flows from the lake that is Kuttarpur's chiefest beauty. Within, a multitude of dwellings huddles, all interpenetrated by streets and backways so straitened and sinuous as scarcely to permit the passage of an elephant from the Maharana's herd; congested in the bottom of the valley, the houses climb tier upon tier the flanking hillsides, until their topmost roofs threaten even the supremacy of that miracle in white marble, the Raj Mahal.

Northwards the palace of Khandawar's kings stands, exquisite, rare, and marvellous, unlike any other building in the world. White, all white, from the lake that washes its lowest walls to the crenellated rim of its highest roof, it sweeps upward in breath-taking steps and wide terraces to the crest of the western hill, into which it burrows, from which it springs; a vast enigma propounded in white marble without a note of colour save where the foliage of a hidden garden peeps over the edge of a jealous screen—a hundred imposing mansions merged into one monstrous and imperial maze.

Impregnable in the old days, before cannon were brought to India, Kuttarpur lives to-day remote, unfriendly, inhospitable. Within its walls there is no room for many visitors; they who come in numbers, therefore, must perforce camp down before the gates.

Now figure the city to yourself, seeing it as Sophia was later to see it in the light of day; then drench it with blue Indian night and stud it with a myriad eyes of fire—lamps, torches, candles, blue-white electric arcs, lights running up and down both hillsides and fringing the very star-sheeted skies, clustering and diverging in vast, bewildering, inconsequent designs, picking out the walls and main thoroughfares, shining through coloured globes upon the palace terraces, glimmering mysteriously from isolate windows and balconies; and add to these the softly illuminated walls of a hundred silken state marquees and a thousand meaner canvas tents arrayed south of the city.... And that is Kuttarpur as it first revealed itself to Amber and Sophia Farrell.

But for a moment were they permitted to gaze in wonderment; Ram Nath had little patience. When he chose to, he applied his whip, and the ponies stretched out, the tonga plunging on their heels down the steep hillside, like an ungoverned, ungovernable thing, maddened. Within a quarter of an hour they were careering through the city of tents on the parked plain before the southern wall. In five minutes more they drew up at the main city gate to parley with the Quarter Guard.

Here they suffered an exasperating delay. It appeared that the gates were shut at sundown, in deference to custom immemorial. Between that hour and sunrise none were permitted to pass either in or out without the express sanction of the State. The commander of the guard instituted an impudent catechism, in response to which Ram Nath discovered the several identities and estates of his charges. The commander received the information with impartial equanimity and retired within the city to confer with his superiors. After some time a trooper was sent to advise the travellers that the tonga would be permitted to enter with the understanding that the unaccredited Englishman (meaning Amber) would consent to lodge for the night in no other spot than the State rest-house beyond the northern limits of the city.

Amber agreed. The trooper saluted with much deference and withdrew. And for a long time nothing happened; the gates remained shut, the postern of the Quarter Guard irresponsive to Ram Nath's repeated summons. His passengers endured with what patience they could command; they were aware that it was necessary to obtain from some quarter official sanction for the opening of the gates, but they had understood that it had already been obtained.

Abruptly the peace of the night was shattered, and the hum of the encampment behind them with the roar of the city before them was dwarfed, by a dull and thunderous detonation of cannon from a terrace of the palace. The tonga ponies, reared and plunged, Ram Nath mastering them with much difficulty. Sophia was startled, and Amber himself stirred uneasily on his perch.

"What now?" he grumbled. "You'd think we were visitors of state and had to be durbarred!"

Far up on the heights a second red flame stabbed the night, and again the thunder pealed. Thereafter gun after gun bellowed at imperative, stately intervals.

"Fifteen," Amber announced after a time. "Isn't this something extraordinary, Miss Farrell?"

"Perhaps," she suggested, "there's a native potentate arriving at the northern gate. They're very punctilious about their salutes, you know."

Another crash silenced her. Amber continued to count. "Twenty-one," he said when it seemed that there was to be no more cannonading. "Isn't that a royal salute?"

"Yes," said the girl; "four more guns than the Maharana of Khandawar himself is entitled to."

"How do you explain it?"

"I don't," she replied simply. "Can you?"

He was dumb. Could it be possible that this imperial greeting was intended for the man supposed to be the Maharana of Khandawar—Har Dyal Rutton? He glanced sharply at the girl, but her face was shadowed; and he believed she suspected nothing.

A great hush had fallen, replacing the rolling thunder of the State ordnance. Even the voice of the city seemed moderate, subdued. In silence the massive gates studded with sharp-toothed elephant-spikes swung open.

With a grunt, Ram Nath cracked his whiplash and the tonga sped into the city. Amber bent forward.

"What's the name of that gate, Ram Nath—if you happen to know?"

"That," said the tonga-wallah in a level voice, "is known as the Gateway of Swords, sahib." He added in his own good time: "But not *the* Gateway of Swords."

Amber failed to educe from him any satisfactory explanation of this orphic utterance.

CHAPTER XIII

THE PHOTOGRAPH

That same night Amber dined at the Residency, on the invitation of Raikes, the local representative of Government, seconded by the insistence of Colonel Farrell. It developed that Sophia's telegram had somehow been lost in transit, and Farrell's surprise and pleasure at sight of her were tempered only by his keen appreciation of Amber's adventitious services, slight though they had been. He was urged to stay the evening out, before proceeding to his designated quarters, and the reluctance with which he acceded to this arrangement which worked so happily with his desires, may be imagined.

Their arrival coincided with the dinner-hour; the meal was held half an hour to permit them to dress. Raikes put a room at Amber's disposal, and the Virginian contrived to bathe and get into his evening clothes within less time than had been allowed him. Sophia, contrary to the habit of her sex, was little tardier. At thirty minutes past eight they sat down to dine, at a table in the garden of the Residency.

Ease of anxiety was more than food and drink to Amber; his feeling of relief, to have convoyed Sophia to the company and protection of Anglo-Saxons like himself, was intense. Yet he swallowed his preliminary brandy-peg in a distinctly uncomfortable frame of mind, strangely troubled by the reflection that round that lone white table was gathered together the known white population of the State; a census of which accounted for just five souls.

In the encompassing, exotic gloom of that blue Indian night—the kind of night that never seems friendly to the Occidental but forever teems with hints of tragic mystery—the cloth, lighted by shaded candles, shone as immaculate and lustrous as an island of snow in a sea of ink—as a good deed in a naughty world. Its punctilious array of crystal and silver was no more foreign to the setting than were the men who sat round it, stiff in that black-and-white armour of civilisation, impregnable against the insidious ease of the East, in which your expatriate Englishman nightly encases himself wherever he may be, as loath to forego the ceremony of "dressing for dinner" as he would be to dispense with letters from Home.

Raikes presided, a heavy man with the flaming red face of one who constitutionally is unable to tan; of middle-age, good-natured, mellow, adroit of manner. On his one hand sat Amber, over across from Sophia. Next to Amber sat Farrell, tall and lean, sad of eye and slow of speech, his sun-faded hair and moustache streaked with grey setting off a dark complexion and thin, fine features. He wore the habit of authority equally with the irascibility of one who temporizes with his liver. Opposite him was a young, mild-eyed missionary, too new in the land to have lost his illusions or have blunted the keen edge of his enthusiasms; a colourless person with a finical way of handling his knife and fork, who darted continually shy, sidelong glances at Sophia, or interpolated eager, undigested comments, nervously into the conversation.

The table-talk was inconsequent; Amber took a courteous and easy part in it without feeling that any strain was being put upon his intelligence. His attention was centred upon the woman who faced him, flushed with gaiety and pleasure, not alone because she was once more with her father, but also because she unexpectedly was looking her best. If she had been well suited in her tidy pongee travelling costume, she found her evening gown no less becoming. It was a black affair, very simple and individual; her shoulders rose from it with intensified purity of tone, like fair white ivory gleaming with a suggestion of the sleek sheen of satin; their strong, clean lines rounded bewitchingly into the fair, slender neck upholding the young head with its deftly coiffed crown of bronze and gold....

Tall, well-trained, silent servants moved like white-robed wraiths behind the guests; the dishes of the many courses disappeared and were replaced in a twinkling, as if by slight of hand. They were over plentiful; Amber was relieved when at length the meal was over, and Miss Farrell having withdrawn in conformance with inviolable custom, the cloth was deftly whisked away and cigars, cigarettes, liqueurs, whiskey and soda were served.

Amber took unto himself a cigar and utilised an observation of the Political's as a lever to swing the conversation to a plane more likely to inform him. Farrell had grumbled about the exactions of his position as particularly instanced by the necessity of his attending tedious and tiresome native ceremonies in connection with the *tamasha*.

"What's, precisely, the nature of this *tamasha*, Colonel Farrell?"

"Why, my dear young man, I thought you knew. Isn't it what you came to see?"

"No," Amber admitted cautiously; "I merely heard a rumour that there was something uncommon afoot. Is it really anything worth while?"

"Rather," Raikes interjected drily; "the present ruler's abdicating in favour of his son, a child of twelve. That puts the business in a class by itself."

"There's been one precedent, hasn't there?" said the missionary, pretending to be at ease with a cigarette. "The Holkar of Indore?"

"Yes," agreed Farrell; "a similar case, to be sure."

"But why should a prince hand over the reins of government to a child of twelve? There must be some reason for it. Isn't it known?" asked Amber.

"Who can fathom a Hindu's mind?" grunted Farrell. "I daresay there's some scandalous native intrigue at the bottom of it. Eh, Raikes?"

The Resident shook his head. "Don't come to this shop for information about what goes on in Khandawar. I doubt if there's another Resident in India who knows as little of the underhand devilment in his State as I do. His Majesty the Rana loves me as a cheetah loves his trainer. He's an intractable rascal."

"They grease the wheels of the independent native States with intrigue," Farrell explained. "I know from sore experience. And your Rajput is the deepest of the lot. I don't envy Raikes, here."

"The man who can guess what a Rajput intends to do next is entitled to give himself a deal of credit," commented the Resident, with a short laugh.

"I've travelled a bit," continued Farrell, "and have seen something of the courts of Europe, but I've yet to meet a diplomat who's peer to the Rajput. You hear a great deal about the astuteness of the Russians and the yellow races, and a Greek or Turk can lie with a fairly straight face when he sees a profit in deception, but none of them is to be classed with these people. If we English ever decide to let India rule herself, her diplomatic corps will be recruited exclusively from the flower of Rajputana's chivalry."

"I'll back Salig Singh against the field," said Raikes grimly; "he'll be dean of the corps, when that time comes. He'd rather conspire than fight, and the Rajputs—of course you know—are a warrior caste. I've a notion"—the Resident leaned back and searched the shadows for an eavesdropper—"I've a notion," he continued, lowering his voice, "that the Rana has got himself in rather deep in some rascality or other, and wants to get out before he's put out. There's bazaar gossip…. Hmm! Do you speak French, Mr. Amber?"

"A little," said Amber in that tongue. "And I," nodded the missionary.
The talk continued in the language of diplomacy.

"Bazaar gossip——?" Farrell repeated enquiringly.

"There have been a number of deaths from cholera in the Palace lately, the grand vizier's amongst them."

"White arsenic cholera?"

"That, and the hemp poison kind."

"Refractory vizier?" questioned Farrell. "The kind that wants to retrench and institute reforms—railways and metalled roads and so forth?"

"No; he was quite suited to his master. But the bazaar says Naraini took a dislike to him for one reason or another."

"Naraini?" queried Amber.

"The genius of the place." Raikes nodded toward the Raj Mahal, shining like a pearl through the darkness on the hill-side over against the Residency. "She's Salig's head queen. At least that's about as near to her status as one can get. She's not actually his queen, but some sort of a heritage from the Rutton dynasty—I hardly know what or why.

90

Salig never married her, but she lives in the Palace, and for several years—ever since she first began to be talked about—she's ruled from behind the screen with a high hand and an out-stretched arm. So the bazaar says."

"I've heard she was beautiful," Farrell observed.

"As beautiful as a peri, according to rumour. You never can tell; very likely she's a withered old hag; nine out of ten native women are, by the time they're thirty." Raikes jerked the glowing end of his cigar into the shrubbery and reverted to English. "Shall we join Miss Farrell?"

They arose and left the table to the servants, the Resident with Amber following Farrell and young Clarkson.

"Old women we are, forever talking scandal," said Raikes, with a chuckle. "Oh, well! it's shop with us, you know."

"Of course.... Then I understand that the *tamasha* is the reason for the encampment beyond the walls?"

"Yes; they've been coming in for a week. By to-morrow night, I daresay, every rajah, prince, thakur, baron, fief, and lord in Rajputana, each with his 'tail,' horse and foot, will be camped down before the walls of Kuttarpur. You've chosen an interesting time for your visit. It'll be a sight worth seeing, when they begin to make a show. My troubles begin with a State banquet to-morrow that I'd give much to miss; however, I'll have Farrell for company."

"I'm glad to be here," said Amber thoughtfully. Could it be possible that the proposed abdication of Salig Singh in favour of his son were merely a cloak to a conspiracy to restore to power the house of Rutton? Or had the *tamasha* been arranged in order to gather together all the rulers in Rajputana without exciting suspicion, that they might agree upon a concerted plan of mutiny against the Sirkar? This state affair of surpassing importance had been arranged for the last day of grace allotted the Prince of the house of Rutton. What had it to do with the Gateway of Swords, the Voice, the Mind, the Eye, the Body, the Bell?

"By the way, Mr. Raikes," said the Virginian suddenly, "what do they call the gate by which we entered the city—the southern gate?"

"The Gateway of Swords, I believe."

Farrell, on the point of entering the house, overheard and turned. "Is that so? Why, I thought *that* gateway was in Kathiapur."

"I've heard of a Gateway of Swords in Kathiapur," Raikes admitted.
"Never been there, myself."

"Kathiapur?"

"A dead city, Mr. Amber, not far away—originally the capital of Khandawar. It's over there in the hills to the north, somewhere. Old Rao Rutton, founder of the old dynasty, got tired of the place and caused it to be depopulated, building Kuttarpur in its stead—I believe, to commemorate some victory or other. That sort of thing used to be quite the fashion in India, before we came." Raikes fell back, giving Amber precedence as they entered the Residency. "By the way, remind me, if you think of it, Colonel Farrell, to get after the telegraph-clerk to-morrow. There's a new man in charge—a Bengali babu—and I presume he's about as worthless as the run of his kind."

Amber made a careful note of this information; he was curious about that babu.

In the drawing-room Raikes and Farrell impressed Clarkson for three-handed Bridge. Sophia did not care to play and Amber was ignorant of the game—a defect in his social education which he found no cause to regret, since it left him in undisputed attendance upon the girl.

She had seated herself at a warped and discouraged piano, for which Raikes had already apologised; it was, he said, a legacy from a former Resident. For years its yellow keys had not known a woman's touch such as that to which they now responded with thin, cracked voices; the girl's fine, slender fingers wrung from them a plaintive, pathetic parody of melody. Amber stood over her with his arms folded on the top of the instrument, comfortably unconscious that his pose was copied from any number of sentimental photogravures and "art photographs." His temper was sentimental enough, for that matter; the woman was very sweet and beautiful in his eyes as she sat with her white, round arms flashing over the keyboard, her head bowed and her face a little averted, the long lashes low upon her cheeks and tremulous with a fathomless emotion. It was his thought that his time was momentarily becoming shorter, and that just now, more than ever, she was very distant from his arms, something inaccessible, too rare and delicate and fine for the rude possession of him who sighed for his own unworthiness.

Abruptly she brought both hands down upon the keys, educing a jangled, startled crash from the tortured wires, and swinging round, glanced up at Amber with quaint mirth trembling behind the veil of moisture in her misty eyes.

"India!" she cried, with a broken laugh: "India epitomised: a homesick, exiled woman trying to drag a song of Home from the broken heart of a crippled piano! That is an Englishwoman's India: it's our life, ever to strive and struggle and contrive to piece together out of makeshift odds and ends the atmosphere of Home!... It's suffocating in here. Come." She rose with a quick shrug of impatience, and led the way back to the gardens.

The table had been removed together with the chairs and candles; nothing remained to remind them of the hour just gone. The walks were clear of servants. Their only light came from the high arch of stars smitten to its zenith with pale, quivering waves of light from the moon invisible behind the hills. Below them the city hummed like a disturbed beehive. Somewhere afar a gentle hand was sweeping the strings of a *zitar*, sounding weird, sad chords. The perfumed languor of the night weighed heavily upon the senses, like the woven witchery of some age-old enchantment....

Pensive, the girl trained her long skirts heedlessly over the dew-drenched grasses, Amber at her side, himself speechless with an intangible, ineluctable, unreasoning sense of expectancy. Never, he told himself, had a lover's hour been more auspiciously timed or staged; and this was his hour, altogether his!... If only he might find the words of wooing to which his lips were strange! He dared not delay; to-morrow it might be too late; in the womb of the morrow a world of chances stirred—contingencies that might in a breath set them a world apart.

They found seats in the shadow of a pepul.

"You must be tired, Mr. Amber," she said. "Why don't you smoke?"

"I hadn't thought of it, and hadn't asked permission."

"Please do. I like it."

He found his cigarette-case and struck a match, Sophia watching intently his face in the rosy glow of the little, flickering flame.

"Are you in the habit of indulging in protracted silences?" she rallied him gently. "Between friends of old standing they're permissible, I believe, but——"

"A day's journey by tonga matures acquaintanceships wonderfully," he observed abstrusely.

"Indeed?" She laughed.

"At least, I hope so."

He felt that he must be making progress; thus far he had been no less inane than any average lover of the stage or fiction. And he wondered: was she laughing at him, softly, there in the shadows?

"You see," she said, amused at his relapse into reverie, "you're incurable and ungrateful. I'm trying my best to be attractive and interesting, and you won't pay me any attention whatever. There must be something on your mind. Is it this mysterious errand that brings you so unexpectedly to India—to Kuttarpur, Mr. Amber?"

"Yes," he answered truthfully.

"And you won't tell me?"

"I think I must," he said, bending forward.

There sounded a stealthy rustling in the shrubbery. The girl drew away and rose with a startled exclamation. With a bound, a man in native dress sped from the shadows and paused before them, panting.

Amber jumped up, overturning his chair, and instinctively feeling for the pistol that was with his travelling things, upstairs in the Residency.

The native reassured him with a swift, obsequious gesture. "Pardon, sahib, and yours, sahiba, if I have alarmed you, but I am come on an errand of haste, seeking him who is known as the Sahib David Amber."

"I am he. What do you want with me?"

"It is only this, that I have been commissioned to bear to you, sahib."

The man fumbled hurriedly in the folds of his surtout, darting quick glances of apprehension round the garden. Amber looked him over as closely as he could in the dim light, but found him wholly a stranger—merely a low-caste Hindu, counterpart of a million others to be encountered daily in the highways and bazaars of India. The Virginian's rising hope that he might prove to be Labertouche failed for want of encouragement; the intruder was of a stature the Englishman could by no means have counterfeited.

"From whom come you?" he demanded in the vernacular.

"Nay, a name that is unspoken harms none, sahib." The native produced a small, thin, flat package and thrust it into Amber's hands. "With permission, I go, sahib; it were unwise to linger——"

"There is no answer?"

"None, sahib." The man salaamed and strode away, seeming to melt soundlessly into the foliage.

For a minute Amber remained astare. The girl's voice alone roused him.

"I think you are a very interesting person, Mr. Amber," she said, resuming her chair.

"Well!... _I_ begin to think this a most uncommonly interesting country." He laughed uncertainly, turning the package over and over. "Upon my word——! I haven't the least notion what this can be!"

"Why not bring it to the light, and find out?"

He assented meekly, having been perfectly candid in his assertion that he had no suspicion of what the packet might contain, and a moment later they stood beneath the window of the Residency, from which a broad shaft of light streamed out like vaporised gold.

Amber held the packet to the light; it was oblong, thin, stiff, covered with common paper, guiltless of superscription, and sealed with mucilage. He tore the covering, withdrew the enclosure, and heard the girl gasp with surprise. For himself, he was transfixed with consternation. His look wavered in dismay between the girl and the photograph in his hand—*her* photograph, which had been stolen from him aboard the *Poonah*.

She extended her hand imperiously. "Give that to me, please, Mr. Amber," she insisted. He surrendered it without a word. "Mr. Amber!" she cried in a voice that quivered with wonder and resentment.

He faced her with a hang-dog air, feeling that now indeed had his case been made hopeless by this contretemps. "Confound Labertouche!" he cried in his ungrateful heart. "Confound his meddling mystery-mongering and hokus-pokus!"

"Well?" enquired the girl sharply.

"Yes, Miss Farrell." He could invent nothing else to say.

"You—you are going to explain, I presume."

He shook his head in despair. "No-o...."

"What!"

"I've no explanation whatever to make—that'd be adequate, I mean."

He saw that she was shaken by impatience. "I think," said she evenly—"I think you will find it best to let me judge of that. This is my photograph. How do you come to have it? What right have you to it?"

"I ... ah...." He stammered and paused, acutely conscious of the voices of the Englishmen, Farrell, Raikes, and young Clarkson, drifting out through the open window of the drawing-room. "If you'll be kind enough to return to our chairs," he said, "I'll try to make a satisfactory explanation. I'd rather not be overheard."

The girl doubted, was strongly inclined to refuse him; then, perhaps moved to compassion by his abject attitude, she relented and agreed. "Very well," she said, and retaining the picture moved swiftly before him into the shadowed garden. He lagged after her, inventing a hundred impracticable yarns. She found her chair and sat down with a manner of hauteur moderated by expectancy. He took his place beside her.

"Who sent you this photograph of me?" she began to cross-examine him.

"A friend."

"His name?"

"I'm sorry I can't tell you just now."

"Oh!... Why did he send it?"

"Because...." In his desperation it occurred to him to tell the truth—as much of it, at least, as his word to Rutton would permit. "Because it's mine. My friend knew I had lost it."

"How could it have been yours? It was taken in London a year ago. I sent copies only to personal friends who, I know, would not give them away." She thought it over and added: "The Quains had no copy; it's quite impossible that one should have got to America."

"None the less," he maintained stubbornly, "it's mine, and I got it in America."

"I can hardly be expected to believe that."

"I'm sorry."

"You persist in saying that you got it in America?"

"I must."

"When?"

"After you left the Quains."

"How?" she propounded triumphantly.

94

"I can't tell you, except vaguely. If you'll be content with the substance of the story, lacking details, for the present——"

"For the present? You mean you'll tell me the whole truth—?"

"Sometime, yes. But now, I may not…. A dear friend of mine owned the photograph. He gave it me at my request. I came to India, and on the steamer lost it; in spite of my offer of a reward, I was obliged to leave the boat without it, when we got to Calcutta. My friend here knew how highly I valued it——"

"Why?"

"Because I'd told him."

"I don't mean that. Why do you value it so highly?"

"Because of its original." He took heart of despair and plunged boldly.

She looked him over calmly. "Do you mean me to understand that you told this friend you had followed me to India because you were in love with me?"

"Precisely…. Thank you."

She laughed a little, mockingly. "Are you, Mr. Amber?"

"In love with you?… Yes."

"Oh!" She maintained her impartial and judicial attitude admirably. "But even were I inclined to believe that, your whole story is discredited by the simple fact that through no combination of circumstances could this picture have come into your possession in America."

"I give you my word of honor, Miss Farrell."

"I wish you wouldn't. If you are perfectly sincere in asserting that, you force me to think you——"

"Mad? I'm not, really," he argued earnestly. "It's quite true."

"No." She shook her head positively. "You say you obtained it from a man, which can't be so. There were only a dozen prints made; four I gave to women friends in England and seven I sent to people out here. The other one I have."

"I can only repeat what I have already told you. There are gaps in the story, I know—incredible gaps; they can't be bridged, just now. I beg you to believe me."

"And how soon will you be free to tell me the whole truth?"

"Only after … we're married."

She laughed adorably. "Mr. Amber," she protested, "you are dangerous—you are delightful! Do you really believe I shall ever marry you?"

"I hope so. I came to India to ask you—to use every means in my power to make you marry me. You see, I love you."

"And … and when is this to happen, please—in the name of impudence?"

"As soon as I can persuade you—to-night, if you will."

"Oh!"

He was obliged to laugh with her at the absurdity of the suggestion. "Or to-morrow morning, at the very latest," he amended seriously. "I don't think we dare wait longer."

"Why is that?"

"Delays are perilous. There might be another chap."

"How can you be sure there isn't already?"

He fell sober enough at this. "But there isn't, is there, really?"

She delayed her reply provokingly. At length, "I don't see why I should say," she observed, "but I don't mind telling you—no, there isn't—yet." And as she spoke, Farrell called "Sophia?" from the window of the drawing-room. She stood up, answering clearly with the assurance that she was coming, and began deliberately to move toward the house.

Amber followed, deeply anxious. "I've not offended you?"

"No," she told him gravely, "but you have both puzzled and mystified me. I shall have to sleep on this before I can make up my mind whether or not to be offended."

"And ... will you marry me?"

"Oh, dear! How do I know?" she laughed.

"You won't give me a hint as to the complexion of my chances?"

She paused, turning. "The chances, Mr. Amber," she said without affection or coquetry, "are all in your favour ... *if* you can prove your case. I do like you very much, and you have been successful in rousing my interest in you to an astonishing degree.... But I shall have to think it over; you must allow me at least twelve hours' grace."

"You'll let me know to-morrow morning?"

"Yes."

"Early?"

"You've already been bidden to breakfast by Mr. Raikes."

"Meanwhile, may I have my photograph?"

"Mine, if you please!... I think not; if my decision is favourable, you shall have it back—after breakfast."

"Thank you," he said meekly. And as they were entering the Residency he hung back. "I'm going now," he said; "it's good-night. Will you remember you've not refused me the privilege of hoping?"

"I've told you I like you, Mr. Amber." Impulsively she extended her hand. "Good-night."

He bowed and put his lips to it; and she did not resist.

CHAPTER XIV

OVER THE WATER

Ram Nath, patient and impassive as ever, had the tonga waiting for Amber before the Residency. Exalted beyond words, the American permitted himself to be driven off through Kuttarpur's intricate network of streets and backways, toward a destination of which he knew as little as he cared. He was a guest of the State, officially domiciled at the designated house of hospitality; without especial permission, obtained through the efforts of the Resident, he could sleep in no other spot in the city or its purlieus. He was indifferent, absolutely; the matter interested him as scantily—which is to say not at all—as did the fact that an escort of troopers of the State, very well accoutred and disciplined, followed the tonga with a great jangling of steel and tumult of hoofs.

He was in that condition of semi-daze which is the not extraordinary portion of a declared lover revelling in the memory of his mistress's eyes, whose parting look has not been unkind. Upon that glance of secret understanding, signalled to him from eyes as brown as beautiful, he was building him a palace of dreams so strange, so sweet, that the mere contemplation of its unsubstantial loveliness filled him with an exquisite agony of hope, a poignant ecstasy of despair. It was too much to hope for, that she should smile upon him in the morning.... Yet he hoped.

Unconscious of the passage of time, he was roused only by the pausing of the tonga and its escort before the Gateway of the Elephants—the main octroi gate in the northern wall of the city. There ensued a brief interchange of formalities between the sergeant of his escort and the captain of the Quarter Guard. Then the tonga was permitted to pass out, and for five minutes rattled and clattered along the border of the lake, stopping finally at the rest-house.

Alighting in the compound, Amber disbursed a few rupees to the troopers, paid off Ram Nath—who was swift to drive off city-wards, in mad haste lest the gates be shut upon him for the night—and entered the bungalow. An aged, talkative, and amiable khansamah met him at the threshold with expressions of exaggerated respect, no doubt genuine enough, and followed him, a mumbling shadow, as the Virginian made a brief round of inspection.

Standing between the road and the water, the rest-house proved to be moderately spacious and clean; on the lake-front it opened upon a marble bund, or landing-stage, its lip lapped by whispering ripples of the lake. Amber went out upon this to discover, separated from him by little more than half a mile of black water, the ghostly white walls of the Raj Mahal climbing in dim majesty to the stars. A single line of white lights outlined the topmost parapet; at the water's edge a single marble entrance was aglow; between the two, towers and terraces, hanging gardens and white scarp-like walls rose in darkened confusion unimaginable—or, rather, fell like a cascade of architecture, down the hillside to the lake. A dark hive teeming with the occult life of unnumbered men and women—Salig Singh the inscrutable and strong, Naraini the mysterious, whose loveliness lived a fable in the land, and how many thousand others—living and dying, working and idling, in joy and sadness, in hatred and love, weaving forever that myriad-stranded web of intrigue which is the life of native palaces ...

The Virginian remained long in rapt wondering contemplation of it, until the wind blowing across the waters had chilled him to the point of shivering; when he turned indoors to his bed. But he was to have little rest that night. The khansamah who attended him had hardly turned low his light when Amber was disturbed by the noise of an angry altercation in the compound. He arose and in dressing-gown and slippers went to investigate, and found Ram Nath in violent dispute with the sergeant of the escort—which, it appeared, had built a fire and camped round it in the compound: a circumstance which furnished food for thought.

Amber began to suspect that the troops had been furnished as a guard less of honour than of espionage, less in formal courtesy than in demonstration of the unsleeping vigilance of the Eye—kindly assisted by the Maharana of Khandawar.

A man who, warmed by the ardour of his first love, feels suddenly the shadow of death falling cold upon him, is apt to neglect nothing. Amber considered that he had given Ram Nath no commission of any sort, and bent an attentive ear to the communication which the tonga-wallah insisted upon making to him.

Ram Nath had returned, he asserted, solely for the purpose of informing Amber in accordance with his desires. "The telegraph-office for which you enquired, sahib, stands just within the Gateway of the Elephants," he announced. "The telegraph-babu will be on duty very early in the morning, should you desire still to send the message."

"Oh, yes," said Amber indifferently. "I'd forgotten. Thanks."

He returned to his charpoy with spirits considerably higher. Ram Nath had not winked this time, but the fact was indisputable that Amber had *not* expressed any interest whatever in the location of the telegraph-office.

Wondering if the telegraph-babu by any chance wore pink satin, he dozed off on the decision that he would need to send a message the first thing in the morning.

Some time later he was a second time awakened by further disputation in the compound. The troopers were squabbling amongst themselves; he was able to make this much out in spite of the fact that the sepoys, recruited exclusively from the native population of Khandawar, spoke a patois of Hindi so corrupt that even an expert in Oriental languages would experience difficulty in trying to interpret it. Amber did not weary himself with the task, but presently lifted up his voice and demanded silence, desiring to be informed if his sleep was to be continually broken by the bickerings of sons of mothers without noses. There followed instantaneous silence, broken by a chuckle and an applausive "Shabash!" and nothing more.

Amber snuggled down again upon his pillow and soothed himself with the feel of the pistol that his fingers grasped beneath the clothes.

A bar of moonlight slipped through the blinds and fell athwart his eyes. He cursed it bitterly and got up and moved his charpoy into shadow. The sibilant lisping of the wavelets against the bund sang him softly toward oblivion … and a convention of water-fowl went into stormy executive session out in the middle of the lake. This had to be endured, and in time Amber's senses grew numb to the racket and he dropped off into a fitful doze....

Footfalls and hushed voices in the bungalow were responsible for the next interruption. Amber came to with a start and found himself sitting up on the edge of the charpoy, with a dreamy impression that two people had been standing over him and had just left the room, escaping by way of the khansamah's quarters. He rubbed the sleep from his eyes and went out to remonstrate vigorously with the khansamah. The latter naturally professed complete ignorance of the visitation and dwelt with such insistence upon the plausibility of dreams that Amber lost patience and kicked him grievously, so that he complained with a loud voice and cast himself at the sahib's feet, declaring that he was but as the dust beneath them and that Amber was his father and mother and the light of the Universe besides. In short, he raised such a rumpus that some of the sepoys came in to investigate and—went out again, hastily, to testify to their fellows that the hazoor was a man of fluent wrath, surprisingly versed in the art and practice of abuse.

Somewhat mollified and reflecting, at the same time, that this was all but a part of the game, to be expected by those who patronise rest-houses off the beaten roads of travel, the Virginian returned to his charpoy and immediately lapsed into a singularly disquieting dream.... He was strolling by the border of the lake when a coot swam in and hailed him in English; and when he stopped to look the coot lifted an A.D.T. messenger-boy's cap and pleaded with him to sign his name in a little black book, promising that, if he did so, it would be free to doff its disguise and be Labertouche again. So Amber signed "Pink Satin" in the book and the coot stood up and said, "I'm not Labertouche at all, but Ram Nath, and Ram Nath is only another name for Har Dyal Rutton, and besides you had better come away at once, for the Eye thou dost wear upon thy finger never sleeps and it's only a paste Token anyway." Hearing which, Amber caught the coot by the leg and found that he had grasped the arm of Salig Singh, whose eyes were both monstrous emeralds without any whites whatever. And Salig Singh tapped him on the shoulder and began to say over and over again in a whisper...

But here Amber another time found himself wide awake and sitting up, his left hand gripping the wrist of a native and his right holding his pistol steadily levelled at the native's breast. While the voice he heard was real and no figment of a dream-mused imagination; for the man was whispering earnestly and repeatedly:

"*Hasten, hazoor, for the night doth wane and the hour is at hand.*"

"What deviltry's this?" Amber demanded sharply, with a threatening gesture.

But the native neither attempted to free himself nor to evade the pistol's mouth. "Have patience, hazoor," he begged earnestly, "and make no disturbance. It is late and the sepoys sleep; if you will be circumspect and are not afraid—"

"Who are you?"

"I was to say, '*I come from you know whom*,' hazoor."

"That all?"

"In the matter of a certain photograph, hazoor."

"By thunder!" Labertouche's name was on Amber's lips, but he repressed it. "Wait a bit." He gulped down the last dregs of sleep. "Let me think and—see."

This last was an afterthought. As it came to him he dropped the pistol by his side and felt for matches in the pocket of his coat, which hung over the back of a bedside chair. Finding one, he struck it noiselessly and, as the tiny flame broadened, drew his captive nearer.

It was a fat, mean, wicked face that stood out against the darkness: an ochre-tinted face with a wide, loose-lipped mouth and protruding eyes that blinked nervously into his. But he had never seen it before.

"Who are you?" He cast away the match as its flame died and snatched up his weapon.

"I was to say—"

"I heard that once. What's your name?"

"Dulla Dad, hazoor."

"And who are you from?"

"Hazoor, I was not to say."

"I think you'd better," suggested Amber, with grim significance.

"I am the hazoor's slave. I dare not say."

"Now look here—"

"Hazoor, it was charged upon me to say, '*I come from you know whom.*'"

"The devil it was.... Well, what do you want?"

"I was to say, '*Hasten, hazoor, for the night—*'"

"I've heard that, too. You mean you're to lead me to somebody, somewhere—you can't say where?"

"Aye, hazoor, even so."

"Get over there, in the corner, while I think this over—and don't move or I'll make you a present of a nice young bullet, Dulla Dad."

"That is as Allah wills; only remember, hazoor, the injunction for haste."

The man, a small stunted Mohammedan, sidled fearsomely over to the spot indicated and waited there, cringing and supplicating Amber with eloquent gestures. The Virginian watched him closely until comforted by the reflection that, had murder been the object, he had been a dead man long since. Then he put aside the revolver and began to dress.

"Only Labertouche would have to communicate with me by such stealth," he considered. "Besides, that reference to the photograph—"

He slipped hurriedly into his clothing and ostentatiously dropped the pistol into his right-hand coat-pocket. "I'm ready," he told the man. "Lead the way; and remember, if there's any treachery afoot, you'll be the first to suffer for it, Dulla Dad."

The Mohammedan bowed submissively. "Be it so, my lord," he said in Hindi, and, moving noiselessly with unshod feet, glided through the door which opened upon the bund, Amber close behind him.

That it was indeed late was shown by the position of the moon; and the sweet freshness of early morning was strong in the keen air. The wind had failed and the lake stretched flawless from shore to shore, a sheet of untarnished silver. Over against them the palace slept, or seemed to sleep, in its miraculous beauty, glacier-like with its shining surfaces and deep, purple-shadowed crevasses. There were few lights visible in the city, and the quiet of it was notable; so likewise with the wards outside the walls and the lakeside palaces and villas. Only in a distant temple a drum was throbbing, throbbing.

In the water at their feet a light boat was gently nosing the marble bund. Dulla Dad, squatting, drew it broadside to the steps and motioned Amber to enter. The Virginian boarded it gingerly, seating himself at the stern. Dulla Dad dropped in forward and pushed off. The boat moved out upon the bosom of the lake with scarce a sound, and the native, grasping a double-bladed paddle, dipped it gently and sent the frail craft flying onward with long, swift, and powerful strokes, guiding it directly toward the walls of the Raj Mahal.

Two-thirds of the way across the Virginian surrendered to his mistrust and drew his pistol. "Dulla Dad," he said gently; and the man ceased paddling with a shudder—"Dulla Dad, you're taking me to the palace."

"Yea, hazoor; that is true," the native answered, his voice quavering.

"Who awaits me there? Answer quickly!"

"Hazoor, it is not wise to speak a name upon the water, where voices travel far."

"Dulla Dad!"

"Hazoor, I may not say!"

"I think, Dulla Dad, you'd better. If I lose patience—"

"Upon my head be your safety, hazoor! See, you can fire, and thereafter naught can trouble me. But I, with a single sweep of this paddle, can overturn us. Be content, hazoor, for a little time; then shall you see that naught of harm is intended. My life be forfeit if I speak not truth, hazoor!"

"You have said it," said Amber grimly, "Row on." After all, he considered, it might still be Labertouche. At first blush it had seemed hardly credible that the Englishman could have gained a footing in that vast pile; and yet, it would be like him to seek precisely such a spot—the very heart of the conspiracy of the Gateway, if they guessed aright.

The boat surged swiftly on, while again and again Amber's finger trembled on the trigger. Though already the white gleaming walls towered above him, it was not yet too late—not too late; but should he withdraw, force Dulla Dad to return, he might miss … what? He did nothing save resign himself to the issue. As they drew nearer the moonlit walls he looked in vain for sign of a landing-stage, and wondered, the lighted bund that he had seen from over the water being invisible to him round an angle of the building. But Dulla Dad held on without a pause until the moment when it seemed that he intended to dash the boat bows first against the stone; then, with a final dextrous twist of the paddle, he swung at a sharp angle and simultaneously checked the speed. Under scant momentum they slid from moonlight and the clean air of night into a close well between two walls, and then suddenly beneath an arch and into a cavernous chamber filled with the soft murmuring of water—and with darkness.

Here the air was sluggish and heavy and dank with the odour of slime. Breathing it, seeing nothing save the spectral gleam of moonlight reflected inwards, hearing nothing save the uncanny lapping and purring of the ripples, it was not easy to forget the tales men told of palace corruption and crime—of lovers who had stolen thus secretly to meet their mistresses, and who had met, instead, Death; of assassins who had skulked by such stealthy ways to earn blood-money; of spies, of a treacherous legion who had gained entry to the palace by such ways as this—perhaps had accomplished their intent and returned to tell the tale, perhaps had been found in the dawn-light, floating out there on the lake with drawn, wan faces upturned to the pallid skies....

"Hazoor!"

It was Dulla Dad's voice, sleek with fawning. For all the repulsiveness of the accents, Amber was not sorry to hear them. At least the native was human and ... this experience wasn't, hardly.... He leaned toward the man, eyes aching with the futile strain of striving to penetrate the blackness. He could see nothing more definite than shadows. The boat was resting motionless on the tide, as if suspended in an abyss of night, fathomless and empty.

"Well, what now?" he demanded harshly. "Be careful, Dulla Dad!"

"Still my lord distrusts me? There is naught to fear, none here to lift hand against you. Your servant lives but to serve you in all loyalty."

"Indeed?"

"My lord may trust me."

"It seems to me I have—too far."

"My lord will not forget?"

"Be sure of that, Dulla Dad.... Well, what are you waiting for?"

"We are arrived, hazoor," said the native calmly. "If you will be pleased to step ashore, having care lest you overturn the boat, the steps are on your left."

"Where?... Oh!" Amber's tentative hand, groping in obscurity, fell upon a slab of stone, smooth and slippery, but solid. "You mean here?"

"Aye, hazoor."

"And what next?"

"I am to wait to conduct you back to your place of rest."

"Um-m. You are, eh?" Amber, doubtful, tried the stone again; it was substantial enough; only the boat rocked. He struck a match; the short-lived flame afforded him a feeble, unsatisfactory impression of a long, narrow, vaulted chamber, whereof the floor was half water, half stone. There was a landing to the left, a rather narrow ledge, with a low, heavy door, bossed with iron, in the wall beyond.

Shaking his head, he lifted himself cautiously out of the boat. "You stay right there, Dulla Dad," he warned the native, "until I see what happens. If I catch you trying to get away—the boat'll show up nicely against the opening, you know—I'll give you cause for repentance."

"I am here, hazoor. Turn you and knock upon the door thus"—rapping the gunwale of the boat—"thrice."

Amber obeyed, wrought up now to so high a pitch of excitement and suspense that he could hardly have withdrawn had he wished to and been able to force Dulla Dad to heed him. As he knuckled the third signal, the door swung slowly inward, disclosing, in a dim glow of light, stone walls—a bare stone chamber illumined by a single iron lamp hanging in chains from the ceiling. Across the room a dark entry opened upon a passageway equally dark.

By the door a servant stood, his attitude deferential. As the Virginian's gaze fell upon him he salaamed respectfully.

Amber entered, his eyes quick, his right hand in his pocket and grateful for the cold caress of nickelled steel, his body poised lightly and tensely upon the balls of his feet—in a word, ready. Prepared against the worst he was hopeful of the best: apprehensive, he reminded himself that he had first met Labertouche under auspices hardly more prepossessing than these.

The clang of the door closing behind him rang hollowly in the stillness. The warder moved past him to the entrance of the corridor. Amber held him with a sharp question.

"Am I to wait here?"

"For a moment, Heaven-born!" He disappeared.

Without a sound a door at Amber's elbow that had escaped his cursory notice, so cunningly was it fitted in the wall, swung open, and a remembered voice boomed in his ears, not without a certain sardonic inflection: "Welcome, my lord, welcome to Khandawar!"

Amber swung upon the speaker with a snarl. "Salig Singh!"

"Thy steward bids thee welcome to thy kingdom, hazoor!"

Dominating the scene with his imposing presence—a figure regal in the regimentals of his native army—the Rajput humbled himself before the Virginian, dropping to his knee and offering his jewelled sword-hilt in token of his fealty.

"Oh, get up!" snapped Amber impatiently. "I'm sick of all this damned tomfoolery. Get up, d'you hear?—unless you want me to take that pretty sword of yours and spank you with it!"

A quiver, as of self-repression, moved the body of the man at his feet; then, with a jangle of spurs, Salig Singh leaped up and stood at a distance of two paces, his head high, his black eyes glittering ominously with well-nigh the sinister brilliance of his vibrating emerald aigrette.

"My lord!" he cried angrily. "Are these words to use to one who offers thee his heart and hand? Is this insolence to be suffered by a Rajput, a son of Kings?"

"As for that," returned Amber steadily, giving him look for look, "your grandfather was a *bunia* and you know it. Whether or not you're going to 'suffer' what you call my insolence, I don't know, and I don't much care. You've made a fool of me twice, now, and I'm tired of it. I give you my word I don't understand why I don't shoot you down here and now, for I believe in my heart you're the unholiest scoundrel unhung. Is that language plain enough for you?"

For an instant longer they faced one another offensively, Amber cool enough outwardly and inwardly boiling with rage that he should have walked into the trap with his eyes open, Salig Singh trembling with resentment but holding himself in with splendid restraint.

"As for me," continued Amber, "I suspect I'm the most hopeless ass in the three Presidencies, if that's any comfort to you, Salig Singh. Now what d'you want with me?"

A shadowy smile softened the blackness of the Rajput's wrath. He shrugged and moved his hands slightly, exposing their palms, subtly signifying his submission.

"Thou art my overlord," he said quietly, with a silky deference. "In time thou wilt see how thou hast wronged me. For the present, I remain thy servant. I harbour no resentment, I owe thee naught but loyalty. I await thy commands."

"The dickens you do!" Amber whistled inaudibly, his eyes narrowing as he pondered the man. "You protest a lot, Salig Singh. If you're so much at my service … why, prove it."

By way of reply Salig Singh lifted his sword in its scabbard from its fastenings at his side and, with a magnificent gesture, cast it clanking to the floor between them. A heavy English army-pattern revolver followed it. The Rajput spread out his hands. "Thou art armed, my lord," he said, "I, at thy mercy. If thou dost misjudge my purpose in causing thee to be brought hither, my life is in thy hands."

"Oh, yes." Amber nodded. "That's very pretty. But presuming I chose to take it?"

"Thou art free as the winds of the morning. See, then." Salig Singh strode to the outer door and threw it open. "The way of escape is clear—not even locked."

The lamplight fell across the stone landing and made visible the waiting boat with Dulla Dad sitting patiently at the oar.

"I see," assented Amber. "Well?"

Salig Singh shut the door gently. "Is there more to say?" he enquired.
"I have shown thee that thou art free."

"Oh, so far as that goes, you've demonstrated pretty clearly that you're not afraid of me. Of course I know as well as you do that at the first shot Dulla Dad would slip out to the lake and leave me here to die like a rat in a corner."

"Thou knowest, lord, that no man in Khandawar would do thee any hurt. Thy person is sacred—"

"That's all bosh. You don't expect me to believe that you still stick to that absurd fiction of yours—that I'm Rutton?"

"Then mine eyes have played me false, hazoor. Shabash!" Salig Singh bowed resignedly.

"Well, then, what do you want? Why have you brought me here?"

"Why didst thou come? There was no force used: thou didst come of thine own will—thine own will, which is the will of the Body, hazoor!"

"Oh, damnation! Why d'you insist on beating round the bush forever? You know well why I came. Now, what do you want?"

"My lord, I move, it seems, in the ways of error. A little time ago the words of the Voice were made known to thee in a far land; thou didst answer, coming to this country. A few days agone I myself did repeat to you the message of the Bell; thou didst swear thou wouldst not answer, yet art thou here in Kuttarpur. Am I to be blamed for taking this for a sign of thy repentance?... Hazoor, the Body is patient, the Will benignant and long-suffering. Still is the Gateway open."

"Is that what you wanted to tell me, Salig Singh?"

"What else? Am I to believe thee a madman, weary of life, that thou shouldst venture hither with a heart hardened against the Will of the Body? I seek but to serve thee in thus daring thy displeasure. Why shouldst thou come to Bharuta [Footnote: India.] at all if thou dost not intend to undergo the Ordeal of the Gateway? Am I a fool or—I say it in all respect, my lord—art thou?"

"From the look of things, I fancy the epithet fits us both, Salig Singh. You refuse to take my word for it that I know nothing of your infamous Gateway and have no intention of ever approaching it, that I have not a drop of Indian blood in me and am in no way related to or connected with Har Dyal Rutton, who is dead—"

"I may not believe what I know to be untrue."

"You'll have to learn to recognise the truth, I'm afraid. For the final time I tell you that I am David Amber, a citizen of the United States of America, travelling in India on purely personal business."

The Rajput inclined his head submissively. "Then is my duty all but done, hazoor. Thrice hath the warning been given thee. There be still four-and-twenty hours in which, it may be, thou shalt learn to see clearly. My lord, I ask of thee a single favour. Wilt thou follow me?" He motioned toward the arched entrance to the passageway.

"Follow thee?" Amber at length dropped into Urdu, unconsciously adopting the easier form of communication now that, he felt, the issue between them was plain, that the Rajput laboured under no further misunderstanding as to the reason of his presence in Khandawar. "Whither?"

"There is that which I must show thee."

"What?"

"My life be forfeit if thou dost not return unharmed to the rest-house ere sunrise. Wilt thou come?"

"To what end, Salig Singh?"

"Furthermore," the Rajput persisted stubbornly, his head lifted in pride and his nostrils dilated a little with scorn—"furthermore I offer thee the word of a Rajput. Thou are my guest, since thou wilt have it so. No harm shall come to thee, upon my honour."

Curiosity triumphed. Amber knew that he had exacted the most honoured pledge known in Rajputana. His apprehensions were at rest; nothing could touch him now—*until* he had returned to the bungalow. Then, he divined, it was to be open war—himself and Labertouche pitted against the strength of the greatest conspiracy known in India since the days of '57. But for the present, no pledge of any sort had been exacted of him.

"So be it," he assented on impulse. "I follow."

With no other word Salig Singh turned and strode down the corridor.

CHAPTER XV

FROM A HIGH PLACE

The passageway was long and dark and given to sudden curves and angles, penetrating, it seemed, the very bowels of the Raj Mahal. It ended unexpectedly in a low arch through which the two men passed into an open courtyard, apparently given over entirely to stables. Despite the lateness of the hour it was tenanted by several wideawake syces, dancing attendance upon a pair of blooded stallions of the stud royal, who, saddled, bridled and hooded, pawed and champed impatiently in the centre of the yard, making it echo with the ringing of iron on stone and the jingling of their silver curb-chains.

Salig Singh paused, with a wave of his hand calling Amber's attention to the superb brutes.

"Thou canst see, hazoor, that all is prepared!"

"For what?"

But Salig Singh merely smiled enigmatically, and shaking a patient head, passed on.

A second arch gave upon a corridor which led upwards and presently changed into a steep flight of steps, of ancient stone worn smooth and grooved with the traffic of generations of naked feet. At the top they turned aside and passed through a deserted hanging garden, and then, through a heavy door which Salig Singh unlocked with a private key, into a vast, vacant room, with a lofty ceiling supported by huge, unwieldy pillars of stone, sculptured with all the loves and wars of Hindu mythology. At one end the fitful, eerie flare of a great bronze brazier revealed the huge proportions of an ivory throne, gorgeous with gems and cloth of gold, standing upon a daïs and flanked by two motionless figures which at first sight Amber took to be pieces of statuary. But they quickened, saluting with a single movement and a flash of steel, as the Maharana drew nearer, and so proved themselves troopers of the State, standing guard with naked swords.

"There is no need, perhaps, to tell thee, hazoor," Salig Singh muttered, bending to Amber's ear, "that sitting upon this throne, in this Hall of Audience, for generations thy forefathers ruled this land, making and administering its laws, meting out justice, honoured of all men—and served, my lord, for generations by my forebears, the faithful stewards of thy House; even as I would prove faithful...."

"Interesting," Amber interrupted brusquely, "if true. Is this what you wanted to show me?"

"Nay, hazoor, not this alone. Come."

The Rajput led him out of the hall by way of a small doorway behind the throne, and after a little turning and twisting through tortuous passages they began to ascend again, and so went on up, ever upwards, the flights of steps broken by other corridors, other apartments, other galleries and gardens, until at length they emerged into a garden laid out in the very topmost court of all—the loftiest spot in all Kuttarpur.

It was a very wonderful garden, a jungle of exotic plants and shrubs threaded by narrow walks that led to secluded nooks and unsuspected pleasaunces, and lighted by low-swung festoons of dim lamps, many-coloured. A banian grew curiously in its midst, and there also they found a great tank of crystal water with a bed of brilliant pebbles over which small golden gleaming fish flashed and loitered. Here, where the walls of acacia, orange, thuia and pepal shut out every breath of wind, the air was dense with the cloying sweetness of jasmine, musk and marigold....

"My lord," said the Maharana, pausing, "if thou wilt wait here for a little, permitting me to excuse myself—?"

"All right," Amber told him tolerantly. "Run along."

Salig Singh quietly effaced himself, and the American watched him go with an inward chuckle. "I presume I'll have to pay for my impudence in the end," he thought; "but it's costing Salig Singh a good deal to hold himself in." He was for the time being not ill-pleased with this phase of his adventure; he had a notion that this must be a sort of very private pleasure-ground of the rulers of Khandawar, and that very few, if any, white people had ever been permitted to inspect it. What the Maharana's next move would be he had not the least suspicion; but since he must be content and abide the developments as they came, he was minded to amuse himself. He moved away from the cistern, idling down a path in a direction opposite that taken by Salig Singh.

An abrupt turn brought him to the outer wall, and he stopped to gaze, leaning upon the low marble balustrade.

From his feet the wall fell away sheer, precipitous, a hundred feet or more, to another hanging garden like that which lay behind him. From this there was another stupendous drop. On all sides the marble walls spread over the hillsides, descending it in great strides broken by terraces, gardens, paved courts, all white and silver and deep violet shadow, with here and there a window glowing softly yellow or a web of saffron rays peeping through the intricacies of a carved stone lattice. Far below, on the one hand, the lake lay like a sheet of steel; on the other the city stretched, a huddle of flat roofs not unlike an armful of child's building blocks. At that great height the effect was that of peering over the upper lip of an avalanche of masonry on the point of tumbling headlong down a mountainside to crush all beneath it.

In the hush there rose to Amber a muted confusion of sounds—the blended voices of the multitude that inhabited the hidden chambers of the palace: the pawing and shrill neighing of the stallions in the lower courtyard, a shivering clash of steel against steel, somewhere the tinkle of a stringed instrument and a soft voice singing, a man's accents weighty with authority, the ripple of a woman's laugh—all relieved against an undertone like a profound sigh, waning and waxing: the breathing of the Raj Mahal ...

Amber turned away to rejoin Salig Singh by the cistern. But the Rajput was not there; and, presently, another path tempting him to unlawful exploration, he yielded and sauntered aimlessly away. A sudden corner cloaked with foliage brought him to a little open space, a patch of lawn over which a canopy had been raised. Beneath this, a woman sat alone. He halted, thunderstruck.

Simultaneously, with a soft swish of draperies, a clash of jewelled bracelets, dull and musical, and a flash of coruscating colour, the woman stood before him, young, slender, graceful, garbed in indescribable splendour—and veiled.

For the space of three long breaths the Virginian hesitated, unspeakably amazed. Though she were veiled, it were deep dishonour for a woman of a Rajput's household to be seen by a stranger. It seemed inexplicable that Salig Singh should have wittingly left him in any place where he might encounter an inmate of the zenana. Yet the Maharana must have known.... Amber made an irresolute movement, as if to go. But it was too late.

With a murmur, inaudible, and a swift, infinitely alluring gesture, the woman swept the veil away from her face, and looked him squarely in the eyes. She moved toward him slowly, swaying, as graceful as a fawn, more beautiful than any woman he had ever known. His breath caught in his throat, for sheer wonder at this incomparable loveliness.

Her face was oval without a flaw, and pale as newly-minted gold, with a flush of red where the blood ran warm beneath the skin. Her hair was black as ebony and finer than the finest silk, rich and lustrous; her jet-black eyebrows formed a perfect arch. Her mouth was like a passion-flower, but small and sweet, with lips full and firm and scarlet. Her eyes were twin pools of darkness lighted with ardent inner fire. They held him speechless and motionless with the beauty of their unuttered desire, and before he could collect his wits she had made him captive—had without warning cast herself upon her knees before him and imprisoned both his hands, burying her face in their palms. He felt her lips hot upon his flesh, and then—wonder of wonders!—tears from those divine eyes streaming through his fingers.

The shock of it brought him to his senses. Pitiful, dumfounded, horrified, he glared wildly about him, seeking some avenue of escape. There was no one watching: he thanked Heaven for that, while the cold sweat started out upon his forehead. But still at his feet the woman rocked, softly sobbing, her fair shoulders gently agitated, and still she defied his gentle efforts to free his hands, holding them in a grasp he might not break without hurting her. He found his tongue eventually.

"Don't!" he pleaded desperately. "My dear, you mustn't. For pity's sake don't sob like that! What under the sun's the trouble? Don't, please!... Good Lord! what am I to do with this lovely lunatic?" Then he remembered that he had spoken in English and thoughtfully translated the gist of his remonstrances, with as little effect as if he had spoken to the empty air.

Though in time the fiercest paroxysm of her passion passed and her sobs diminished in violence, she clung heavily to him and made no resistance when he lifted her in his arms. The error was fatal; he had designed to get her on her feet and then stand away. But no sooner had he raised her and succeeded in disengaging his hands, than soft round arms were clasped tightly about his neck and her face—if possible, more ravishing in tears than when first he had seen it—pillowed on his breast. And for the first time she spoke coherently.

"*Aie!*" she wailed tremulously. "*Aie!* Now is the cup of my happiness full to brimming, now that thou hast returned to me at last, O my lord! Well-nigh had I ceased to hope for thee, O Beloved; well-nigh had this heart of mine grown cold within my bosom, that had no nourishment save hope, save hope! Day and night I have watched for thy coming for many years, praying that thou shouldst return to me ere this frail prettiness of mine, that made thee love me long ago, should wane and fade, so that thy heart should turn to other women, O my husband!"

"Husband! Great—Heavens! Look here, my dear, hadn't you better come to your senses and let me go before—"

"Let thee go, *Lalji*, ere what? Ere any come to disturb us? Nay, but who should come between husband and wife in the first hour of their reunion after many years of separation? Is it not known—does not all Khandawar know how I have waited for thee, almost thy widow ere thy wife, all this weary time?... Or is it that thy heart hath forgotten thy child-bride? Am I scorned, O my Lord—I, Naraini? Is there no love in thy bosom to leap in response to the love of thee that is my life?"

She released him and whirled a pace or two away, draperies swirling, jewels scintillating cold fire in hopeless emulation of the radiance of her tear-gemmed eyes.

"Naraini?" stammered Amber, recalling what he had heard of the woman. "Naraini!"

"Aye, my lord, Naraini, thy wedded wife!" The rounded little chin went up a trifle and her eyes gleamed angrily. "Am I no longer thy Naraini, then? Or wouldst thou deny that thou art Har Dyal, my king and my beloved? Hast thou indeed forgotten the child that was given thee for wife when thy father reigned in Khandawar and thou wert but a boy— a boy of ten, the Maharaj Har Dyal? Hast thou forgotten the little maid they brought thee from the north, *Lalji*—the maiden who had grown to womanhood ere thy return from thy travels to take up thy father's crown?... *Aie!* Thou canst never forget, Beloved; though years and the multitude of faces have come between us as a veil, thou dost remember— even as thou didst remember when the message of the Bell came to thee across the great black waters, and thou didst learn that the days of thy exile were numbered, that the hour approached when again thou shouldst sit in the place of thy fathers and rule the world as once they ruled it."

A denial stuck in Amber's throat. The words would not come, nor would they, he believed, have served his purpose could he have commanded them. If he had found no argument wherewith to persuade Salig Singh, he found none wherewith to refute the claim of this golden-faced woman who recognised him for her husband. He was wholly dismayed and aghast. But while he lingered in indecision, staring in the woman's face, her look of petulance was replaced by one of divine forgiveness and compassion. And she gave him no time to think or to avoid her; in a twinkling she had thrown herself upon him again, was in his arms and crushing her lips upon his.

"Nay," she murmured, "but I did wrong thee, Beloved! Perchance," she told him archly, "thou didst not think to see me so soon, or in this garden? Perchance surprise hath robbed thee of thy wits—and thy tongue as well, O wordless one? Or thou art overcome with joy, as I am overcome, and smitten dumb by it, as I am not? *Aho, Lalji!* was ever a woman at loss for words to voice her happiness?" And nestling to him she laughed quietly, with a note as tender and sweet as the cooing of a wood-dove to its mate.

"Nay, but there is a mistake." He recovered the power of speech tardily, and would have put her from him; but she held tight to him. "I am not thy husband, nor yet a Rajput. I come from America, the far land where thy husband died.... Nay, it doth pain me to hurt thee so, Ranee, but the mistake is not of my making, and it hath been carried too far. Thy husband died in my presence—"

"It is so, then!" she cut him short. And his arms were suddenly empty, to his huge relief. "Indeed they had warned me that thou wouldst tell this story and deny me—why, I know not, unless it be that thou art unworthy of thy lineage, a coward and a weakling!" Her small foot stamped angrily and on every limb of her round body bracelets and anklets clashed and shimmered. "And so thou hast returned only to forswear me and thy kingdom, O thou of little spirit!" The scarlet lips curled and the eyes grew cold and hard with contempt. "If that be so, tell me, why hast thou returned at all? To die? For that thou must surely come to, if it be in thy mind to defy the behests of the Voice, thou king without a kingdom!... Why, then, art thou here, rather than running to hide in some far place, thinking to escape with thy worthless life—worthless even to thee, who art too craven to make a man's use of it—from the Vengeance of the Body?... Dost think I am to be tricked and hoodwinked—I, in whose heart thine image hath been enshrined these many weary years?"

"I neither think, nor know, nor greatly care, Ranee," Amber interposed wearily. "Doubtless I deserve thine anger and thy scorn, since I am not he who thou wouldst have me be. If death must be my portion for this offence, for that I resemble Har Dyal Rutton ... then it is written that I am to die. My business here in Khandawar hath concern neither with thee, nor with the State, not yet with the Gateway of Swords—of the very name of which I am weary.... Now," and his mouth settled in lines of unmistakable resolve, "I will go; nor do I think that there be any here to stop me."

He wheeled about, prepared to fight his way out of the palace, if need be. Indeed, it was in his mind that a death there were as easy as one an hour after sunrise; for he had little doubt but that he was to die if he remained obdurate, and the hospitality of the Rajput would cease to protect him the moment he set foot upon the marble bund of his bungalow.

But the woman sprang after him and caught his arm. "Of thy pity," she begged breathlessly, "hold for a space until I have taken thought.... Thou knowest that if what thou hast told me be the truth, then am I widow before my time—widowed and doomed!"

"Doomed?"

"Aye!" And there was real terror in her eyes and voice. "Doomed to *sati*. For, since I am a widow—since thou dost maintain thou art not my husband—then my face hath been looked upon by a man not of mine own people, and I am dishonoured. Fire alone can cleanse me of that defilement—the pyre and the death by flame!"

"Good God! you don't mean that! Surely that custom has perished!"

"Thou shouldst know that it dieth not. What to us women in whose bodies runs the blood of royalty, is an edict of your English Government? What, the Sirkar itself to us in Khandawar?" She laughed bitterly. "I am a Rohilla, a daughter of kings: my dishonour may be purged only by flame. *Arre!* that I should live to meet with such fate—I, Naraini, to perish in the flower of my beauty.... For I am beautiful, am I not?" She dropped the veil which instinctively she had caught across her face, and met his gaze with childish coquetry, torn though she seemed to be by fear and disappointment.

"Thou art assuredly most beautiful, Ranee," Amber told her, with a break in his voice, very compassionate. And he spoke simple truth. "Of thy kind there is none more lovely in the world ..."

"There was tenderness then in your tone, my lord!" she caught him up quickly. "Is there no mercy in thy heart for me?... Who is this woman across the seas who hath won thy love?... Aye, even that I know—that thou dost love this fair daughter of the English. Didst thou not lose the picture of her that was taken with the magic-box of the sahibs?... Is it for her sake that thou dost deny me, O my husband? Is she more fair than I, are her lips more sweet?"

"I am not thy husband," he declared vehemently, appalled by her reversion to that delusion. "Till this hour I have never seen thee; nor is the sahiba of any concern to thee. Let me go, please."

But she had him fast and he could not have shaken her off but with violence. He had been a strong man indeed who had not been melted to tenderness by her beauty and her distress. She lifted her glorious face to him, pleading, insistent, and played upon him with her voice of gold. "Yet a moment gone thou didst tell me I was greatly gifted with beauty. Have I changed in thine eyes, O my king? Canst thou look upon this poor beauty and hear me tell thee of my love—and indeed I am altogether thine, *Lalji*!—and harden thy heart against me?... What though it be as thou hast said? What though thou art of a truth not of the house of Rutton, nor yet a Rajput? Let us say that this is so, however hard it be to credit: even so, am *I* not reward enough for thy renunciation?"

"I know not thy meaning, Ranee, I—"

"Come, then, and I will show thee, my king. Come thou with me.... Nay, why shouldst thou falter? There is naught for thee to fear—save me." She tugged at his hand and laughed low, in a voice that sang like smitten glasses. "Come, Beloved!"

Unwillingly, he humoured her. This could not last long.... The woman half led, half dragged him to the northern boundary of the garden, where they entered a little turret builded out from the walls over an abyss fully three-hundred feet in depth. And here, standing upon the verge of the parapet, with naught but a foot high coping between her and the frightful fall, utterly fearless and unutterably lovely, Naraini flung out a bare, jewelled arm in an eloquent gesture.

"See, my king!" she cried, her voice vibrant, her eyes kindling as they met his. "Look down upon thy kingdom. North, south, east, west—look!" she commanded. "Wherever thine eyes may turn, and farther than they can see upon the clearest day, this land is all thine ... for the taking. Look and tell me thou hast strength to renounce it ... and me, Beloved!"

A little giddy with the consciousness of their perilous height, his breath coming harshly, he looked—first down to the lake that shone like a silver dollar set in velvet, then up the misty distances of the widening valley through which ran the stream that fed the lake, and out to the hills that closed it in, miles away, and then farther yet over the silvered summits of the great, rough hills that rolled away endlessly, like a sea frozen in its fury.

"There lies thy kingdom, O my king!" The bewitching voice cooed seduction at his shoulder. "There and ... here." She sought his hand and placed it firmly upon her bosom, holding it there with gentle pressure until he felt the thumping of her heart and the warm flesh that heaved beneath a shred of half-transparent lace.

Reddening and a little shaken, he snatched his hand away. And she laughed chidingly.

"From the railway in the north to the railway in the south, all the land is Khandawar, Beloved: thine inheritance—thine for the taking ... even as I am thine, if thou wilt take me.... Look upon it, thy father's kingdom, then upon me, thy queen.... Yea!" she cried, throwing back her head and meeting his gaze with eye languorous beneath their heavy silken lashes. "Yea, I am altogether thine, my king! Wilt thou cast me aside, then, who am faint with love for thee?... Never hast thou dreamed of love such as the love that I bear for thee. How could it be otherwise, when thou hast passed thy days in the chill exile of the North? O my husband, turn not from me—"

He pulled himself together and stood away. "Madam," he said with an absurdly formal bow, "I am not your husband."

She opened her arms with infinite allure. "It is so little that is asked of thee—only to ascend thy father's throne and be honoured of all Bharuta, only to wield the sceptre that is thine by right, only to reign an undisputed king in two kingdoms—Khandawar and thy Naraini's heart!"

"I am very sorry," he returned with the same preciseness. "It is quite impossible. Besides, it seems that you leave the Sirkar altogether out of your calculations. It may not have occurred to you that the Supreme Government of India may have something to say about the contemplated change."

He saw her bite her lips with chagrin, and the look she flashed to his face was anything but kind and tender. "*Arre!*" she laughed derisively. "And of what account is this frail, tottering Sirkar's will besides the Will of the Body? Of what avail its dicta against the rulings of the Bell? Thou knowest—"

"Pardon, I know nothing. I have told thee, Ranee, that I am not Har Dyal Rutton."

She was mistress of a thousand artifices. Brought to a standstill on the one line of attack, she diverged to another without the quiver of an eyelash to betray her discomfiture.

"Yea, thou hast told me," she purred. "But I, Naraini, *I* know what I know. Thou dost deny thyself even as thou dost deny me, but ... art thou willing to be put to the proof, my king?"

"If you've any means of proving my identity, I would thank you for making use of it, Ranee."

"There is the test of the Token, *Lalji.*"

"I am not aware of it."

"The test of the Token—the ring that was brought to thee, the signet of thy House. Surely thou hast it with thee?"

Since that night in Calcutta Amber had resumed his habit of carrying the Token in the chamois bag. Now, on the reflection that it had been given him for a special purpose, which had been frustrated by the death of Dhola Baksh, so that he had no further use for it, he decided against the counsels of prudence. "What's the odds," he asked himself, "if I do lose it? I don't want the damn' thing—it's brought me nothing but trouble, thus far." And he thrust a hand within his shirt and brought forth the emerald. "Here it is," he told the woman cheerfully. "Now this test?" "Place it upon thy finger—so, even upon thy little finger, as was thy father's wont with it. Now lift up thine arm, so, and turn the stone to the west, toward Kathiapur."

Without comprehension he yielded to this whim, folding up his right arm and turning the emerald to the quarter indicated by Naraini.

The hour had drawn close upon dawn. A cold air breathed down the valley and was chill to them in that lofty eyrie. The moon, dipping towards the rim of the world, was poised, a globe of dull silver, upon the ridge of a far, dark hill. As they watched it dropped out of sight and everything was suddenly very bleak and black.

And a curious thing happened.

Naraini cried out sharply—"*Aho!*"—as if unable to contain her excitement.

Somewhere in the palace behind them a great gong boomed like thunder.

A pause ensued, disturbed only by the fluttering of the woman's breath: for the space of thirty pulse-beats nothing happened. Then Naraini's fingers closed like bands of steel about Amber's left wrist.

"See!" she cried in a voice of awe, while the bracelets shivered and clashed upon her outstretched arm, "The Eye, my king, the Eye!"

Amber shut his teeth upon an exclamation of amaze. For just above the far, dark mountain ridge, uncannily brilliant in the void of the pale, moonlit firmament, a light had blazed out; a vivid emerald light, winking and stabbing the darkness with shafts of seemingly supernatural radiance.

"And thy ring, lord—look! The Token!"

The great emerald seemed to have caught and to be answering the light Naraini called the Eye; in the stone's depths an infernal fire leaped and died and leaped again, now luridly blazing, now fitfully a-quiver as though about to vanish, again strong and steady: even as the light of the strange emerald star above the mountains ebbed and flowed through the night.

Naraini shuddered and cried out guardedly for very fear. "By Indur, it is even as the Voice foretold! Nay, Heaven-born"—she caught his sleeve and forcibly pulled down his hand—"tempt not the Unseen further. And put away this Token, lest a more terrible thing befall us. There be mysteries that even we of the initiate may not comprehend, my lord. It is not well to meddle with the unknown."

The ring was off his finger now and the woman was cramming it into his coat-pocket with tremulous hands. And where the Eye had shone, the sky was blank. They stood in darkness, Amber mute with perplexity, Naraini clinging to his arm and shaking like a reed in the wind.

"Now am I frightened, lord of my heart! Lead me back to the garden, for I am but a woman and afraid. Who am I, Naraini, to see the Eye? What am I, a weak woman, to trespass upon the Mysteries? I am very much afraid. Do thou take me hence and comfort me, my king!" She drew his arm about her waist, firm, round, and slender, and held it so, her body yielding subtly to his, her head drooping wearily upon his shoulder.

They moved slowly from the turret and back along the lighted walks of the garden, the woman apparently content, Amber preoccupied—to tell the truth, more troubled than he would have been willing to confess. As for the intimacy of their attitude, he was temporarily careless of it; it meant less to him than the woman guessed. It seems likely that she inferred a conquest from his indifference, for when they had come back to the tank of the gold-fish beneath the banian she slipped from his embrace and confronted him with a face afire with elation.

"See now how thou art altogether controverted, *Lalji!*" she cried joyfully. "No longer canst thou persist that thou art other than thy true self, the lord of Naraini's heart, the king returned to his kingdom.... For who would dare give the lie to the Eye?... Indeed," she continued with a low, sighing laugh, "I myself had begun to doubt, my faith borne down and overcome by thy repeated denials; but now I know thee. Did not the Bell foretell that the Eye should be seen of men only when Har Dyal Rutton had returned to his kingdom, and then only when he wore the Token? Even as it was said, so has it been.... And now art thou prepared to go?"

"Whither?"

"To Kathiawar—even to the threshold of the Gateway?... There is yet time, before the dawn, and it were wise to go quickly, my king; but for one night more is the Gateway open to receive thee. Thou didst see the saddled stallions in the courtyard? They wait there for thee, to bear thee to Kathiawar.... Nay, it were better that thou shouldst wait, mayhap, for the hours be few before the rising of the sun. Go then to thy rest, heart of my heart, since thou must leave me; and this night we shall ride, thou and I, together to the Gateway."

"So be it," he assented, with a grave inclination of his head. Convinced of the thanklessness of any further attempt to convince the woman against her will, he gave it up, and was grateful for the respite promised him. In twelve or eighteen hours he might accomplish much—with the aid of Labertouche. At worst he would find some means to communicate with the Farrells and then seek safety for himself in flight or hiding until what he had come to term "that damned Gateway-thing" should be closed and he be free to resume his strange wooing. Some way, somehow, he could contrive to extricate himself and his beloved.

111

Therefore he told the woman: "Be it so, O Queen! Now, I go."

"And leave me," she pouted prettily, "with no word but that, my king? Am I not worth a caress—not even when I beg for it?"

He smiled down at her, tolerant and amused, and impulsively caught her to him. "The point's well taken," he said. "Decidedly you're worth it, Naraini. And if you were not, the show was!"

And he kissed and left her, all in a breath.

CHAPTER XVI

SUNRISE FOR TWO

I

Amber found his way out of the garden without difficulty; at the doorway an eunuch waited. The Maharana himself, perhaps in deference to the dictates of discretion, did not reappear, and Amber had no desire to see him again. He was eager only to get away, to find a place and time to think, and to get into communication with Labertouche.

The eunuch bowed submissively to his demand to be shown out, and silently led him down through the echoing marble corridors and galleries of the many-tiered palace. They took a different way from that by which Amber had ascended; had his life depended on it, he could not have found his way back to the garden of Naraini, but by accident.

As they passed through the lower court of stables he remarked the fact that the stallions were being led away to their stalls. The circumstances confirmed Naraini's statement; the hour of their usefulness was ended for the day—or, rather, for the night.

The Virginian wondered dully if ever he would find himself astride one of the superb animals. After what he had witnessed and been a part of there was for him no longer any circumscribing horizon to the world of possibility. For him the improbable no longer existed. He had met the incredible face to face and found it real.

In the cavern-like chamber at the water-level Dulla Dad had the boat in readiness. Amber embarked, not without a sigh of relief, and the Mohammedan with his double-bladed paddle drove the boat out of the secret entrance, in an impassive silence. In the stern Amber watched the indefinite grey light of dawn wavering over the face of the waters and wondered …

The boat swung in gently to the marble steps of the bund. Amber rose and stepped ashore, very tired and very much inclined to believe he would presently wake up to a sane and normal world.

"Hazoor," the voice of Dulla Dad hailed him. He turned. "Hazoor, I was to say that at the third hour after sunset to-night this boat will be in waiting here. You are to call me by name, and I will put in for you, hazoor."

"What's that? I don't understand…. Oh, very well."

"And I was to say further, my lord, these words: 'You shall find but one way to Kathiapur.'"

Amber shook his head, smiling. "If you don't mind getting yourself disliked on my account, Dulla Dad, you may take back to the author of that epigram this answer: 'You shall find but one way to Jehannum, and that right speedily.' Good-morning, Dulla Dad."

"The peace of God abide always with the Heaven-born!"

With a single, strong stroke the creature of the palace sent the boat skimming far out from the bund, and, turning, headed for the palace.

112

Amber entered the bungalow, to find the khansamah already awake and moving about. At the Virginian's request he shuffled off to prepare coffee—much coffee, very strong and black and hot, Amber stipulated. He needed the stimulant badly. He was sleepy and his head was in a whirl.

He sat lost in thought until the khansamah brought the decoction, then roused and drank it as it came from the pot, without sugar, gulping down huge bitter mouthfuls of the scalding black fluid. But the effect that he expected and desired was strangely long in making itself felt. He marvelled at his drowsiness, nodding and blinking over his empty cup. Out of doors the skies were hot and blue—white with forerunners of the sun, and the world of men was stirring and making preparation against the business of the day; but Amber, who had a work so serious and so instant to his hand, sat on in dreamy lethargy, musing....

The faces of two women stood out vividly against the misty formless void before his eyes: the face of Naraini and that of Sophia Farrell. He looked from one to the other, stupidly contrasting them, trying to determine which was the lovelier, until their features blurred and ran together and the two became as one and ...

The khansamah tiptoed cautiously into the room and found the Virginian sleeping like a log, his head upon the table. His face was deeply coloured with crimson, as if a fever burned him, and his breathing was loud and stertorous.

Pausing, the native beckoned to one who skulked without, and the latter entering, the two laid hold of the unconscious man and bore him to the charpoy. The second native slipped silver money into the khansamah's palm.

"He will sleep till evening," he said. "If any come asking for him, say that he has gone abroad, leaving no word. More than this you do not know. The sepoys have an order to prevent all from entrance."

The khansamah touched his forehead respectfully. "It is an order. Shabash!" he muttered.

A shaft of sunlight struck in through the window and lay stark upon the sleeper's face. He did not move. The khansamah drew close the shades, and with the other left the room in semi-dusk.

II

Beneath the spreading banian, by the cistern of the goldfish, Naraini with smouldering eyes watched Amber disappear in the wilderness of shrubbery. He walked as a man with a set purpose, never glancing back. She laughed uneasily but waited motionless where he had left her, until the echo of his boot-heels on the marble slabs had ceased to ring in the neighbouring corridor. Then, lifting a flower-like hand to her mouth, she touched her lips gently and with an air of curiosity. The resentment in her eyes gave place to an emotion less superficial. "By Indur and by Har!" she swore softly. "In one thing at least he is like a Rajput: he kisses as a man kisses."

She moved indolently along the walk to the rug beneath the canopy where he had found her, her lithe, languid, round body in its gorgeous draperies no whit less insolent than the flaming bougainvillea whose glowing magenta blossoms she touched with idle fingers as she passed.

The east was grey with dusk of dawn—a light that grew apace, making garish the illumination of the flickering, smoking, many-coloured lamps in the garden. Naraini clapped her hands. Soft footsteps sounded in the gallery and one of her handmaidens threaded the shrubbery to her side.

"The lamps, Unda," said the queen; "their light, I think, little becomes me. Put them out." And when this was done, she composedly ordered her pipe and threw herself lazily at length upon a pile of kincob cushions, her posture the more careless since she knew herself secure from observation; the garden being private to her use.

When the tire-woman had departed, leaving at Naraini's side a small silver *huqa* loaded with fine-cut Lucknow weed, a live ember of charcoal in the middle of the bowl, she sat up and began to smoke, her face of surpassing loveliness quaintly thoughtful as she sucked at the little mouthpiece of chased silver and exhaled faint clouds of aromatic vapour. From time to time she smiled pensively and put aside the tube while she played with the rings upon her slender, petal-like fingers; five rings there were to each hand, from the heavy thumb circlet that might possibly fit a man's little finger to the tiny band that was on her own, all linked together by light strands of gold radiating from the big, gem-encrusted boss of ruddy gold midway between her slim round waist and dimpled knuckles....

The tread of boots with jingling spurs sounded in the gallery, warning her. She sighed, smiled dangerously to herself, and carelessly adjusted her veil, leaving rather more than half her face bare. Salig Singh entered the garden and found his way to her, towering over her beneath the canopy, brave in his green and tinsel uniform. She looked up with a listless hauteur that expressed her attitude toward the man.

"*Achcha*!" she said sharply. "Thou art tardy, Heaven-born. Yet have I waited for thee this half-hour gone, heavy with sleep though I be—waited to know the pleasure of my lord."

There was a mockery but faintly disguised in her tone. The Maharana seemed to find it not unpleasant, for he smiled grimly beneath his moustache.

"There was work to be done," he said briefly—"for the Cause. And thou—how hast thou wrought, O Breaker of Hearts?"

The woman cast the silver mouthpiece from her and clasped her hands behind her head. "Am I not Naraini?"

"The man is ours?"

"Mine," she corrected amiably. His face darkened with a scowl of jealousy and she laughed in open derision. "Were I Naraini could I not divine the heart of a man?"

"By what means?"

"What is that to thee, O Heaven-born?" She snuggled her body complacently into the luxurious pile of cushions. "If I have accomplished the task thou didst set for me, what concern hast thou with the means I did employ? Thou art only Salig Singh, Maharana of Khandawar, but I am Naraini, a free woman."

"Thou—!" Rage choked the Rajput. "Thou," he sputtered—"thou art—"

"Softly, Heaven-born, softly—lest I loose a thunderbolt for thy destruction. Is it wise to forget that Naraini holds thy fate in the hollow of her hands?" She sat forward, speaking swiftly and with malice. "Thou art pledged to produce Har Dyal Rutton in the Hall of the Bell before another sunrise, and none but Naraini knows to what a perilous resort thou art driven to redeem thy word."

"I was lied to," he argued sullenly. "A false tale was brought me—by one who hath repented of his error! If I was told that Har Dyal Rutton would be in India upon such-and-such a day, am I to blame that I did promise to bring him to the Gateway?"

"And seeing that the man is dead, art thou to blame for bringing in his place a substitute, even so poor a changeling as this man Amber? Nay, be not angry; do I blame thee? Have I done aught but serve thee to the end thou dost desire?... Thou shouldst be grateful to me, rather than menace me with thine anger.... And," she added sweetly, "it were well for thee that thou shouldst bear always in mind my intimacy with thy secret. If thou art king, then am I more than queen, in Khandawar."

"I am not angry, Naraini," he told her humbly, "but mad with love for thee—"

"And lust, my lord, for—power," she interpolated.

"But if what thou hast said be true—"

"'Who lies to the King, is already a dead man.' Why should I trouble to deceive thee, Heaven-born? I tell thee, the man is won. The day shall declare it: this night will he ride with me to Kathiapur. Why didst thou not tarry to eavesdrop? Indeed thou hast lost an opportunity that may never a second time be thine—to learn of the wiles of woman."

"There was work to be done," he repeated. "I went to take measures against thy failure."

"O thou of little faith!"

"Nay, why should I neglect proper precautions? Whether thy confidence be justified or no, this night will Har Dyal Rutton—or one like him—endure the Ordeal of the Gateway."

"So I have told thee," she assented equably. "He will come, because Naraini bids him."

"It may be so. If not, another lure shall draw him."

She started with annoyance. "The Englishwoman of the picture?"

"Have I named her?" He lifted his heavy brows in affected surprise.

"Nay, but—"

"Secret for secret," he offered: "mine for thine. Is it a bargain, O Pearl of Khandawar?"

"Keep thy silly secret, then, as I will keep mine own counsel," she said, with assumed disdain. It was no part of wisdom, in her understanding, to tell him of her interview with Amber. A man's jealousy is a potent weapon in a woman's hands, but must be wielded with discretion.

He was persistent: "I will back my plan against thine, Ranee."

"So be it," she said shortly. "Whichever wins, the stake is won for both. What doth it matter?"

She rose and moved impatiently down the walk and back again, bangles tinkling, jewels radiant on wrist and brow, ankle and bosom. The man watched her with sulky eyes until she turned, then bent his head and stood glowering at the earth and twisting his moustache. She paused before him, hands on hips, and raised her eyes in silent inquiry. He pretended not to notice her. She sighed with a pretence of humility thinly disguised. "Thy trouble, my lord?" she rallied him.

"I have wondered," he said heavily: "will he pass?"

"If not, it were well for thee to die this night, O Heaven-born."

"That was my thought."

"Thou hast little need to worry, lord." Woman-like she shifted to suit his humour. "He is a man: I answer for that, though ... he is no fool. Still, when the hour strikes, what he must, that will he endure for the sake of that which Naraini hath promised him."

"Or for another," Salig Singh growled into his beard.

"I did not hear."

"I said naught. I am distraught."

"Be of good heart," she comforted him still further. "If he doth fail to survive the Ordeal—Har Dyal Rutton hath died. If he doth survive—"

"Har Dyal Rutton shall die within the hour," Salig Singh concluded grimly. "But ... I am troubled. I cannot but ask myself continually: Were it not wiser to confess failure and abide the outcome?"

"How long wouldst thou abide the outcome, my king, after thou hadst informed the Council of this deception to which thou hast been too willing and ready a party?... He who misled you died a dog's death. But thou—art thou in love with death?"

"Unless thy other name be Death, Naraini ..."

"Or if the Council should spare thee—as is unlikely? The patience of the Body is as the patience of Kings—scant; and its mercy is like unto its patience.... But say thou art spared: what then? How long art thou prepared to wait until the Members of the Body shall again be in such complete accord as now? When again shall all Hindustan be ripe for revolt?... *Aho!* Thou wouldst have sweet patience in the waiting, Salig Singh!... Let matters rest as they be, my lord"—this a trace imperiously. "Leave the man to me: I stand sponsor for him until the Gateway shall have received him and—and perhaps for a little afterwards."

"Thou art right as ever." He lifted his gaze to meet hers and his eyes flamed. "I leave my life on your knees, Naraini. I love thee and ... by all the gods, thou art altogether a woman!"

"And thou ... a man, your Highness?" she countered provokingly. "Nay!" she continued, evading him with a supple squirm, "be content until this affair be consummated. Wait until the time when an empress shall reign over all Bharuta and thou, my lord, shall be her Minister of State."

The man's voice shook. "That hour is not far off, my queen. Thou wilt not keep me waiting longer?"

She gave him the quick promise of her eyes. "Thou shouldst know—thou of all men, my lord.... But see!" It was necessary to distract him and she seized hastily upon the first pretext. "The last day of the old order dawns ... and the dawn is crimson, my lord, as with blood!" Her soft scarlet lips curled thirstily and showed her teeth, small, sharp and white as pearls. "I think," she added with somber conviction, "this omen is propitious!"

She swept away from him, toward the parapet. He took a single step in pursuit and halted, following her with a glance that was at once a caress and a threat.

She paused only when she could go no further, and stood in silent waiting.

Deep down in the valley the city was stirring from its sleep; the dull and peaceful humming of its hived hordes rose to her, pulsating in the still air. Above the eastern ridge the sky was hot and angry, banded with magenta, scarlet, and cadmium, and shot with expanding shafts of fierce radiance, like ribs of a fan of fire. In a long and breathless instant of suspense the hilltops blushed with the glare and threw down the light to the night mists swimming in the valley, rendering them opalescent, as with a heart of flame.

With eyes half-veiled by long languorous lashes the woman threw back her head until her swelling throat was tense. She raised her arms and stretched them wide. The sun, soaring suddenly, a crimson disk above the ridge, seemed to strike fire from her strange, savage beauty as from a jewel. Bathed in its ruddy glare she seemed to embody in her frail, slight form all that was singular to that cruel, passionate land of fire and steel. Her face became suffused, her blood leaping in response to the ardour of the sun.

Her parted lips moved, but the man, who had drawn near enough to hear, caught two words only.

"*Naraini!... Empress!*"

CHAPTER XVII

THE WAY TO KATHIAPUR

Gall and wormwood in his mouth, more bitter than remorse, Amber became conscious. Or perhaps it were more true to say that he struggled out of unconsciousness, dragging his ego back by main will-power from the deep oblivion of drugged slumber. One by one his faculties fought their way past the barrier, until he was fully sentient, save that his memory drowsed. His head was hot and heavy, his eyes burned in their sockets like balls of live charcoal, a dulled buzzing sounded in his ears, his very heart felt sore and numb; he was as one who wakes from evil dreams to the blackness of foreknown despair.

He lay for a time without moving. Because it was dark and his memory not working properly, time had ceased to be for him, and to-day was as yesterday and to-morrow. The ceiling-cloth above him was blood-red with light from the sepoys' fire in the compound, and all was as it had been when he had first lain down the night before. And yet....

Suddenly he raised himself upon the charpoy and called huskily for the khansamah. Promptly the squat white figure that he remembered appeared in the doorway. "Bring lights," Amber ordered, peremptory.

"Bring lights quickly—and water." And when the man had returned with a lamp, which he put on the table, Amber seized the red earthenware water-jug and drained it greedily. Returning it, empty, to the brown hands, he motioned to the man to wait, while he consulted his watch. It had run down. He thrust it back into his pocket and enquired: "What's o'clock?"

"Eight of the evening, sahib."

Amber gasped and stared. "Eight of the ... Let me think. Go and bring me food and a brandy-peg—or, hold on! Bring a bottle of soda-water and a glass only."

The khansamah withdrew. Amber fell back with his shoulders to the wall and stared unwinking at the lamp. He distinctly remembered undressing before going to bed; he now found himself fully clothed. He felt of his pocket, and found the emerald ring there, instead of in its chamois case. Then it had not been a nightmare!

He had a bottle of brandy which had never been uncorked, in his travelling-kit. Rising, he found it and inspected the cork narrowly to make sure it had not been tampered with; then he drew it.

The khansamah returned with the glass and an unopened bottle of Schweppe's, and prepared the drink under eyes that watched him narrowly. While Amber drank he laid a place for him at the table. When he left the room a second time the Virginian produced his automatic pistol and satisfied himself that it remained loaded and in good working order.

In the course of a few minutes the native reappeared with a tray of food and pot of coffee. These arranged, he stood by the chair, ready to serve the guest. Then he found himself looking into the muzzle of Amber's weapon, and became apparently rigid with terror.

"Sahib—!"

"Make no outcry, dog, and tell me no lies, if you value your contemptible life. Why did you drug me—at whose instance?"

"Sahib!..."

"Answer me quickly, son of vipers!"

"By Dhola Baksh, hazoor, I am innocent! Another has done these things—he who served you last night, belike, and whose place I have taken."

Now the oaths of India are many and various, so that a new specimen need not be held wonderful. But Amber sat bolt upright, his eyes widening and his jaw dropping. "Dhola—!" he said, and brought his teeth together with an audible click, staring at the khansamah as if he were a recrudescence of a prehistoric mammal. He caught a motion of the head and a wave of the hand toward the window, warning him that there might be an eavesdropper lurking without, and rose admirably to the emergency.

"That is a lie, misbegotten son of an one-eyed woman of shame! By the Gateway at Kathiapur, that is a lie! Speak, brother of jackals and father of swine, lest my temper overcome me and I make carrion of you!"

"My lord, hear me!" protested the man in an extremity of fright. "These be the words of truth. If otherwise, let my head be forfeit.... Early in the morning you returned from the lake, heavy with sleep, and so soundly have you slept since that hour that no effort of mine could rouse you, though many came to the door, making inquiry. I am Ram Lal, a true man, and no trafficker in drugs and potions."

"Even so!" said Amber, ironic. "But if, on taking thought, I find you've lied to me ... Go now and hold yourself fortunate in this, that I am not a man of hasty judgment."

"Hazoor!" Like a shadow harried by a wind of night, the khansamah scurried from the room. But on the threshold he paused long enough to lay a significant finger upon his lips and nod toward the table.

Amber put away his pistol, sighed from the bottom of his soul, and, seating himself, without the least misgiving, broke his long fast with ravenous appetite, clearing every dish and emptying the coffee pot of all save dregs. Then, with a long yawn of satisfaction, repletion, and relief, he lighted a cigarette and stretched himself, happily conscious of returning strength and sanity.

From the khansamah's quarters came an occasional clash of crockery and pattering of naked feet. Outside, in the compound, the sepoys were chattering volubly; their words were indistinguishable, but from their constantly increasing animation Amber inferred that they were keenly relishing the topic of discussion. He became sure of this when, at length, his curiosity roused, he went to the window and peered out between the wooden slats of the blind. The little company was squatting in a circle round the fire, and a bottle was passing from hand to hand.

He turned back, puzzled, to find the khansamah calmly seated at the table and enjoying one of Amber's choicest cigarettes.

"Thank God," he said, with profound emotion, "for a civilised smoke!"

"Labertouche!" cried Amber.

The pseudo-khansamah rose, bowed formally, and shook hands with considerable cordiality. "It's good to see you whole and sound," he said. "I had to wait until Ram Nath's work began to show results. He's out there, you know, keeping the bottle moving. I don't believe those damned sepoys will bother us much, now, but we've got no time at all to spare. Now tell me what you have to tell, omitting nothing of the slightest consequence."

Amber dropped into a chair, and the Englishman sat near to him. "I say, thank God for you, Labertouche! You don't know how I've needed you."

"I can fancy. I've had a ripping time of it myself. Sorry I couldn't communicate with you safely before you left Calcutta. But we've not a minute to waste. Get into your yarn, please; explanations later, if we can afford 'em."

Inhaling with deep enjoyment, he narrowed his dark eyes, listening intently to Amber's concise narrative of his experiences since their parting before the stall of Dhola Baksh in the Machua Bazaar. Not once was he interrupted by word or sign from Labertouche; and even when the tale was told the latter said nothing, but dropped his gaze abstractedly to the smouldering stump of his cigarette.

"And you?" demanded the Virginian. "Have pity, Labertouche! Can't you see I'm being eaten alive by curiosity?"

Labertouche eyed him blankly for an instant. "Oh!" he said, with an effort freeing his mind from an intense concentration of thought. "I? What's there to tell? I've been at work. That's all.... I was jostled off to one side when the row started in the bazaar, and so lost you. There was then nothing to do but strike back to the hotel and wait for a clue. You can figure my relief when you dropped out of that ticca-ghari! I gave you the word to go on to Darjeeling, intending to join you *en route*. But you know why that jaunt never came off. I found out my mistake before morning, wired you, and left Calcutta before you, by the same train that conveyed his Majesty the Maharana of Khandawar. Fortunately enough we had Ram Nath already on the ground, working up another case—I'll tell you about it some time. He's one of our best men—a native, but loyal to the core, and wrapped up in his work. He'd contrived to get a billet as tonga-wallah to the Kuttarpur *bunia* who has the dâk-service contract. I myself had arranged to have the telegraph-babu here transferred, and myself appointed in his place. So I was able to attach myself to the 'tail' of the Maharana without exciting comment. Miss Farrell came by the same train, but Salig Singh was in too great a hurry to get home to pay any attention to her, and I, knowing you'd be along, arranged that tonga accident with Ram Nath. He bribed his brother tonga-wallah to bring it about."

"Thank you," said Amber from his heart.

Labertouche impatiently waved the interruption aside. "I looked for you at the telegraph office this morning, but of course when you didn't appear I knew something was up. So I concocted a message to you for an excuse, came down, engaged the khansamah in conversation (I think he had some idea I was an agent of the other side) and ... he is an old man, not very strong. Once indoors, I had little trouble with him. He's now enjoying perfect peace, with a gag to insure it, beneath his own charpoy. Ram Nath happened along opportunely and created a diversion with his gin-bottle. That seems to be all, and I'm afraid we mayn't talk much longer. I must be going—and so must you."

He glanced anxiously at his watch—a cheap and showy thing, such as natives delight in. Both men rose.

"You return to the telegraph station, I presume?" said Amber.

"Not at all. It wouldn't be worth my while."

"How's that?"

"The wires haven't been working since ten this morning," said Labertouche quietly. Amber steadied himself with the back of his chair. "You mean they've been cut?"

"Something of the sort."

"And that means—"

"That this infernal conspiracy is scheduled to come to a head to-night—as you must have inferred, my dear fellow: this is the last night of your probation. The cutting off of Khandawar from all British India is a bold move and shows Salig Singh's confidence. It means simply: 'Governmental interference not desired. Hands off.' He knows well that we've spies here, that enough has leaked out, unavoidably, to bring an army corps down on his back within twenty-four hours, if he permitted even the most innocent-seeming message to get out of the city."

Amber whistled with dismay. "And you—"

"I'm going to find out for myself what's towards in Kathiapur."

119

"You're going there—alone?"

"Not exactly; I shall have company. A gentleman of the Mohammedan persuasion is going to change places with me for the night. No; he doesn't know it yet, but I have reason to believe that he got an R.S.V.P. for the festive occasion and intends to put in a midnight appearance. So I purpose saving him the trouble. It's only a two-hour ride."

"But the risk!"

Labertouche chuckled grimly. "It's the day's work, my boy. I'm not sure I shan't enjoy it. Besides, I mayn't hang back where my subordinates have not feared to go. We've had a man in Kathiapur since day before yesterday."

"And I? What am I to do?"

"Your place is at Miss Farrell's side. No; you'd be only a hindrance to me. Get that out of your thoughts. Three years ago I found time to make a pretty thorough exploration of Kathiapur, and, being blessed with an excellent memory, I shall be quite at home."

Amber made a gesture of surrender. "Of course you're right," he said. "You're always right, confound you!"

"Exactly," agreed Labertouche, smiling. "I'm only here to help you escape to the Residency. Raikes and Colonel Farrell have already been advised to make preparations for a siege or for instant flight, if I give the word. They need you far more than I shall. It would be simple madness for you to venture to Kathiapur to-night. The case is clear enough for you to see the folly of doing anything of the sort."

"It may be clear to you...."

"See here," said Labertouche, with pardonable impatience; "I'm presuming that you know enough of Indian history to be aware that the Rutton dynasty in Khandawar is the proudest and noblest in India; it has descended in right line from the Sun. There's not a living Hindu but will acknowledge its supremacy, be he however ambitious. That makes it plain, or ought to, why Har Dyal Rutton, the last male of his line, was—and is—considered the natural, the inevitable, leader of the Second Mutiny. It devolved upon Salig Singh to produce him; Salig Singh promised and—is on the point of failure. I can't say precisely what penalty he'll be called upon to pay, but it's safe to assume that it'll be something everlastingly unpleasant. So he's desperate. I can't believe he has deceived himself into taking you for Rutton, but whether or no he intends by hook or crook to get you through this Gateway affair to-night. He's got to. Now you are—or Rutton is—known to be disloyal to the scheme. Inevitably, then, the man who passes through that Gateway in his name is to be quietly eliminated before he can betray anything—in other words, as soon as he has been put through the 'Ordeal,' as they call it, for the sake of appearances and the moral effect upon the Hindu race at large. Now I think you understand."

"I think I do, thanks," Amber returned drily. "You're quite right, as I said before. So I'm off to the Residency. But how to get through that guard out there?"

He received no response. In as little time as it took him to step backwards from Amber, Labertouche had resumed his temporarily discarded masquerade. Instantaneously it was the khansamah who confronted the Virginian—the native with head and shoulders submissively bended, as one who awaits an order.

Amber, surprised, stared, started to speak, received a sign, and was silent, the excuse for Labertouche's sudden change of attitude being sufficiently apparent in an uproar which had been raised without the least warning in the compound. The advent of a running horse seemed to have been responsible for it, for the clatter of hoofs as the animal was checked abruptly in mid-stride was followed by a clamour of drunken cries, shrieks of alarm, and protests on the part of the sepoys disturbed in the midst of their carouse. Over all this there rang the voice of an Englishman swearing good, round, honest British oaths.

"Stand aside, you hounds!"

Amber turned pale. "That's Farrell's voice!" he cried, guessing at the truth.

Labertouche made no answer, but edged toward the khansamah's quarters.

The din subsided as Farrell gained the veranda. His feet rang heavily on the boards, and a second later he thrust the door violently open and slammed breathlessly into the room, booted, spurred, his keen old face livid, a riding-whip dangling from one wrist, a revolver in the other hand.

He wheeled on the threshold and lifted his weapon, then, with a gasp of amazement, dropped it. "By Heaven, sir!" he cried, "that's odd! Those damned sepoys tried to prevent my seeing you and now they've cleared out, every mother's son of them!"

Amber stepped to his side; to his own bewilderment, the compound was deserted; there was not a sepoy in sight.

"So much the better," he said quickly, the first to recover. "What's wrong, sir?"

"Wrong!" Farrell stumbled over to the table and into a chair, panting. "Everything's wrong! What's gone wrong with you, that we haven't been able to find you all day?"

"I've been lying there," Amber told him, nodding to the charpoy, "drugged. What's happened? Is Miss Farrell—?"

"Sophia!" The Political lifted his hand to his eyes and let it fall, with an effect of confusion. "In the name of charity tell me you know where she is!"

"You don't mean—"

"She's gone, Amber—gone! She's disappeared, vanished, been spirited away! Don't you understand me? She's been kidnapped!"

In dumb torment, Amber heard a swift, sharp hiss of breath as pregnant with meaning as a spoken word, and turned to meet Labertouche's eyes, and to see that the same thought was in both their minds. Salig Singh had found the way to lure Amber to Kathiapur.

No spoken word was needed; their understanding was implicit on the instant. Indeed the secret-agent dared not speak, lest he be overheard by an eavesdropper and so be the cause of his own betrayal. With a flutter of white garments he slipped noiselessly from the room, and Amber knew instinctively that if they were to meet again that night it would be upon the farther side of the Gateway of Swords. For himself, his path of duty lay clear to the Virginian's vision; like Labertouche's, it was the road to Kathiapur. He had no more doubt that Sophia had been conveyed thither than he had of Farrell's presence before him. And in his heart he cursed, not Naraini, not Salig Singh, but himself for his inept folly in bringing to India the photograph which had been stolen from him and so had discovered to the conspirators his interest in the girl.

He thought swiftly of Dulla Dad's parting admonition: "*You shall find but one way to Kathiapur.*"

"Well, sir? Well?" Exasperated by his silence the Political sprang to his feet and brought the riding-crop against his leg with a smack like a gun-shot. "Have you nothing to say? Don't you realise what it means when a white woman disappears in this land of devils? Good God! you stand there, doing nothing, saying nothing, like a man with a heart of stone!"

"Speak French," Amber interposed quietly. He continued in that tongue, his tone so steady and imperative that it brought the half-frantic Englishman to his senses. "Speak

French. You must know that we're spied upon every instant; every word we speak is overheard, probably. Tell me what happened—how it happened—and keep cool!"

"You're right; I beg your pardon." Farrell collected himself. "There's little enough to go on…. You disappointed us this morning. During the day we got word from a secret but trustworthy source to look out for trouble from the native side. Nevertheless, Raikes and I were obliged, by reason of our position, representing Government, to attend the banquet in honor of the coronation to-morrow. We called in young Clarkson—the missionary, you know—to stay in the house during our absence. When we returned the Residency was deserted—only we found Clarkson bound, gagged, and nearly dead of suffocation in a closet. He could tell us nothing—had been set upon from behind. Not a servant remained…. But, by the way, your man Doggott came in by the evening dâk-tonga."

"Where's Raikes?"

"Gone to the palace to threaten Salig Singh with an army corps."

"You know the telegraph wires are cut?"

"Yes, but how—"

"Never mind how I know—the story's too long. The thing to do is to get troops here without a day's delay."

"But how?"

"Take Raikes, Clarkson, and Doggott and ride like hell to Badshah Junction. Telegraph from there. The four of you ought to be able to fight your way through."

"But, man, my daughter!"

"I know where to find her—or think I do. No matter which, I'll find her and bring her back to you safely, or die trying. You spoke just now of a secret but trustworthy source of information: I work with it this night. I can't mention names—you know why; but that source was in this room ten minutes ago. He's gone after your daughter now. I follow. No—I go alone. It's the only way. I know how you feel about it, but believe me, the thing for you to do is to find some way to summon British troops. Now the quicker you go, the quicker I'm off. I can't—daren't move while you're here."

Farrell eyed him strangely. "I'll go," he said after a pause. "But … why can't I—"

"There are just two white men living, Colonel Farrell, who can go where I am going to look for your daughter to-night. I'm one of them. The other is—you know who."

"One of us is mad," said Farrell with conviction. "I think you are."

"Or else I know what I'm talking about. In either event you only hinder me now. Please go."

His manner impressed the man; for a moment Farrell lingered, doubting, then impetuously offered his hand. "I'm hanged if I understand why," he said, "but somehow I believe you know what you're about. Good-night and—and God be with you, Amber."

The Virginian followed him to the doorway. Farrell's horse, a docile, well-trained animal, had come to the edge of the veranda to wait for his master. Otherwise the compound was as empty as the night was quiet. Mounting, the Political waved a silent farewell and spurred off toward the city. Amber passed back through the bungalow to the bund.

It was a wonderful blue night of clear moonlight, quickened by a rowdy wind that rioted down the valley from the north. The roughened surface of the lake was dark save where the moon had blazed its trail of shimmering golden scales. There was no boat visible, and for the first time Amber's heart misgave him and he doubted whether it were not best to seek a mount from the stables of the Residency and try to reach Kathiapur on his own initiative. But his ignorance of the neighbouring topography was too great a handicap to be overcome; and now that Labertouche had gone, he was without a friendly, guiding hand. He could but deliver himself into the hands of the enemy and do what he might thereafter.

He lifted his voice and called: "*Ohé*, Dulla Dad!"

There came a soft shuffle of feet on the stones behind him, and the stunted, white-clad figure of Dulla Dad stood at his side, making respectful obeisance. "Hazoor!"

"You damned spying scoundrel!" Amber cried, enraged. "You've been waiting there by the window, listening!"

"Hazoor," the native quavered in fright, "it was cold upon the water and you kept me waiting over-long. I landed, seeking shelter from the wind. If your talk was not for mine ears, remember that you used a tongue I did not know."

"So you were listening!" Amber calmed himself. "Never mind. Where's your boat?"

"I thought to hide it in the rushes. If the hazoor will be patient for a little moment …" The native dropped down from the bund and disappeared into the reedy tangle of the lake shore. A minute or so later Amber saw the boat shoot out from the shore and swing in a long, graceful curve to the steps of the bund.

"Make haste," he ordered, as he jumped in and took his place. "If I have kept you waiting, as you say, then I am late."

"Nay, there is time to spare." Dulla Dad spun the boat round and away. "I did but think to anticipate your impatience, knowing that you would assuredly come."

"Ah, you knew that, Dulla Dad? How did you know?"

The man giggled softly, plying a busy paddle. "Am I not of the palace, hazoor? What are secrets in the house of kings? Gossip of herders and bazaar-women!"

"And how much more do you know, Dulla Dad?" Amber's tone was ominous.

"I, hazoor? Who am I to know aught?… Nay, this have I heard"—he paused cunningly: "'*You shall find but one way to Kathiapur.*'"

Amber, realising that he had invited this insolence, was fair enough not to resent it, and held his peace until he could no longer be blind to the fact that the native was shaping a course almost exactly away from the Raj Mahal. "What treachery is this, dog?" he demanded. "This is not the way—"

"Be not mistrustful of your slave, hazoor," whined the native. "I do the bidding of those before whose will I am as a leaf in the wind. It is an order that I land you on the bund of the royal summer pavilion, by the northern shore of the lake. There will you find one waiting for you, my lord."

Amber contented himself with a fresh examination of his pistol; it was all one to him, whatever the route by which he was to reach Kathiapur, so long as the change involved no delay. But this way across the water was so much longer than that which he had anticipated that he had time to work himself into a state of fuming impatience before the boat finally ranged alongside a pretentious marble bund backed by ragged plantations of palms and bananas. To the left the white-columned facade of the Maharana's stately pleasure-house glimmered spectral in the moonlight. It showed no lights, and Amber very naturally concluded that it was unoccupied.

He landed on the steps of the bund and waited for Dulla Dad to join him; but when, hearing a splash of the paddle, he looked round, it was to find that the native had already put a considerable distance between himself and the shore. Amber called after him angrily, and Dulla Dad rested upon his paddle.

"Nay, Heaven-born!" he replied. "Here doth my responsibility end. Another will presently appear to be your guide. Go you up to the jungly path leading from the bund."

The Virginian lifted his shoulders indifferently, and ascended to discover a wide footpath running inland between dark walls of shrubbery, but quite deserted. He stopped with a whistle of vexation, peering to right and left. "What the deuce!" he said aloud. "Is this another of their confounded tricks?"

A low and marvellously sweet laugh sounded at his elbow, and he turned with a start and a flutter of his pulses. "Naraini!" he cried.

It had been impossible to mistake the gracious lines of that slight, round figure, cloaked though it was in many thicknesses of white veiling. She had stolen upon him without a sound, and seemed pleased with the completeness of his surprise, for she laughed again before he spoke.

"Tell me not thou art disappointed, O my king!" she said, placing a soft hand firmly upon his arm. "Didst thou hope to meet another here?"

"Nay, how should I expect thee?" His voice was gentle though he steeled his heart against her fascinations; for now he had a use for her. "Had Dulla Dad conveyed me to the palace, then I should have remembered thy promise to ride with me to Kathiapur. But, being brought to this place…"

"Then thou didst wish to ride with me?" She nodded approval and satisfaction. "That is altogether as I would have it be, Lord of my Heart. By this have I proven thee, for thou hast consented to approach the Gateway, not altogether because the Voice hath summoned thee, but likewise, I think, because thine own heart urged thee. Nay, but tell me, King of my Soul, did it not leap a little at the thought of meeting me?"

With a quick gesture she threw her veil aside and lifted her incomparably fair face to his, and he was conscious that he trembled a little, and that his voice shook as he answered evasively: "Thou shouldst know, Ranee."

"*Ahi!* Then am I a happy woman, to think that, though thou wert in open mutiny against the Voice, when I called, thou didst yield…. And thou art ready?"

"Am I not here?"

"Now of a verity do I know that thou art a man, my king!—a Rajput, a son of kings, and … my husband!" Pitched to a minor, thrilling key, her accents were as musical as the singing of a 'cello. "For thou dost know what thou must dare this night of nights, and he is a brave man who can dare so much, unfaltering. Tell me thou art not afraid, my king?"

"Why should I be?"

"Thou wilt not draw back in the end?" Her arms clipped him softly about the neck and drew his head down so that her breath was fragrant in his face, her lips a sweet peril beneath his own. "Thou wilt brave whatever may be prepared for thy testing, for the sake of Naraini, who awaits thee beyond the Gateway; O my Beloved?"

"I shall not be found wanting."

Lithe as a snake, she slipped from his arms. "Nay, I trust thee not!" she laughed, a quiver of tenderness in her merriment. "Let my lips be mine alone until thou hast proven thyself worthy of them." She raised her voice, calling: "*Ohé*, Runjit Singh!"

The cry rang bell-clear in the stillness, and its silver echo had not died before it was answered by one who stepped out from the black shadow of a spreading banian, some distance away, and came toward them, leading three horses. As the moonlight fell upon him, Amber recognised the uniform the man wore as that of the Imperial Household Guard of Khandawar, while the horses seemed to be the stallions he had seen in the palace yard, with another but little their inferior in mettle or beauty.

"Now," announced the woman in tones of deep contentment, "we will ride!"

She turned to Amber, who took her up in his arms and set her in the saddle of one of the stallions; who, his bridle being released by the trooper, promptly leaped away and danced a spirited saraband with his shadow, until Naraini, with a strength that seemed incredible when one recalled the slightness of her wrists, curbed him in and taught him sobriety.

"By Har!" she panted, "but I think he must know that he carries to-night the destinies of empire! Mount, mount, my lord, and bear me company if this son of Eblis tries to run away with me!"

The sowar surrendered to Amber the reins of the other stallion, and stepped hastily aside. The Virginian took the saddle with a flying leap, and a thought later was digging his knees into the brute's sleek flanks and sawing on the bits, while the path flowed beneath him, dappled with moonlight and shadow, like a ribbon of grey-green silk, and trees and shrubbery streaked back on either hand in a rush of melting blacks and greys.

Swerving acutely, the path ran into the dusty high-road. Amber heard a rush of hoofs behind him, and then slowly the gauze-wrapped figure of the queen drew alongside.

"*Maro!* Let him run, my king! The way is not far for such as he. Have no fear lest he tire!"

But Amber set his teeth and wrought with the reins until his mount comprehended the fact that he had met a master, and, moderating his first furious burst of speed, settled down into a league-devouring stride, crest low, limbs gathering and stretching with the elegant precision of clockwork. His rider, regaining his poise, found time to look about him and began to enjoy, for all his cares, this wild race through the blue-white night.

Behind them, carbine on saddle-bow, the sowar thundered in pursuit, at an interval of about a hundred yards—often greater, when the stallions would have it so and spent their temper in brief, brisk contests for the leadership. On Amber's left the woman rode as one to the saddle born, her face turned eagerly to the open road, smiling a little with excitement beneath the tissue of thin veiling which the speed-bred breeze moulded cunningly to the contour of her flawless features. The fire in her blood shone lambent in the eyes that now and again met Amber's. More than once he heard her laugh low, with a lilt of happiness.

For himself he was drunk with the spirit of adventure. Bred of the moonlit sky and the far shy stars, of the flooding moonlight breaking crisply against impenetrable shadows like surf against black rocks, of the tune of hoofs, of the singing wind and sighing waters, a wild and reckless humor possessed him, ran molten in his veins, swam in his brain like fumes of wine.

As the tale of miles increased, the valley opened out, and presently they swung to the west from the northerly track, branching off into a rougher way through a wilder countryside. Rugged hilltops marched beside them, looming stark black against the silvered purple of the sky. They met no one, their road winding through a land whose grandeur was enhanced by its positive desolation—a land tenanted only by a million devils of loneliness with naught to do save to fling back mocking echoes of the road-song of the flying hoofs....

Toward the close of the second hour the valleys began to widen, the hills to be less lofty and precipitous. The horses swung up gentler ascents, down slopes less sharp. The road ran for a time along the bank of a broad and placid river, then crossed it by a massive arch of masonry as old as history. They circled finally a great, round, grassless hillside, and pulled rein in the notch of a gigantic V formed by two long, prow-like spurs running out upon a plain whose sole, vague boundary was the vast arc of the horizon.

Before them loomed dead Kathiapur, an island of stone girdled by the shallow silver river. Like the rugged pedestal of some mammoth column, its cliffs rose sheer threescore feet from the water's edge to the foot of the outermost of its triple walls. From the notch

125

in the hills a great stone causeway climbed with a long and easy grade to the level of the first great gate, spanning the chasm over the river by means of a crazy wooden bridge.

Above the broken rim of the three-fold walls the moon's unearthly splendor made visible a vast confusion of crumbling cornices, blank walls, turrets, domes, and towers, the gnarled limbs of dead trees, the luxuriant dark foliage of banian and pepal, palm and acacia. But nothing moved and there was not a light to be seen. These things with the silence told the tale of death. With the cessation of the ringing hoofbeats the stillness had closed down upon the riders like a spell to break the which were to invite the wrath of the undying gods themselves. Other than the silken breathing of the horses, an occasional muffled thud or the jingle of a bridle-chain as one pawed the earth or tossed his head, they heard no sound. The unending hum of a living city was not there. Sister of Babylon, Nineveh and Tyre, kin to Chitor and that proud city of the plains that Jai Singh abandoned when he built him his City of Victory, Kathiapur is as Tadmor—dead. The shell remains; the soul has flown.

A gasp from the woman and an oath from the sowar startled Amber out of somber apprehensions into which he had been plunged by contemplation of this impregnable fortress of desolation. Gone was his lust for peril, gone his high, heedless joy of adventure, gone the intoxication which had been his who had drunk deep of the cup of Romance; there remained only the knowledge that he, alone and single-handed, was to pit his wits against the invisible and mighty forces that lurked in hiding within those walls, to seem to submit to their designs and so find his way to the woman of his love, tear her from the grasp of the unseen, and with her escape...

Naraini had, indeed, no need to cry aloud or clutch his hand in order to apprise him that the Eye was vigilant. He himself had seen it break forth, a lurid star of emerald light suspended high above the dark heart of the city—high in the air where the moment gone there had been nothing; so powerful that it shaded with sickly pallor the face of the woman, who clung shuddering to Amber; so unpresaged its appearance and so malign its augury that it shook even the skepticism of him whose reason had been nourished by the materialism of the Occident.

Slowly, while they watched, the star descended, foot by foot dropping until the topmost pinnacle of a hidden temple seemed to support it; and there it rested, throbbing with light, now bright, now dull.

Amber shook himself impatiently. "Silly charlatanry!" he muttered, irritated by his own susceptibility to its sinister suggestion.... "I'd like to know how they manage it, though; the light itself's comprehensible enough, but their control of it.... If there were enough wind, I'd suspect a kite...."

"Thou art not dismayed, my king?"

He laughed, not quite as successfully as he could have wished, and, "Not I, Naraini," he returned in English: a tongue which seemed somehow better suited for service in combating the esoteric influences at work upon his mind. "What's the next turn on the programme?"

"I like not that tone, nor yet that tongue." The woman shivered. "Even as the Eye seeth, my lord, so doth the Ear hear. Is it meet and wise to speak with levity of that in whose power thou shalt shortly be?"

"Perhaps not," he admitted, thoughtful. "'In whose power I shall shortly be.' ... Well, of course!"

"And thou wilt go on? Thou art not minded to withdraw thy hand?"

"Not so that you'd notice it, Naraini."

"For the sake of the reward Naraini offers thee?" she persisted dangerously.

"I don't mind telling you that you'd turn 'most any man's head, my dear," he said cheerfully, and let her interpret the words as she pleased.

She was not pleased, for her acquaintance with English was more intimate than she had chosen to admit; but if she felt any chagrin she dissimulated with her never-failing art. "Then bid me farewell, O my soul, and go!"

"Up there?" he enquired, lifting his brows.

"Aye, up the causeway and over the bridge, into the city of death."

"Alone?"

"Aye, alone and afoot, my king."

"Pleasant prospect, thanks." Amber whistled, a trifle dashed. "And then, when I get up there—?"

"One will meet thee. Go with him, fearing naught."

"And what will you do, meanwhile?"

"When thou shalt have passed the Gateway, my lord, Naraini will be waiting for thee."

"Very well." Amber threw a leg over the crupper, handed the stallion's reins to the sowar, who had dismounted and drawn near, and dropped upon his feet.

Naraini nodded to the sowar, who led the animal away. When he was out of earshot the woman leaned from the saddle, her glorious eyes to Amber's. "My king!" she breathed intensely.

But the thought of Sophia Farrell and what she might be suffering at that very moment was uppermost—obtruded itself like a wall between himself and the woman. He had no further inclination for make-believe, and he saw Naraini with eyes that nothing illuded. Quite as casually as though she had been no more to him than a chance acquaintance, he reached up, took her hand, and gave it a perfunctory shake.

"Good-night, my dear," he said amiably; and, turning, made off toward the foot of the causeway.

When he had gained it, he looked back to see her riding off at a wide angle from the causeway, heading out into the plain. When he looked again, some two or three minutes later, Naraini, the sowar, and the horses had vanished as completely as if the earth had opened to receive them. He rubbed his eyes, stared, and gave it up.

So he was alone!... With a shrug, he plodded on.

CHAPTER XVIII

THE HOODED DEATH

The causeway down which the horsemen of forgotten kings of Khandawar had clattered forth to war, in its age-old desuetude had come to decay. Between its great paving blocks grass sprouted, and here and there creepers and even trees had taken root and in the slow immutable process of their growth had displaced considerable masses of stone; so that there were pitfalls to be avoided. Otherwise a litter of rubble made the walking anything but good. Amber picked his way with caution, grumbling.

The grade was rather more steep than it had seemed to be from the plain. Now and then he stopped to regain his breath and scrub a handkerchief over his forehead, on which sweat had started despite the cold. At such times his gaze would seek inevitably and involuntarily, the lotus-pointed pinnacle whereon the Eye was poised, blazing. Its baleful

127

emerald glare coloured his mood unpleasantly. He had a fancy that the thing was actually watching him. The sensation was creepy.

For that matter, nothing that met his eye was calculated to instil cheer into his heart. Desolation worked with silence sensibly upon his thoughts, so that he presently made the alarming discovery that the bottom had dropped completely out of his stock of scepticism, leaving him seriously in danger of becoming afraid of the dark. Scowling over this, he stumbled on, telling himself that he was a fool: a conclusion so patent that neither then nor thereafter at any time did he find reason to dispute it.

After some three-quarters of an hour of hard climbing he came to the wooden bridge, and halted, surveying it with mistrust. Doubtless in the olden time a substantial but movable structure, strong enough to sustain a troop of warriors but light enough to be easily drawn up, had extended across the chasm, rendering the city impregnable from capture by assault. If so, it had long since been replaced by an airy and well-ventilated latticework of boards and timbers, none of which seemed to the wary eye any too sound. Amber selected the most solid-looking of the lot and gingerly advanced a pace or two along it. With a soft crackling a portion of the timber crumbled to dust beneath his feet. He retreated hastily to the causeway, and swore, and noticed that the Eye was watching him with malevolent interest, and swore some more. Entirely on impulse he heaved a bit of rock, possibly twenty pounds in weight, to the middle of the structure. There followed a splintering crash and the contraption dissolved like a magic-lantern effect, leaving a solitary beam about a foot in width and six or eight inches thick, spanning a flight of twenty and a drop of sixty feet. The river received the rubbish with several successive splashes, distinctly disconcerting, and Amber sat down on a boulder to think it over.

"Clever invention," he mused; "one'd think that, after taking all this trouble to get me here, they'd changed their minds about wanting me. I've a notion to change mine." He looked up at the cusped and battlemented gateway opposite him, shifted his regard to the Eye, and shook his fist vindictively at the latter. "If ever I get hold of the chap that invented you...!" An ingenious imagination failing to suggest any form of torture commensurate with the crime, he relapsed into gloomy meditation.

There seemed to be no possibility of turning back at that stage, however. Kuttarpur was rather far away, and, moreover, he doubted if he would be permitted to return. Having come thus far, he must go on. Moreover, Sophia Farrell was on the other side of that Swordwide Bridge, and such being the case, cross it he would though he were to find the next world at its end. Finally he considered that he was presently to undergo an Ordeal of some unknown nature, probably extremely unpleasant, and that this matter of the vanishing bridge must have been arranged in order to put him in a properly subdued and tractable frame of mind.

He got up and tested the remaining girder with circumspection and incredulity; but it seemed firm enough, solidly embedded in the stonework of the causeway and immovable at the city end. So he straddled it and, averting his eyes from the scenery beneath him, hitched ingloriously across, collecting splinters and a very distinct impression that, as a vocation, knight-errantry was not without its drawbacks.

When again he stood on his feet he was in the shadow of the outer gateway, the curtain of the second wall confronting him. The stillness remained unbroken but the moonlight illuminated with startling distinctness the frescoes, half obliterated by time, and they were monstrous, revolting and obscene, from a Western point of view. A bastion of the third wall hid the Eye, however; he was grateful for that.

Casting about, he discovered the second gateway at some distance to the left, and started toward it, forcing a way through a tangle of scrubby undergrowth, weeds, and thorny acacia, but had taken few steps ere a heavy splash in the river below brought him up standing, with a thumping heart. After an irresolute moment he turned back to see for himself, and found his apprehension only too well grounded; the Swordwide Bridge was gone, displaced by an agency which had been prompt to seek cover—though he confessed himself unable to suggest where that cover had been found. There was no one visible on the causeway, and nobody skulked in the shadows of the bastions of the main gate. Furthermore it seemed hardly possible that in so scant a space of time human hands could have worked that heavy beam out of its sockets. And if the hands had been human (of course any other hypothesis were ridiculous) what had become of their owners?

He gave it up, considering that it were futile to badger his wits for the how and the wherefore. The important fact remained that he was a prisoner in dead Kathiapur, his retreat cut off, and—Here he made a second discovery, infinitely more shocking: his pistol was gone.

Amber remembered distinctly examining the weapon in Dulla Dad's boat, since when he had found no occasion to think of it. Now either it had jolted out of his pocket in that wild ride from Kuttarpur, or else Naraini had managed deftly to abstract it while in his arms by the summer palace, or when, later, she had shrunk against him in real or affected terror of the Eye. Of the two explanations his reason favoured the second. But he made no audible comment, though his thoughts were as black as his brow and as grimly fashioned as the set of his jaw.

Turning back at length he made his way to the second gateway and from it to the third, under the lewdly sculptured arch of which he stopped and gasped, forgetting himself as for the first time Kathiapur the Fallen was revealed to him in all the awful beauty of its naked desolation.

A wide and stately avenue stretched away from the portals, between rows of dwellings, palaces of marble and stone, tombs and mausoleums, with meaner houses of sun-dried brick and rubble, roofless all and disintegrating in the slow, terrible process of the years. Here a wall had caved in, there an arch had fallen out. The thoroughfare was strewn with fallen lintels, broken marble screens, blocks of red sandstone, bricks, and in between them the fig and pipal nourished with the bebel-thorn, the ak, the mimosa, the insidious convolvulus twining everywhere. At the far end of the street a yawning black arch rose in the white, beautiful façade of a marble temple on whose uppermost pinnacle the Eye hovered, staring horridly.

As Amber moved forward small, alert ghosts rose from the undergrowth and scurried silently thence: a circumstance which made him very unhappy. Even a brilliant chorus of sharp barks from an adjacent street failed to convince him that he had merely disturbed a pack of jackals, after all, and not the disconsolate brooding wraiths of those who had died and been buried in the imposing ruined tombs, what time Kathiapur boasted ten thousand swords and elephants by the herd.

The way was difficult and Amber tired. After a while, having seen nothing but the jackals, an owl or two, several thousand bats and a crawling thing which had lurched along in the shadow of a wall some distance away, giving an admirable imitation of a badly wounded man pulling himself over the ground, and making strange gutteral noises—Amber concluded to wait for the guide Naraini had promised him. He turned aside and seated himself upon the edge of a broken sandstone tomb. The silence was appalling and for relief he took refuge in cheap irreverence. "Home," he observed aloud, "never was like this."

A heart-rending sigh from the tomb behind him was followed by a rattle of dislodged rubbish. Amber found himself unexpectedly in the middle of the street and, without stopping to debate the method of his getting there with such unprecedented rapidity, looked back hopefully to the tomb. At the same moment a black-shrouded figure swept out of it and moved a few paces down the street, then paused and beckoned him with a gaunt arm. "I wish," said Amber earnestly, "I had that gun."

The figure was apparently that of a native swathed in black from his head to his heels and seemed the more strikingly peculiar in view of the fact that, as far as Amber could determine, he had neither eyes nor features although his head was without any sort of covering. He gulped over the proposition for an instant, then stepped forward.

"Evidently my appointed cicerone," he considered. "Unquestionably this ghost-dance is excellently stage-managed.... Though, of course, I *had* to pick out that particular tomb."

He followed in the wake of the figure, which sped on with a singular motion, something between a walk and a glide, conscious that his equanimity had been restored rather than shaken by the incident. "You wouldn't think," he reflected, "that a man like Salig Singh would lend himself to anything so childish. Still, I'm not through with it yet." He conceived a scheme to steal up behind his guide and strip him of his masquerade, but though he mended his pace he got no nearer, and eventually abandoned it on the consideration that it was probably most inadvisable. After all, he had to remember that he was there for a purpose, and a very serious one, and that properly to further that purpose he must comport himself with dignity, submissively, accepting, at least with a show of ease, each new development of the affair along its prearranged lines. And so he held on in pursuit of the black shadow, passing forsaken temples and lordly pleasure-houses, all marble tracery and fretwork, standing apart in what had once been noble gardens, sunken tanks all weed-grown and rank with slime, humbler dooryards and cots on whose hearthstones the fires for centuries had been cold—his destination evidently the temple of the unspeakable Eye.

As they drew nearer the leading shadow forsook the shade of the walls which he had seemed to favour, sweeping hastily across a plaza white with moonglare and without pause on into the black, gaping hole beyond the marble arch.

Here for the first time Amber hung back, stopping a score of feet from the door, his nerves a-jangle. He did not falter in his purpose; he was going to enter the inky portal, but ... would he ever leave it? And the world was still sweet to him. His quick, darting gaze registered a dozen impressions in as many seconds: of the silver splendour spilled so lavishly upon the soulless corpse of the city, of the high, bright sky, of dead black shadows sharp-edged against the radiance, of the fleet flitting spectre that was really a flying-fox....

Afar a hyena laughed with a sardonic intonation wholly uncalled-for—it was blood-curdling, besides. And down the street a melancholy air breathed gently, sighing like a soul astray.

"This won't do," he told himself; "it can't be worse inside than out here."

He took firm hold of his reason and went on across the dark threshold, took three uncertain strides into the limitless unknown, and pulled up short, hearing nothing, unable to see a yard before him. Then with a terrific crash like a thunder-clap the great doors swung to behind him. He whirled about with a stifled cry, conscious of a mad desire to find the doors again, took a step or two toward them, paused to wonder if he were moving in the right direction, moved a little to the left, half turned, and was lost. Reverberating, the echoes of the crash rolled far away and back again, diminishing in volume, dying until they were no more than as a whisper adrift in the silence, until that was gone....

Profound night enveloped him, vast, breathless, without dimensions. One can endure the blackness that abides within four well-kenned walls; but night unrelieved by the least gleam of light, night without bounds or measurements, enfolding one like a stifling blanket and instilling into the brain the fear of nameless things, quickening the respiration and oppressing the heart—that is another thing entirely, and that is what Amber found in the Temple of the Bell. Darkness swam visibly before his eyes, like a fluid. The sound of his constrained breathing seemed most loud and unnatural. He could hear his heart rumbling like a distant drum.

Digging his nails into his palms, he waited; and in the suspense of dread began to count the seconds.

One minute ... two ... three ... four....

He shifted his weight from one foot to the other....

Seven ...

He passed a hand across his face and brought it away wet with perspiration....

Nine ...

In some remote spot a bell began to toll; at first slowly—*clang!... clang!... clang!*—then more quickly, until the roar of its sonorous, gong-like tones seemed to fill all the world and to set it a-tremble. Then, insensibly, the tempo became more sedate, the fierce clamour of it moderated, and Amber abruptly was alive to the fact that the bell was *speaking*—that its voice, deep, clear, sound, metallic, was rolling forth again and again a question couched in purest Sanskrit:

"*Who is there?... Who is there?... Who is there?...*"

The hair lifted on his scalp and he swallowed hard in the effort to answer; but the lie stuck in his throat: he was not Rutton and ... and it is very hard to lie effectively when you stand in stark darkness with a mouth dry as dust and your hair stirring at the roots because of the intensely impersonal and aloof accents of an inhuman Bell-voice, tolling away out of Nowhere.

"*Who is there?*"

Again he failed to answer. Somewhere near him he heard a slight noise as of a man moving impatiently; and then a whisper: "Respond, thou fool!"

"Art thou come, O Chosen of the Gateway?" the Bell-voice rang.

"I ... I am come," Amber managed to reply. And so still and small sounded his own voice in the huge spaces of the place that he was surprised to find he had been heard.

"Hear ye!" rang the Bell. "Hear ye, O Lords and Rulers in Medhyama! O Children of my Gateway, hear ye well! He is come! He stands upon the threshold of the Gateway!"

Resonant, the echoes of those awe-inspiring tones died upon the stillness, and in response a faint sighing rose and, momentarily growing in volume, became as the roaring of a mighty wind; and suddenly it was abrupted, leaving only a ringing in the ears.

A great drum roared like the crack of Doom; and Amber's jaw dropped. For in the high roof of the temple a six-foot slab had been noiselessly withdrawn, and through it a cold shaft of moonlight fell, cutting the gloom like a gigantic rapier, and smote with its immaculate radiance the true Gateway of Swords.

Not six paces from him it leaped out of the darkness in an iridescent sheen: an arch a scant ten feet in height, and in span double the width of a big man's shoulders, woven across like a weaver's frame with ribbons of pale fire. But the ribbons were of steel—steel blades, sharp, bright, gleaming: a countless array of curved tulwars and crescent scimetars, broad jataghans, short and ugly kukurees, long kutars with straight ends, slender deadly patas, snake-like bichwas; swords with jewelled hilts and engraved and damascened blades; sabres with channels cut from point to guard wherein small pearls ran singing; khands built for service and for parade; swords of every style and period in all the history of India. With their pommels cunningly affixed so that their points touched and interlaced, yet swung free, they lined the piers of the arch from base to span and all the graceful sweep of the intrados, a curtain of shimmering, trembling steel, barring the way to the Mystery beyond. Which was—darkness.

"O ye Swords!" belled the Voice.... "O ye Swords that have known no dishonour! O ye Swords that have sung in the grasp of my greatest! Swords of Jehangar, Akbar, Alamgir! Swords of Alludin, Humayun, Shah Jehan! Swords of Timur-Leng, Arungzeb, Rao Rutton!..."

The invocation seemed interminable. Amber recognised almost every name noted in the annals and legends of Hindustan....

"Hearken, O my Swords! He, thy Chosen, prayeth for entry! What is thy welcome?"

One by one the blades began to shiver, clashing their neighbours, until the curtain of steel glimmered and glistened like phosphorescence in a summer sea, and the place was filled with the music of their contact; and through their clamour boomed the Bell:

"O my Chosen!" Amber started and held himself firmly in hand. "Look well, look well! Here is thy portal to kingship and glory!"

He frowned and took a step forward as if he would throw himself through the archway; for he had suddenly remembered with compelling vividness that Sophia Farrell was to be won only by that passage. But as he moved the swords clattered afresh and swung outwards, presenting a bristle of points. And he stopped, while the Voice, indifferent and remote as always, continued to harangue him.

"If thy heart, O my Chosen, be clean, unsullied with fear and guile; if thy faith be the faith of thy fathers and thy honour rooted in love of thy land; if thou hast faith in the strength of thy hands to hold the reins of Empire ... enter, having no fear."

"Trick-work," he told himself. He set his teeth with determination. "Hope they don't see fit to cut me to pieces on suspicion. Here goes." He moved forward with a firm step until his bosom all but touched the points.

Instantaneously, with another clash as of cymbals, the blades were deflected and returned to their first position, closing the way. He hesitated. Then, "That shan't stop me!" he said through his teeth, and pushed forward, heart in mouth. He breasted the curtain and felt it give; the blades yielded jealously, closing round his body like cold caressing arms; he felt their chill kisses on his cheeks and hands, even through his clothing he was conscious of their clinging, deadly touch. Abruptly they swung entirely away, leaving the entrance clear, and he was drawing a free breath when the moon glare showed him the swords returned to position with the speed of light. He jumped for his life and escaped being slashed to pieces by the barest inch. They swung to behind him; and again the drum roared, while afar there arose a furious, eldritch wailing of conches. Overhead the opening disappeared and the light was shut out. In darkness as of the Hall of Eblis the conches were stilled and the echoes ebbed into a silence that held sway for many minutes ere again the Bell spoke.

"Stretch forth thy hand."

Somewhat shaken, Amber held out an open palm before him. A second time the gusty sighing arose and breathed through the night, increasing until the very earth beneath him seemed to rock with the magnitude of the sound, until, at its highest, it ceased and was as if it had not been; not even an echo sang its passing. Then out of nothingness something plopped into Amber's hand and his fingers closed convulsively about it. It was a hand, very small, small as a child's, gnarled and hard as steel and cold as ice.

Amber sunk his teeth into his lower lip and subdued an almost uncontrollable impulse to scream and fling the thing away; for his sense of touch told him that the hand was dead. And yet he became sensible that it was tugging at his own, and he yielded to its persuasion, permitting himself to be led on for so long a journey that his fingers clasping the little hand grew numb with cold ere it was over. He could by no means say whither he was being conducted, but was conscious of a long, gradual descent. Many times he swept his free arm out round him, but touched nothing.

Abruptly the guiding hand was twisted away. He stopped incontinently, and possessed himself with what patience he could muster throughout another long wait tempered by strange sibilant whisperings and rustlings in the void all about him.

Without any forewarning two heavy hands gripped him, one on either shoulder, and he was forced to his knees. At the same instant, with a snapping crackle a spurt of blue flame shot down from the zenith, and where it fell with a thunderclap a dazzling glare of emerald light shot up breasthigh.

To his half-blinded eyes it seemed, for a time, to dance suspended in the air before him. A vapour swirled up from it, a thin cloud, luminous. By degrees he made out its source, a small, brazen bowl on a tripod.

A confusion of hushed voices swelled as had the sound of that mighty, rushing, impalpable wind, and died more slowly.

Conscious that his features were in strong light, he strove to exhibit an impassiveness that belied his temper; then glancing round beneath lowered eyelids he sought to determine something of the nature of his surroundings, but could see little. The hands had left his shoulders the minute his knees touched the floor; he knelt utterly alone in the middle of what seemed to be a vast hall, or cavern, of which the size was but faintly suggested. As his eyes became accustomed to the chiaroscuro he became aware of monstrous images of stone that appeared to advance from and retreat to the far walls on either hand as the green light flared and fell, and of a great silent and motionless concourse of people grouped about the massive pedestals—a crowd as contained and impassive as the gods that towered above its heads, blending into the gloom that shrouded the high roof of the place.

In front of him he could see nothing beyond the noiselessly wavering flame. But presently a hand appeared, as if by magic, above the bowl—a hand, bony, brown, and long of finger, that seemed attached to nothing—and cast something like a powder into the fire. There followed a fizz and puff of vapour, and a strong and heady gust of incense was wafted into Amber's face. Again and again the hand appeared, sprinkling powder in the brazier, until the smoke clouded the atmosphere with its fluent, eddying coils.

The gooseflesh that had pricked out on Amber's skin subsided, and his qualms went with it. "Greek fire burning in a bowl," he explained the phenomenon; "and a native with his arm wrapped to the wrist in black is feeding it. Not a bad effect, though."

It was, perhaps, as well that he had not been deceived, for there was a horror to come that required all his strength to face. He became conscious that something was moving between him and the brazier—something which he had incuriously assumed to be a piece of dirty cloth left there carelessly. But now he saw it stir, squirm, and upend, unfolding itself and lifting its head to the leaping flame: an immense cobra, sleek and white as ivory, its swelling hood as large as a man's two hands, with a binocular mark on it as yellow as topaz, and with vicious eyes glowing like twin rubies in its vile little head.

Amber's breath clicked in his throat and he shrank back, rising; but this instinctive move had been provided against and before his knees were fairly off the rocky floor he was forced down again by the hands on his shoulders. He was unable to take his eyes from the monster, and though terror such as man is heir to lay cold upon his heart, he did not again attempt to stir.

There was now no sound. Alone and undisturbed the bleached viper warmed to its dance with the pulsing flame, turning and twisting, weaving and writhing in its infernal glare....

"Hear ye, O my peoples!"

Amber jumped. The Voice had seemed to ring out from a point directly overhead.

He looked up and discovered above him, vague in the obscurity, the outlines of a gigantic bell, hanging motionless. The green glare, shining on its rim and partly illumining its empty hollow (he saw no clapper) revealed the sheen of the bronze of which it was fashioned.

Out of its immense bowl, the Voice rolled like thunder:

"Hear ye, O my peoples!"

A responsive murmur ascended from the company round the walls:

"We hear! We hear, O Medhyama!"

"Mark well this man, O Children of my Gateway! Mark well! Out of ye all have I chosen him to lead thee in the work of healing; for I thy Mother, I Medhyama, I Bharuta, I the Body from which ye are sprung, call me by whatever name ye know me—I am laid low with a great sickness.... Yea, I am stricken and laid low with a sickness."

A great and bitter wailing arose from the multitude.

"Yea, I am overcome with a faintness, and my strength is gone out from me, and my limbs are as water; I am sick with a fever and languish; in my veins runs the Evil like fire and like poison; and I burn and am stricken; I toss in my torment and murmur, and the sound of my Voice has come to thine ears. Ye have heard me and answered. The tale of my sufferings is known to ye. Say, shall I perish?"

In the brazier the flame leaped high and subsided, and with it the cobra leaped and sank low upon its coils. From the people a mighty shout of negation went up, so that the walls rang with it, and the echoes were bandied back and forth, insensibly decreasing through many minutes. When all was still the Voice began to chant again, and the flames blazed higher and brighter, while the cobra resumed its mystic dance.

Amber knelt on in a semi-stupor, staring glassily at the light and the serpent.

"I, thine old Mother, have called ye together to help in my healing. From my feet to my head I am eaten with pestilence; yea, I am devoured and possessed by the Evil. Even of old was it thus with thy Mother; long since she complained of the Plague that is Scarlet— moaned and cried out and turned in her misery.... But ye failed me. Then my peoples were weaklings and their hearts all were craven; the Scarlet Evil dismayed them; they fled from its power and left it to batten on me in my sickness."

A deep groan welled in uncounted throats and resounded through the cavern.

"Will ye fail me again, O my Children?"

"Nay, nay, O our Mother!"

"Too long have I suffered and been patient in silence. Now must I be cleansed and made whole as of old time; yea, I must be purged altogether and the Evil cast out from me. It is time.... Ye have heard, ye have answered; make ready, for the day of the cleansing approacheth. Whet thy swords for the days of the healing, for my cleansing can be but by steel. Yea, thy swords shall do away with the Evil, and the land shall run red with the blood of Bharuta, the blood of thy Mother; it shall run to the sea as a river, bearing with it the Red Evil. So and no otherwise shall I, thine old Mother, be healed and made whole again."

"Aye, aye, O our Mother!"

The flames, dying, rose once more, and the Voice continued, but with a change of temper. It was now a clarion call, stirring the blood like martial music.

"Ye shall show me your swords for a token.... Swords of the North, are ye ready?"

"We are ready, old Mother!"

With a singing shiver of steel, all around the walls, in knots and clusters, naked blades leaped up, flashing.

"Swords of the East, are ye loyal?"

"Aye, old Mother!"

And the tally of swords was doubled.

"Swords of the South, are ye thirsty?"

A third time the crashing response shattered the echoes.

"Swords of the West, do ye love me?"

With the fourth ringing shout and showing of steel, a silence fell. The walls were veritably hedged with quivering blades, all a-gleam in the ghastly glare of green. Over the sculptured faces of the great idols flickering shadows played, so that they seemed to move and grimace, as if with approbation.

Amber was watching the serpent—dazed and weary as if with a great need of sleep. Even the salvos of shouts came to him as from a great distance. To the clangour of the Bell alone he had become abnormally sensitive; every fibre of his being shuddered, responsive to its weird nuances.

It returned to its solemn and stately intoning.

"Out of ye all have I chosen and fixed upon one who shall lead ye. Through him shall my strength be made manifest, my Will be made known to my peoples. Him must ye serve and obey; to him must ye bow down and be humble. Say, are ye pleased? Will ye have him, my Children?"

Without an instant's delay a cry of ratification rang to the roof. "Yea, O our Mother! Him we will serve and obey, to him bow down and be humble."

The Voice addressed itself directly to the kneeling man. He stiffened and roused.

"Thou hast heard of the honour we confer upon thee—I Medhyama, thy Mother, and these my children, thy brothers. Ye shall lead and shall rule in Bharuta. Are ye ready?"

Half hypnotised, Amber opened his mouth, but no words came. His chin dropped to his breast.

"Thy strength must be known to my peoples; they must see thee put to the proof of thy courage, that they may know thee to be the man for their leader.... Ye are ready?"

He was unable to move a finger.

"Stretch out thine arms!"

He shuddered and tried to obey. The Voice rang imperative.

"Stretch forth thine arms for the testing!"

Somehow, mechanically, he succeeded in raising his arms and holding them rigid before him. Alarmed by the movement, the cobra turned with a hiss, waving his poisonous head. But the Virginian made no offer to withdraw his hands. His eyes were wide and staring and his face livid.

A subdued murmur came from the men clustered round the idols, in semi-darkness.

The Bell boomed forth like an organ.

"O hooded Death.... O Death, who art trained to my service! Thou before whom all men stand affrighted! Thou who canst look into their hearts and read them as a scroll that

135

is unrolled ... Look deep into the heart of my Chosen! Judge if he be worthy or wanting, judge if he be false or true ... Judge him, O Death!"

Before Amber the great serpent was oscillating like a pendulum, its little tongue playing like forked red lightning, its loathsome red eyes holding his own. Terror gripped his heart, and his soul curdled. He would have cried out, but that his tongue clave to the roof of his mouth. He could not have moved had he willed to.

"Look well, O Death, and judge him!"

The dance of the Hooded Death changed in character, grew more frenzied; the white writhing coils melted into one another in dizzying confusion; figure merged into figure like smoke.... The suspense grew intolerable.

"Hast thou judged him, O Death?"

Instantly the white cobra reared up to its utmost and remained poised over Amber, barely moving save for the almost imperceptible throbbing of the hood and the incessant darting of the forked tongue.

"If he be loyal, then spare him ..."

The hood did not move. Amber's flesh crawled with unspeakable dread.

"If he be faithless, then ... *strike!*"

For another moment the cobra maintained the tensity. Then slowly, cruel head waving, hood shrinking, eyes losing their deathly lustre, coil by coil it sank.

A thick murmur ran the round of the walls, swelling into an inarticulate cry, which beat upon Amber's ears like the raving of a far-off surf. From his lips a strangled sob broke, and, every muscle relaxing, he lurched forward.

Alarmed, in a trice the cobra was up again, hood distended to the bursting point, head swinging so swiftly that the eye could not follow it. In another breath would come the final thrust....

A firearm exploded behind Amber, singeing his cheek with its flame. He fell over sideways, barely escaping the head of the cobra, which, with its hood blown to tatters, writhed in convulsions, its malignant tongue straining forth as if in one last attempt to reach his hand.

A second shot followed the first and then a brisk, confused fusillade. Amber heard a man scream out in mortal agony, and the dull sound of a heavy body falling near him; but, coincident with the second report, the brazier had been overturned and its light extinguished as if sucked up into the air.

CHAPTER XIX

RUTTON'S DAUGHTER

In darkness the blacker for the sudden disappearance of the light, somebody stumbled over Amber—stumbled and swore in good English. The Virginian sat up, crying out as weakly as a child: "Labertouche!" A voice said: "Thank God!" He felt strong hands lift him to his feet. He clung to him who had helped him, swaying like a drunkard, wits a-swirl in the brain thus roughly awakened from semi-hypnosis.

"Here," said Labertouche's voice, "take my hand and follow. We're in for it now!"

He caught Amber's hand and dragged him, yielding and unquestioning, rapidly through a chaotic rush of unseen bodies.

The firing had electrified the tense-strung audience. With a pandemonium of shrieks, oaths, shouts, orders unheard and commands unheeded, a concerted rush was made from every quarter to the spot where the doomed man had been kneeling. Men running blundered into running men and cannoned off at direct angles to their original courses, without realising it. Disorder reigned rampant, and the cavern rang with a thousand echoes, while the Bell awoke and roared a raging tocsin, redoubling the din. No man could have said where he stood or whither he ran—save one, perhaps. That one was at Amber's side and had laid his course beforehand and knew that both their lives depended upon his sticking to it without deviation. To him a rush of a hundred feet in a direct line meant salvation, the least deviation from it, death. He plunged through the scurrying masses without regard for any hurt that might come either to him or to his charge.

A red glare of torches was breaking out over the heads of the mob before they gained their destination. Amber saw that they were making for a corner formed by the junction of one of the pedestals with a rocky wall. He was now recovering rapidly and able to appreciate that they stood a good chance of winning away; for the natives were all converging toward the centre of the cavern, and apparently none heeded them. Nevertheless Labertouche, releasing him, put a revolver in his hand.

"Don't hesitate to shoot if any one comes this way!" he said. "I've got to get this door open and..."

He broke off with an ejaculation of gratitude; for while he had been speaking, his fingers busily groping in the convolutions of the sculptured pedestal had encountered what he sought, and now he pulled out an iron bar two feet or so in length and as thick as a woman's wrist. Inserting this in a socket, as one familiar with the trick, he put his weight upon it; a carved sandstone slab slid back silently, disclosing a black cavernous opening.

"In with you," panted Labertouche, removing the lever. "Don't delay...."

Amber did not. He took with him a hazy impression of a vast, vaulted hall filled with a ruddy glare of torchlight, a raving rabble of gorgeously attired natives in its centre. Then the opening received him and he found himself in a black hole of an underground gallery—a place that reeked with the dank odours of the tomb.

Labertouche followed and with the aid of a small electric pocket-lamp discovered another socket for the lever. A moment later the slab moved back into place, and the Englishman dropped the metal bar. "If there were only some way of locking that opening," he gasped, "we'd be fairly safe. As it is, we'll have to look nippy. That was a near call—as near a one as ever you'll know, my boy; and we're not out yet. What are you doing?" he added, as Amber stopped to pick up the lever.

"It isn't a bad weapon," said the Virginian, "at a pinch. You'll want your gun, and that she-devil, Naraini, got mine."

"Keep the one I gave you and don't be afraid to use it. I've another and a couple of knives for good measure. That Mohammedan prince whom I persuaded to change places with me was a walking arsenal." Labertouche chuckled. "Come along," he said, and drew ahead at a dog-trot.

They sped down a passage which delved at a sharp grade through solid rock. Now and again it turned and struck away in another direction. Once they descended—or rather fell down—a short, steep flight of steps. At the bottom Amber stopped.

"Hold on!" he cried.

Labertouche pulled up impatiently. "What's the matter?"

"Sophia—!"

"Trust me, dear boy, and come along."

Persuaded, Amber gave in, blundering on after Labertouche, who loped along easily, with the confidence of one who threads known ways, the spot-light from his lamp dancing along the floor several feet before him. Otherwise they moved between walls of Stygian darkness.

It was some time later that Labertouche extinguished his lamp and threw a low word of warning over his shoulder. Synchronously Amber discerned, far ahead, a faint glow of yellow light. As they bore down upon it with unmoderated speed, he could see that it emanated from a rough-hewn doorway, opening off the passage. Before it a man stood guard with a naked sword.

"*Johar!*" he greeted them in the Mahar form: "O, warrior!"

"*Johar!*" returned Labertouche, panting heavily. He closed upon the native confidently, but was brought up short by a peremptory sweep of the sword, coupled with an equally imperative demand for an explanation of their haste. The Englishman replied with apparent difficulty, as if half-winded. "It is an order, *Johar*. The woman is to be brought to the Hall of the Bell."

"You have the word?" The Mahar lowered his sword. "It hath been said to me that—"

Labertouche stumbled over his feet, and caught the speaker for support. The native gurgled in a sodden fashion, dropped his sword, stared stupidly at Labertouche, and put an uncertain hand to his throat. Then he lurched heavily and collapsed upon himself.

The secret-agent stepped back, dropping the knife he had used. "Poor devil!" he said in a compassionate undertone. "That was cold-blooded murder, Mr. Amber."

"Necessary?" gasped Amber, regarding with horror the bloodstained heap of rags and flesh at his feet.

"Judge for yourself," said Labertouche coolly, stepping over the body. "Here," he added, pausing by the doorway, "you go first; she knows you."

He pushed Amber on ahead. Stooping, the Virginian entered a small, rude chamber hollowed out of the rock of Kathiapur. A crude lamp in a bracket furnished all its illumination, filling it with a reek of hot oil. Amber was vaguely aware of the figures of two women—one standing in a corner, the other seated dejectedly upon a charpoy, her head against the wall. As he lifted his head after passing under the low lintel, the woman in the corner fired at him point-blank.

The Virginian saw the jet of flame spurt from her hand and felt the bullet's impact upon the wall behind his head. He flung himself upon her instantly. There was a moment of furious struggle, while the cell echoed with the reverberations of the shot and the screaming of the woman on the charpoy. The pistol exploded again as he grappled with the would-be murderess; the bullet, passing up his sleeve, creased his left arm as with a white-hot iron, and tore out through the cloth on his shoulder. He twisted brutally the wrist that held the weapon, and the woman dropped it with a cry of pain.

"You would!" he cried, and threw her from him, putting a foot upon the pistol.

She reeled back against the wall and crouched there, trembling, her cheeks on fire, her eyes aflame with rage. "You dog!" she shrilled in Hindi—and spat at him like a maddened cat. Then he recognised her.

"Naraini!" He stepped back in his surprise, his right hand seeking instinctively the wrist of his left, which was numb with pain.

His change of position left the pistol unguarded, and the woman swooped down upon it like a bird of prey; but before she could get her fingers on its grip, Labertouche stepped between them, fended her off, and quietly possessed himself of the weapon.

"Your pardon, madam," he said gravely.

Naraini retreated, shaking with fury, and Amber employed the respite to recognise Sophia Farrell in the woman on the charpoy. She was still seated, prevented from rising by bonds about her wrists and ankles, and though unnaturally pale, her anguish of fear and despair had set its marks upon her face without one whit detracting from the appeal of her beauty. He went to her immediately, and as their eyes met, hers flamed with joy, relief and—he dared believe—a stronger emotion.

"You—you're not hurt, Mr. Amber?"

"Not at all. The bullet went out through my sleeve. And you?" He dropped on his knees, with his pocket-knife severing the ends of rope that bound her.

"I'm all right." She took his hands, helping herself to rise. "Thank you," she said, her eyes shining, a flush of colour suffusing her face with glory.

"Did you cut those ropes, Amber?" Labertouche interposed curtly.

"Yes. Why?"

The Englishman explained without turning from his sombre and morose regard of Naraini. "Too bad—we'll have to tie this woman up, somehow. She's a complication I hadn't foreseen.... Here; you'd better leave me to attend to her—you and Miss Farrell. Go on down the gallery—to the left, I'll catch up with you."

The pistol which he still held lent to his demand a sinister significance of which he was, perhaps, thoughtless. But Sophia Farrell heard, saw, and surmised.

"No!" she cried, going swiftly to the secret-agent. "No!" She put a hand upon his arm, but he shook it off.

"Did you hear me, Amber?" said Labertouche, still watching the queen.

"What do you mean to do?" insisted Sophia. "You can't—you mustn't—"

"This is no time for half-measures, Miss Farrell," Labertouche told her brusquely. "Our lives hang in the balance—Mr. Amber's, yours, mine. Please go."

"You promise not to harm her?"

"Amber!" cried the Englishman impatiently. "Will you—"

"Please, Miss Farrell!" begged Amber, trying to take the girl's hand and draw her away.

"I won't!" she declared. "I'll not move a step until he promises. You don't understand. No matter what the danger she's—"

"She's a fiend incarnate," Labertouche broke in. "Amber, get that girl—"

"She's my sister!" cried Sophia. "*Now* will you understand?"

"What!" The two men exclaimed as one.

"She's my sister," the girl repeated, holding up her head defiantly, her cheeks burning— "my sister by adoption. We were brought up together. She was the daughter of an old friend of my father's—an Indian prince. A few years ago she ran away—"

"Thank God!" said Amber from the bottom of his soul; and, "Ah, you would!" cried Labertouche tensely, as Naraini seized the opportunity, when his attention was momentarily diverted, to break for freedom.

Amber saw the flash of a steel blade in the woman's hand as she struck at the secret-agent, and the latter, stepping back, deflected the blow with a guarding forearm. Then, with the quickness of a snake, Naraini stooped, glided beneath his arms, and slipped from the cell.

With a smothered oath Labertouche leaped to the doorway, lifting his pistol; but he was no quicker than Sophia, who caught his arm and held him back. "No," she panted; "not even for our lives—not at that price!"

He yielded unexpectedly. "Of course you are perfectly right, Miss Farrell," said he, with a little bow. "I'm sorry that circumstances … But come! She'll have this hornet's nest about our ears in a brace of seconds. Hark to that!"

A long, shrill shriek echoed down the gallery. Labertouche shrugged and turned to the left. "Come along," he said. "Amber, take Miss Farrel's hand and keep close to me." He led the way from the cell at a brisk pace—one, indeed, that taxed Sophia's powers of endurance to maintain. Amber aided her as much as he might, but that was little; the walls of the passageway were too close together to permit him to be by her side much of the time. For the most part he had to lead the way, himself guided by the swiftly moving patch of light cast by Labertouche's bull's-eye. But through it all he was buoyed up and exhilarated out of all reason by the consciousness of the hand that lay trustfully in his own; a hand soft and small and warm and (though he could not see it) white, all white! More, it was the hand of his wife to be; he felt this now with an unquestioning assurance. He wondered if she shared the subject of his thoughts …

The gallery sloped at varying grades, more or less steep—mostly more—and minute by minute the air became more dank and cold. At an unseen turning, where another passage branched away, a biting wind swept out of the black nowhere, chilling them to the marrow. Deeper and still deeper, into the very bowels of the earth, it seemed, the secret-agent led them, finding his way with an unfaltering confidence that exalted Amber's admiration of him to the pitch of hero-worship.

At length the gallery dipped and ran level, and now, while still cold, the wind that blew in their faces was cleaner, burdened with less of the clammy effluvium of death and decay; and then, abruptly, the walls narrowed suddenly, so that Amber was forced to surrender possession of the girl's hand and to fall behind her. She went forward without question, following the dancing spotlight.

Amber paused to listen for sounds of pursuit, but hearing nothing save the subdued sigh of the draught between the straitened walls of rock, followed until the walls fell away and his hands, outstretched, failed to touch them, and he was aware that the stone beneath his feet had given way to gravel. He halted, calling guardedly to Labertouche.

The secret-agent's voice came from some distance. "It's all right, my boy. Miss Farrell is with me. Come along."

There was an *élan* in his tone that bespoke a spirit of gratulation and relief and led Amber to suspect that they were very close upon the end of their flight, near to escape from the subterranean ways of Kathiapur the dead. He proceeded at discretion in the direction of Labertouche's voice—the light being invisible—and brought up flat against a dead wall. Coincidently he heard Sophia exclaim with surprise and delight, somewhere off on his left, and, turning, he saw her head and shoulders move across a patch of starlit sky. In half a dozen strides he overtook her.

They stood on a low, pebbly ledge, just outside the black maw of the passage—an entrance hidden in a curtain-like fold in the face of the cliff that towered above them, casting an ink-black shadow. But beyond it the emblazoned firmament glowed irradiant, and at their feet the encircling waters ran, a broad ribbon of black silk purling between the cliff and the opposing shores, where a thicket of tamarisks rose, a black and ragged wall.

Labertouche strode off into the water. "Straight ahead," he announced; "don't worry— 'tisn't more than knee-deep at the worst. I've horses waiting on the other side—"

"Horses!" Amber interrupted. "Great heavens, man, you're—you're omniscient!"

"No—lucky," Labertouche retorted briskly. "Where'd I've been without Ram Nath? He's taking care of the animals…. Come along. What're you waiting for? Don't you know—" He turned to see the girl hesitant, though with lifted skirts. "Oh," he said in an accent of understanding, and came back. "If you'll help me, Amber, I daresay we can get Miss Farrell across without a wetting."

He offered to clasp hands with the Virginian and so make a seat; but Amber had a happier thought.

"I think I can manage by myself, thank you—if Miss Farrell will trust me."

His eyes met the girl's, and in hers he read trust and faith unending: he was conscious of a curious fluttering in his bosom.

"Trust *you!*" she said, with a little, broken laugh, and gave herself freely to his arms.

Labertouche grunted and turned his back, wading out into the stream with a great splashing.

Amber straightened up, holding her very close to him, and that with ease. Had she been thrice as heavy he could have borne her with as little care as he did his own immeasurably lightened heart in that hour of fulfilment. And she lay snug and confident, her arms round his neck, the shadowed loveliness of her face very near to him. The faint and elusive fragrance of her hair was sweet and heady in the air he breathed; he could read her eyes, and their allure and surrender was like a draught of wine to him. He felt the strength of ten men invigorate him, and his soul was sober with a great happiness. But a little while and she would be in safety; already her salvation seemed assured.... The further bank neared all too quickly. He would willingly have lingered to prolong the stolen sweetness of that moment, forgetful altogether of the danger that lay behind them.

Ahead, he saw Labertouche step out upon a shelving shore and, shaking his legs with an effect irresistibly suggestive of a dog leaving the water, peer inland through the tamarisks. His low, whistled signal sounded as Amber joined him and put down the girl—reluctantly. Her whispered thanks were interrupted by an exclamation from Labertouche.

"Hang it all! he can't've mistaken the spot. I told him to wait right here, and now … We daren't delay." He cast an apprehensive glance across the stream. "Look lively, please."

He shouldered away through the thicket, and for several moments they struggled on through the hindering undergrowth, their passage betrayed by much noisy rustling. Then, as they won through to open ground, Labertouche paused and whistled a second time, staring eagerly from right to left.

"I'm blessed!" he declared, with a vehemence that argued his desire for stronger language. "This is bad—bad—bad! He never failed me before! I—"

A mocking chuckle seemed to break from the ground at their feet, and in the flicker of an eyelash a shadow lifted up out of the scrub-encumbered level. Sophia cried aloud with alarm; Labertouche swore outright, heedless; and Amber put himself before her, drawing his revolver, heartsick with the conviction that they were trapped, that their labour had gone all for naught, that all futilely had they schemed and dared....

But while his finger was yet seeking the trigger the first shadow was joined by a score of fellows—shades that materialised with like swiftness and silence from the surface of the earth—and before he could level the weapon Labertouche seized his wrist. For an instant he resisted, raging with disappointment; but the Englishman was cool, strong, determined; inevitably in the outcome the weapon was pointed to the sky.

"Steady, you ass!" breathed the secret-agent in his ear. "Can't you see—"

And Amber gave over, in amazement unbounded, seeing the starlight glinting down a dozen levelled rifle-barrels, glowing pale on the spiked, rounded crowns of pith helmets, and striking soft fire from burnished accoutrements; while a voice, thick with a brogue that was never bred out of hearing of Bow Bells, was hectoring them to surrender.

"'Ands up, ye bloomin' black beggars! 'Ands up, I s'y!"

"Tommies!" cried Amber; and incontinently he dropped the revolver as though it had turned hot in his hand.

"Steady, my man!" Labertouche interrupted what threatened to develop into a string of intolerable abuse. "Hold your tongue! Can't you see we've a lady with us?"

"Ul-*lo!*" The soldier lowered his rifle and stepped closer, his voice vibrating with astonishment. "Blimme, 'ere's a go!... beggar of a nigger givin' me wot-for 's if 'e was a gent! 'Oo in 'ell d'ye think y'are, yer 'ighness?'

"That'll do. Put down those guns, and call your commanding officer. I'll explain to him. Where is he? What troops are you? When did you arrive?"

Such queries and commands discharged quickly in crisp English from the mouth of one who wore the color and costume of a Mohammedan of high degree, temporarily dazed his captors. In a body they pressed round the three, peering curiously into their faces—the two white and the one dark; and their murmurings rose and swelled discordant. "Blimme if 'e *ain't* a gent!" "T'other un is!" "An this un a leddy!"...But to his interrogations Labertouche got no direct reply. While as for Amber, he could have laughed aloud from a heart that brimmed with thanksgiving for the honest sound of their rich rough voices; besides which, Sophia stood very close to him, and her fingers were tight about his....

"What's this?" A sharp voice cut the comments of the Tommies, and they were smitten silent by it. An officer, with jingling spurs and sword in hand, elbowed through the heart of the press. "Stop that row instantly. What's this? Who are you, sir?"

"I sent the message from Kathiapur, and I'm uncommonly happy to meet you, whoever you may be, sir. Tell your men to fall back, please, and I'll introduce myself properly."

Two words secured the secret-agent the privacy he desired; the officer offered him an ungloved hand as the troopers withdrew out of hearing.

"Happy, indeed!" he said cheerfully. "I'm Rowan, Captain, Fourteenth Pioneers."

"I'm Labertouche, I.S.S. This is Miss Farrell, daughter of Colonel Farrell, and this Mr. Amber, of New York. We're just escaped from that rock over there and—if you'll pardon—I'd suggest you set a strong guard over the ford behind those tamarisks."

"One moment, please." The officer strode off to issue instructions in accordance with Labertouche's advice. "We got here only a quarter of an hour ago," he apologised, swinging back as the men deployed into the thicket, "and haven't had time to nose out the lay of the land thoroughly."

"I infer you got my man with the horses—native calling himself Ram Nath?"

"He's with the Colonel-commanding now, Mr. Labertouche. As I was saying, we've hardly had time to do more than throw a line of pickets round the rock. It's been quick work for us—marching orders at midnight yesterday, down by train to Sar, and forced march across the desert ever since daybreak."

"I'd hardly hoped the thing could be done so quickly. If I had been able to get the information an instant earlier, my mind would've been easier, captain, but—Hello!"

From the ford an abrupt clamour of voices interrupted. The officer hooked up his scabbard. "Sounds as if my men had gathered in somebody else," he said hastily. "If you'll excuse me, I'll have a look." He trotted off into the shade of the tamarisks.

As he disappeared the disturbance abated somewhat. "False alarm," Amber guessed.

"I fancy not," said Labertouche. "If I'm not mistaken our friend Naraini left for the special purpose of raising the hue and cry. This should be the vanguard of the pursuit."

Amber looked upward. Overhead the soulless city slumbered in a stillness apparently unbroken, yet he who saw its profile rugged against the stars, could fancy what consternation was then, or presently would be, running riot through its haunted ways.

"How many of 'em are there, do you reckon?" he asked.

"Three or four hundred," replied the secret-agent absently; "the pick and flower of Indian unrest. My word, but this will kick up a row! Think of it, man! three hundred and fifty-odd lords and princes bagged all at once in the act of plotting the Second Mutiny! What a change it will work on the political face of the land! ... And the best of it is, they simply can't get away."

"Is this the only exit, then—the way we escaped?"

"Not by three—all on the other side of the rocky where they rode up and left their horses. And that's where the most of 'em will come out, by twos and threes, like the animals out of the Ark, you know. What a catch!"

"And we've you to thank!"

"I? Oh, dear boy, thank the Tommies!"

"But what would we have done, or the Tommies either, without you?"

"What indeed!" Sophia echoed warmly. "I've had no chance, as yet—"

"Not another word, my dear Miss Farrell!" Labertouche protested, acutely uncomfortable. "To've been able to help you out of the scrape is enough."

"But I must—" she began, and stopped with a little cry as a shot rang out from the heart of the thicket, to be followed by another and then by a shriek of agony and a great confusion of sounds—shouts and oaths and noisy crashings in the tamarisks as of many men blundering hither and yon.

Silenced, with a slight shudder of apprehension, the girl drew to Amber's side, as if instinctively. He took her hand and drew it through his arm.

"Run to earth at last!" cried Labertouche. "I wonder—"

"If my hope's good for anything," Amber laughed, less because he felt like laughing than for the purpose of reassuring Sophia, "this will be the gentleman who trained the Hooded Death to dance, or else he who—"

He was thinking with vindictive relish of what fate he would mete out to the manipulator of the Bell, were it left to him to pass sentence. But he broke off as a body of soldiery burst from the tamarisks, and, headed by young Rowan, hurried toward the three, bringing with them a silent and unresisting prisoner.

"I say," the officer called excitedly in advance, "here's something uncommon' rum. It's a woman, you know."

"Aha!" said Labertouche, and "Ah!" said Amber, "with a click of his teeth, while the woman on his arm clung to him the closer.

"I thought we'd better bring her to you, for she said ..." Rowan paused, embarrassed, and took a fresh start. "My men got to the ford just as she was coming ashore with three other men, and the whole pack took to cover on this side. Two of the men are still missing, but we routed out the other just now with this—ah—lady. He showed fight and got bayonetted. But the woman—excuse me, Mr. Amber—she protests—by George, it's too ridiculous!—"

"I have claimed naught that is not true!" an unforgettably sweet voice interrupted from the centre of the group. It opened out, disclosing Naraini between two guards, in that moment of passion and fear perhaps more incomparably beautiful than any woman they had ever looked upon, save her who held to Amber's arm, a-quiver with womanly sympathy and compassion.

143

During her flight and her resistance Naraini's veil had been rent away; in the clear starlight her countenance, framed in hair of lustrous jet and working with uncontrollable rage and despair, shone like that of some strange tempestuous Aphrodite fashioned of palest gold. Beneath its folds of tightly drawn, bespangled gauze her bosom swelled and fell convulsively, and on her perfect arms, more softly beautiful than any Phidias ever dreamed to chisel, the golden bracelets and bangles clashed and tinkled as she writhed and fought to free herself of the defiling hands. Half-mad with disappointment, she raged amid the scattered shreds of her dream of power like a woman hopelessly deranged.

"Aye, I have claimed!" she stormed. "I have claimed justice and the rights of wifehood, the protection of him whose wife I am; or, if he deny me, I claim that he must suffer with me—he who hath played the traitor's part to-night, betraying his Cause and his wife alike to their downfall!... I claim," she insisted, lifting, in spite of the soldiers' restraining hands, one small quivering arm to single Amber out and point him to scorn, "that this is the man who, wedded to me by solemn right and the custom of the land, hath deserted and abandoned me, hath denied me even as he denies his birthright, when it doth please him, and forswears the faith of his fathers! I claim to be Naraini, Queen, wife to Har Dyal Rutton, rightful ruler of Khandawar—coward, traitor, renegade—who stands there!"

"For the love of Heaven, Rowan, shut her up!" cried Labertouche. "It's all a pack of lies; the woman's raving. Rutton's dead, in the first place; in the second, he's her father. She can't be his wife very well, whether he's alive or dead. It's simply a dodge of hers to gain time. Shut her up and take her away—she's as dangerous as a wildcat!"

"Nay, I will not be gagged nor taken hence till I have said my say!" With a sudden furious wrench Naraini wrested her arms from the grasp of the guards and sprang away, eluding with lithe and snake-like movements their attempts to recapture her. "Not," she cried, "until I have wrought my will upon the two of them. Thou hast stood in my light too long, O my sister!"

A hand blazing with jewels tore at the covering of her bosom and suddenly came away clutching a dagger, thin, long, and keen; and snarling she sprang toward the girl, to whose influence, however unwitting, she rightly ascribed the downfall of her scheme of empire. Rowan and Labertouche leaped forward and fell short, so lightning swift she moved; only Amber stood between her and her vengeance. Choking with horror, he put the girl behind him with a resistless hand, and took Naraini to his arms.

"Ah, hast thou changed thy mind, Beloved?" The woman caught him fiercely to her with an arm about his waist, and her voice rose shrill with mocking triumph, "Are my lips become so sweet to thee again? Then see how I kiss, thou fool!"

She thrust with wicked cunning, twice and again, before the men tore her away and disarmed her. For an instant wrestling like a demon with them, still animated by her murderous frenzy, still wishful to fill her cup of vengeance to the brim with the blood of the girl, she of a sudden ceased to resist and fell passive in their hands, a dying flicker of satisfaction in the eyes that watched the culmination of her crime....

To Amber it was as if his body had been penetrated thrice by a needle of fire. The anguish of it was exquisite, stupefying. He was aware of a darkening, reeling world, wherein men's faces swam like moons, pallid, staring, and of a mighty and invincible lethargy that pounced upon him, body, brain and soul, like a black panther springing from the ambush of the night. Yet there were still words that must be spoken, lest they live in his subconsciousness to torment him through all the long, black night that was to receive him. He tried to steady himself, and lifted an arm that vibrated like the sprung limb of a sapling, signing to the secret-agent.

"*Labertouche*," he said thickly ... "*Sophia ... out of India ... at once ... life ...*"

The girl's arms received him as he fell.

CHAPTER XX

A LATER DAY

A man awoke from a long dream of night and fear, of passion, pain, and death, and opened eyes whose vision seemed curiously clear, to realise a new world, very unlike that in which the incoherent action of his dream had moved—a world of light and lively air, as sweet and wholesome as glistening white paint, sunshine, and an abundance of pure, cool air could render it.

Because he had known these things in a former existence, he understood that he lay in the lower berth of a first-cabin stateroom, aboard an ocean steamship; a spacious, bright box of a room, through whose open ports swayed brilliant shafts of temperate sunlight, together with great gusts of the salt sweet breath of the open sea. Through them, too, he could see patches of unclouded blue, athwart which now and again gulls would sweep on flashing, motionless pinions.

The man lay still and at peace, watching, wondering idly, soothed by the sense of being swung through space, only vaguely conscious of the plunging pulsations of the ship's engines, hammering away indomitably far in the hold beneath him. His thoughts busied themselves lightly with a number of important questions, to whose answers the man realised that he was singularly indifferent. Who was he? What had happened to bring him back to life (for he was sure that he had died, a long time ago)? How had he come to that stateroom? What could the name of the vessel be? Where ... Deep thoughts were these and long; the man drowsed over them, but presently was aroused by the sensation of being no longer alone, of being watched.

His eyeballs seemed to move reluctantly in their sockets, and his head felt very light and empty, although so heavy that he could not lift it from the pillow. But he managed to shift his gaze from the window until it rested upon a man's face—a gaunt, impassive brown face illuminated by steady and thoughtful eyes, filled with that mystic, unshakable spirit of fatalism that is the real Genius of the eastern peoples. The head itself stood out with almost startling distinctness against the background of pure white. It was swathed with an immaculate white turban. The thin, stringy brown neck ran into a loose surtout of snowy white.

The sick man felt that he recognised this countenance—had known it, rather, in some vague, half-remembered life before his latest death.
The name...? He felt his lips move and that they were thin and glazed.
Moistening them with his tongue he made another attempt to articulate.
A thin whisper passed them in two breaths: "Ram ... Nath ..."

Hearing this, the dark man started out of his abstraction, cast a swift, pitiful glance at the sick man's face, and came to hold a tumbler to his lips. The liquid, colourless, acrid, and pungent, slipped into his mouth, and he had to swallow whether he would or no. When the final drop disappeared, Ram Nath put down the glass, smiled, laid a finger on his lips, and went on tiptoe from the stateroom.

After awhile the man without an identity fell asleep, calmly, restfully, in absolute peace. When again he awakened it was with the knowledge that he was David Amber, and that a woman sat beside him.

Her face was turned from him, and her brown eyes, clouded with dreams, were staring steadfastly out through the open port; the flowing banners of sunshine now and again touched her hair with quick fire—her wonderfully spun hair, itself scarcely less radiant than the light that illumined it. Against the blue-white background her gracious profile showed womanly and sweet. There was rich colour in cheeks fresh from the caress of the sea wind. She smiled in her musing, scarlet lips apart.

"Sophia..."

His voice sounded in his own hearing very thin and brittle. The girl turned her gaze upon him swiftly, the soft smile deepening, the dream-light in her eyes burning brighter and more steady. She bent forward, placing over his wasted hand a hand firm and warm, strong yet gentle, its whiteness enhanced by the suggested tracery of blue veins beneath the silken skin, and by the rosy tips of her slender, subtle fingers.

"David!" she said.

He sighed and remembered. His brows knitted, then smoothed themselves out; for with memory came the realisation that, since he was there and she by his side, God was surely in his Heaven, all well with the world!

"How long...Sophia?"

"Five days, David."

"Where...?"

"At sea, David, on a *Messageries* boat for Marseilles. Dear ..."

He closed his eyes in beatific content: "David ... Dear ...!"

"Can you listen?"

"Yes ... sweetheart."

Her voice faltered; she flushed adorably. "You mustn't talk. But I'll tell you.... They refused to let us go back to Kuttarpur; an escort took us across the desert to Nok, you in a litter, I on horseback. There we took train to Haidarabad and Karachi. Ram Nath came with us, as bearer, it being necessary that he too should leave India. My father and your man Doggott joined us at Karachi, where this steamer touched the second day."

"You understand, now—?"

"Everything, dearest."

"Labertouche—?"

"He told me nothing. I haven't seen him since that morning, when, just after you were wounded, we started for Nok. He posted off to Kuttarpur to find my father.... No; it was you who told me—everything—in your delirium."

"And ... you forgive—?"

"Forgive!"

He smiled faintly. "That photograph?"

"I had it ready to return to you that morning, David."

"Knowing what it meant to me?"

"Knowing what it meant to *me*—what it meant to both of us, David."

"So you weren't offended, that night?"

"I loved you even then, David. I think I must have loved you from that first day at Nokomis. Do you remember...?"

His eyes widened, perplexed, staring into her grave, dear eyes. "Then why did you pretend—?"

With the low, caressing laugh of a happy child, the girl knelt by the side of his berth, and laid her cheek against his own. "Oh, David, my David! When do you expect to understand the heart of a woman, dear heart of mine?"

CHAPTER XXI

THE FINAL INCARNATION

About five o'clock of an evening in April the Cunarder *Caronia*, four hours out from Queenstown and buckling down to a night's hard work against the northwesterly gale, shipped a sea. It was not much of a sea—merely a playful slap of a wave that broke against the staunch black side and glanced upward in a shower of spray, spattering liberally a solitary passenger who had been showing enough interest in the weather to remain on deck until that particular moment. Apparently undisconcerted by the misadventure, he shook himself and laughed a sober, contented laugh, found a handkerchief and mopped his face with it, then, with a final approving survey of the lowering and belligerent canopy of wind-cloud that overhung the tortured ocean, permitted himself to be blown aft to the door of the first-cabin smoking-room. Opening this by main strength, he entered. The gale saved him the bother of closing it.

Removing his rain-coat and cap and depositing them on a convenient chair, he glanced round the room and discovered that he shared it with a single passenger, who was placidly exhausting the virtues of an excellent cigarette. Upon this gentleman the newcomer bent a regard steadfast and questioning, but after returning it casually the smoker paid him no further attention. Dissatisfied, the other moved toward him, and the deck slanted suddenly and obligingly the better to accelerate his progress, so that he brought up with a lurch in the seat next the smoker. The latter raised the eyebrows of surprise and hoped that the gentleman had not hurt himself.

"I didn't, thank you, Mr. David Amber."

Mr. David Amber looked the gentleman over with heightened interest. He saw a man of medium height, with a sturdy figure that bore without apparent fatigue the years that go with slightly greyish hair. He was quietly dressed and had intelligent eyes, but was altogether unimpressive of manner, save for a certain vague air of reserve that assorted quaintly with his present attitude.

"You've the advantage of me, sir," Amber summed up the result of his scrutiny.

"It's not the first time," asserted the other, with an argumentative shake of his head. "No-o?" Light leaped in Amber's eyes. "Labertouche!"

"Surprised you, eh?" The Englishman grinned with pleasure, pumping Amber's arm cordially. "I don't mind owning that I meant to."

"Well, considering that this is positively your first appearance as yourself on the stage of my life, you don't deserve any credit for being able to deceive me. When one gets accustomed to remembering you only as a native—generally as a babu in dirty pink satin—...Do you know, I made all sorts of enquiries after you, but they told me, in response to my wires to Calcutta, that you'd dropped out of the world entirely. I had begun to fear that those damned natives must have got you, after all, and that I'd never see you again."

"I'd almost given up hope of ever seeing myself again," said Labertouche drily.

"But why didn't you—?"

"Business, dear boy, business.... I was needed for several days in the neighbourhood of Kathiapur."

"It seems as though I'd waited several years for news of Kathiapur. The papers—"

"There are a good many things that happen in India that fail to get into the newspapers, Amber. It wasn't thought necessary to advise the world, including Russia, that half the native potentates in Hindustan had been caught in the act of letting the Second Mutiny loose upon India." A network of fine wrinkles appeared about his eyes as he smiled enjoyment of what he seemed to consider a memorable joke.

"Go on," pleaded Amber.

"Kathiapur was a sort of mousetrap; the brutes came out by twos and three, just as I said they would, for the better part of three days. It was either surrender or starve with them, and after five-sixths of them had elected not to starve we turned a couple of companies of Tommies into the place, and I don't believe they left unturned a stone big enough to hide a rabbit. One by one they routed 'em out and booted 'em down to us. Meanwhile we had rushed enough troops to Kuttarpur to keep their tails quiet."

"And Salig Singh—and Naraini?"

"Salig Singh, it turned out, was the chap that got bayoneted in the tamarisks. Naraini managed somehow to steal away the next night, under the noses of any number of sentries; beauty such as hers would bribe her way out of hell, I think. What became of her I don't know, but I can prophesy that she won't live long. She was rather too advanced in her views, for India—some centuries ahead of her race. She and Salig Singh had it all planned, you know; his was the master-mind, hers the motive-power. They were to crown you, instead of Salig's son, the next day—in the name of Har Dyal Rutton; and then you were to die suddenly by virtue of hemp poison or some other contagious disease, and Salig was to step into your shoes as Emperor of Hindustan, with Naraini as his Empress.... She should have stayed home and been a suffragette."

"Better for her," said Amber. "Of course I've found out about her, from Farrell. It seems that she was brought up in England, with Sophia, and always given to believe she was his own daughter, but she was a wild thing and hard to handle. One day she found out about her parentage—how, it's not known, but Farrell suspects that the men who were hounding Rutton got into communication with her. At all events, she brooded over the thing, and when, five years or so ago, Mrs. Farrell died and the Colonel sent for Sophia to join him in India, Naraini—well, she rebelled. He refused to let her leave England, and she finally took the bit in her teeth and ran away—vanished and was never heard of again until Sophia recognised her in Kathiapur."

"I myself can fill in the gap," Labertouche volunteered. "She joined some of Salig's underlings in Paris and went thence direct to Khandawar, assuming the name of one of the old queens who had elected opportunely to die.... Queer case—singular instance of reversion to type."

"A mighty distressing one to the old colonel; you know Rutton kept religiously to his promise not to see the child after he'd given her into Farrell's care. Farrell lost all track of him and was unable to communicate with him, of course, when Naraini chose to strike out for herself.... One thing has always puzzled me; the girl called me by her father's name, pretending to recognise me as her husband; you can't reconcile such conduct."

"You can, easily enough—beg pardon, my dear fellow. Neither she nor Salig Singh was for an instant deceived. But Salig *had* to deliver up *a* Har Dyal Rutton to the Council, so Naraini was set to seduce you. Their plans only required that you should be madly infatuated with her for a couple of days; after that ..." Labertouche turned down his thumb significantly. "I fancy there must have been a family secret or tradition, handed down from father to son in the Rutton line, that some day one of the family would be called upon to raise the standard of the Second Mutiny. That will explain why Har Dyal Rutton, a gentleman of parts and cultivation, dared not live in India, and why—because he was sworn to keep the secret—he laid stress on the condition that you were not to mention his name."

"Still, he gave me permission to talk to Dhola Baksh."

"True; but it seems that Dhola Baksh had been his confidential body-servant in Kuttarpur, during his too-brief reign. Rutton thought he would be able to help you, and knew that he would be loyal to his master's memory."

"Finally, what about that photograph?"

"You've Salig Singh to thank for its return, I fancy. I had nothing to do with it. But they were bent on luring you to Naraini's bower, and they figured that after receiving it you'd go anywhere to meet the man who returned it. By the way, where's Ram Nath?"

"He's staying in England as body-servant to Colonel Farrell."

"He's well off, so; his sphere of usefulness in India was at an end. So, in fact, was mine. That's why I'm here—on indefinite leave of absence. One or two things grew out of the affair of the Gateway to make me a person of interest to the natives, and when that happens in India it's just as well for the interesting person to pack up and get thence with all possible expedition. It's too bad; I was really doing some good work there. Well…! When the East gets into a fellow's blood, he's a hopeless, incurable case; I shall go back, I presume, some day. If the big trouble comes in my lifetime—and I think it will; come it will unquestionably, soon or late—I shan't be able to keep away, you know." He glanced at his watch and rose. "Time to dress for dinner," said he; and as they were moving to the door, he added: "What ever became of that emerald ring, Amber?"

"The Eye?" Amber laughed. "Well—it was silly enough; but women are superstitious, you know—Sophia dropped it overboard one day as we were coming through the Mediterranean. She said she was afraid of it … and I don't know but I sympathise with her."

"I'm certain I do. And yet, in your case, it was the means of introducing you, wasn't it?… But there! It's been on the tip of my tongue a dozen times to ask, but other things got in the way…. How *is* Mrs. Amber?"

"You shall see for yourself," said Amber, "when we meet for dinner."

CPSIA information can be obtained
at www.ICGtesting.com
Printed in the USA
LVOW13s0022260117
522209LV00006B/480/P

9 781516 892372